MIKE4

MISSION POINT PRESS

Readers are encouraged to go to www.MissionPointPress. com to contact the author or to find information on how to buy this book in bulk at a discounted rate.

Published by Mission Point Press
2554 Chandler Rd.
Traverse City, MI 49696
(231) 421-9513
www.MissionPointPress.com

ISBN: 978-1-950659-17-3
Library of Congress Control Number
available upon request

Printed in the United States of America

MIKE4

J. R. Seeger

book 1 in the   MIKE4 series

MISSION POINT PRESS

To the men and women of Special Operations and the Intelligence Community who have fought America's shadow wars and collected intelligence since 1942 expecting no recognition while risking everything.

Their feats, their fortunes and their fames
Are hidden from their nearest kin;

No eager public backs or blames,
No journal prints the yarn they spin
(The Censor would not let it in!)
When they return from run or raid.

Unheard they work, unseen they win.
That is the custom of "The Trade."

— *Rudyard Kipling*

CONTENTS

AAR: after action report

Alpha: Surveillance terminology for a target location of interest.

Bravo: Surveillance terminology for a person of interest.

BTK: Acronym for below the knee amputation.

Charlie: Surveillance terminology for a vehicle of interest.

COS: Chief of Station. The senior CIA officer in a field station.

CPU: car pickup

CQB: Close quarters battle aka urban assault operations.

CSM: Command Sergeant Major. The senior non-commissioned rank in the US Army.

CWO: Chief Warrant Officer. A military rank with ratings from CWO1 to CWO5

DCOS: Deputy Chief of Station. The number two officer in a CIA station.

Downrange: A generic term applied to any combat tour.

FOB: forward operating base

Foxtrot: Surveillance term for walking surveillance, in contrast to vehicle surveillance.

FWD: forward. When a command is split in multiple locations, each of the locations outside the main headquarters are listed as "fwd." In this story, both Balad airbase and Bagram airbase have a SOF(FWD) contingent.

Glock: An Austrian pistol manufacturer. Glock pistols in this book are Glock19 (a compact pistol) and Glock26 (a subcompact pistol). Both are chambered in 9mm.

Green eyes: Night vision goggles, aka NVG.

Head of station: UK term for the head of the British intelligence in a field station. Also, "station commander."

HF: high frequency radio transmission.

HOA: Horn of Africa

HUMINT: human intelligence

Klingon: Military terminology for intelligence collectors, especially CIA operators in the field (see also OGA).

Makarov: a small, Russian officer's pistol. Similar to the Walther PP in design, it is chambered in a 9mm x 18mm cartridge

M4: US Army military rifle with a collapsible stock and short barrel chambered in 5.56mm.

MP5: A short-barreled submachine gun chambered in 9mm.

NAVSPECWAR: US Navy Special Warfare Command

NVG: Night vision goggles

OP: Observation point

OGA: "Other government agency" — a military term for the CIA.

One up: Surveillance term for working in a vehicle without a partner.

PCS: Permanent change of station — a long term assignment.

QRF: Quick reaction force. A military unit on standby to support a smaller force if necessary.

Red Gun: A non-functioning plastic training weapon with approximately the same weight as the real gun. Originally, all training weapons were colored red. They come in other colors as well, but are still called "red guns."

RTU: "return to unit." If a SOF operator does not meet the necessary requirements, he or she can be returned to their parent unit in the conventional forces.

SAP: "Special access program" — a program which has a limited and classified audience.

SAS: Special Air Service — a UK Special Operations unit.

SBS: Special Boat Service — a UK Special Operations unit.

Selection: A formal training program used by special operations units to select candidates.

Serial: A surveillance term used for a single, continuous shift following a target or observing a location.

SF: US Special Forces, aka Green Berets.

Shooters: Special Operations teams specifically trained to conduct raids.

SIGINT: signals intelligence

Six: The call sign for any commander of any military unit. Therefore, if the overall call sign for a unit is Mike, then Mike6 is the commander of that unit.

SMG: Submachine gun

SOF: Special Operations Forces

Squint: A less than positive name for analysts focused on imagery intelligence.

Standby: A surveillance communication term implying new information.

S&R: Surveillance and Reconnaissance — a fictitious US special operations unit.

SVTC: Secure Video Teleconference

Tag: An electronic tracking device.

TDY: Temporary Duty. A short-term assignment.

TF160: A unit from the US Army Special Operations Aviation Regiment. In this novel, they fly MH60 "Blackhawk" or MH8 "Little Bird" helicopters

TOC: Tactical Operations Center

Two up: Surveillance term for working in a vehicle with a partner.

Victor: Vehicle

VSO: village stability operations, a Special Forces counterinsurgency mission

Zero: The call sign for the team leader on a surveillance team.

ZULU: Greenwich Mean Time. When operations are conducted across multiple theatres, they are all linked to Zulu time so there is no confusion on what time they are starting.

OPERATOR

Sue O'Connell was not enjoying her shift. The room smelled of sweaty humans and creeping under the door was the smell of urine. There was little in the way of comfort in the room other than a case of bottled water and a box of granola bars. Sue hadn't eaten any of the granola bars because she was convinced that the bugs that scurried around the floor at night had already invaded the aluminum wrapped bars and taken the best parts. She had a thermos of coffee and two peanut butter sandwiches in a reinforced canvas shoulder bag, but that was for mid shift when she needed some energy. Her eyes hurt from staring into the spotting scope. She had shifted from the straight scope to the night vision scope an hour ago and the change from normal light to the green glow of the night vision scope helped some, but she was tired of this shift and tired of staring at a warehouse from a fourth-floor window in a wrecked apartment building with no running water and no electricity. Sue was sitting behind a black screen that covered the window — only the scope peered through the screen and saw the outside world.

No fresh air penetrated the screen, which added to the claustrophobic atmosphere. Next to her was her computer, capturing the images from the scope, her suppressed MP5 submachinegun, and her radio. She was sitting on a straight-backed chair wearing a t-shirt, cargo pants, black trainers and her Glock 26 in her nylon shoulder holster. The door behind her was "locked and chocked" with two old locks and a set of steel chocks wedged in top and bottom to insure no intruders could get in before Sue could kill them.

Night shift was never fun and any sort of observation point work was not what Sue liked. After selection and the yearlong training course that followed, when she arrived at her squadron in S&R, the Command Sergeant Major had warned her about what Squadron work was like.

"Chief O'Connell, welcome to S&R. You are one of our first chief warrant officers to come from Army military intelligence, so I want to warn you ahead of time about what you are getting into."

He didn't need to say that Sue was also the first female warrant

15

officer to pass selection. The shock on the faces of S&R leadership when she passed selection was something she had gotten used to after six years in the Army. Sue found out soon enough in the Special Operations Forces (SOF) once you passed any selection program, most of that gender prejudice went away. Unless you demonstrated that the prejudice was well founded. Sue remembered what her mom had said years ago about her work. She said she saw the world for women in the government as a "Ginger Rogers" world. Ginger Rogers had to be as good a dancer as Fred Astaire, but she had to do everything backwards in high heels.

"Thanks, Sergeant Major. I thought selection made it pretty clear — our job is to find and fix the bad guys so that the raid teams can finish them."

"Too true, but find and fix sometimes means find, watch and wait. I hope you have patience, because patience is the single most important attribute you need here."

Sue had been in Nairobi for eight weeks assigned to the embassy as a logistics staffer to the military assistance and advisory group, the MAAG, at the embassy. Her real job was as part of a team designed to find and track members of the al-Qaida infrastructure that had attacked the embassy in 1998. The President was determined to bring the terrorists to justice and SOF's role as the premier anti-terrorism arm of the US military meant that this became their job. Once the targets were found and could be fixed in place, SOF raid teams would "finish" the targets one way or the other.

They started with a few leads eight weeks ago — suspected supporters of the network provided, according to the morning briefing, by "the Klingons." Back in May, Sue was still new enough that she didn't mind asking dumb questions. Her boss, Chief Warrant Officer 5 William Jameson, had more time in SOF than anyone else. He had spent ten years with the raid teams and now five in S&R and he was a good liaison between the shooters and S&R. He looked about 50 but was only 40. "Time in the harness" was his only explanation. He didn't seem to mind dumb questions — at least not from Sue.

"Chief, Klingons?" Jameson smirked.

"Come on, Sue. Klingons. Star Trek? Cloaking device? Cloak and dagger?"

"The station, right?"

"Brilliant deduction, Holmes. I assumed you knew that simply because you are a child of a pair of Klingons."

"Don't remind me, Chief. It is burned into my head." Sue had spent years avoiding being called the "daughter of the O'Connells" or even the "granddaughter of Peter O'Connell." She had been able to avoid this sort of legacy discussion in conventional military intelligence, but the links between the special operations community and the CIA were far deeper and more profound.

"Well, I could think of worse things to have burned into your head. I have my drill instructor's face burned into my head…"

"Fair enough, Chief. Fair enough."

It turned out the Klingon leads had been very good and the two S&R teams started building out the full network of active AQ targets and local supporters working 24/7. Surveillance operations on the street were challenging in Nairobi. Most of her team were very fit, very large, very white guys — hard to blend into the markets and coffee houses where the Arabs and Kenyans met unless you were trying to look like oil or dock workers on holiday, but hard even then. She and Joe Billings, the single black guy on the team, were out every day. Sue had been used on the street more than most of the team, including Joe, simply because she could fit into nearly any market place as a woman shopper. She used that cover story over and over again by buying cloth, cheap jewelry and trinkets while watching a target attend a meeting. The guys operated from Toyota Hilux pickups and from small Suzuki and Indian Enfield motorcycles. They still stuck out, but looked more like their peers from the oil fields or the docks.

This was a far cry from her work as a conventional military intelligence warrant officer at Ft. Bragg and Sue loved it. The adrenaline rush when you were following a target in a foreign country was transformative. When she was working at the Corps level at Ft. Bragg, her work had been primarily on force protection operations and counterintelligence operations. She was loaned out once to the airborne battalion at Vincenza when they went into Bosnia and once to the Berlin brigade, but mostly she trained and did paperwork. In SOF, she was either "downrange" someplace, preparing to go to downrange or on block leave. It was focused work and she loved it. She could feel her senses being enhanced the more she practiced her new trade. She thrived on the street work and, just as the CSM had warned her, hated the watching and waiting when you were located in a fixed-point observation point. Worse still when you were in a "night standing observation point" forced to stay awake watching nothing through the green world of night vision waiting for something to happen. Generally speaking, it never did.

Each shift of 12 hours had a five-man S&R team and a full raid team of 10 building the network that would eventually result in some sort of take-down in Nairobi or wherever the target took them. The end result of their surveillance efforts to date had been identifying a warehouse on the edge of town near a truck depot that ran authorized convoys of supplies from Nairobi to Mombasa as well as smuggled cargo to the warlords in Somalia. The warehouse was now designated Alpha6 — and Jameson decided that this had to be either a safe house or a bed down location — either way, it was better than trying to follow young Kenyans on the streets going nowhere fast. Eventually, it would all end up at Alpha6.

The ear bud in her left ear clicked twice, bringing her back to the present, the room and the green viewer of the NVGs attachéd to the spotting scope.

"All stations, this is Zero. 22hrs. Time check." Jameson's voice came through the earpiece as clearly as if he was whispering in her ear. Jameson was in a van about a half mile away. His driver was Terry. They would be cruising the neighborhoods, circling the area and staying just in range of the radios. Inside the van with Jameson and Terry was Johnny Marshall, the raid team liaison officer operating on a different set of communications with his raid team leader located someplace else in the city. Sue had no idea how or where they were hiding a dozen operators in black nomex flight suits kitted out for war.

"Mike8" George was located on the roof of the building she was watching. He had it far worse than Sue. He had to be outside among the mosquitoes and various other creepy crawlies dressed in his black jumpsuit and facemask. Sometimes you just had to embrace the suck.

Sue spoke into her headset, "Mike4."

"Mike7" Nate was in an old, apparently abandoned 12 passenger van down the street. He could drive anywhere, anytime with anything. He would either recover the team or, if necessary, follow a vehicle. In the passenger seat next to him was Jim Massoni, the senior NCO for the team.

"Mike9" Joe was on a rooftop down the street. Enjoying the same lovely vermin as George. Over the past week, he and George had a competition to see who had the most and diverse bug bites.

"Mike 3" Deke was in a hotel room in the same building as George. Like Sue, he had been staring into the spotting scope since they took over from the other team at 1800hrs. Deke had avoided the rooftop service because on a previous rotation he had come down with Dengue fever. The second infection could be fatal. Even Jameson thought that was a good reason to keep him inside.

"Folks, we just heard from the Klingons that one of their sources has report of a meeting at our Alpha tonight. Meeting is set for ca. 24hrs, but that would be Arab time. Keep alert because we don't know when we will start to see visitors. Out."

Jameson was mission focused, but also determined to keep his team in the loop. He was currently located with the raid team commander on the first floor of Sue's building. Even though the radios were encrypted to an NSA standard, he didn't say much on the radio unless it was needed. Arab time meant it could be anywhere from 22hrs to 03hrs or tomorrow or the next day. "Bukhra, inshallah" — tomorrow, god willing — seemed to be the motto for anything dealing with Arabs.

Two clicks in the ear bud

"Boss, our Klingons or the Klingons?"

George was asking if the info was coming from the SOF team on the ground or the Station.

"Not that it matters, but ours. Zero out." Jameson was not big on chatter on the net.

It was 0125hrs and Sue was working on a sandwich and a cup of coffee when she saw a light blast out of the warehouse door. In the night vision screen, even a 60w bulb seemed like a searchlight.

"Stand by Stand by. Mike4. Someone just opened the door at Alpha6. We have a bravo standing in the door — it looks like he is waiting for someone."

"Mike4, this is Zero. Roger. Everyone confirm and then leave the channel open for 4."

"8"

"7"

"2"

"3"

"9"

Sue watched the street and the door. The single bravo, silhouetted in yellow against the green of the NVG, was clearly armed. He had an AK with its distinctive banana magazine slung over his shoulder.

"Zero this is 4"

"Go"

"Bravo at Alpha6 is armed. AK is visible. Slung over his shoulder."

"Roger. Bravo is armed. Slung over right or left shoulder?"

"Right shoulder."

Sue blamed the time of night for not reporting that initially. Of course the raid team, especially the snipers located on the same roof-top as George and on the roof of her building, would need to know that important fact. Assuming he was right handed, it meant that he was not ready to put the AK into action.

An old Mercedes taxi cab rolled up in front of the door with its lights off. All four doors opened and six separate figures left the car.

"Standby Standby. A Charlie just pulled up. Mercedes Taxi. Old style — heavy. Six bravos just entered the building. Two were armed with AKs — carried at the ready. Both right handed. Four were in thobes and pulled bags out of the car boot."

"Roger. Six bravos plus the one in the building. Any other seen?"

"No."

"3 this is Zero. Do you see any Charlies at your end of the street that look like blocking elements?"

"No, Boss. Nothing at my end."

There was a pause. No one wanted to break the silence as they waited for Jameson's orders. It didn't take long. Jameson keyed the comms 90 seconds later.

"Zero to all — main team is taking over. 8, 4, 3 and 9, pack up your kit and be prepared for pickup from 2. We have ten, rpt ten minutes. Clear and sanitize your space. We won't be coming back. Confirm."

"2"

"8"

"4"

"3"

"9"

Sue was more than a bit pissed off that she was not going to get to watch the assault. She knew better — their positions needed to be clear and they needed to be out of the area before any shit storm with the locals started, but still, this was the first time she had been directly involved in this sort of find, fix AND finish operation. Still, she wanted to watch.

She started by taking down the spotting scope and NVGs. These along with the collapsible tripod went into a small black Pelican case on wheels. Next, she put on a smaller set of NVGs and searched the room for debris. The water and the granola bars went into smaller pelican that fit on top of the wheeled case. This case also carried the garbage bag and the urine relief bottle that they all carried so that they didn't have to leave their position during a 12-hour shift. She checked around her chair — thermos and food were already in her shoulder bag.

She pulled the chocks from the door and put them in her backpack. She collapsed the stock on the MP5 and attachéd the SMG on two straps on her shoulder holster harness with the rifle facing down. Finally, she pulled a dark cotton smock from her shoulder bag, put it on and buttoned the top button. She pulled the NVGs off her head and they hung by their strap around her neck. She disguised that by pulling a headscarf around her neck and over her hair. Sue waited a full two minutes to let her eyes readjust to the dark.

Finally, she pulled the black window cover off the window and over her shoulders and attachéd it at the Velcro strip. It wasn't exactly an abaya, but at this time of night, it would have to do. She pulled out her Glock and stood next to the door.

"Time to go." She said to herself as she checked the hallway and, since it was clear, she holstered the Glock, walked out the door, down the hall and to the stairs.

She was down the stairs and standing next to the door when Nate pulled up on what appeared to be a decrepit minibus — a bus that sounded surprisingly well tuned. Just as she jumped into the bus, she heard the door to the warehouse being blown in by the team. Even from the other side of the building, the flash and noise of the explosion was deafening. She thought she might have heard a round go off, but that may have been her imagination. What she did hear was a 5-ton cargo truck pull up in front of the warehouse. Everyone — alive or dead was going to leave.

Nate pulled down the street, turned right on a very dark highway with the lights of the Nairobi airfield at the end of the road and started to drive carefully toward the lights.

Afghanistan in February 2003 was cold and damp. The mountains of the Hindu Kush hold the snow for months after the winter is gone and the dark skies of winter are still common in February. Also, the winter sun comes up too late and too far south to bring much heat into the valleys or, for that matter, into the narrow alleys of Afghan cities. Jalalabad is one of those cities that were probably designed by Afghans who watched the forces of Alexander the Great pass through on their way to Hindustan. The city extends out in all directions from the Kabul River and slowly evaporates as the Kabul and Konar rivers join in the East. Except for the main highway which was the remnant of the Moghul Grand Trunk road, Jalalabad streets were narrow, poorly (or unpaved) tracks that wander seemingly following the high walls of the various households rather than the more likely idea of streets first then homes. The February sun, when it rarely appears, never reaches into these streets and the mix of gray snow, garbage and sewage masses against the walls waiting for spring to thaw it. Inside the households, it is not any better. The best of homes was constructed during the 1970s of concrete brick. Most of the homes were mud brick. Cold in the winter and blazing hot in the summer. Only the rich homeowners enjoyed some respite from either discomfort by having wood trucked in from the Konar valley and shade inside their compounds created by trees planted when the first British invaders tried to conquer Afghanistan early in the 19th century.

Jalalabad for all its limitations was a rich city in 2003 — at least rich by Afghan standards. It was the major transportation hub for the agricultural products of the Kabul river — fruit and vegetables as well as fodder for animals. It was also the hub for smugglers who drove large, hand painted and decorated 10-ton cargo trucks between Peshawar in Pakistan and Kabul in Afghanistan. The economic role of Jalalabad had made it a target in virtually every conflict over the past three hundred years, but it also made it the least likely to suffer the extreme destruction caused by rival Afghan warlords or even outsider attacks whether British in the 19th and early 20th centuries or the Americans in 2001. The Arabs who were the targets of the American anger were kind enough to build their compounds outside of the city — more likely to keep Afghans out than to protect Jalalabad from any attack. So, while Kabul might have sections of town, including the King's palace ruined by the civil war in the 1990s, Jalalabad remained more or less intact — basically the truck stop that everyone in every conflict wanted to keep open.

Trucks moved to and from the city every hour of daylight in every season. Most winter days in February, the truckers had to use their headlights to peer through the mix of dust, charcoal and wood smoke and pollution. One bit of evidence of wealth in Jalalabad was the number of cars, scooters and pickup trucks that also occupied the highway with the donkeys and the occasional camel as well as men and women who walked to whatever daily toil they had outside their homes. In the middle of this mass of human, animal and machine traffic was a brightly colored truck driven by truckers who were known both for their reliability as local delivery vehicles and their willingness to avoid asking questions if someone wanted to pay to move cargo between Pakistan and Afghanistan.

Inside a small, disguised compartment in the front of the bed of a 10ton cargo truck, it was neither cold nor noisy. It was hot, it smelled bad and the eight SOF operators were packed shoulder-to-shoulder, sitting on their rucksacks, with their long guns (a mix of M4 carbines and MP5 machine pistols) between their legs, barrels down. Seven men and one woman were jostled every minute of the hour-long ride. The Stanakzai clan driver was reliable but just barely safe. A mix of naswar snuff was always sliding out of his mouth and he viewed the side mirrors of the truck simply as devices used to view his own lovely face as he careened down the highway. It didn't seem to matter if he was going a mile or 100 miles — it was always full throttle with horn blaring. The concealment included a small video screen that allowed the team to see what the driver saw on the highway. No one ever turned it on — the view was simply too terrifying and only amplified the nausea. The only time anyone had the screen on was anytime the truck was stopped for more than a minute — generally to make a delivery along the route. There was a second camera mounted in the bed of the truck on the concealment wall allowing the team to watch any loading or unloading process. Still, it was an ugly hour out and a worse 2-hour return trip; the transfer was referred to as "the ride on the vomit comet."

The truck was registered to a cargo hauler family in Tor Kham on the Afghan side of the Khyber Pass called Stanakzai Haulers. Stanakzai Haulers had been running Nangarhar fruit and vegetables East to Pakistan and Pakistani manufactured goods and engine parts West to Jalalabad since 1982. They also happened to be part of the Klingon infrastructure recruited in late 2001 after the SOF and Agency operators moved from Kabul to Jalalabad to hunt for Al Qaida agents on the run from the Northern Alliance forces that had swept down from the Panjshir. Local extremists had tried several times to convince the Stanakzai that they should allow the truck to become a bomb. They refused that offer, but, of course, promised to report on the compound to the Arabs every Friday after prayers. The SOF handler for the Stanakzai provided the necessary "feed material" for their reports to the Arabs and doubled the Stanakzai payment every time there was a meeting with the Arabs.

The truck delivered fresh fruits and vegetables to dozens of normal Afghan compounds every day and one delivery of fruit and vegetables to the American Special Operations forward operating base on the edge of town. The base had been an old Afghan Air Force helicopter base during the Soviet occupation and it was now easy to identify as a US base. The area was surrounded by 10-foot-high brown Hesco barriers (a mix of cardboard and fencing that was filled with dirt to make nearly instant and bullet proof barriers) topped by barb wire and covered on all sides by armored sentry posts guarding with .50 caliber machine guns. The approach highway also had a separate set of Hesco barriers creating a chicane so that no one could approach the FOB at full speed. It was particularly difficult for the Stanikzai truck to negotiate the chicane and especially hard on the crew inside the concealment. The FOB housed the command post, maintenance crew, and the crews for the TF160 helicopters, two teams equipped for raids from SOF, one troop from the SOF Surveillance and Reconnaissance (S&R) squadron and a Ranger company serving as base security and quick reaction force (QRF). 6 MH8 Little birds and two drones were housed in separate hangers inside the wire. That compound had consistent power and real food — more or less as well as electronic connectivity to the US and to SOF headquarters in Bagram airfield north of Kabul. The goal of the SOF element in Jalalabad was the same as any other in country. Their job was to find, fix, and finish any high value targets who were remnants of Al Qaida and then exploit and analyze anything found either on the HVTs or their quarters. S&R had one job only — find and fix the targets. Once that was accomplished, the raid teams would "finish" the mission.

By definition, the S&R operations had to be clandestine — find the HVTs and follow them without being seen. Given the high profile of the SOF base, S&R missions could not start and finish from the FOB. Instead, every ten days, the teams rotated in and out of the FOB to a safe house in the city using the Stanikzai cargo truck. On "moving day" while the truck was delivering fresh fruit and vegetables to the American compound, the team loaded into the concealment in the truck. It sucked moving from the air-conditioned compound to the safe house and sucked even worse moving from the team house to the compound. While the incoming team simply rode from the compound to the Stanakzai truck park, the outgoing team left early the next morning and had to ride a full day in the concealment as the truck made deliveries in Jalalabad before his final delivery to the FOB. It was hot, claustrophobic and necessary if the team was going to have a clean start from a location that was not associated with any NATO forces.

After departing from the FOB, the driver returned to the walled Stanakzai compound on the opposite side of the city and parked the truck next to three identically painted trucks. The end of the trip was timed for approximately sundown. Once signaled by the driver, the team left the concealment and walked to a Mitsubishi minivan that looked like it had been rolled end over end down the Khyber Pass. The only complete sheet of glass in the vehicle was the driver's windshield. Every door and window in the truck was crushed, rusted and looked inoperable. In fact, the van was mechanically one of the most sophisticated in the team inventory and was almost as fast as the two Nissan sedans and two Toyota Hilux pickups they had at the safe house.

The team house was only 2km from the truck parking lot, so the last bit of the travel was not unpleasant and easy enough. The admin staff would be signaled before the van arrived and they would open the ten-foot tall metal gates on the walled compound and the van would pull into the interior courtyard. After that, it was just a matter of pulling kit out of the van, conducting a lengthy debriefing with the outgoing team, dinner and heading to the sleeping quarters inside the compound.

The new team pulled into the compound just after sunset to start their 10 days of surveillance on foreign fighters in search of the main headquarters of al-Qaida in Jalalabad. The gates closed and locked, the team was now inside the 10' high walled compound with three buildings inside — team quarters, command post and admin/maintenance shop. The team quarters and the maintenance shop were well lighted, but the command post windows were covered so it was never clear if anyone was working or not.

As they approached the door to the command post, Frank Sinatra's voice started singing a Bossa Nova tune.

"What the fuck is that?" Billy was the newest member of the team — on his first rotation to Jalalabad. He arrived for this rotation directly from selection. He was very new to SOF, but not to Afghanistan. He had been with the Rangers since '97. He was still trying to figure out how to work with a team where everyone was older than he was, in some cases old enough to be his father. This was his first ride on the vomit comet and he was definitely green around the gills.

"Chill, Billy. Remember, we only stay here for ten days at a pop; these guys are here for an entire rotation 120 days. This is their home. If they want to do weird shit when we arrive, I say let them." Jameson was definitely "the Man" downrange and he made sure everyone knew it.

"Hey, Billy, it could be worse. Last rotation, Chief Dolan used to play Edith Piaf when we arrived. It got ugly a couple of times, but Dolan was the best admin chief we ever had and a terrific cook. Plus, you just don't mess with a Command Master Chief — remember that."

Jim Massoni had been the number two on the team for nearly five years and was unofficially the team comedian. He regularly delivered windup toys and other bits of childhood to the team. On one TDY, he formally issued red clown noses as part of the "disguise package" on surveillance serial. In the world of Ft. Bragg, Jim was a senior command sergeant major with a dozen years and two combat jumps with the Rangers now eight more in SOF. He had more time in Army SOF units than anyone else in S&R. He said he decided to end his career in S&R because he couldn't hang with the cool guys anymore. No one who saw him workout during off hours thought that was the reason he was on the team. He and Jameson had been together in SOF units longer than most of the rest of the team had been in the Army.

"Billy, do you want me to carry your ruck for you? You look a little green." Sue was on her third 120-day rotation to Jalalabad and was just looking forward to her cot in her plywood cubicle that served as her room inside the house, a shower and just maybe a cold soda if she could get it down and keep it down after the ride. She didn't need to hear any whining right now, especially from the most junior guy on the team.

Sue had learned a long time ago that to survive life in a SOF unit she always had to be tougher, faster, and smarter than the guys if she was going to get any respect at all. At 5'10" and with her short haircut, she often was mistaken for "one of the guys" when she was in body armor and gunned up. Sue suffered through five years in an MI company in the 18th Airborne Corps and then fought to go to selection for S&R. She thrived in the SOF world where competence and intelligence always trumped spit and polish. She hated the formal nature of the conventional Army and especially the formal structure of military intelligence. A year after selection bouncing around various jobs at S&R headquarters, she found a home and a family when she was assigned to Jameson's team. She had been on TDY in Kosovo, Nairobi and now Jalalabad over the last five years with the guys. There was nothing you could do to her to get her to leave this team. Also important to Sue was her team had been tracking the same network of Al Qaida terrorists since the Nairobi bombing. They were slowly wrapping up all of the assholes who attacked Americans. Jalalabad was just one more stop hunting these guys.

"Never mind." Billy ended with "bitch" added just under his breath. He may be the new guy on the team, but after 6 years at special operations, he figured he had earned his right to complain a bit after that stinking trip in the back of the truck. He didn't like working with a woman and didn't understand why any Tier unit would allow women in; eventually, they would fail in the crunch. He sure as hell wasn't going to take any crap from her and he intended to make that clear now.

Jim came up to Billy and put his arm around his shoulder. He bumped heads with Billy in a friendly manner and whispered in his ear "If you use that tone or those words again with anyone on this team, first I will stick a finger in your eye and dial a number and, once the medics are through with you, I will make sure you return to Group or some conventional unit before we are even through with this rotation. Clear?"

"Check, Sergeant Major." Billy was more than a little shaken by the transformation of Jim the team sergeant to Jim the command sergeant major. He grabbed his kit and moved into the quarters. Jim ended the conversation with his normal voice saying, "Billy, if you want some of your Nashville torch and twang next time, just ask. Dolan loves being a DJ."

"A little harsh?" Jameson asked as he shouldered his ruck and joined Jim before entering the house.

"We don't have time for this guy right now. Either he is in or out. In the old days, we had a couple of training cycles to test him, but not anymore. This is the real deal, Boss, and we have to be sure he knows where we stand. After five years of the shit, Sue has more than earned her status on the team. Right now, all he needs to do is ruck the fuck up and learn from her and the rest of us."

Jameson smiled. He hadn't heard RTFU in years, but sometimes Jim jumped into his Ranger NCO role and couldn't help it. Jameson would leave Billy to Jim. He had other things to think about — right now, he wanted dinner and coffee and then a debrief from the out-bound team on the last ten days. The debrief was in the main TOC and would be linked by secure video teleconference to the FOB. Everyone in the chain of command would have the same level of situational awareness at that point. After that, he would sit with out-bound team leader and listen to the stuff that wouldn't go out on SVTCs. Then some sleep, maybe.

The safe house had room for thirty though rarely were all the bunks filled. Typically the mix was one surveillance team, six admin staff (one team leader, three communicators and two mechanics), and a team of eight contractors who served as security officers and shared in the cooking responsibilities. Other than the contractors, everyone inside the compound was part of the larger S&R squadron assigned to Jalalabad. The contractors were all retired SOF operators. The admin and security members of the team house all claimed to be chefs, but none of them seemed to deliver the goods. There was a lot of rice and beans served for dinner. Occasionally a real meal was assembled. "Moving day" was one of those times when the staff worked hard to create a meal worth eating. After all, one team was leaving and another arriving. The compound was full of operators for the night and it almost seemed like a party. Almost.

In the interior courtyard, three of the security team were working in front of two 55-gallon drums cut in half and serving as a six-foot long grill. The glow from the charcoal was coupled with the fading light struck their bare arms as they worked on the mystery meat and bread, an Afghan meal. A blackened pot was boiling on separate pro-pane stove soon to deliver the rice for the meal. It was already starting to get cold, but they were plenty warm working on what appeared to be two sides of beef. The smell of the charcoal from the grills mixed with wood smoke from the houses, the low rumble from the gener-ators powering the compound and the city noise from motorcycles and trucks created an environment every operator who smelled meat on a charcoal grill for the rest of his life would relate to his days in Jalalabad. "Mad Max" Creeter, the head of the security team was running the show at the grills. He was dressed in green cargo pants and a stained gray sweatshirt. He waved to Jameson.

"Boss, dinner in 30, OK?"

"Check, Max. We'll be recovered by that time and have appetites for sure."

Jameson knew Creeter from his days in his earliest days in SOF. Creeter was a terrific operator and an even better leader. He retired as a CSM and started working almost immediately for a security contractor providing "close protection" (bodyguard) work for oil companies. After 9/11, he quit that job, reached out to SOF and offered to build security teams for SOF forward bases so they didn't have to use conventional troops to guard inside the wire. At 60, he was still downrange and still running the show inside a safe house. No matter what the team leaders thought, Creeter was in charge inside the compound walls. Jameson was fine with that because it was one less thing to think about during a rotation.

Jameson walked directly into the TOC, set down his ruck, pulled out and opened his Toughbook and plugged into the LAN. The rooms inside this old Afghan residence were divided in 2002 by the first team in the safe house using plywood and simple 2x4 frames. In most of the rooms, carpets purchased in the market and tacked to the walls by staple guns covered the plywood. The TOC walls were covered by maps, overhead photography and grainy pictures printed from the online feed of the Predators. Two white boards on either end of the room were filled with notes. Some were serious (B4 is left RPT left handed and keeps his AK under his left shoulder) and some less so (B2 drinks too much tea, he pisses in the jube every twenty minutes — watch out or you will stumble over him, and the definition of insanity is doing the same experiment over and over again expecting different results, so why am I here... again!). Directly in front of the main desk was a flat screen and camera that was used for the SVTC with the FOB. The same link could be fed into the SOF commander's headquarters and Ft. Bragg as well. When the light went red and the screen went on, everyone put on the serious face.

Jameson could unpack later; right now he needed to get up to speed so that he could ask reasonable questions during the debrief. No one wanted to look like a bonehead during the debriefing. He and

Chief Berry, the outgoing S&R team leader, would eat in the TOC tonight while the two teams ate in the only large room in the compound that served as briefing room, mess hall, and general assembly room. They would clean up and log into the SOF net precisely at 2020hrs local so that the link was complete by 2030hrs local exactly 1600hrs Z which was one of the times that SOF main would monitor the network.

Master Chief Dolan walked into the TOC with a mug and a thermos. "Boss, here is your tea. The TOC has its own coffee pot, but I remembered you prefer tea — black and sweet." Dolan was from Naval Special Warfare and responsible for communications and maintenance. He had been a special boat squadron Master Chief, but Afghanistan was the SOF war, so he left the boat squadron to run the Jalalabad safe house with Max Creeter. Dolan was still active duty, so he could make official requests for supplies and funds. His work with the small boats in his old squadron turned out invaluable as he worked with the maintenance team to modify and enhance the wrecks they called vehicles here.

"You know what the Brits say, Chief? If there is tea, there is hope." Jameson had learned to drink tea during a rotation with the UK Special Reconnaissance Regiment, probably the best military surveillance and reconnaissance organization in the world. Jameson was convinced his team was as good as the average SRR team — just barely.

"Well, we got plenty of both, Boss. I'll make sure someone feeds you and Chief Berry before too long. You want me to get the space heater going? Gonna be cold tonight."

"Chief, I think it will be plenty warm in here until after the SVTC, so no need right now."

"Check, Boss. Food on its way. Don't miss out on the barbecue. Max has pride in his work."

"Will do. Thanks."

The team here was like a second family. Of course, Dolan and Creeter's bunch were super close and two teams were like cousins who were regular visitors, but the place had a friendly feel to it and this, coupled with the adrenaline rush of the work, made these sort of TDYs addictive. No wonder most of his team was either single or divorced. Nothing back home matched living downrange unless you had kids and an understanding spouse drawing you back into normal life through SKYPE and emails. Jameson wondered about Sue. He wasn't as worried as Jim about guys like Billy and how they would treat her. Sue would take care of him soon — in fact he intended to start Billy's education process tomorrow when he and Sue would go 'two up' on the street. She was like a sister to everyone on the team. She kept to herself and early on inside the unit the word got out that she was not interested in "sex inside the regiment" so that made it easier for the old timers and amusing for everyone as newcomers arrived and tried to hit on this tall redhead — one of dozen women in S&R. Jameson was too old to fret about that but he did worry about how she could keep grounded over the next few years in the TDY cycle. This was going to be a long war, he was certain of that no matter what the Generals or the press said. S&R would be used in every theater as they hunted Al Qaida. If all you had was warzone relationships and adrenaline, how long would you last on the TDY addiction?

He heard that she had a mother and a brother, but little else. One of the squints in the intel shed at SOF main told him when she first arrived that she was second-generation spook with her family working with the Klingons. She never said and he never asked. Sue was a good operator, a good, if conservative driver and the best on his team when it came to stake outs and observation posts. She had a tendency to be just a bit too aggressive on foot surveillance: too close and too willing to take risks. So far, that hadn't resulted in any trouble. She never seemed to tire and always picked out small, critical facts that others missed because they got bored and assumed they understood the target. She was also the best technical operator on the team. She knew how, where, and when to use the tracking and locating gizmos that were part of the team kit. Maybe that would be good enough for a couple of years, but then what? He couldn't imagine her as a team leader yet, too distant, too clinical in her engagement with team members. Jim would need to have a discussion with her. She was a junior warrant and if she wanted to make WO3 in the unit or in SOF proper, she needed to be able to move troops.

Jameson turned to his Toughbook that had booted up and opened the serial logs. He started his second cup of tea and scrolled through ten days of reports. Chief Berry walked into the TOC as he read through day 3 of Berry's team's logs.

"Wally, how are you doing, brother?" Mike Berry was a Chief Petty Officer from NAVSPECWAR and his team was part of the Navy contingent that included the half dozen SEAL teams in country based in Bagram airfield. He had been on a CQB team for years and decided to shift to S&R in 2000. As he put it, he was bored with the "finish piece" and wanted to work on "finding and fixing the bastards." Mike was 5'9" and was built like a refrigerator with a head. Not all SEALS were as obviously muscular, but he looked like what most folks expected when they thought of SEALS — men who could swim a mile ashore from a submarine dragging a sea bag of equipment behind them and then hump a ruck, ammo, and weapons all day to the target, execute the operation and then return by sea. On arrival at S&R, he had decided that Jameson looked like a Wally to him and he refused to change his mind. Jameson was not going to leg wrestle over that decision because he knew he would lose.

"Mike, when are you going to realize that you belong near a body of water? The Kabul River is thataway." Jameson pointed roughly north.

"Wally, you push 'em into the river, I will be happy to drown 'em. Until that time, I figure we just have to follow the bastards until you do your job." Greetings completed, Berry started into his summary of the last ten days as Dolan brought in their plates. He didn't interrupt and they left the plates where they were as they focused on the evolving story of the life of their targets — Bravo 1 through Bravo8.

Just before dawn, Sue crawled up the ladder on the third floor of the main house to a hatch on the roof. This was her third rotation to Afghanistan in the last four years and the third time in this rotation into the safe house. She never slept well on TDY no matter the venue and the safe house was not a sleep friendly place. She liked the guys and her plywood cubicle was fine, but the roof was the only place to get some peace and quiet. The living quarters echoed snores and after last night's meal there were plenty of that. Also, outgoing operators left at 0400 and though they tried to keep it quiet, the plywood walls just vibrated as they left with rucks over their shoulders. Sue had a small electric kettle and a one-cup French press. She made coffee, read for a while using her headlamp, and finally decided the roof was the only alternative. The house was cold and climbing out of the sleeping bag was painful, but once in her sweats and fleece, she was ready to move.

There was a high wall surrounding the roof, so you could sit outside, watch the sunrise, sunset or the night sky and have no fear of observation. The romance of an early morning in Afghanistan was limited by the fact that the concrete walls were lined with sandbags and there was a pair of M60 machine guns covered in canvas ready to go. During holidays and wedding season, you could watch the tracer rounds running across the sky at night — "festive fire" was the description from their interpreter. Everywhere else in the world, people dance at weddings. In J-bad, they opened up with Kalashnikovs. Go figure.

Mad Max Creeter was already up there watching the beginning of the day — dressed in black converse high tops, black sweat top and bottom and a watch cap. He had his sidearm in a drop holster and team radio on a duty belt hanging from the arm of a locally made bench and weight set. His M4 was leaning against the bench. He was doing a standing yoga pose (Sue wasn't surprised it was the warrior pose) while facing the Safed Koh and watching as the dark eastern sky turned purple. The mix of dust, diesel and cooking fires made the sunrises and sunsets spectacular though in the summer, the rooftop

35

would be an oven day or night. Creeter always took the night shift on the roof. Whatever the season, it didn't seem to matter to him.

Creeter suffered a bit from being trapped inside the compound for 120 days, but he understood how to keep quiet when quiet was required and how to keep his team and the visiting surveillance teams loose and focused on their job. Last night was a good example — his team liked the break in the routine and the visitors seemed to appreciate the effort. It didn't cost much to feed thirty here and the Stanikzai truckers delivered good food at a fair price. The kabobs and rice plus the stew fed everyone and would continue to feed them for two more days as his guys created various casseroles from the leftovers.

At stand to this morning, Berry's team was fed a quick breakfast, while a pair of Creeter's team dressed in local kit wandered the neighborhood insuring the outgoing team's trip to the truck yard was uneventful and, equally important, unobserved. There was always something that needed attention and it kept the support team plenty busy. They would repeat the same routing this morning as Jameson's team departed the back gate on their first serial of the rotation.

Creeter looked ten years younger than his 60 years at six foot, 190 pounds, with short-cropped hair and a week of gray beard. Sue had heard from teammates that Creeter was in class two of SOF selection — attending selection when the first SOF teams were in Iran on Operation EAGLE CLAW in 1979. He had been an operator, a team leader and a Troop CSM. He had stayed with the raid teams for twenty of his thirty years in service and then served as an instructor at the JFK center for his last two years. Everyone she knew saw him as the ultimate SOF warrior.

"Howdy, Sue. Welcome back."

"Thanks, Max. You are looking fit."

"Sue, you know the drill. Get up on the roof early, workout, make sure you guys deploy out of the nest, listen to the serial transmission, and make sure you get back, get some sleep, cook dinner and then workout, and pull the night shift. I brought a pelican case of books with me this time already read every book, twice."

"Last time I was here, you were working on some historical research, right?"

"Yup. History of the Knights Templar. Warrior monks in a time of the rise of Islamic warriors threatening Europe. It kept me busy. This time, I am simply reading Tolstoy and Kipling short stories as well as some histories about the Brits working on both sides of the border. I like Tolstoy; his stories as a Russian soldier in Dagestan let you know what it's like to live surrounded by enemies. Hey, let me know if you run out of reading material."

"Thanks. I would offer to share my books, but they are all brain candy.

A mix of mysteries and SCI FI."

"All good, but I run through them too quickly. I will let you know."

Sue had always wondered, so she just asked. "Hell, Max. Don't you ever go home?"

"Our rotations are 120 just like yours. I don't really have much at home, so I do doubles and then either do a couple of weeks in Spain or a month at home before coming back. When I'm home, I leave Southern Pines on my bike and drive to the mountains for a couple of weeks. After two weeks I'm ready to come back."

Sue understood the seduction of working downrange. Life was simple, the mission was clear and if there was no one home to return to, downrange became the only family you knew. Sue had her mom taking care of all the bills and her apartment in Fayetteville was a simple studio that served as a place to stack the duffle bag and little more. Still, Max was 60, had been retired for at least 10 years, and was still a nomad. It was not a promising future to consider.

"Why do you do it, Max?"

He looked puzzled. "To keep you and the guys safe."

That was more words than Max had offered since she had known him. He must be getting pretty tired of this rotation. Dawn was just starting to hint at the horizon, the mountains turned purple and a crescent moon was setting as well. She could see he wasn't through with his morning workout and it was time for a quick breakfast and the morning briefing. Sue turned back to the hatch and climbed down the ladder.

The teams had been working the same target for six weeks, so there was little change in the protocols or operational goals during the morning briefing. The SOF team BAKER had identified an Arab facilitator in Jalalabad (identified as B2) who also may be a courier between local Haqqani network infrastructure and a foreign HVT (high value target identified as B1) known only as Abdullah Bukhari who was supposed to be located somewhere in the city. Subsequent rotations between Berry and Jameson's teams identified three other targets, Bravos 3-5. The mission of this particular operation was to follow at least one of the targets every day until he led you to an HVT safe house or another facilitator. Berry's team had focused on B3, an Afridi trader known locally as Nader, for the last ten days and their work argued that he should remain the target during this rotation as well. B4 and 5 were interesting but more challenging. Berry's team had put a beacon on the vehicle they had seen at their bed down location. No one knew yet who owned the vehicle, but it was associated with the BDL and that was good enough for S&R. B4 and B5 were a pair of Uzbeks who were fighting alongside Al Qaida. The Uzbeks and the Chechens had survived years being hunted by the KGB, so they were far more security conscious and far tougher to find, much less fix. If they used the vehicle, no one would have to follow too close.

B3 was an Afghan living a relatively normal life moving from bed down location (identified as A3) to a tea house (A7) and then to mosque (A1). The previous week-long serial had identified a new safe house location (A4) with other suspicious Afghan targets (identified as B6-8). The SIGINT team was monitoring the land lines used in the Alphas and identified a possible SAT phone link to B3. Berry's serials had observed B3 use a SAT phone which was something no Afghan should own. Someone was paying a lot of money for B3 to be in contact with the world.

Chief Jameson started the morning meeting at 0600 by rapping his spoon on the metal coffee mug. He looked over the picnic table at his operators who were working on coffee, tea, or power drinks.

"OK, it's time to earn our pay. You got the current sitrep yesterday, so let's outline the plan for the day. We are going to establish a stakeout at A3 at 0800hrs. B3 hasn't left his bed down location any earlier than 0930hrs for the past two weeks, so if we are in place at 8 it should be good to go. We continue the serial until he returns to A3 or until we identify critical information that might justify a drone or technical coverage.

First serial will be Jim, call sign Mike2 in the Toyota corolla, Sue, call sign Mike4 and Billy, call sign Mike5 in the Magic Bus, and George, call sign Mike8 in a Nissan pickup. Deke and Joe, you will be Mike3 and Mike9. Deke, you are in the Lada and number three in the follow. Joe, you are in the Niva and on standby here at base. I will be call sign 0 operating in the commo van with Nate. Be prepared to switch out as needed as soon as the serial starts. Jim, set up the stake-out as you see fit, just let me know as soon as you can where everyone is located. Remember, our cousins said our Bravo is not surveillance aware, but we know that Bravo 2 and 3 and Bravo 4 and 5 are very aware. Be prepared as well to shift priorities if it looks like our Bravo meets someone new. George and Joe, you both have Bunions to use as quick plant tags if we see any car worth tagging. In the last rotation, they tagged Charlie1.

Billy, you drive the Magic Bus two up with Sue who will use the Equipment to monitor any mobile phone or handheld radio signals and monitor the tag on Charlie 1. Billy, this is your first day here so use it to get familiar with the streets. I know you used the simulator at Bagram, but today it will be a chance to get used to the real J-bad. Listen to Sue and follow her directions. Clear?"

Sue returned to her cubicle and switched out of her sweats and into her shalwar pajama pants. She knew the orders were no need for local garb today and, especially for her since she was going inside the Magic Bus. Still, you never knew when there might be a follow and she didn't want to be unprepared to get out on the street. The support staff had modified the shalwar pants so that they looked exactly like women's pajama trousers, but they were belted and designed to fit more like martial arts pants than the ungainly bloomers that Afghan and Pakistani women wore. She switched from her trainers to a set of what appeared to be Afghan women's shoes — more or less regular shaped women's plastic flats made in China. Again, modified by the support staff so that they worked well (more or less) as running shoes. Over her t-shirt, she pulled on her second chance vest — good for knife and 9mm threats, worthless for much else unless you added the plate designed to protect from rifle rounds. Unfortunately, the plate was big, awkward and made you look like you had a chicken breast Given the fact that the vehicles were already armored and the street work was unlikely to result in a full-fledged firefight, everyone on the team used the soft vest and hoped for the best.

Sue opened two Velcro pockets in the vest. Left side held her team radio with the mike and earpiece wires already threaded through the vest. Right side held the smaller GPS that she turned on as she put it in the pocket. The GPS would allow everyone on the team and, most probably, everyone in country to monitor her movements on the street. In the center of the vest, she had added another pocket, just the right size for a four-inch flat throwing knife. She never expected to have to use it, but it was her talisman against trouble. Next, the long shirt and her shoulder holster with her Glock 26 and two spare magazines. Finally, the long wool kurta jacket to cover it all, her gray wig and glasses, and her dupatta — they would all go in a gym bag in the back. If needed, she could put them on in a few seconds. The first time she had put the entire outfit on and looked at herself in the small mirror on one of the plywood walls, Sue had been amazed at the transformation.

"You look like a typical grandmother here in J-bad, except you should have a Kalashnikov."

She picked up her M4 carbine and the gym bag and headed down the stairs to the parking lot.

Billy had returned to his room. He had no idea what the Magic Bus was but after the confrontation yesterday with Massoni, he figured he would avoid stupid questions. Anyhow, he knew how to drive and figured the Magic Bus had to be just another vehicle. Sue was waiting for him at the Magic Bus. From the outside, it looked like any cargo van in the city. It was right hand drive as were most of the work trucks in the city even though Afghanistan was a left-hand drive country. Work trucks almost always came from Pakistan where right hand drive was the standard. The van was sprung like a cargo hauler, riding slightly higher than the other van in the inventory which was a micro-van that was the common bus on the streets of Peshawar. As with all of the vehicles inside the compound, the truck looked like it had been beaten with baseball bats, which, in fact it had been.

The van had light armor on the doors, but the front and side windows were normal glass. It was a panel van with no windows behind the driver including no rear windows. Sue opened the sliding door on the left side of the van and Billy saw her sit down on a single bucket seat surrounded by communications gear and a small work table with an LED desk lamp. She locked her M4 into a carry position on the ceiling, pulled down her headscarf and put on a headset and mike that was plugged into the onboard radio. Billy closed the door and went over to the driver's side of the vehicle. He climbed, clipped the M4 into the carry position under the dashboard, climbed into the van and started the vehicle up. Like all of the vehicles, it started immediately. In the winter, Creeter's team started all the vehicles at dawn and let them run for 10 minutes to get them ready for the day. They also fueled the vehicles from the tanks inside the compound — no watered gas or diesel for the S&R vehicles as long as Creeter and Dolan were around.

The Magic Bus had a series of small electronics in the passenger side of the van including a backup camera, an onboard radio and his own version of the intercept capability. Billy did a radio check with the base, and then turned around to see if there was any visibility into the back. There was none. Suddenly, Sue's voice came through a speaker in the headrest of his seat.

"Billy, I have full viz from a front camera mounted in the windshield washer port on your side of the truck so I can see more or less what you see. I will be focused on the intercept and the beacons more than anything else, but if you get turned around in the city, I can help. Meanwhile, please hit the lock override button that is next to your left knee. That inserts steel bars between the doors and the door frames. No one gets in or out unless you let them. OK?"

"Check. You do the magic in the back, I'll do the driving."

Billy, still didn't understand why he was working the intercept van today instead of working one up on the target, but he certainly didn't need any help from the chick in the back. Sue knew what was going on, but was too busy already working the communications and the tracking computers to worry about Billy's ego.

The vehicles left the compound in 10 minute intervals. Billy and Sue were the last ones out. By the time they were headed into Jalalabad, the network was alive with voice traffic as everyone identified their stakeout locations. The van had a modified fuel tank designed for the vehicle to run all day on one tank of gas. This meant they would be seeing the city again and again as they ran along the outskirts of the town and progressively worked towards the city center.

Billy knew the biggest problem he faced today would be avoiding traffic that would slow him down to a crawl. He was also unfamiliar with driving a right-hand drive vehicle on left hand drive streets. It wasn't a big deal, but it was certainly different than the simulator in Bagram. Given the size, shape and condition of the van, if they slowed down, he could expect local men and women to work the van door and try to get in. The van looked just like the others that were used as local cargo haulers. The locals didn't care if the vehicle was carrying sheep, food, or anything else. They would try to squeeze into any remaining space. Billy had been warned in Bagram that locals filled the interior, exterior, roof and sometimes hood as passengers kept coming on board.

The support team had solved some of that problem. First, none of the exterior door handles worked. The only way in or out of the van was with remotes that both Billy and Sue kept in their pockets and only then if Billy or Sue released the override. The van also had none of the normal access points like bumpers or roof racks that people could hold on for a free ride. She was very busy today watching the various electronics that were used to track the targets and monitor the local airwaves. After two years of successes, al-Qaida had shifted from hand held radios to other mobile technology, but their Afghan infrastructure hadn't made the shift and so the van served as a radio intercept platform as well as the main receiver for the beacons.

"Billy, take the 3 o'clock exit on the next round about, we have to head north to keep up with the signals."

"Roger." Billy was still pissed at the Massoni and his selection as the driver for what he saw as a "dial spinner" not a real operator. He decided that this was something he would have to handle internally with the rest of his teammates in the near term, but talking to Sue was not going to help.

"There is an alley that cuts through from Phase line Boston to Phase Line Chicago in about 100 meters, take that right turn and we will avoid the traffic that jams at the junction of Route Miami and Route Atlanta."

Billy decided that he didn't need that sort of guidance from someone who was focused on the dials and gizmos, so he blasted by the alley and continued toward Boston. He had a map on a pilot's knee board on his right leg against the door. He looked down at the map and was certain that he could go right at the next intersection and end up at on Route Atlanta quicker and cleaner.

As he drove past the alley, Sue realized what had happened and why. She was not going to fight this right now. She would not lose signal if Billy decided to travel on his route, so the mission would not be compromised, but it would make his life and hers more difficult in a few minutes. Billy was the sort of guy who would have to learn by bad experience and nothing Sue could do would change that.

Billy looked up from the map and realized that he was about to run the van into the back of the last camel in a camel caravan. There were six camels carrying cargo lumbering along the street shared with other vans, motorcycles, and cars all ignoring the lanes of the road. As he slowed down, locals walking along the street decided to jump on the hood of the van for a brief ride. In a minute, he was looking through a windshield obscured by three men, two women in burkas and six young boys who were making faces at him. Sue could no longer see what was going on because one of the boys was sitting on the forward camera. All she could do was focus on tracking the beacon that was moving away.

Sue switched over from the internal to the team net. "Stand by, stand by. Mike4."

"4 this is 0, go."

"Charlie1 has left A3 and is headed West, West along route Atlanta. Currently between Phase line Boston and Chicago."

"Roger. That is Charlie1 heading West, West between Boston and Chicago. Who can?"

"Mike8 can."

"Roger, 8 can. Everyone else stay on Alpha 3 stakeout until 8 determines who is in Charlie1. 4, focus on the Charlie. Do not lose the signal. We have to split the team. Confirm."

"2"

"3"

"4"

"5"

"8"

"9, this is 0"

"9"

"Join us at A3. Confirm." Jameson was convinced he would need all his resources in this serial.

"9"

Sue switched from the team net to the internal.

"Billy, turn right at the next intersection. That should get most of the barnacles off our vehicle and then turn right again when the streets intersect with the route New York. New York parallels Atlanta. We need to do this soonest because the signal is receding pretty quickly and we need to get in the chase."

"Check."

Billy was sweating and mostly wanted to reach through the windshield and choke at least one if not all the kids who were staring at him. The best he could do was turn on the windshield wipers and sprayer and give them a quick bath. They thought that was great fun and grabbed the wipers. He turned hard right at Sue's direction and every one of the folks who had been grabbing a free ride jumped off. They did not want to go back the way they came and they knew the street was taking them away from whatever destination they had. Billy had turned too hard on the right and ran over a curb or some obstacle which dumped the kids off. He accelerated along the street and finally made it back to Route New York. He knew Sue didn't have a map in the back. How did she know this city so well?

"OK, we are on track and we should be good to go." Her voice was calm and helped Billy calm down as well.

"0, 4"

"4, go"

"Charlie1, continuing straight, straight."

"Charlie1, straight, straight"

"8 has Charlie1" George's Alabama drawl was distinctive.

"Roger. 8 has Charlie 1. 9 are you in place?"

"5Mike's out."

"Roger, 2 this is 0. Move out and join 8 in the hunt. Confirm."

"2"

"4, this is 0. Any ICOM traffic?" Jameson was expecting some handheld intercepts from the Afghan's ICOM radio.

"Nothing. It doesn't look like it is on at all."

"Roger. Keep on the Charlie."

"4"

Sue switched back over to the internal net.

"Billy, you can slow down a bit now. George has eyes on, so all we have to do is maintain speed and distance from the Charlie and we are golden."

"Roger. Sorry about the mess back there."

"No dramas. First day in Jalalabad, I nearly killed an elephant that had been brought into the city as part of a wedding party."

"Really?"

"Well, I thought it was an elephant, but lost the thread when I got caught behind the dancers and the band. Anyhow, I barely avoided a collision, but lost my place in the serial. It took me an hour to get back in the chase."

"Shit, girl."

"Yup. Now, watch out at Phase Line Denver where New York junctions with Route Miami. There is a roundabout that comes in from the villages and some of the old villagers' brains are not calibrated for vehicle speeds. They expect you to arrive at donkey speed."

"Check."

The chase of Charlie1 had led to a new location — a warehouse on the Western edge of Jalalabad on the Kabul river. The warehouse was called Sorubi industries and was named A5. B3 and B4 were in the car and picked up a new passenger at A5 and then returned to A3. The new individual was named B6. George got a grainy shot of B6 as he entered Charlie1. Billy was still fuming when he returned to base that night — more at himself than anything else. Jameson had been right, there was quite a difference between the simulator at Bagram and the streets of Jalalabad. He was beginning to realize how hard it would be to work these streets until he got a street map locked into his head. You just couldn't drive and navigate with a map on your lap. It had to be all in your head. Sue had saved him and hadn't said a word about his missing the turn or about the extra passengers they picked up.

The team on the stakeout didn't have anything to report. B5 never left the Alpha until after B3, 4 and 6 returned. They all went to mosque, went to the market, bought food, and returned to the bed down location. After an hour on sight with no further activity, Jameson ended the surveillance serial. He had Deke emplace a video sensor disguised in simulated human dung on the edge of the road across the street from Alpha and the team pulled off to return to base one at a time. The sensor would alarm at the safe house if there was any activity as would the beacon on Charlie1.

Jameson started the morning meeting with a brief summary of the day's activities and a report that the video sensor had not shown any entrances or departures from the Alpha. He pointed out that this didn't mean that the Bravo didn't jump the fence, but given the long-term goals of the operation, he wasn't yet willing to set up an observation point both at the front of the house and in the alley behind the house. One thing at a time.

"The mission today is the same as yesterday. We find Bravo 3, we track him, we record any contacts and hope he takes us to another safe house or meets contacts with a new face. Now that we have done our warmup serial, we need to be prepared to work a full serial on foot if need be. We will start with George in the Lada, Nate in the Nissan sedan as Mike7 today, and yours truly with Billy will be in the radio van call sign Zero unless I am on the street when I am Mike6 and Billy will remain Mike5. Jim, you are two up with Sue in the Toyota taxi. Sue, you need to transfer the small comms package from the van to the taxi. Priority goes to the beacon tracker."

Sue nodded. She would have a smaller box today and could put it in the front seat of the taxi and operate it remotely from the back. If she had to go on foot, foxtrot in their lingo, Jim could run the tracker from the driver's seat.

Jameson continued after seeing everyone was tracking on his plan.

"I don't know how long we will be running today, so pack expecting to run a 4-5-hour shift. As we approach 4 hours, I will start to change out vehicles with Joe in the Toyota Hilux and Deke in the Niva. If we start a foxtrot surveillance, Jim dump Sue as close as possible and then either George or Nate will carry on as soon as they can dump their trucks. Everyone is full local today. I don't know how many of us will be on the street."

The groan from the team was loud and long. Full local meant shalwar kamise, the long shirt and baggy pants used by all men in Jalalabad, with wool vests both because that's what locals wear and that's how you conceal body comms and weapons. The local wool cap, a pakol, may have made the image complete, but it also meant a very hot head. Of course, Sue's groan was loudest and longest because full local for her meant a burqa. Better to disguise equipment but basically a black wool bag that she would wear from her head to her ankles.

On her first tour in Afghanistan, she was usually two up in a vehicle or sometimes working at the safe house with a drone operator running over the city. On the second tour, she was one up wearing a rubber full face mask making her look like another bearded male driving another beat up truck in the street. What she hadn't realized was how claustrophobic the burka would be during a surveillance run until she had to do it at the end of the last rotation. Instead of a well fitted mask, she was looking through a mesh screen that barely allowed a view directly to her front. It smelled like wet sheep and it was hot. Mix that with the street smells of burning charcoal, cooking meat, raw sewage and human sweat and it was delightful.

They had not established the stakeout when Nate drove by the Bravo already out on the street at 0750hrs and walking along a new route that he had not previously used in the last two weeks. The team had moved quickly, Jameson mobilized Jim and Deke from the team house and Sue was dropped off approximately a half mile ahead of the Bravo on the other side of the street. She confirmed his speed and direction, reported he had a canvas shoulder bag over his right shoulder and his gait did not suggest any change in his normal pattern of life. She let him pass by her and then crossed the street crowded with taxis, jingle trucks, donkey carts and people and resumed a conventional follow approximately 50m behind the Bravo.

This was not going to be a follow where she could speed up to close with the target if he started to move quickly. Her burqa seemed to work on its own to tie up her legs wrapped in the baggy pajama pants and force her to walk at a slow and deliberate pace. Sue decided then and there this was nothing like tracking terrorists in Kosovo on one of her tdys two years ago. The only good thing was that she was one of fifty burqas on the street out for morning shopping.

"4, do you have Bravo3?" The voice was too loud in the earpiece. She had to restrain herself from reaching up to her ear to make it stop or reaching on her hip to turn down the volume.

Instead, she pushed two clicks to confirm on the transmission key that was concealed in her left hand.

Another loud transmission. "All stations this is 0, 4 has Bravo3. Her GPS identifies her on Route Miami near Phase Line Niagara. 4, confirm this is correct."

Two clicks.

Luckily, the burqa was a loose garment which disguised her kit which today included an MP5 in a chest harness; she just looked like every other female black bag walking to the market. She had been following the Bravo for a half hour now since he was sighted on the street. It was entirely possible that he was going to the central market as well given the route he was taking. She focused on what she could see and didn't try to assume anything. That was the job of Zero. Her job was to keep track of the Bravo, observe and, as appropriate, report.

Bravo3 turned into a narrow alley to her left; just before he turned, he met Bravo2 coming from the opposite direction. It was no more than 2 meters wide, with a small ditch, known as a jube, running down the center filled with sewage. She couldn't see much as she approached the alley.

In a whisper, Sue said, "Bravo3 and 2, left, left in an alley near junction of Niagara and route Detroit."

"That is 4. Bravo3 and 2, left, left in an alley near Niagara and Detroit." She passed the alley and tried to get a glimpse of Bravo2, but the burqa eliminated any chance of a peripheral vision. She continued down the street for a few seconds then keyed the mike.

"I can't see him inside this crap. I'm going to turn around and go down that alley to see if I can sort out where he went."

"4, this is 0. Do not repeat do not follow them in the alley. Confirm, Mike4."

Too late. She had already entered the alley.

No longer looking like just another burqa clad female on the way to the market, she was moving quickly along one side of the alley, avoiding the sewage rut called a jube and trying to see where her Bravos went. The alley was a creation of the walls of two compounds, 3 meters high, brown mud brick with stains on the side of the walls in front of her where the locals had poured their nightsoil toward, but generally not into the sewage rut. No doors on either side. She could see the alley made a hard-right turn about 25 meters in front probably following the compound wall and connecting with a street perpendicular to the market street.

"Bravos have followed the alley which turns right, right heading north toward Route Detroit — I think."

"That is 4 saying Bravos heading north toward Route Detroit. Who can intercept at Phase line Dallas?"

"2 can."

"Roger, 2 can. Mike4, get out of the alley, do not continue the follow and go back to Niagara for pickup. Confirm."

She was about to key the mike, when her left leg collapsed. She was confused for a second. Why did it collapse and why couldn't she feel her leg? She was lying on her back in the jube. Then she heard the shots flying over her head, hitting the mud walls, careening down the alley and out into the street. Rifle fire — Kalashnikov. The assholes definitely couldn't shoot straight when they fired full auto. Bravo3 had pulled a AKMS out of the shoulder bag and was spraying the alley and the street beyond with 7.62 x 39 rounds. She could hear the screams behind her as some of the stray rounds hit people, cars and donkeys.

She keyed the radio. "Mike4 down. Mike4 down."

No more transmissions. She was on her back with her wounded leg underneath her. She pulled the burqa off and released the MP5 harness. Two bursts of three down the alley toward the shooter. The casings were hitting her in the face and she could smell the sewage as well as the gunpowder. Two more bursts of three down the alley. This time she heard a scream. Her attacker hadn't heard the first set of shots because of the suppressor. He had been approaching for his kill when the second set of rounds stitched his chest. He was down; she put another three in the body to be sure and waited to see if he would move or if someone else would enter the alley. He didn't move and no one else arrived to visit him

Less than a minute later, they blocked the alley with the commo van and Jameson rolled out with his M4. He found her in the jube in the alley. He saw Bravo3, dead, about 10 meters from Mike4. She was unconscious from blood loss and on the way to shock. He pulled her out of the sewage and put her inside the armored radio van. Her earpiece fell out as they placed her in the back of the van. The door had barely closed when the van took off, horn and a loud siren blaring driving pedestrians, vehicles and animals off the street.

Chief Jameson applied a pressure bandage to her leg and pulled a plasma bag out of the med kit and stuck the catheter into the first available vein he could find. He covered her upper body with a space blanket from the med kit. The pressure bandage did its job and stopped the bleeding. The van was filled with commo gear as well as his wounded operator. He switched to the local SOF command net.

"Sabre6, Sabre6, this is Mike6. We have an operator down. Mike4, she's alive but has gsw to the left leg. One dead Bravo. No further casualties. We need a medevac arriving at EVAC site Falls on Route Niagara now. We are enroute."

"Roger Mike6. Medevac enroute. Mike6 pull your team. Hotel6, you are the cleanup team. Confirm."

"Mike6"

"Hotel6"

He wasn't surprised that Sabre6 had been monitoring his internal net. That was the sort of boss Sabre6 was. He expected the medevac Blackhawk and little bird gunship had been launched as soon as Mike4 had transmitted her last message. They would be waiting at the evac site. Hotel6 was the current shift team leader at Jalalabad. He and his team would be onsite in minutes to police up Bravo3 and anything else they could find.

The Chief switched back over to the team internal net. "Mike2, Zero. Are you at Detroit?"

"Roger, Zero. I'm waiting at Detroit to intercept Bravo2."

"All stations, all stations, this is Zero. RTB, I say again, return to base. Mike4 is wounded and Bravo3 is dead. RTB and we will meet you there as soon as we meet the medevac bird and transfer Mike4. Be aware of possible surveillance on your victors. It is not yet clear if this was planned ambush. Do not repeat do not take surveillance back to the team house. If you are under or suspect surveillance, move directly to Sabre6 location. Confirm."

"Mike2"

"Mike3"

"Mike5"

"Mike7"

"Mike8"

"Mike9"

Chief Jameson turned back to Mike4. She was pale and clammy, but not as symptomatic of shock as he had feared. He started his SOF career as an SF medic and this gunshot wound was bad, but not as bad as some he had seen in a career that had taken him to Bosnia, Afghanistan, and Iraq.

He expected to see Mike4 back on the team in a few months. The wound was angry, it would be painful, but it would not stop Mike4 from staying with S&R. He was certain of that.

Sue was coming to terms with her injury. She was a BTK patient. BT — below the knee — amputations at Walter Reed Army Hospital were all too common. They knew how to handle them and they knew how to handle the victims of catastrophic injury. Sue had almost avoided the amputation. The AK round had broken her shin and torn a hole in her calf the size of a golf ball. But, her team had stabilized her and the medevac had her in Bagram mobile hospital in less than a half hour. The problem had been the infection. Bad luck falling into the sewage. On the other hand, if she hadn't fallen into the sewage ditch, the asshole might have killed her in his second burst. Something to be said for sewage.

They had tried to save the leg at Langstuhl hospital in Germany and at Walter Reed, but in the end, the infection ended up in the bone and they told her that they were going to have to amputate. It was not a choice — either amputate or die from the infection. It was the Army and they were not going to give Sue a choice, Special Operator or not. When she came out of the anesthetic, her mom was waiting for her at the hospital bed and within a month, they were fitting her with the initial prosthetic. After that she started to walk all over the hospital. First with a walker, then a cane, eventually on her own. The physical therapists told her that she was making real progress and, slowly, she saw the progress as well. Initially her walk was really a hobble. Then, a heavy limb where she swung the entire leg forward in a way that identified her as wearing a prosthetic. Now, no limp at all.

Through it all, her mom had been at her side. Her mom retired to Chicago, but she moved to a local hotel near Walter Reed as soon as Sue arrived from Germany. As Sue progressed, her mom started looking for a more permanent solution and, after a few weeks, she found and leased a two bedroom, ground floor townhouse in old town Alexandria. They worked together and cried together and made progress together. The relationship was a revival of her childhood memories of her mom and dad caring for her and her brother Bill when they were sick from some local crud that was common everywhere they lived. Common, but potentially deadly for children and there was always time for mom or dad to spend in the kid's rooms watching and helping them through fevers that only those who have lived in South Asia or Africa could know. Her folks were always busy with work, but if she or Bill were sick, everything stopped and Barbara and Peter focused on their kids.

In November 2003, when the team rotated back to Ft. Bragg, Chief Jameson and CSM Massoni came up to DC and told her silly stories that are the most common shared by war veterans. In a serious tone, Jameson told her that they had identified the terrorist safe house in J-bad and the squadron finished the mission "kinetically." In fact, because of her gunfight with Bravo3, the rest of the AQ target started talking on ICOM radios and that lead the team to the safe house. Jameson was also the first person to tell her that one of the reasons she was still alive was because after the first round from Bravo3 hit her leg and dropped her, Bravo3's second round glanced off the knife she kept in the sheath attachéd to her armor. Jameson said they found the hilt and broken blade on site later and he gave it to her mounted on a small wooden frame and brass plaque saying — "Don't leave home without me!" Massoni also gave her a small windup toy a blue plastic stegosaurus. "Hey, you need a pet," was all he said.

The next day, Jameson and Massoni returned with the Commander of the US Special Operations Forces who pinned the Purple Heart and a Bronze Star with V device on her gray Army sweat suit that served as her duty uniform at Walter Reed. Sue's mom and her brother were standing in the room near the door. This was the first-time Sue had ever met the three star that ran the entire SOF enterprise. He was a huge man who filled the room both with his muscular presence and his personality. He read a citation and then talked to Sue about the fight. Finally, he said "We need you back. Get healthy and rejoin the Command."

This had been the first-time Sue had heard anyone say she could be healthy enough to return to SOF. It was another emotional moment with Sue barely able to get out "Yes, sir." The Commander left with Jameson and Massoni. Sue had heard other members of SOF had recently arrived in the ward from Iraq, victims of a new terror weapon, the improvised explosive device or IED; no doubt he had other folks to see that day. Roadside bombs and ambushes were starting to make amputees the most common wounded warriors at Walter Reed.

After they left, Sue and her mom and brother walked down to the cafeteria for lunch. It was hard work and she needed a cane, but Sue was determined to walk with her family. Bill turned to Sue.

"You are looking a little pale, sis. You need to get out more."

"Thanks, asshole."

"Sue!" Barbara O'Connell had more than enough profanity in her vocabulary in at least three languages, but she had never tolerated profanity inside the family. Bill was separated from the Marines after a tour in Afghanistan and a tour in Iraq and he had just finished Quantico as a newly minted FBI special agent. He appeared in what Sue assumed was the "duty uniform" of a special agent — dark suit, white shirt, striped tie, with his sidearm and badge attachéd too obviously on his belt.

"So, Willie, now that you are part of the world's finest, what are you actually doing for a living?"

"Sue, I almost prefer asshole to Willie. Anyhow, I chase villains. I was assigned to the VCMO squad at Washington field office and we have plenty of bad men out there in DC and Northern Virginia."

"VCMO?"

"Violent crimes and major offenders."

Barbara winced slightly at the thought of her son chasing hardened criminals down dark alleys in Washington, DC.

"Mom, it's really not like it sounds. My squad supervisor and the seniors on the squad have rarely drawn their sidearms and none of them have ever had to use one. Mostly what we do is arm's length investigations and let the local PD do what they do best — put cuffs on offenders. It is a long ways from my time as a platoon commander in the Helmand."

"It's not about who you shoot, dear, it's about who is shooting at you."

"She has a point, Wyatt Earp."

"Thanks to you both and I still prefer asshole."

A month after the Walter Reed ceremony and after the excitement of her first Christmas in the US in years, Sue had a particularly bad set of days. At this point, she was living with her mom in the condo and spending her days in physical therapy at the hospital. Her mom would drive her to the hospital and leave her with the various doctors, nurses and physical therapists. Her new prosthetic didn't fit, the pain was worse than usual and then she started to have what she called "the dreams." Sometimes they were simple, childlike terror dreams of being chased along dark alleys and not being able to stay ahead of the enemy who she never saw but knew were behind her. Sometimes they were frustration dreams. She would be back with her team and Massoni would be ordering everyone to grab their kit and load up in the truck to go home. First, she wouldn't be able to find her ruck, then, once she found her ruck, she couldn't find her rifle, then she couldn't find her sidearm, eventually, she was ready and then realized she hadn't strapped on her prosthetic. She was hobbling over and over again in a team house with empty rooms and long corridors. All she could hear was Massoni saying "Come on, Sue. We got to leave. Come on!"

She woke each time when in the dream she fell and couldn't get up. She soaked her new pajamas, the pillow and usually the top sheet. To get back to bed, she had to call her mom to help change the bed and Sue simply didn't want to do that. She would spend the rest of the night in the chair in her room reading or in the kitchen drinking coffee from her French press. Sue had already received some psychological counseling about both the trauma of an amputation as well as PTSD, but Sue still figured she was failing herself. If she just was "an adult" the nightmares would go away and the pain would recede as she got used to the new prosthetic. The doctors didn't support that view. It was not about being an adult, it was about letting the wounds — physical and mental — heal. That would take time.

Sue was on her sixth night without any real sleep and walking like a zombie on the way to physical therapy at Walter Reed when she received an unexpected early morning visitor. Max Creeter appeared in the hallway. Or, at least, it more or less looked like Creeter. He was in a dark blue suit, blue shirt, a tie with small parachutes or balloons embossed over navy blue and wearing half glasses looking at a map of the hospital. He had a small bag in his hand and he definitely looked lost.

"Max?"

"Hey, Sue, I have been looking for you all over this place. Found some other folks I know who probably needed the visit more than you, but I'm pleased to find you."

"I didn't know you had hair and what's with the business armor?"

"I suspect you don't know, but I have given up the tdy circuit — at least for a while."

"Really?"

"Yup. The bases expanded, our job got folded into the expansion so conventional guys are now running the places. I could have gone to work for OGA, but that just didn't seem right. No offence to your family."

"None taken." OGA or "other government agency" was another SOF way of saying CIA. Hardly a secret code, but it did include a slight insinuation of "less than straight" when most operators said it as in "that other government agency." Max had simply used the letters as a descriptor the same way he had used Klingon.

"So, what do you do for a living?"

"Sue, I am mostly a mere, wretched, federal pensioner these days, though I do have a job as a part time instructor at CSIS."

The Center for Strategic and International Studies was the premier think tank in Washington loosely affiliated with Georgetown University. It was where the big brains of Washington addressed strategic issues; when CSIS called politicians and government officials, the phone was answered.

"CSIS? No offense, Max, but I never thought of you as an egghead."

"I prefer warrior scholar, thank you." Max smirked. "I suspect you were headed to PT and I don't want to delay you too much. I just wanted to give you a couple of things and then we can meet another time."

Max reached into the canvas tote he had in his left hand and handed two neatly wrapped presents. Sue was overwhelmed and had to sit down in the bank of chairs in the hallway, both because she wanted to open the presents now and because she felt a little carried away by Max's gift.

"Hey, it's not like the rest of the stuff that was in the tote — I brought novels, flowers, candy, and a small bottle of Jack to various pals in here today. You got the nicely wrapped stuff."

Sue opened the first package and it was a small paperback published by a Washington based academic press. *The Dogma of the Warrior: The Knights Templars During the Crusades* by James M. Creeter, PhD.

"Max, you are an egghead!"

"Yes, I admit to the crime now that you have the proof. It is my dissertation and there was sufficient interest that I decided to see if I could get it published. I signed it for you."

Sue looked at the title page. To Mike4, from one warrior to another.

Sue started to cry — not just sniveling, but really crying. Max sat next to her, he looked a little lost and looked a little like a grandfather that might have been foolish in giving the wrong gift to the wrong child.

"You OK?" was all he said.

"Max, it is fantastic."

"Well, if you think that is fantastic, then open the other present."

The second wrapped package was small, about the size of a deck of cards. She opened it to find a green leather box. Inside the box was an old coin.

"When the Templars were based in Malta, they were wealthy warrior priests or, perhaps, wealthy pirates. It depends on your perspective. They had gold and silver coins struck during their Malta days. This is one of the silver ones. I love you as a daughter, Sue, but not enough to mortgage the house to give you a gold Templar coin."

"You don't own a house, Max."

"OK, so I wouldn't sell my Norton Commando for you."

Sue reached over and hugged Max with all her energy. She had never actually touched him before and she was not surprised that hugging him was like trying to hug a tree trunk.

"Sue, I haven't lived through what you are living with right now, but I did have a chest wound that took me out of action for a while.

You need to read the book, think about who you want to be now and remember, that one thing you will always be is a warrior. Now, get over to therapy on the double and get better. Your mates are waiting for you to come back."

O f course, her days as an S&R operator were over. That was just a fact of life. Sue was cleared to return to duty on 11 April and she drove herself down to Bragg. She could no longer drive her beloved Mazda Miata, but Bill had found a vintage 1965 Thunderbird convertible, had it repainted an electric blue, and had the engine reworked to the point where it was both fast and a dream to drive. Barbara and Bill presented it to her on April Fool's Day. The Spring weather was perfect and she took two days to drive from Northern Virginia to Fayetteville driving first to the Shenandoah and along Interstate 81 until she hit the Virginia — North Carolina border and then headed South and East along state roads through Winston Salem, Greensboro and Chapel Hill. Sue had not been pleased with Bill getting her a Virginia plate identifying her as a purple heart recipient, but it had more than paid its dues on several occasions at gas stations in Virginia and in North Carolina when Sue had lost track of the speed her T-bird was traveling. The North Carolina state policeman had been polite and warned her to "tone it down" and then spent another half hour looking at the T-bird. He said that the plate would nearly guarantee she would go unmolested by any lawman in North Carolina, but he still wanted her to drive safe and get to her destination alive. Sue agreed that this was a good idea.

Sue had maintained her condo in Southern Pines and moved back in with little drama. Her previous TDY lifestyle was such that the condo looked more like a hotel room than a house, but her cleaning service had prepared the place including stocking the fridge with fresh food, milk and diet soda. There was a note inside thanking her for her service and letting her know that they would do anything for her. The ladies of Merry Maids had previously adopted her as their daughter and the time at Walter Reed clearly hadn't changed that view.

The morning of 14 April, Sue put on her walking prosthetic, her fatigues and boots and drove on post. Her first stop was SOF main headquarters where she walked into J1 shop and reported in for duty. She had an appointment with a personnel counselor who was responsible for handling returning "wounded warriors." The only good thing about the meeting was when Master Sergeant Silver reached out with his left hand to shake hers. His right hand was a sophisticated prosthetic, but not sophisticated enough to shake hands. His army combat uniform fatigues had a master parachutist badge, a combat infantry badge, a halo badge, and on his right sleeve was a Special Forces combat patch.

"Chief, welcome back to the Command. I have heard from your unit that they miss you and want you to know that when we are through here today, they want to see you." Sue was pleased that things were returning to normal — at least as normal as you can get in SOF during two different wars. The Master Sergeant outlined the options that the Army and SOF were offering to her. First, he wanted her to know that if she wanted to leave service and start a new life, everyone would understand. She would leave with 100% disability and with the new GI Bill, she would be able to start a new career after any type of school she wanted. Sue was polite, but her face gave away her disappointment. She wanted to get back into the fight and was certain that she could still jump, still shoot and still do her job. Her interlocutor looked her in the eyes.

"I'm glad to hear it. So is the Command leadership. Still, you need to know that your days in S&R are over and I'm sure you know why. The job requires lots of street work and at least in the near term, you don't have the stamina or the balance to do the job. That doesn't mean that you can't work in the command, but not at S&R."

This hit Sue hard. She had a family in S&R and she wanted to return to them. They certainly wanted to see her, how could they believe that she couldn't hold up her end of the bargain?

"Chief, I don't make the rules or cut the orders. I just give the bad news. Here are your options. You can always return to the 525th. They would take you back in a second."

He saw that was a non-starter and before Sue could say anything, he raised his hand.

"There are two other options available. We can get you involved here at the Command or forward as an intelligence targeter. We need folks who are experienced and understand what the operators need."

He paused. "Or, we can put you in a slot in the next running of the

Agency HUMINT course and, assuming you pass, the Command will deploy you as one of our Klingons." He smiled. "I understand you come from a family of Klingons?"

Sue knew there was no real choice here. She certainly wasn't going to return to the 525th and she definitely did not want to spend her days working in the SOF analyst shop known as "the tank" because it was a windowless room where analysts worked 12 hour shifts, seven days a week. It was a box inside a box — whether it was at Ft. Bragg or Bagram or Balad, she didn't want to live in a box. She was a SOF field body and if they would keep her as a Klingon, then that was what she was going to be.

"Klingon is in the blood."

"We thought that would be the answer, Chief. You need to report to in-process for the Command training tomorrow at 0900hrs in building E4605. In the meantime, there are a couple of things you need to do today. First, you need to get a new ID card. You are now a Chief Warrant Officer 3 and you need to get an ID card that says that. You need to get a new access card for the compound that lets you in and out without that silly Visitor No Escort badge you are wearing and you need to talk to the air ops NCO to sort out when you can get your jump status back."

Sue looked at him. "Really?"

"Chief, we have several BTK jumpers in the command. Of course, if you don't want to…"

"Who says I don't, jumpmaster?" They both laughed as MSG Silver handed her a packet of personnel papers and a map of the various stops in the building.

SOF was determined that their students at the Farm were going to be prepared and would graduate with their civilian counterparts no matter what. During her in-briefing at the J3, she received a detailed outline of what would need to happen between 15 April and 10 August. She would start with classroom work, then practical exercises, and written tests. She had already received clearance for a series of Hollywood jumps including a water jump to determine if she could remain on jump status. She would receive additional driving and shooting training as well as advanced hand to hand combat training.

Still, for the next four months, Sue was going to be focused on preparing for the Farm. Sue attended the six-week prep school with the other five operators. There were two from her old S&R unit, two from an Army special operations group and two from NAVSPECWAR. The training was designed to test their writing skills and teach them the formats that would be used in the course. There had been little time for socializing or to sort out anything but names and service. The instructor cadre were a mix of trainers from the JFK Special Warfare Center and Schools and contractors who were former CIA and FBI source handlers. Any extra time gave Sue additional time to rebuild her strength and get used to her prosthetics. She was determined that by the time she started the Farm, no one was going to know she was a BTK wounded warrior.

STUDENT

S ue walked from the dormitory to the newest building on campus, three stories of dull gray concrete with large tinted windows identifying each floor. The auditorium was through the main doors and immediately to the front. Unlike any other building that Sue had observed so far, this was carpeted in a light gray. White walls covered with empty bulletin boards. No doubt those would fill up quickly as the course proceeded. An instructor in chinos and a blue polo shirt with the NCS spearhead logo asked her name, gave her a folder, and directed her down to the front — seat B5. Sue hated the mix of angled floor with periodic shallow steps, but she was damned if she was going to walk along the ramp that was on the side of the auditorium.

The auditorium at the Farm was small but still dwarfed the 30 students in the class who sat in the first two rows auditorium. She had not met her fellow students yet. She arrived last night and received an envelope at the gate. Inside was her dorm room key, a base badge — bright yellow badge with an alphanumeric — H23, a computer logon, and two sets of what appeared to be Vietnam era jungle fatigues in men's size small/long. The in-processing officer told her these were only for specific exercises and she was expected to report to class in "Farm casual." When she asked what he meant, he replied "any shirt with a collar and any pants that are long enough to cover your shins. We don't expect you to look like anyone special here for now." The thirty students in the auditorium were a mix of civilians and the six SOF operators Sue had met at Ft. Bragg.

A man in his mid-50s got up on stage. He was dressed in black suit, white shirt and gray tie. Highly shined black shoes. Rolex watch, stainless steel glasses. A short haircut and equally short, gray beard. Sue was already wondering where in the world they got this dinosaur.

"Ladies and gentlemen. Welcome to the Farm. You are about to spend 24 weeks here learning the art of espionage. My name is Lester Bayard and I am the chief of the Farm. I have served as a case officer, a branch chief, a group chief, a COB and a COS. Like the rest of my staff, I volunteered to come down here and teach my trade to a new generation of officers.

"You are entering this world at a time of world crisis and unrest that is probably worse than any time in my lifetime. We still have strategic adversaries like Russia, China, and North Korea. We have regional adversaries like Iran, Venezuela and Cuba. We also have non-state adversaries too numerous to count including terrorists, insurgents, transnational criminal organizations and cyber anarchists. These organizations and individuals are determined to do harm to the US and to our allies. Our job is to steal their secrets and to do so in a way so that they are not aware we know their plans and intentions.

"You already know that the CIA partners with our colleagues in DoD to conduct paramilitary operations and we partner with our colleagues in DoJ to disrupt terrorist operations against the home-land. We are not going to teach you how to do either of these oper-ations during this course. We are here to teach you one thing and one thing only — how to conduct espionage. If for some reason you came here to become the next thriller hero, please let us know sooner rather than later. There are parts of the intelligence community and the special operations community who need future heroes. This is just not the place.

"Espionage is not science; espionage is an art. You are going to learn over the next 24 weeks the case officer's motto: It depends. How you conduct an operation depends on the requirement. It depends on the situation. It depends on the target. It depends on the security ser-vice you are trying to defeat and the friendly services you are trying to avoid. We are not going to teach you a recipe on how to conduct espi-onage. We are going to teach you principles and some techniques that have worked in the past. You will have develop your own techniques over time that will likely be quite different from those we teach here. Just remember, if you violate the principles, you put yourself at risk, you likely will kill your assets and you may end up delivering faulty or even false intelligence to the Nation.

"Today, I want you to remember two things. Everything you do for the next 24 weeks is under scrutiny. We have one four-day break in the middle of the course where you can go and do as you please.

Otherwise, there is no time off and virtually everything that you do will be under some type of surveillance. Secondly, we are not looking for perfection here. Now, the second motto of the case officer: the perfect is the enemy of the good. We rarely have enough information to do a perfect job in any case. We only expect you to think through each problem, resolve quickly how to handle the problem and afterwards to report accurately what happened — good, bad or ugly.

"There are many ways that you might not pass this course, but there is one certain way to fail this course. That is to lie to an instructor or to your peers about an operational act. In espionage, there is no one out there but you — your bosses must be certain that when you talk to them, you will tell them what actually happened, not what you wish happened. We are going to test this aspect of the case officer's requirement over and over again. We are going to design events that are certain to fail. There will be other training events where you will fail because you haven't prepared enough or you didn't understand the requirement. That is expected. What is not expected or accepted is an unwillingness to report what went wrong.

"I will be seeing you over the next few weeks as an instructor. I will also see you in the cafeteria and likely in the gym or the pool. I hope to get a chance to have a one on one conversation with each of you. Best of luck."

The dinosaur left the stage and a younger version of the dinosaur came to the podium. This time a woman with more hair, no glasses, but still the dark suit.

"Ladies and gentlemen, my name is Martha Anderson. I am the chief instructor for your class. I am responsible for the training and will be the one who signs the certificate that certifies you as a strategic HUMINT collector. Over the next thirty minutes, I will go over the basic outline of the course and what you can expect from the instructor cadre. I believe we have created a course that is…"

She droned on for nearly 45 minutes. Sue couldn't stand this sort of presentation — after all, they handed each student a course schedule when they entered the auditorium this morning. It was clear enough to serve as a basic plan and vague enough to insure the students received nothing useful. Now the chief instructor was reading this to the students — Sue hated formal military training for the same reason — military pedagogy said, "say what you are going to teach, teach it, and then say what you taught." It was mental root canal work.

The pain ended just before 1100hrs. The chief instructor told the students to take the time to visit their advisor in the Admin building, have lunch and return to the auditorium for the first class at 1300hrs.

Sue walked down the hall toward her advisor's office. The admin building was perhaps the oldest building she had seen so far. It was a classic military style building from the 1940s — tile floors and pale green walls. Typical USG facility — nothing expensive and nothing attractive. Still, the tile floors were useful — Sue had learned that predictable surfaces were important. When she was walking and even running on a predictable surface, no one could tell she had a prosthetic. Of course, her advisor's office would be the last room at the end of the hall. She walked down the hall, the solid glass cube window throwing light on the tile floor.

Mary Sanderson looked up as Sue knocked on the open door. Mary had seen more than a couple students in her tenure at the Farm over the last two years and this was her last class before returning to the field. She liked the training program and felt she was making a difference, but it was time to get back into the trade. Sue would be part of the last set of students to be mentored; she intended to be certain that she made a difference. Mary's last assignment had been as a chief in Dubai and she was angling for a chief of station job in either Kuwait or Sana'a, but she would take a chief job anywhere to get back into the field.

Mary thought of herself as pretty fit for a fifty-year-old, but she knew her face looked older. Too much sun, too many late nights, too many bad tours in the "night soil" circuit in Central and South Asia. And, two divorces didn't help much either. Still, she no longer drank, no longer smoked, and during her two years at the Farm, she had become a runner and a kayaker. Her arms and shoulders were just this side of masculine which, added to the wrinkles on her face and her nearly six-foot frame, made her an imposing figure for her student mentors and even scarier for the students when she was role playing against them.

"Sue, come in and sit down." Mary looked at Sue carefully. This was the first time she had seen the girl up close. Her file picture was in uniform. Her SOF unit sent a half dozen of their best people to the Farm every class and SOF operators were usually in the top 10 percent of the class. They were motivated, well prepared, and far more mature than most of the civilian students that arrived at the Farm from Wall Street, law firms, and academia. Only the "internals," students who already had five years of service in the CIA or DIA before their selection to become case officers, were as prepared for the Farm.

Sue was different. Mary knew about the BTK, about the shooting and about her options in SOF once she left the Farm. More importantly, Mary knew Sue's parents and her grandfather. This was a secret that they alone would share and she wanted to use this introductory meeting to explain.

While Mary was watching Sue, Sue was scanning the room for something that would give her an idea who Mary was. In the conventional Army, senior officers had an "I like me" wall which usually included a couple of diplomas, some plaques from former units and maybe a couple of signed pictures of Army or civilian seniors. Mary's office was spartan. On the bookcase, there were about a dozen books which Sue could not make out and an Arabic-English dictionary. On the wall to the right of the desk was what looked liked a framed antique lithograph and next to it a framed US military Joint Operational Graphic map of Northern Saudi Arabia and Southern Iraq. Next to the map was a small black and white picture of what looked like a squad of British SOF operators in desert camouflage kit circa 1990. Desert Storm was Sue's best guess, but it could just as easily be anywhere in North Africa.

"Sue, let's cut the crap and any attempt to build rapport. I know more about you than you think. Of course, I have your complete military file. I am the only instructor here who will know who you are and where you come from. In fact, as you already know, I am the only one who knows your true name. To everyone else, you are Sue Richards and the only way that anyone is going to know otherwise is if you tell them. No one knows about your injury. The only thing they do know is you are a military student. They will know you for the length of the course as Hotel23. Is that clear?"

"Check, ma'am."

"OK, now get rid of the military response right now. Here at the Farm and in any station you go to in the future, your colleagues are all going to address you by your first name and you need to respond in kind. Of course, each COS may be a little different, but you'll sort that out soon enough. And, by the way, please never, ever refer to the COS as the 'CAUSE' — spell out the initials, don't try to make it a word. It gives the military guys away every time."

"Next, what you don't know is that I knew your parents and your grandfather. I served with your parents on my first tour in Nairobi — they were on their third tour as a tandem couple having served in Delhi and Moscow in what we call today "the bad old days" though I don't know when Moscow has had good days. You were ten. I worked with them again in headquarters when you were a teenager and then we lost touch. Of course, you know why I know your grandfather — he was head of the Farm when I was a student here."

Sue was not excited about this entire conversation. She had been a CIA brat growing up, served as CIA intern while in college and everyone she knew at college had been expected to be a CIA officer shortly after graduation. She knew stations and bases and the Farm as part of her life and, honestly, didn't want any of that to be part of her life today. She joined the Army out of college and built her own career in SOF. She didn't need a conversation about the "good old days" to motivate her to work hard for the family name. She didn't like the discussion of the "CIA family" and hadn't expected to hear it from an instructor.

"Your grandfather was famous. He was an OSS Jedburgh, one of the early case officers of the CIA, a Cold Warrior, often called COS "the world" because he was a chief in many different places and Farm chief before he retired. He was a tough instructor and even tougher on female students. After he retired, he lived in an old Victorian house just north of here until he left a couple of years ago. Used to work in the Farm archives for years as an annuitant — working for a dollar a year. Came to work down the coast in a beautiful old speedboat from the 40s. Quite the hero."

"Yes, ma'am. Quite the hero." She remembered Pete O'Connell as a short-tempered man who treated her father with contempt simply because he had never been in the military and never went "downrange" to serve in a warzone. Her mother tried everything to build bridges between father and son and her own career suffered as she tried to pick and choose places where Sue could have an education and Peter Jr. could have a chance at promotion. The only good thing she could say about her grandfather was he was an indulgent grandparent. When she was a William and Mary student, he often provided his house to serve as a safe haven away from her peers. The two of them didn't talk a lot. He could be sullen, but they did spend time on the Potomac river in his 1950s Cris-Craft. Peter Senior was crushed when his son died of cancer in 2000.

Sue came back for the funeral; SOF had arranged her space available on every available air force and navy aircraft from her tdy in Nairobi to Norfolk. She arrived in time to buy a dark pants suit and join the family at the residence that Peter Sr. had on the river. They took her dad's ashes, went out on the river in the Cris-Craft and sent her dad on his way to the Atlantic Ocean. Her grandfather docked the boat, walked into the house and got quietly and thoroughly drunk. Barbara and Bill joined her mom in the family car and drove up to Northern Virginia where her mom and dad had been living while serving a final tour in Headquarters.

"Sue, you have nothing to prove to me and I doubt you have anything to prove to anyone here. What I want you to know is that I owe your family a debt that I can't ever repay from that tour in Nairobi and I want you to know that I'm ready to repay that debt as well as serve as your advisor over the next 6 months."

Sue puzzled over this. Her mom never told her anything about a Mary Sanderson or about the Nairobi tour and she had never asked about their first tours in Delhi and Moscow. They had carpets and brass in the house picked up in India and more carpets and other stuff from tours in Central Asia in the early 90s, but no stories. Up until now, she had never thought it important. However, it was beginning to be important.

"What's the next step here… Mary."

Mary smiled. Sue was cautious (a good thing) and probably would take some development before she would open up. That was fine — there were months to go; Mary started on her standard pitch that she used for every new student.

"You start with the basics. You are going to learn by doing. You will have a few classes, but mostly you will get the principles of espionage tradecraft, some recommendations on specific tradecraft and then you will practice and practice and practice. We use a case study methodology at times and you will hear about your grandfather in one of the case studies — his work is still held as a standard.

You will work alone though you may work as part of a team in specific problems — those will be rare. Everything you do here is evaluated and watched. You will not have a private moment for the next few months except in the bathroom and the shower and the break after week 12. Remember that the next time you start to gossip with another student."

"This trade requires a degree of commitment. It is more than a profession, it has to become your life if you are going to succeed. As a third-generation member of this community, you already know the toll it takes on your life. I also know that your SOF time has taught you a commitment to an organization and a lifestyle. We are going to be testing you to see if you can apply the discipline you already have demonstrated in your previous life to our trade. I have no doubt you will succeed, but don't expect it to be easy."

Sue thought back about going through S&R selection — two women, thirty men when they started, she and six men survived selection. She doubted that this course would be much of a challenge after selection, but she knew enough about the Agency to avoid that comparison. She looked Mary in the eyes and nodded.

"Of course, you think SOF selection was hard and this will be easy. Your Selection was hard and designed to be hard." Mary paused to see if Sue would react — she didn't.

"Here, we are not going to put you through physical challenges other than lack of sleep and plenty of time on the street. Our challenges are based on demands on production and an exceptionally high standard of performance. Tradecraft keeps you and your assets alive. Nothing more complicated than that. Different kinds of challenges than you had in the past. Not easier and certainly not harder, just different."

Sue had seen this sort of bait and switch technique during her own selection course, so she was prepared to avoid a confrontation with this instructor and play the committed student. Still, she had never been clear what "tradecraft" meant when her mom talked about it or the SOF "secret squirrels" talked about it when they did joint operations with S&R. So, perhaps, she might learn something here.

"Sue, don't be angry with me, your parents, or your grandfather. Just do your job here and leave the rest for after graduation."

This did surprise Sue. Did she look angry? She had spent her military career living inside herself and avoiding expressing any emotion; defeating the hard-core bone heads who didn't believe women belonged in special operations through not taking the bait when they tried to get her angry. So, how did Mary know after a few minutes where she was doing all the talking?

"Sue, it is part of the trade you are about to learn. You will learn to read people quickly and determine whether they will commit treason and why. Reading your mind wasn't half as hard as that. Now, tell me why you want to be in this trade."

She started into her standard answer that she gave to everyone in the chain of command, the shrinks who reviewed her file, and the instructor cadre who determine which operator gets to go to the Farm.

"It is a natural extension of my previous work in S&R. We are collectors of intelligence — we watch our targets and collect small data points about their lives, their colleagues and their jobs. After Walter Reed, when they offered me this chance, I took it as a way to go to the next step — to become a human intelligence collector. Someone who would acquire intelligence not simply by observation but by debriefing." She went on and on — not really thinking about what she said, just saying the standard pitch which worked before with all the other players.

"Not good enough Sue. In fact, that is crap. Your answer only explains why you might want to stay a military intelligence officer. Why do you want to be a case officer — convincing someone to commit treason?"

This was the first time Sue had heard anyone talk about "treason." Previously, the targets were "sources" or "assets" or even "agents" but no one talked about spies and treason.

"I don't have a choice — I either become a recruiter of spies or I have to leave my unit. If they told me to learn to be a surgeon or a jet pilot or a garbage man so that I could stay in the unit, I would do that too. Nothing more to it than that."

"Well, Sue, that might be enough. You'll have to see for yourself as we move into the course. I suspect there is nothing more to talk about today. Your first class is tomorrow at 0800hrs and then your first practical exercise is this Friday night. Over the weeks in practical exercises, you will see me there, but I will be in role, so don't expect me to be me.

One final point: after every exercise, you and I will meet to review your performance. Your evaluations are called blue sheets simply because we use blue paper to identify evaluations once we put them in your file. You will not talk to the role player/evaluator. You will only talk to me. So, let's plan on meeting on next Thursday at 1800hrs. By that time, you will have completed the exercise and completed your write ups, they will be graded and we will know how you did. Until then, cheers."

Sue got up and left. She walked down the hall with a slight limp. This was likely to be harder than she thought.

Lunch in the mess hall at the Farm was the first time Sue saw how active the facility was. The venue was traditional US military dining facility. A long serving line, followed by a cash register and open seating. The facility could be found on every Army post in CONUS and in the big facility at Bagram and Balad. What made the facility different was the clientele. The students from her class were all in casual clothes wearing the bright colored badges that identified them by program (H — which she assumed was for HUMINT) followed by a student number. Other students in orange badges with 10S appeared to be from some ongoing class as did students in green fatigues with red badges marked 6CB. The red-badged students were all carrying "red guns"plastic simulation weapons — in concealed carry holsters. The fatigues were curious because they appeared to have red permanent marker marks on their arms, legs and across their chests. The instructor cadre all wore 5.11 cargo pants and blue polo shirts with blue photo ID badges with their names — all clipped to their collars. The cadre were the only ones who had to pay for their meals.

Members of her class sat at two of the open tables. At this point, they were all uncomfortable with the setting, the crowd and each other and it didn't offer much in the way of social time. Sue sat with her SOF colleagues. At least they had been together for more than a day and had more than enough shared background to trust each other, at least more than the rest of their new colleagues.

"You think these kids know anything about anything?" Joe Billings was an Army Master Sergeant, SOF operator who looked at the change to HUMINT as a means of sustaining a career that had taken its toll on his back and every joint in his body.

"Hey, you jealous of their age?" Jerry Ackers was a SEAL who always seemed to have a smirk on his face and a quick response ready during their preparatory training.

"I think a balding man in his 40s is sexy, don't you Sue?"

Sue had just taken a mouth full of salad, so she avoided entering this bit of macho stupidity.

"Somebody talking about sexy men?" A young lady in her late 20s sat down at their table. She was slim, had long hair pulled into a pony tail and wore very "sensible" black framed glasses.

"Melissa Hosteen. Not my real name, but I am a Navajo. Pleased to meet you all. I don't know anyone, so I figured I would join your tribe."

She looked at them offering anyone the chance to take in that challenge. No one did.

"I'm Sue. These madmen at Peter, Joe, Jerry, Sandy, Ginger (cause of his red hair) and Pigpen (you can figure that one out). Don't expect them to be polite, they were all raised by wolves."

"Wolf tribe, I like it." Sue blushed, she hadn't thought about Native American iconography when she added the epithet.

"Sue, your job is to teach me your tribal rules. I need someone here I can trust and I figured hanging out with the guys from the pyramid of cool will keep me safe." At the time, Sue thought nothing of this comment and couldn't quite figure out the pyramid comment.

At the end of lunch, an instructor made an announcement.

"Class 2, get on the bus outside."

The bus traveled along a two lane highway on post and pulled up at a medium sized, brick building surrounded by a wall and concrete obstacles.

It was a good simulation of most US facilities Sue had visited in Africa or Central Asia. Outside the building was a sign:

United States Embassy. Republic of Zed.

"Ladies and gentlemen, welcome to your new life assigned to the Republic of Zed." The instructor spoke from the front of the bus. "Today, you begin work in Zed by in processing at the embassy annex which is the building to the left of the chancery. After that, I will take you to ROZ station to meet the chief. You will begin classes back at the auditorium tomorrow at 0800hrs, but all practical exercises will start and finish from the Embassy. Clear?"

"Please take this seriously. We certainly do." The bus pulled forward into the main gate of the walled compound. Guards in full combat uniform conducted a sweep of the bus for explosives, checked the driver and instuctor's ID and then allowed the bus into the inner courtyard. The door opened and the instructor simply said "Follow me."

The embassy annex was a large warehouse with a high bay door and a smaller personnel door on the side of the embassy. Parked behind the warehouse were five rows of compact sedans in various colors. Once they entered the warehouse they were faced with four tables.

"Please move to an open table and start your in-processing."

Sue walked across the warehouse to a table with what appeared to be electronic gear. Melissa followed her. A middle-aged woman greeted Sue as she arrived.

"OK, Hotel23, first question. Do you want a messenger bag or a backpack to hold your gear?"

"Messenger bag."

The woman pointed to a box with 20 bags.

"Pick one from our highly attractive selection." Sue picked a well worn sand colored bag with a broad shoulder strap.

"Next, put the following in your bag. One iPhone with charger, one iPad with charger, one digital camera, one ICOM encrypted radio, one vest for the radio, two ear pieces, multiple batteries for the radio, earpieces and camera. Then sign here and move to the table to your left."

Sue grabbed the equipment as quickly as she could without dropping the individual pieces and placed each in the bag. She noticed the sheet she was signing was simply a log of students. She had to think for a second because she was now Sue Richards and everything she signed here would be in that name — she would definitely have to practice the signature.

"Where do I sign for the specific pieces of equipment?"

"Dear, this is the Republic of Zed. We aren't worried that you are going to lose the equipment or sell it. Just plan to return it in whatever condition it is when you PCS out of Zed."

Sue walked to her left doing a quick calculation of the material in her bag. As near as she could tell, she just picked up $2500 worth of kit and nobody made her accountable. This was definitely not the Army. As she walked away, she heard the lady repeat the performance for Melissa: "OK, Hotel 16, what will it be…"

Next desk. A 60 year-old in mechanics overalls looked at her and spoke in a deep Southern drawl.

"Ford or Volkswagon?"

"Excuse me?"

He slowed his speech as if speaking to a non-native speaker or a child. "Do you want a Ford Fiesta or a Volkswagon Golf?"

"Ford will be fine."

He threw her a set of marked keys.

"There ya go. Parked in slot 27. Sign here and move on. Next!"

The next table was easy to sort out. Another woman, this time who looked to be nearly 70 stood in front of 30 red guns, 30 concealment holsters, 30 sure fire flashlights, and 30 simulated red batons still in their plastic.

"Glock 19 or 26? Remember, what you pick is what you get issued for real on the range."

"26"

"Right or left handed?"

"Right"

She handed Sue a simple, plastic waistband holster with a simulated Glock 26.

Next she handed Sue a sure fire flashlight and the baton.

"Do not take the baton out of its packaging until you are instructed to do so."

"Yes, ma'am."

"Sign here. Next."

Sue looked over her shoulder and said to Melissa "take the 19, you'll do better on the range when you get the real thing." She heard Melissa say "26" before she walked away. When Melissa caught up to her at the next desk, she said "I know a little bit about guns, but thanks for the advice."

The final desk looked very much like a desk at a DMV anywhere in the US. A young man who looked about 15 ran the desk. Still, he had the Farm field badge so Sue assumed he had to be at least 25.

"Name"

"Sue Richards" quickly typed in. "Date of Birth — month, date, year?"

"03 12 1971"

"Place of birth?"

"Weisbaden, Federal Republic of Germany"

"Please pick a US city, OK?"

"Richmond, Virginia."

"Great. Now, which of these photos do you want to use?"

While he had been asking her questions, he had been also taken photos from the small camera next to his desk. None of the photos would take a prize; any of the photos would be useful to identify her.

"First one is fine"

"Foreign travel in the last five years?" Her natural suspicion took over.

"None."

"Look, ma'am. Either you tell me or I get it out of the file or I make it up. You don't want the last option."

"OK. Kenya 2000, Kosovo, and Germany 2000, Afghanistan 2001, Dubai 2002, Afghanistan 2003 direct into theater.

"Got it."

After about a minute listening to the printer behind him reel off pages, he turned away from her, cut the pages and ran them through the laminator. Five minutes later, he handed her a red and green Republic of Zed (ROZ) diplomatic driver's license and a black US diplomatic passport with entry/exit stamps for Kenya, Germany, Uzbekistan and Dubai plus multiple entry stamps into the US at Washington Dulles International. A quick check surprised Sue. Except for the ROZ entry stamp into her passport, the rest of the stamps looked real and the passport was as real as any passport she had previously except it had a series of holes punched into the front cover and a front page that said FOR EXERCISE ONLY. She shoved it into her new bag.

"Next."

Sue returned to the entrance where the rest of the crew were gathering. This wasn't like any bus she had been on in training before, but it wasn't a party bus either, that was for sure. Next stop was the office of the COS of ROZ.

The office of the Chief of Station in the Republic of Zed was similar to her father's office when he was COS in Baku. Basic government furniture. A desk placed in front of a set of bookcases. Two couches on either side of the room, one set against windows that overlooked the forest outside the compound. Directly in front of the desk were two straight backed chairs. The office walls were filled with pictures of various foreign field locations, a few family pictures and a couple of "I like me" pictures that were placed on the wall next to the book case. The case itself had a mix of books, family pictures and what appeared to be a pair of wooden awards cases open to show the awards.

The COS sat at the desk as the class crowded into the room. The room was barely big enough for the class, but assuming everyone stood still, it would be tolerable. Sue made sure she was near a wall at the rear of the room in case she had to lean a bit to take weight off the prosthetic. Of all the challenges she faced with the prosthetic, prolonged standing still was the worst — if she stood in a traditional military stance with weight distributed on both legs, after a while, the prosthetic attachment point started to throb. Luckily, in the civilian world, she rarely had to stand at attention or parade rest and could shift her weight. Still, she had learned over time to make sure she was in a place where she could do that without making it look like she was fidgeting.

"Welcome to Zed. My name is Barry Johnson and I am the COS here. I realize this room is not designed for this many people and I will keep this short so that we don't all faint from lack of oxygen."

Nervous laughter from some of the men and women in the room. Slight looks of suffering among the SOF and any other students who had lived through this sort of speech before.

"I expect to see each of you daily as you progress on operations in my country. I won't expect a lengthy report, simply a report that focuses on answering three questions: What happened? Why did it happen? And What's next? Simple points. I will be reading your reporting which will be more detailed, so don't spend a lot of time on things here. Is that clear?"

Nodded and verbal assent worked its way around the room.

"Now, I want to emphasize one thing about life in Zed Station. You are here to do two things. You are here to recruit spies and collect intelligence. We expect you to do so while defeating the Zed service. You have two things to think about as you work here:

"First, how do you convince someone to commit treason? What are the inner flaws or inner desires in a target's character that will convince him or her to make this irrational jump into treason and to trust you to keep them safe?

"Secondly, how will you keep a recruited asset safe? Once that person agrees to help the United States government understand the workings of Zed, its political, military and economy, your primary obligation is to make sure this relationship remains hidden from the Zed security services. Traitors in Zed are hung. Traitors to the extremist cause working against Zed are beheaded. Anyone who says yes to you is placing their life in your hands. You need to be certain that what they are going to give you is worth that risk and, if it is, then you have to be certain that they will survive this decision.

"I won't work to ask you this question every time we meet, but you can expect it to be part of my calculations as I understand the nature of your operations and what you want to do to move forward on these cases. Often, people ask me why you are called case officers. It sounds so bland compared to special agent as used by our law enforcement colleagues or operator as used by the Special Operations community. You are case officers because you are responsible for your espionage cases — people who trust you and who share both their government's secrets and their own darkest secrets. In a sense, you are their confessor, their parent, and often their only friend. Handling these cases is what you do for a living.

"OK, you will hear more from me in your one on one sessions. I expect each of you to be prepared when you come into this office. I expect you to be serious about your cases, no matter how weird or absurd the individuals may be. Good luck in Zed and I will see you soon."

The students filed out of the office, past empty offices filled with computers, down the hallway, through "the hard line" (a metal door that looked more like a bank vault door than a normal door) and down the stairs to "Post One" where a Security guard nodded to them as they exited through the hardened door with bullet proof glass. Sue and her fellow students didn't have much to say to each other as they got near the bus.

"OK, you have your kit and you have your vehicles. They are parked behind the embassy and you can make your way back to the housing compound on main post on your own. You have the rest of the day to explore the roads on post so that you won't get lost. Do not, repeat, do not go off post tonight. You have a full day tomorrow."

"Here are some rules you need to follow:

"Your kit is your responsibility. You have a small locker in your room. Keep your kit locked up. That locker is your safe site. We don't go into it for any reason. If we find your kit unattended anytime, anywhere else during the class, you have to explain to the COS why your stuff is missing somewhere in RoZ. You don't have to carry any of it around if you don't need it. That's your call.

"There is only one other exception to this rule: when you are inside hard line and in station, you can leave your bags unattended. This is the only place that is secure. The rest of the base and the outside world is filled with hostiles.

"Your only personal time will be before breakfast and after dinner. Of course, if you are working on a case after hours, that is entirely different — then you don't get any time off. So, if you want to work out or relax or have a beverage of choice, you need to do that between the hours of 1900 and 0800hrs.

"We post a class schedule for each week in your room, in classroom 1, and on the video monitor in the dining facility. We switch week schedules at 1800hrs on Saturday so you will know where you are expected to be each day for the next week after dinner on Saturday. We do not tolerate late students. We will give you a COS briefing schedule for each practical exercise. As you might imagine, the COS is a busy person and you are expected to be in his office on time. Tomorrow morning, classes start in Classroom 1 at 0900hrs. We start with a security briefing — both real world and RoZ threats. After that, we start training. No need to bring your kit with you tomorrow. All you need is something to write with and one of the notebooks that is in the desk drawer in your room.

"Good luck to you all. I will be seeing you later in the program." The instructor got on the bus and it left through the main gate.

After the bus pulled away, Sue let out a deep breath. She realized that after all these years, she had been convinced somehow that she would end up on day one with a sand bag over her head in a dark room with an instructor screaming at her. No sign of that… yet.

Sandy walked over to her. "So, they aren't going to punish us, today? I don't think I can stand this sort of kindness."

Melissa looked up at Sandy and asked "Punish?"

Sue interjected "Usually on day one of these sorts of classes, if you get on a bus, you end up in some sort of jail cell or workout pit where the instructors are not very nice."

"Really?"

Pigpen walked by, headed to his car.

"Yes, really."

Sue explained "In most selection courses, they want to sort out the posers from the folks who really want to be there. Some sort of punishment is usually the tool they use early in the course to sort out one from the other. Posers usually quit in the first couple of days. After that, the instructors realize they are going to have to shoot you to get you to quit. It doesn't get any easier, but it tends to get less randomly brutal. So far, it doesn't look like that is the technique they are going to use here."

Pigpen looked over his shoulder as he headed to the parking lot.

"You realize of course, we still have to make it back to the barracks on our own in one of these cars."

Melissa immediately ran to catch up with Pigpen."I will follow you, OK?"

Martha Anderson stood in front of the class in the main auditorium. She was no longer dressed in business attire; she was wearing what Sue had come to realize was the instructor uniform — flats, chinos and a navy blue shirt with the OSS spearhead on the left side of the shirt and her blue badge hanging from a lanyard that identified her "home" division in the directorate of operations. Sue couldn't make out the lanyard markings, but she knew already that home division meant everything to case officers. Her parents and her grandfather were from the Soviet division and in rare moments of candor, they would tell Sue that a visitor was from this division or that division rather than telling her where the visitor physically came from in the US. It was as if the division was more important culturally than the station or university or home town.

Martha started the lecture precisely at 0900hrs even though there were three empty seats of students who were probably running from the mess hall right now after enjoying an extra cup of coffee. Since the students had assigned seats, their absence would be noted by the two instructors sitting on the side watching. Sue expected Mary to be one of those two instructors and, she was not disappointed. After years of Army instruction and a life with parents from the Agency, Sue knew that if you were only five minutes early to an appointment, you were already late. Luckily, none of her new friends were late. SOF folks knew better and so did Melissa Nez.

"Ladies and gentlemen, today's presentation is one that I like to give myself. It is at the heart of your training and it is one of the three major principles of my trade and, if you pass, your future trade. This is a discussion of the nature of treason. After all, the creation of traitors, the management of traitors, and the safety of traitors is the core of our business.

"I like to start this discussion by using this term that has so pejorative a reputation. After all, when we think of traitors we think of all of the Americans arrested by the FBI, convicted, and serving in one of the two maximum security prisons that hold our traitors. When I joined the Agency, the names Julius and Ethel Rosenberg still resonated — they were the last traitors we executed for working for the Soviets. They are most often depicted as demented people who were alcoholics or maladapted loners who never appreciated America. All true, but only from our perspective. From the perspective of our adversaries, these American traitors were their assets, their agents, their key sources of information and brave men and women who served another country."

Martha stopped at this point as the three latecomers arrived in the hall. She quietly watched them walk down the stairs and take their seats in auditorium. She waited while they pulled out their notebooks and pens and settled into their seats. She watched them as they seemed to shrink into their seats as the nervous silence spread across the auditorium from the three to the rest of the students and eventually to the instructors on the side of the hall. Martha did not say anything nor did she show any emotion at all at being interrupted. She simply started again.

"So, what is the nature of treason? Or, better discussed, why do individuals commit treason? How do we get individuals with access to information to commit treason? These questions are central to what we do for a living. And, honestly, it is one of the reasons why we often lose some of our best students. In nearly every class, one of our students tells their advisor — I know how to do this, I think I'm pretty good at it, but I can't bring myself to convince another human to betray his country. We prefer you face this question soon and if you decide during the class that you are one of the folks who can't do this central task, there are many other jobs in the Directorate of Operations and in the rest of the Agency. There will be no penalty for facing this personal decision and realizing you are not a good fit for this behavior. We want you to think about it and we want you to face the challenge before you graduate and we send you to the field.

"Why do people commit treason? For nearly a century, our British and Russian colleagues have been using the acronym MICE to explain motivations of traitors. MICE stands for money, ideology, compromise, and ego. I also have a colleague who says that treason is an irrational act that is never easy to understand. I disagree with both depictions and offer the following: individuals who are dissatisfied with their lives, who have reached a point where they have come to realize they are not going to arrive at their hoped for level of status will always look for alternatives that help them come to terms with their desires: financial, ideological or egotistical. These are the people who embezzle funds. These are also the people who suddenly have affairs or take risks with alcohol, drugs, or high adrenaline activities.

"It is not always a decision based on what we would consider immoral motivations. Sometimes, that decision can be entirely honorable. For example, the true believer who finds himself surrounded by corrupt officials from his own party and decides the only way he can change the system is to work with the US. Or, the official who needs special health care for a family member and has received no support or even acknowledgment of his fears that he is about to lose a close family member unless someone helps. Sometimes, the decisions are dishonorable. The mediocre bureaucrat or scientist who thinks they should be more senior than they actually deserve to be or the terrorist who simply wants revenge on his peers. Honorable or dishonorable, it is up to the case officer to identify the motivation and then use that motivation to convince the target that it is in his best interest to cooperate.

"One thing we do not do is place people under duress. This is the 'compromise' part of MICE. Many services do. They structure elaborate schemes to catch targets in compromising positions and then blackmail them to deliver information. That may work for some countries and may work in some cases, but our analysis over sixty years of operations is that blackmail may get a person to say yes, but you will never know precisely what "yes" means. They will always be looking for ways to get out from under the compromising situation and, honestly, the best way to get out from under the situation is to turn you into the host nation security service. We are going to teach you how to find a person who actually wants to commit treason — even though he may not know it — and then to convince him that treason is in his best interest.

"So, the basic question is how? This is where the world of the case officer is built around the saying "It depends." It depends on you. It depends on your target. It depends on their frustrations and it depends on the security service you are facing. I say it depends on you because you have to decide who you are going to engage and how. There are far more people in the world who are capable of treason than you think. You will have to pick an individual and, also, you have to decide what you will do to get to know this individual. I know many successful case officers who will not work certain kinds of targets or certain kinds of people simply because they will not go the full measure required to recruit that specific target. Over time, you realize how successful you are is not necessarily dependent on being able to work every target every time.

"You have to be willing to give much of yourself to this effort. You have to share confidences and you have to be precisely what the target is looking for in a confidential relationship. You have to get to know your target better than anyone else in the world. Better than his mother. Better than her spouse. You need to become the closest friend, the secret confidant, even the person they confess to when they sin. When they confess their sins or describe their most secret desires, you have to be prepared to use these confessions to your advantage. You have to guide the target. You have to explain that you are offering the target a chance to exchange a "normal" though disappointing life with a extraordinary though dangerous life. You have to do so without appearing to judge them, but you still are judging them — not on their moral values, but on whether they are willing, whether they are capable, and whether they can do the job and remain safe. This is the world you are entering.

"You must engage people at a level far deeper than you have ever before. Our work is similar to seduction, but it is more complicated. The seducer has a simple mission really — gain a target's confidence and offer some type of excitement and gratification at a very basic level. In our world, we are always working the personal and the professional at the same time — always. From the minute you meet a likely target, through your effort to gain confidence, to the moment of recruitment and then every time you see your new recruit until he is an established asset and then over and over again you have to explore emotions, fears and desires, to make sure the asset remains productive and safe.

"I keep mentioning safe because one of our key goals in espionage is longevity. We are training you to find and recruit assets who will work for years. We do not play checkers in this trade. We play chess. We plan many moves ahead and we expect our recruited assets to remain productive for an entire career. We decide when the relationship should end. They do not. We decide if they can remain safe and remain productive. We assess their efforts every time we meet them. And we assess their motivations every time we meet them because people change and their motivations change as well. If you assume the motivations of an asset are static, you will end up arrested and the asset will end up dead. It is that simple and that complicated."

Throughout the lecture, Martha had been making direct eye contact with each student — in a way that surprised Sue. She had thought that her time in William and Mary and her time as a student in the Army that she had seen just about every instructor technique there could be. Some professors were good showmen, others were not. Some military instructors were almost robotic in following the rules of military instruction, others were more comfortable with their subject matter and seemed committed to passing on the Army "wisdom." Martha's lecture was more pointed, more personal and more disturbing. When she made eye contact, it was not for a brief moment, it was for an entire sentence or sometimes two. She appeared to be talking to you personally, not to a room of students in an auditorium. Sue had seen this level of intensity in her grandfather and in her mother. It was scary as a child and, honestly, even more scary now. Martha left the podium and Sue's advisor Mary walked over and started her portion of the lecture.

"Thanks, Martha. So, for those of you who are wondering what's next in this lecture on horrors, I'm next. This is your first lecture on how to build trust sufficient that you can take a target by the hand and lead him or her into the darkness that is espionage. We use the same method that you all have used before when you seduced a man or a woman. First, you have to know the person. Know them better than they know themselves. Know their most intimate desires and their greatest fears. It sounds dramatic, but remember, we are talking about convincing a person to commit a very dramatic and, likely life-threatening act.

"In the movies, the target is always obviously vulnerable and the ops officer always brilliant. That is not more true than any movie portrayal of lawmen or soldiers. Super vulnerable people don't have access to secrets or, if they do, they are watched by their security service. It's up to you to find a person who does not appear to be vulnerable to recruitment and yet, someone who has secret desires that are not being met by their everyday life.

"How do you do that? You work hard to understand everyone you meet, let experience teach you the signs of vulnerabilities and then slowly, carefully reveal those vulnerabilities to both yourself and your target. We all have secrets we hide, but wish we could share. It is your job to be the person that the target feels he can share those personal secrets. This is one of the reasons that most extroverts do badly in this course and, if they pass, do badly in the field. The internal voice of the extrovert drowns out the voice of the target and an extrovert never really gets to hear the secret that will motivate the target to take your hand and go over to the darkness."

Sue listened to Mary as she used the rest of the hour to describe methods of elicitation and manipulation that were common sense, but methods she had never used in this way. She also thought about her parents. So quiet, so ordinary, but apparently working this task for years while she and her brother were growing up, taking dance lessons, horseback riding, and playing soccer. Sue had no memory of any of this. Her parents had friends, entertained, went to different lectures and receptions. When did they transform into manipulative agents of the CIA? Or, as Martha said, were they always day in, day out, both loving parents and hunters of human vulnerability. What did two decades of doing this do to your real persona? Or, did that become who you were?

Sue also thought about Mary. She was so confident and so much more direct than her parents had been. Sue realized that part of this was Mary was playing the role of instructor and had to be direct. Still, there was a hard edge to her that she had not seen in her parents when she was growing up. Was that a function of their commitment to being good parents or was there something about Mary that was different from her parents — perhaps because of her assignments, perhaps because she was a single woman who never had a chance to share some of her own doubts with anyone. Sue wondered if Mary was the person that she would become if she remained on this career path and remained a single woman.

In 13 August, each student had an appointment with COS, Zed. Each student was issued a target folder and given a location where to find the target. Sue had been through this sort of exercise over and over again in S&R selection so she assumed this would be an easy day. Instead, she found it a real challenge. Her target, Vasily Andropov, was a Russian scientist who might or might not be going to work for a nuclear facility in Zed and might or might not have access to the nascent Zed weapons program. She had a picture and a venue — a coffee shop on base in a simulated village known as "the ville." Her job was to identify him, establish contact and get a second meeting.

Sue walked into the full coffee shop at 1100hrs expecting room for her to first identify the target and sit next to him. Instead, the shop was full and the target was playing chess with a young man who looked like the dictionary definition of a bohemian. Sue ordered coffee and walked out onto the patio and sat down. Almost immediately another young Bohemian sat down next to her.

"You are new here? Are you a student at the university of Zed?"

"No." Sue hadn't expected to have to explain herself while waiting for an opening to meet Dr. Andropov.

"Graduate student?"

"No." Her mind juggled with two challenges — she had to formulate some sort of story, get rid of her new "best friend" and get back into the shop. She had to time the coffee she had at the table to be sure she had an excuse to go back inside, yet she didn't want to be obvious about her interests in the scientist.

"A writer then? Who else comes to the Café Central? Surely not for the coffee, though it is the cheapest and worst in town. What do you write? Novels of course, but what? Historical fiction? Political fiction? Careful not to be too political, the Zed censors will be after you." He was wagging a finger at her and smiling.

Sue decided to go with it. "I'm doing research on women in Zed history. My partner is a young lawyer who says she can't make history. I want to show her that she isn't the first woman in Zed to try."

He looked disappointed. "Your partner?"

"We share everything. Surely you must have the same relationship with you man?"

He shifted from disappointment to discomfort. "I do not live with a man."

"Your mother, then? Don't worry, you will find your soul mate."

"Perhaps, but not here I suppose." He almost knocked over the chair

as he stood up. Sue noticed the chess game was over and the student was leaving. She finished her coffee and stood up as well.

She walked inside the shop, talking deep breaths to calm herself as she ordered another coffee. There was no open seat except at Andropov's table. As she paid for her coffee in Zed currency (in the local Zed currency zuks, of course), she barely made it to the table before it was taken by another bohemian.

"May I take this seat?"

"Only if you play chess." His breath smelled of onions, garlic and something else. Perhaps cabbage? Sue realized that he was just as bohemian as the rest of the crowd except he was definitely less clean. He had greasy hair, a full beard and thick, smeared glasses.

"I just want to sit and drink my coffee."

"Go someplace else then. This is where I play chess."

Behind Sue, a young man's voice said "I want to play chess, Doctor." Sue realized it was either chess or nothing. She relented.

"I play chess and sat here to play chess with this man."

"Man? don't you know who I am?"

"Not a clue, but you seem committed to the game and I am as well Sue." She offered her hand, he took it and smirked.

"Andropov." He looked over her shoulder at the man behind her. "Come back in ten minutes, I will be done with her by then."

Sue decided that she was going to be there for more than ten minutes and set up the board so that she had the opening move.

The exercise was exhausting and the write up worse. Sue had to remember information that she elicited from her target while trying to stay in the chess game. In the long run, well after ten minutes, she could see she was going to lose the game, but she was sufficiently good that when they were done, Andropov asked her to return on 15 August for another game. Sue returned to the station, wrote up her summary of the meeting, turned it into the COS and went home to shower. Everything she was wearing smelled of garlic.

The morning class on 14 August was offered by another instructor named Stacy Mackenzie. She was a thin athletic blonde in her early 40s and rumor had it that she had just returned from a tour as chief of base in Ramadi, Iraq. Sue was looking forward to some insight into life for a case officer in a warzone. She didn't get it.

"Colleagues, today we are going to talk about you, your self-image and how you project that image."

Sue was less than pleased. The last thing she wanted to listen to was a lecture on getting in touch with yourself through emotional intelligence. She almost missed the curve ball as it went past her.

"You are all successful, determined and committed individuals. You look like you are, you act with confidence, and you are proud of your accomplishments. This is especially true if you come from the military where you are used to the respect that comes from you rank and your uniform. Fine, except, if you continue to act this way, you will be the first person identified by a hostile service as "suspect IO" — meaning suspected intelligence officer. If you are identified early on as an IO, the security, or worse, the counterintelligence service will focus their resources on you. Remember, this is their country and if they decide they want to hunt you, they will do so with no mercy. The best you can hope for at that point is a short, unsuccessful tour. The worst is arrest."

Stacy paused and walked from behind the podium. She was wearing the "instructor uniform" but unlike some of the instructors, she made sure the uniform fit well. The polo fit perfectly and the khakis were just a shade tighter than they were for the other instructors. This was a woman who knew the power of her appearance.

"As you can see, I am not hard to spot, especially in an Arab or Asian country. I have to change my appearance to work in these countries, but more importantly, I have to change my persona. I cannot appear to be a self-confident woman. I may have to appear to be a weak old woman or even a young man. I cannot appear to be a successful diplomat. A young, successful female diplomat becomes the target of every skirt chaser in the local foreign ministry and every surveillance team in country. If they are looking for you, they will find you.

Give up your egos and start to think about how you balance this challenge. On the one side, you have to be sufficiently dull the service doesn't make you as an IO. On the other side, you have to be interesting to your targets and coldly professional to your assets so they trust you. You must start now realizing you will project many personalities to many people. Schizophrenia is hard, but multiple personality disorder is harder. Here are some suggestions..."

At the end of the lecture, Sue was so lost in thought she nearly knocked over Melissa.

"Hey! Trying out your rude persona?"

"Sorry. This lecture got me thinking how hard it is to live this life."

Melissa was totally deadpan. "It can't be that hard. Otherwise, they wouldn't have recruited me."

Sue smiled at Melissa. Early days, yet, but she could see Melissa was going to do fine with the SOF crew, even if she didn't do well in the class.

"It has to be hard to figure out over the years who you really are or who you want to be."

"I think you live in the moment and work out who you are in each moment. Of course, I went to school in California — home of the New Age."

"I thought you went to Stanford — home of the silicon age?"

"That too. Still, we try not to think too much about how we make the electrical charges make zeros or ones. If we do, it is a short step to candles and Rumi poetry."

Sue had survived the first month of school with a few bumps and bruises on her ego and a growing appreciation of the art of espionage. She found some of the parts of tradecraft easy enough to learn to Agency standard — after all, many of the techniques used in S&R work were nearly the same. She had no trouble with the assessment side of the equation — again, she had learned to watch and listen to people years ago as a survival trait in the Army. Writing for her was no problem at all — she was an English major after all. The Agency style and format took some getting used to and it wasn't any fun to get reports marked up with red pen, too much like college, but eventually she cracked the code and now her reports made it through first time.

The last few weeks hadn't been all classrooms. They had already completed one block on asset development and two of the six required blocks of instruction on surveillance detection. Of all the classes, these could be the most stressful. The first block was primarily theory and riding with an instructor. Block two was the first "one up" block and most students found it challenging.

Both Nancy and Melissa had barely passed and Sue had taken them out late night after night to determine the problem and show them how to "see" surveillance. Nancy was a lawyer by training and had problems with surveillance and with learning to write concise reports rather than painfully thorough arguments and assessments. The three lived in the same hallway and at any given evening, they were usually together in one of the three rooms. They had grown closer over the last two weeks as they started out the windshield on the pitch-black roads of the Farm. Nancy used the night driving school as her classroom to teach introverts how to engage a stranger even when you don't want to do so. Just for fun, Sue had given both ladies instruction on how to do reverse 180 turns out on one of the skid pads at the driving track — useful perhaps, but also a great confidence builder. Sue was more terrified than either Melissa or Nancy at first, but eventually, they both could execute the turn as well as anyone Sue knew in SOF. The nights ended with smiling ladies returning to the dorm. Cooperate and graduate became their motto.

The SOF students also stuck close together. Most of the guys lived in the same dorm one floor below and they worked out together from 05000600hrs each morning. Sue wasn't able to keep up with their runs, so she met them at 0530hrs in the weight room. Ginger was the only SOF operator having difficulties in the class. He was not very good at elicitation and Sue had matched him up with Nancy. As a lawyer, she had been very good at elicitation in Wall Street. This informal seminar helped Ginger and there was something growing between the two of them. Sue thought it might be function of the class, but they were starting to make "moon eyes" at each other, so she stayed clear of them when they were on break.

Sue felt a growing attachment to Sandy. He was quieter than most of the Army operators she knew and had a quirky sense of humor which he attributed to mixed gas diving as a SEAL. His work habits were a good match for hers and they often ended up in station spaces writing their reports together. One thing that made Sue more comfortable with Sandy than some of the male civilian students was Sandy already knew about her BTK status and there wasn't any tension about that secret.

Her meetings with COS, ZED had been uneventful. He treated her just like any other new officer — with limited time on his hands and focusing on what was wrong and spending little time on what was right. The real feedback she received over time had been from Mary. Sue's dreams had changed from having Massoni yelling at her to Mary and the COS searching for her and not able to see her because she was never in the right room. It was not a pleasant change in her nightmares. They still ended with Sue unable to find her prosthetic and missing the shouting people.

One of the real sessions with Mary had been nearly as uncomfortable as her dreams.

"You don't like Andropov do you?"

"He smells bad, he is rude and he leers at me. So far, I haven't seen anything that I like about him."

"Do you think any of this matters to me? Is he a validated target?"

"Yes."

"So, what makes him tick? What are his vulnerabilities?"

"He likes chess."

"Not exactly a vulnerability. You have met him four times for chess games. Surely he has talked about something."

"He is convinced he is the smartest man in Zed and no one realizes it. He plays chess simply to demonstrate to any of the students or other visitors at the coffee house that he can beat them while still drinking coffee and reading scientific journals."

"So he has an ego."

"Sure. Don't we all?"

"Yes, we all do. But how are you going to use that ego to convince him that he needs to be our source? After all, this is the game we are playing — we play with people's inner most desires and their inner most fears. Both work."

Sue could see the lesson here, but she wanted to hear something more personal.

"Do you ever find it hard to play that game?"

Mary looked her in the eyes. The gaze was an uncomfortable mix of engagement, assessment, and candor. Not exactly a loving gaze, nor a collegial gaze, something entirely different. Almost the gaze you expected to see from a big cat staring at you through the bars in a zoo. The eyes seemed to ask: Friend or lunch?

"Sue, it becomes who you are. The game defines who a case officer is. If you came here to be a patriot, you need to return to the conventional military and be a military intelligence officer giving briefings to your commanding officer. Patriotism isn't enough. This trade is about taking people where they don't know they want to go and don't believe they can go. It is the ultimate chess game. I think you can do this, but you need to be certain that this is your world. Otherwise, you will not survive and neither will the people that you handle."

"I want this job. I think I am good at this job." It was all she could get out though there was more going on inside her head. Mary never broke eye contact with Sue though the gaze softened a bit.

"I believe you do want this job and I think you can be good at it. It is going to take more commitment than you have realized so far. That is your biggest hurdle."

The meeting ended shortly with Sue receiving her guidance from Mary on how she can manipulate Andropov into recruiting himself.

When she returned to the barracks, she sat down on the bed, pulled out her headphones and iPod and dialed in a Bach cantata. A bit of mathematical precision was what she needed for her thoughts. She had been preoccupied over the past few weeks, but she had cracked open the book on the Knights Templar. Creeter's style was very academic and she had trouble following all the references. Still, his premise was useful right now. Creeter saw the Knights as a warrior caste made up of men focused almost maniacally on their mission and saw their mission as their way to praise their God. Sue wasn't exactly a devout Christian, but she could see how focusing on a mission provided clarity in a world with shades of gray. In the case of the Knights it was the medieval world where Greco-Roman laws were no longer applicable and the rise of Islam threatened everything they believed to be true. Of course, there were plenty of ways to compare the post 9/11 world with the world of the late Crusades and the conflict between Christianity and Islam.

Sue kept returning to what Max called the "inner conflict" of mental focus when your senses described a world of disorder. There were many aspects of the Knights that were dangerously monomaniacal and that made them enemies. In Sue's case, the "world of disorder" right now was linked to the world of espionage where nothing and no one was entirely what they seemed to be. Focusing on the day to day mission and Bach were two things keeping her sane. She didn't have to worry too much about maniacal commitment — the cadre were doing that for her.

Sue's primary difficulty at present had little to do with the basic skills or as the military would say the "tactics, techniques, and procedures" or TTPs. She was committed to demonstrating excellence in these skills and, so far, had done well. Another part of this training had nothing to do with TTPs. It had to do with engaging people, learning who they were and using that knowledge to recruit them.

Sue was an introvert at heart and she had to really push herself to engage with a stranger. Of course, once she engaged a stranger, her introversion meant that she was a good listener and could pick out the vulnerabilities. But, she had to get over that first hurdle. In this problem, she had a fellow sufferer. Melissa turned out to be even more introverted and she struggled to get a conversation started in the practical exercises.

Melissa knocked on the door. Sue put down Creeter's book and returned to the present from her visit to the Medieval world and the war between two religions. Melissa was concerned over her recent discussions with Mary and wanted to know how Sue worked through her own difficulties with engaging targets. Melissa also had trouble with Mary because of the eye contact and her mentoring style.

"How can you have so much trouble? You just walked up to us the first day and, blam, you were talking to us like we were your old pals."

"I never said I can't do it, I simply said that I have to work twice as hard to make it happen. It takes enormous energy to be outgoing. I was terrified that first day and I didn't know what to do. So, I saw you and joined your clan."

Melissa had taken her normal position during these visits — right on the edge of Sue's bed.

"Melissa, you have nothing to worry about here. I've watched you work in the exercises that are taped and shown to the class. You are great one on one."

"It is not the one on one I worry about, it's getting from the room full of folks to the one on one that I hate."

Sue knew that each exercise was graded and you were expected to pass the exercise sooner or later. Sue had made that jump first time, but just barely. Melissa finally made it happen on the last and final exercise. Two failed attempts had not boosted her ego, that was for sure. Sue decided it was time to share problems. It was time to share a secret.

"Melissa, there is nothing that can hold you back if you want it bad enough. You are smart, you write well, and you listen with a degree of internal silence that I wish I had. I always have a little voice going on in my head as I try to listen to the role player."

"Thanks, but it seems to me that you don't have a lot of obstacles holding you back. You are a special forces operator and have faced challenges that I hope I never have to face and succeeded. You wouldn't be here if you hadn't succeeded. I'm a geek at heart. A Navajo geek is a strange bird indeed, but that's what I am. Here I am learning to be a spy and I don't like any of it very much. If it wasn't for you guys, I will would have left a while ago."

Sue knew there was no going back now; she had to share with Melissa or this could spiral into a lecture which might do more harm than good. She had tried over the past few weeks to keep her own secret to herself. It was just getting harder and harder and, honestly, she wanted to share with someone. Melissa seemed the right person.

"Melissa, let me show you an obstacle that I live with every day." Sue raised up her pants leg and revealed the prosthetic. Sue was wearing her running prosthetic which was made up of flesh colored plastic, titanium and a series of artificial joints. The gasp from Melissa was audible.

"Sue, I never knew. Believe me, I never knew. I must have sounded like such a self-absorbed little shit."

"Yeah, you did."

Melissa was starting to cry and that made Sue even more uncomfortable than ever.

"Girl, I need someone to talk to, I don't need someone to cry with…are you in or are you out?"

Melissa stopped with a snuffle. "So much for the taciturn Navajo, huh?"

"You are really part of our wolf tribe now, kid. All the SOF guys know the deal and now you really know that sometimes when I am a bitch it isn't because of hormones, it's because of the leg. Either way, the guys give me a wide berth, but I needed you to know."

"So you aren't just a natural jerk, then?"

"It's a knack. Some of it is inherited, some of it is learned, OK?"

"Deal." Melissa held out a fist and Sue responded in kind.

"Now, what was the complaint that brought you into my room?"

"Somehow, I don't remember. Tell me this: what do you know about Pigpen? Is he married? Is he as much of a catch as he looks?" Now Sue was the one looking uncomfortable.

Mike Robinson was on the stage. He was the primary instructor for the counterintelligence staff. He had been the face of their threat briefings, their discussions on hostile intelligence service tactics, and the cyber security briefing. He was Melissa's favorite because he was the tech threat guy which was her primary interest. His presentation was on asset validation and counterintelligence operations. It was nearly an hour long when he had just finished the portion of his lecture about Angleton, Golitsyn, and Nosenko. Sue was trying desperately to stay awake.

"My point is that Angleton, the head of counterintelligence, decided that one KGB defector, Golitsyn, was telling the truth and another, Nosenko was not only telling lies, but was a provocation designed by the KGB to lead us astray. They detained Nosenko in solitary confinement and it took years to sort out what was fact and what was conjecture. Please note, folks: I didn't say what was true and what was false. We never did sort out "truth" in this case. Too many officers assumed too much for too long and, by the time this was sorted out years later, there was no good way to identify fact from fiction.

"You might say, who cares, they were just KGB defectors who left a vicious service for their own, likely questionable reasons. Perhaps, but let me tell you another story of why this case is important for other reasons. In 1966, a senior officer working in headquarters named Peter O'Connell, was working in the Soviet Eastern European division as a group chief responsible for Poland, Czechoslovakia, and Hungary. He had previously served as COS in Budapest in 1956 and had recently served in Berlin in 1961. He was successful though he lost his wife in a car accident in Berlin."

After about the first 5 minutes of the presentation, it seemed pretty clear that the point was you should test your agents before you trusted them, but Robinson had presented this as if it was a revelation. Sue had dozed a bit hoping that, eventually, he would offer some specific examples of operational testing that she could use. Instead, she realized he was talking about her grandfather.

"O'Connell was an OSS Jedburgh whose last mission in Europe

was in support of the allied invasion of Southern France — Operation Dragoon. He and two other allied officers, one British, one French, inserted into Southern France in July 1944 and linked up with a French resistance circuit. Their goal was to disrupt rail and road traffic north of Avignon just prior to the invasion. The team landed as scheduled. One of the five known resistance circuits served as their reception committee. Within days, they expanded their contacts to include all the resistance units into one network committed to conducting operations. Unfortunately, Avignon resistance efforts were split into resistance supporting the Free French (De Gaulle's army) and the communist resistance.

"O'Connell was interested in the successful accomplishment of the mission not in politics. He supported training any resistance group willing to fight. His French counterpart, Captain Broumand wanted nothing to do with the communists and, instead, it was uncovered later instructed the Free French resistance to attack the communists before Dragoon. O'Connell and his British counterpart, Lieutenant Colonel Barker, were caught in the middle of a firefight and barely escaped with their lives. Broumand was killed under suspicious circumstances.

"Everyone back in England thought that the communist resistance had killed Broumand. O'Connell's report was classified in ways that we still can't sort out. War zones are not the place for a deliberate investigation, particularly when you have a mission to accomplish. O'Connell and Barker ended up conducting most of the demolition operations themselves, but when they returned to England, they were investigated for the murder of Broumand. Eventually, they were both reassigned to the China, Burma, India theater and ran operations there for the rest of the war. O'Connell and Barker were exonerated and both went on to careers in intelligence: O'Connell in the CIA and Barker in MI5.

"O'Connell was the COS in Budapest in 1956 during the uprising against the communist government and reported successfully on the Soviet invasion. He also served in West Berlin as the wall was being built in the early 1960s. But, his experiences in France colored his 'hall file' and Angleton's counterintelligence staff ran a second investigation of O'Connell in 1966 as a follow up when Golitsyn stated that there was a mole inside CIA headquarters. Everyone in the East Bloc division was investigated and the Broumand case was once again considered as evidence of O'Connell's collaboration with the French communists. O'Connell was reassigned to the historical archives staff in headquarters for two years while under investigation and did not return to operational activities until an assignment in Laos in 1968. What was the proof used to pull a well-respected officer off line for two years? Nothing, ladies and gentlemen. Nothing. Simply conjecture that a wartime event pointed to a willingness to be associated with communists. And, unfortunately, when the CI staff finally admitted this was a weak reed in their investigation, O'Connell was considered "damaged goods" and the only place he was allowed to go was a war zone and, honestly, a remote and peripheral part of a war zone at that. Eventually, he served as a COS again in Bangkok and New Delhi, and served as Chief at the Farm and you are sitting in the O'Connell lecture hall right now.

"So, what do we learn from this little tragedy from a time well before you were born? No matter how much you might trust an asset, no matter how good his reporting may be, you need to conduct operational testing.

"Assets lie, they fabricate, they confuse facts, and, sometimes, they are even directed double agents. If you don't test them, you simply don't know. And if you don't know, how can you expect managers and analysts in headquarters to know. And if there is not testing, there is no way to determine reliability. That's all. Please return to your homerooms where your instructor will give you specific operational testing techniques that you will be expected to use with your current agent this week. Thank you."

Sue stood up slowly and was the last one to leave the lecture hall. Her grandfather was investigated as a traitor? He lived with that accusation for two years? Her father at that point would have been in college. As an only child with no mother and a father living with daily accusations? What did Peter tell his son? What could he tell him? Family history was folding into training and making it harder and harder to sort out truth from lies. Sue was tired, the course was harder than she thought and now she had to deal with a family legacy that she had never known.

Pigpen walked up to Sue. "Rough day?"

"You have no idea."

Sue walked into Warehouse 8 at 0850hrs. The POI stated the 0900hrs class was titled "Street Defense — Class 1." Her only instruction was to show up in green fatigues and gym shoes. She hadn't been in fatigues in a while and the old set was soft and loose and reminded her of her past life. After some of the academic and practical exercises on spotting and assessment, she was ready for something a bit more physical and this uniform made it just that much easier. She was actually hoping she would finally get a chance to hit something or someone.

The warehouse could have housed a basketball court and bleachers for a small college. It was lit by large halogen lights suspended from the ceiling. The floor and all four walls up to shoulder height were covered with blue wrestling mats. A small "class room" was at the end of the warehouse, simply another wrestling mat rolled up serving as a seating area. About half of the class was already there with the rest arriving shortly after Sue. Sue took a seat next to Sandy and Melissa sat down next to her. It was tight seating but Sue figured they wouldn't be sitting for long. Nancy arrived just in time and ended up in the front row. Her fatigues didn't fit and if she had been wearing a feather boa and a hard hat, she couldn't have seemed more uncomfortable.

At 0900hrs exactly, a cadre of instructors walked in wearing navy blue fatigues and black converse high tops. There were five of them, ranging in apparent age from 40 to 60. All fit, but none heavily muscled. They reminded Sue of the fitness instructors in selection. Guys that could run all day and all night carrying the safety radio on their backs while you fought to keep up.

"This might not be as much fun as I hoped..." Sue whispered to Melissa.

"Why? They look like my uncles and aunts."

"Ever see your uncles and aunts in a fight?"

"Oh..." Melissa's demeanor changed to the serious Melissa who focused on staying in the course.

"Class 2, welcome to the Forum and to Street Defense. My name is

Joe and I am the chief instructor. Over the next six weeks, we will be meeting twice a week here. These two gentlemen and two ladies are my instructors: Bill, Dave, Molly, and Gail." Joe was the oldest, probably 60, gray hair cut short and probably no more than 5'8." The biggest of the five was Dave at 6'2" and Gail was the smallest at 5 feet in her sneakers. None of the men could have weighed more than 190 and Gail probably looked to weigh about 110 pounds at most.

"I know we have a mix of military and new hires here. I expect you all to pay attention and follow our instructions even if you are a black belt in some martial art and even if you have killed someone with your bare hands. We are going to teach you survival skills that are not in any book or in any dojo and are very much focused on your life as a case officer. So, let's get started."

"Hotel 16, please come forward."

Pigpen stood up and walked cautiously toward Joe. Pigpen had a good notion that he had been picked because he was one of the largest men in the class. He had spent an entire military serving as the "tackling dummy" for instructors trying to show smaller students that they could beat up guys the size of Pigpen. He knew the drill, but also knew that if he didn't play the game, sooner or later one of these instructors would punish him.

"Relax, H16, I'm not going to hurt you." Pigpen was already on the balls of his feet waiting for some sort of attack. "Seriously, this will be a simple demonstration that won't hurt."

Joe pulled out a rubber training knife which he held in his right hand in a classic knife fighter stance. "H16, I have just confronted you in an alley. Please respond and don't break any of my parts as you do it."

Pigpen was very quick for his size and before even Sue knew it, he had Joe's knife hand in a wrist lock and Joe was already on one knee trying to relieve the pressure of the wrist lock. Equally fast, Joe's left hand passed along the inside of Pigpen's thigh and Sue realized that Joe had concealed a red marker in his left hand and Pigpen's fatigue pants now had a red line from crotch to knee.

"Perfect. Please, let go now."

"Folks, here is lesson one. People who confront you intend to do you serious harm. No matter how good you are and, by the way, H16 is very good, you will be harmed if you let them get close to you. H16, if that was a knife instead of a marker, what would have been the result?"

"Worst case, femoral artery puncture and I bleed out in 4 minutes."

"Precisely. Now in that remaining time he had left to live, H16 would certainly kill me, but that is not the point, ladies and gentlemen. We are not here to make you killers and we really don't care if street punks live or die. We are here to make you survivors. The United States government is spending time, money and effort to teach you how to commit espionage. We can't afford to have you hurt by some street punk who is not afraid to die."

"So, let's start again." He tossed the knife and the marker to H16. "Your turn." Pigpen approached Joe with exceptional caution. Suddenly, Joe let out a loud, frantic childlike cry "Don't kill me!" and dropped what appeared to be his wallet on the mat in front of Pigpen. For a split second, Pigpen looked down at the wallet. Joe struck another marker along Pigpen's right arm — now he had a long red mark from his elbow to his wrist — as soon as the mark was made, Joe pivoted and ran away at a dead sprint. He was at the end of the warehouse when he started to speak again.

"Break contact and run away. If you can leave a reminder with the guy that he shouldn't follow, great. But, break contact and run away. We are not law men and we are not warriors. We don't stand and fight. Why? The most important reason is we have no partners, no backup, no QRF, and no hope of a medic keeping us alive. We just run away to live another day. If you have to fight, you have to kill the attacker quickly with the best weapon you have available, but the best plan is to run away"

Sue could see how this was going to get very interesting.

"Alright, I want you to break up into four groups. Bill, Dave, Molly, and Gail are going to lead you through some stretching exercises and then some practice confrontations. Pick up you training knives and your markers from the boxes at the end of the mat and let's get going. And, H16, thank you for not breaking me. I am, after all, an old man."

They survived the first class with only a few bumps and bruises. Still, it was as Sue expected a good break from the more cerebral work they had been doing for the past six weeks. Most of the students were covered in red ink. Some of her more cerebral colleagues looked like zebras, but they were learning fast. Sue and her SOF colleagues picked up the idea fairly quickly and only had stripes on their arms and a few tears on shirts where the initial confrontation resulted in some judo throws.

During the session, Sue had been careful not to plant her prosthetic out too far from her body, though as a right-handed fighter, she should have been in a balanced stance with left foot forward. She was afraid that any sort of twist would put her in more than the usual pain. Early in the breakout, Joe walked over to her.

"Plant your left foot under your hip and accept the fact that you are not going to get the sort of pivot you need from your left leg. You might even have to back pedal a bit off your right foot before you can turn. You may have to learn to knife fight with your left hand. Remember, your goal is to get away. If you can incapacitate, then do so, but get away. I recommend a quick knife thrust up under the chin — it will definitely convince your attacker that you are serious. Whatever you do, it has to be fast and then you need to get out of reach. That's especially true for you with your prosthetic."

Sue flashed hot for a moment. Does everyone in the cadre know she is a wounded warrior? Are they adjusting the course for her to be sure she is not going to "hurt herself?" It was already hard enough to keep this a secret within her small set of friends in the class. It would be harder if she had to worry about every instructor.

Joe noticed the look. He reached down to his right foot and pulled up his pants leg. To the rest of the room, it would look like he was tying his sneaker. To Sue, it was clear what he was doing. He was showing her his prosthetic. His started right above the ankle and went into the sneaker.

"Land mine in Somalia in '92. I was lucky. My partner didn't make it. You are well on your way to recovery and I doubt any of my cadre noticed and probably the only peers who know are those you have told. Still, I know what it looks like to compensate for the loss and I could see you were favoring the leg the same way I did at first. Of course, when they gave me my first prosthetic, it didn't fit like this one or like yours. In a few months, maybe a year tops, you will be able to do everything you did before — possibly even a bit better.

If you ever want to talk, let me know. There are three of us on post. One is a legend. He lost his leg in the 70s and is still flying for air branch. He comes down here sometimes when they are outloading one of our birds. He still flies anything he wants, though he has a little trouble with the controls of helicopters. Anyhow, it is all about carrying off the disguise. No different from anything else you do here. It's all in your mind."

Before Sue could speak, Joe had whipped out a marker and caught her across the chest.

"Don't trust anyone, young lady." He moved on to another set of students and didn't look back.

The previous two weeks had been an intense series of agent meetings, communications training and writing exercises. Sue had worked her way back into Mary's graces, more or less, through the successful recruitment of her scientist. Sue almost viewed the firearms training as a reward for surviving another two weeks of Mary's tough love.

The paramilitary instructor cadre were at the front of the class with their backs to the 50m covered range. Each cadre member had a pistol in a duty belt holster. There were 20 lanes and tables at the end of each lane with a pistol and four magazines. At the far end of the range was a berm and a set of targets currently turned so only the edges of the targets were visible. The students in their green fatigues, now covered with red marks on arms and legs waited for the start of the class.

A senior instructor with a gray crew cut stepped forward.

"Ladies and gentlemen, welcome to your firearms instruction. We are going to be working with you over the next eight weeks. Our goal is to teach you when and how to use a firearm to save your life or the life of another U.S. citizen. We are not going to teach you how to fight in combat. We are going to teach you how to survive a gunfight.

"We will start with your primary firearm, the Glock semiautomatic pistol. We will transition to the Mossberg 500 shotgun and eventually to the M4 carbine. These are the only weapons you will ever be issued. We are also going to familiarize you with the AK rifle platform, the MP5 and Beretta sub machine guns and several pistols, but the Glock will be the weapon you will practice with every time you are on the range. Starting today and until the final exercise, you will carry your Glock red gun in concealed carry at all times during exercises. Are we clear?"

The students agreed.

"I know many of you are very experienced with firearms and that is good news. It will mean we can work quickly through the basics and spend more time improving your skills…"

He started with a fairly lengthy firearms safety discussion first about the Glock and then in more detail about concealed carry and the way to safely carry the Glock while not revealing its existence.

"Remember, we are intelligence officers, not soldiers or lawmen. We carry a weapon to protect ourselves and the weapon is absolutely the last resort. If you can avoid trouble, do so. If you can't avoid trouble, run away. If you can't run away, then eliminate the threat with your weapon. Notice, I didn't say 'kill.' We eliminate the threat so that we can break contact and leave the scene. We are not going to stand and fight and we are not going to wait for the locals to come and arrest us for carrying a weapon.

"Mr. Jacobs is currently at the ready line and he will demonstrate what we expect you to do here and in the future. Please put on your quiet ears and safety glasses."

He checked the crowd to be sure they obeyed, then he checked Jacobs.

He put on his own "ears" which had an attachéd microphone.

"Stand by, stand by. The line is hot. The line is hot. Mr. Jacobs load and holster your weapon. Now, when a target appears, I want you to draw your weapon and fire two rounds, center mass in the target. You will have two seconds."

Shortly after the senior spoke a target still on edge in Jacobs lane began to move forward toward him. It appeared as a full target at 20 meters. Jacobs drew and fired two rounds. As he drew his weapon, another target to his right appeared, he fired a second pair of rounds and at the 50m line a third target appeared, he moved to his left, took a position behind a table and fired two more rounds.

"Cease fire, cease fire, cease fire. Holster your weapon."

The instructor took off his headphones and motioned for everyone to do the same.

"That full series of six rounds was fired in a total of 4 seconds. We want you to always scan to your left and right to determine if there are other threats. Do not assume you have only one enemy out there or only enemies out there. Mr. Jacobs always fired two rounds in each target. If the target keeps coming you fire two more until you have eliminated the threat. Now we are going to start with the first 10 of you up on the firing line.

"Hotel 1 through 10, please move forward and take a position on the odd lanes."

In the first group were Nancy and Ginger and Stan, an "Agency internal." Internal meant he was already an Agency employee. Sue knew from her previous training at Bragg that Ginger was one of the best shots in S&R and she expected Stan to be a solid shot based on her expectation that Stan had already received this training sometime in the past. Nancy was the one she worried about.

In a few minutes, Sue realized that she had nothing to worry about when it came to Nancy's ability to use a pistol. After the first two magazines, the instructors pulled the targets to the students. Stan and Ginger's 30 rounds were in the center of the target and all 30 could be covered by a saucer from a dinner set. Nancy's shots were all on the X ring of the target and could have been covered by an index card. Sue should have realized something was up when she saw Nancy's smooth, steady draw from the holster and relaxed isosceles stance.

As the next set of ten moved up to the firing range, Nancy sat down next to Sue.

"Where did you learn to shoot like that?"

Nancy turned to Sue, pulled back the right headphone and whispered in her ear.

"Dad was a Newark cop. I was the New Jersey pistol champ for under 16 year olds and on the Cornell modern pentathlon and biathlon teams. I've had a concealed carry permit since I was 20. Basically, I'm the ringer in the crowd."

There was always something new to learn about her fellow students. It made Sue smile that most of her military colleagues in the past assumed the "Klingons" knew nothing about the military or weapons. The first military operator who decided Nancy was an easy mark on the range would be sorry.

Mary walked into the meeting feeling very good about her students. Each mentor handled four and she had three women and one man. They were progressing well. She knew of three in the class who would not make it, one of which had been given Mary as his recruitment target. He had never been able to get past talking to a woman of status (she was playing a senior diplomat) who was also 10 years older than he was. Better to get dropped now, find another home in the intel community and leave espionage to folks who had the knack.

Like most rooms in the Farm, this one had the feel of a college classroom rather than a business boardroom. The tables and chairs had a semi-permanent feel to them as if they might be cleared tomorrow to open the room for something entirely different — perhaps a photography class or day care. The Farm might be the premier spy school in the USG, but it was still a school with an infrastructure budget similar to a community college. Mary walked into the room with a brief case with the three student files. Across the table from her sat the chief of the Farm, the course lead, and the head of tradecraft instruction. "Mary, thanks again for your work here. I want you to know up front that you have significantly transformed our program with your time here."

Mary was so tired of Lester's smarmy crap she could throw a chair at him. But, he was the chief and it would be his evaluation of her that gets her the next assignment.

"Thanks, Lester."

"Lester, I don't think Mary knows yet." Martha was at the end of her career and had been a model for Mary's generation of female case officers. Martha had served hard, denied area tours, hunted terrorists in the 80s and served as COS in Miami. Mary was convinced that if she had been a man, her COS job would have been one of the big stations in LA division — Mexico City or Buenos Aires.

"Mary, we just got the cable today. It's in your queue, but I suspect you have been working on the mid-cycle reviews. You have been selected for COS, Tunis. The senior PMC hasn't formally passed the

COS assignments to the DDO yet, so please don't plan the champagne breakfast at the Club yet, but congratulations!"

Mary was pleased and shocked at the same time. Tunis was a terrific assignment. All the targets of a Gulf assignment without any of the hardline difficulties for a woman that an assignment in Arabia would deliver. It was more than she expected. The caveat about the senior personnel manning choice decision was the real deal. She knew there was no guarantee their recommendations would get approval and bragging about a PMC before the deputy director for operations signed the paperwork was one of the ways to insure he wouldn't approve it.

Martha looked like a mother who just heard her daughter won a scholarship to an Ivy League school.

"Congratulations, Mary."

Barry Johnson looked like someone just spit in his lemonade. He was also a Near East Division body, also at the end of the assignment at the Farm and also competing for COS jobs. He choked out "Well done, Mary." Lester interjected "Barry is going to be the DCOS in Riyadh, Mary.

Great job as well!"

Mary knew that DCOS in Riyadh was a career enhancing selection that would likely get Barry promoted faster than her. But, it also meant he would be someone's deputy, following someone's direction, and living in the Kingdom where his wife couldn't drive and his family life would be circumscribed by the diplomatic quarter except when he went out to see liaison or went to the airport. Mary figured she got the better deal and Barry knew it.

"Barry, that's fantastic. The work in the Kingdom is central to everything we do against Al Qaida." Not exactly true, Al Qaida was far more than Bin Laden and his family ties to the Kingdom and most of the high value targets had never set foot in Arabia, but it was the best she could do. "Alright, let's get to work." Lester may have been a politician at heart, but he knew this exchange could only get more poisonous if he let Mary and Barry trade empty platitudes.

"This will be a short brief. I am recommending all four of my students to continue in the course. All four have passed the key initial tradecraft gateways and they have all completed their first recruitment exercise. All four have made mistakes and shown where we need to focus attention, but my assessment and my discussion with the instructors who have been role players against them suggest they are right about where they should be. No superstars here, just average students with a good chance to make solid case officers."

"Excellent and given the fact that you have never been a pushover, I'm ready to accept the recommendation. Still, I want to hear one by one: strengths and weaknesses."

Lester's focus was always on how to best use the second half of the course to improve the student. The first half was a straightforward set of gateways; the second half was tuned to the students. They might not see it, but they were given very specialized training in the last twelve weeks. This was Mary's sixth time briefing at mid cycle. She knew Martha and Barry, like their predecessors, would follow Lester's lead, so she had prepared the briefing for him. Simple bullets, strengths and weakness.

"I'll do it in alphabetical order: Stan Cyzneski:

"Strengths: surveillance detection, CI, agent handling. He is one of our internal students, works inside the CI shop at Headquarters and is a former Marine. He will do anything to pass and, more importantly, to get any skill right. Determined is the key word here: I think we would have to shoot him to eliminate him from the course.

"Weaknesses: Asset development. I am working with him on how to build rapport. He is a detail oriented person, so he sounds a little robotic with his target. Both his target and I agree he just needs practice. He needs to get two or three more runs at a target in the second half. Otherwise, he is good to go. His writing is to standard and his tech ops are fine.

"Nancy Garrison:

"Strengths: she was a corporate lawyer and her asset developmental work as well as her tradecraft are excellent. She knows how to 'get to yes' with both male and female targets. I say this because Nancy is strikingly good looking and charming so I wanted to see if her good grades were just because her male role players were stunned. Not so, her female role players said the same thing as the males: she is charming, but she is well prepared and all business. This lady will be a terrific hunter for us. She is the daughter of a police detective from Newark. He gave her plenty of street smarts. Weaknesses: she had some trouble early on in identifying surveillance. We worked with her and I asked one my other students, Sue O'Connell, to help. We will talk about Sue later, but she was a SOF surveillance operator so I had her work with Nancy. It helped, but she needs more practice and, if we build exercises that force her to practice that skill, she will be fine."

"If she can't see surveillance, she can't be a case officer." Mary knew she could count on Barry to say the obvious in these briefings. She had prepared the defense.

"No argument, Barry. She will get there if for no other reason than I know she has the determination to put in the extra work. She wants to beat the male students in the course."

Martha decided it was her turn to send the two fighters to their corners.

"The last two are our second-generation operators, right?"

Mary really hadn't been finished with Barry, but she knew that part of the problem was his irritation at their respective follow on assignments and that wasn't going to go away.

"Correct. Melissa Nez is the granddaughter of a code talker and the daughter of two linguists at the Fort. She has been very good about keeping quiet about both her grandfather's heroism and her parents' jobs at NSA. I don't think I need to explain Sue O'Connell's heritage.

"Melissa Nez:

"Strengths: this lady is a tech ops wizard. She comes from Silicon Valley. She was both a software and hardware developer. We were lucky to find her before the Fort got their hooks into her. The tech team here says after hours she has already taught them how to improve COVCOM. She is also one determined lady. She is like Stan. If she doesn't get something, she will put in the time to get it right. She had some trouble up front with standard tradecraft, but she is now one of the top three in the class.

"Weaknesses: she is an introvert. I don't know if this is because she is an engineer, because of her culture, or just because she is wired that way. She is having trouble with asset development. She passed the gateway, but just barely. I recommend we match her up with Nancy and see if that helps. Honestly, as long as she can pass this require- ment, we need to pass her because the information operations folks need her, today."

Mary saw Barry ready to interject, but Lester gave him "the look" that he used when he wanted consensus. Barry was a standard case officer, hated tech ops, really hated the idea that the Internet was becoming a new operational environment and a woman like Melissa was truly a challenge for him to understand. Lester, for all his weak- nesses, had embraced this new world and forced a reluctant training cadre to include "cyberspace" (everyone grimaced when he used the term — like nails on a chalkboard) as part of the instruction.

"OK, last one in the box is Sue O'Connell.

"Strengths: surveillance detection and tech ops. Neither should be a surprise given her previous jobs for SOF. She is average on all of the other gateways. No real problems and, honestly, no great successes. All of her instructors say she will be a good, though not great, ops officer.

"Weaknesses: she has a hard time hiding her prejudices. Lester, you were the first one to see this in the first exercise when you played the "stinky professor" role. She had a hard time getting past her dis- gust. I hate to say it, but you are very good at that role."

Lester smirked. "I spent half a lifetime working against WMD sci- entists who had poor personal hygiene. I don't like it any better than the students, but the disguise folks do their magic and I just channel the scientists from long ago. She did have some trouble, but eventu- ally figured out my interest in chess and she did use the chess as a start point for the operational relationship. Still, you are right that she was clearly disgusted with me and her write ups were particularly venomous. A good DCOS would fix all those problems. I agree she needs to meet more disgusting people. We can make that happen, can't we Martha."

"Oh, yes indeed, Lester."

Barry fired another salvo. "What's with her posse? I mean, the SOF crew and Melissa and Nancy seem to be inseparable. This is a singleton trade and I hate to see too much collaboration to the exclusion of individual performance."

"Barry, you raise this every time we have military special operators." Martha had decided to address this. "There is no way we are going to separate the SOF folks outside of the exercises. And, given the fact that Sue is a wounded warrior, I think the guys are especially protective. As to Melissa and Nancy, Mary already said Sue was helping them. Give it a rest."

Barry tried not to sulk, but he wasn't succeeding.

"Mary, thanks for the briefing. I recommend we accept Mary's four into the final problem. Any disagreement?" Barry knew better. "Excellent. We have a half hour before Mike brings in his four. Coffee sounds like a plan."

The flight from Reagan International to Midway had been uneventful. The businessman sitting next to her had immediately opened his laptop and tapped away on a proposal for one company to buy another one based in Chicago. Sue always took a window seat; she always liked to watch as the plane took off and as it landed. Even as a child on their various tours abroad, Sue fought to get the window seat and watch the world go by. It wasn't more than five minutes after takeoff and she was asleep.

The nightmare started quietly enough. She was in some strange mix of the Farm and Ft. Bragg. She was in woods enjoying a walk along a forest trail. She knew she needed to find her way back to some base camp, but the trail never seemed to get anywhere. The sun went down and the forest turned from light to dark in a minute. She was lost and disoriented and couldn't find her way back. She didn't have a flashlight and the forest kept getting darker and darker. She started to hear voices — voices calling for her in the forest, but every time she tried to determine where they were coming from, they were less distinct. They were calling her name, but she couldn't quite make out who they were until suddenly she knew they were her team from S&R. They were looking for her, they needed her and she couldn't get to them. Suddenly, Mary showed up directly in front of her. "What are you going to do now, Sue? Don't you know?" Sue didn't know and wanted Mary's help. Instead, she got a shove from Mary and fell down a gully.

Sue woke with a start and looked over at the businessman who was staring directly at her. No telling what she had said or done. These dreams were not getting any more understandable. At least in this one, she had two feet.

Sue walked out of Chicago Midway airport and into a winter sleet storm that slashed her face. The transformation from mid-Atlantic late fall to Midwest early winter over a three-hour plane ride was unpleasant. She was dressed appropriately for Virginia but not at all for Chicago. Her fleece vest inside the Gore-Tex parka barely kept the wind out and her watch cap just barely covered her ears. Worse still, her jeans were no match at all for the wind out of the Canada

She caught a cab and headed "home." Well, as much of home as she had shared with her family over the last five years. As soon as she retired, Barbara O'Connell sold the house in Reston and used the money to buy a turn of the century old bungalow on the north shore. Like most arts and crafts bungalows of the time, it was a small two bedroom house with an associated "carriage house" that now served as the home of her mother's fifteen year old Range Rover. The house was especially pleasant in the summer because it had a small screened in porch that originally was a sleeping porch before the arrival of air conditioning. Though not directly on the water, it was close enough that in the summer you could sit on the porch and listen to the waves of Lake Michigan. It was almost the perfect definition of cozy. Now, an early winter storm made the area bleak, gray and grim.

Sue had an hour to watch first the industrial parks around O'Hare and then the suburbs race by the window of the Lincoln Towncar that she had hired. The driver had tried to start a conversation with her, but she cut the conversation short and the rest of the ride was in silence. She would tip him well and ask him to pick her up early Monday morning if he was willing to do so. That was as close to polite as she was going to get.

Her mom greeted her at the door and welcomed her into the small bungalow. There was a fire going in the fireplace and the French doors looked down to the lakefront. Despite her tensions from the previous twelve weeks, as soon as she pulled her roller board suitcase over the threshold, Sue began to relax as she stripped off the layers and walked over to the fireplace.

"Mom, the place looks terrific. I see you have been working the antique shops again — finding period pieces to go with the house."

"Suzie, the arts and crafts style matches my needs now and, honestly, the stuff goes well with the Central Asian carpets and Indian brass. What the heck, I hope you like it because it is going to be yours someday."

"Not anytime soon, mom." Sue looked at her mom. They had

spent plenty of time together at Walter Reed, but all Sue remembered from that time was how worried and tired her mother looked every day. Barbara was a fit lady in her early 60s, still over 5'10," gray hair having taken over the brunette, dressed in jeans, a white men's dress shirt and slippers. Surrounded by the arts and crafts interior, she looked like she belonged in a layout for Architectural Digest. The house, the interior furnishings, and the small garden had become her mom's passion and it was hard to imagine that she had been a case officer for nearly 30 years. A lifetime ago. Along with an opportunity to get away from the Farm, Sue now needed to know about that lifetime and this weekend would have to be the start of that search, even if it was difficult.

They started with lunch. No one ever visited the house without either tea or food. That was simply the way that the O'Connell household worked. Barbara O'Connell had made goulash and fresh rolls. They ate it with mugs of tea and ended with oatmeal cookies — Sue's favorite when she was a kid. It was Barbara's way of welcoming her daughter back home and trying to reestablish a past that only existed in memory, not in fact. Sue took her carry-on bag to the ground floor guest bedroom — another perfect arts and crafts room — and took a hot bath in the claw foot tub. She never really got used to seeing her left leg without a foot, but it no longer ached as much and she could get around just fine in the bathroom without the prosthesis as she toweled off and watched the travel grime go down the drain.

After putting on sweats and her "running foot" with a sock on her left leg, she returned to the living room where her mom was reading and drinking another mug of tea.

"I made another pot if you like. Earl Grey."

Sue grabbed another mug and then settled into a leather chair near the fire. She was starting to relax after the trip and, more importantly, after 12 weeks of intense training. She told Barbara the basics of her experience. The course wasn't physically hard, but it was mentally tough and the fact that you were always under observation made it worse. The first half of the course focused on the basics of "the trade." Everything you wanted to know about spotting, assessing, developing, recruiting, and handling an asset was covered. At each step, you learned how to report what you did in a level of detail that Sue had never seen in her time in SOF. These Agency folks wanted to know everything that happened in chronological order with few adjectives and no adverbs. The emphasis was on what you knew about the case and then ending briefly on what you thought about the case. Facts first, opinions second. Both equally important. Sue was surprised that her mother remained interested and asked hard questions about the training.

"Dear, this was my trade for most of my life. You can't expect me to forget everything just because I am spending my days arranging flowers and dusting furniture now, can you?"

Dinner was a delicious coq au vin served with a French wine and French bread that her mom made that afternoon. They ended back in the living room in front of the fire with glasses of port. Sue had always assumed port was an "old man's drink" but it seemed like a nice ending to a great day. She was nearly asleep when her mom coaxed her back from the land of Nod.

"Suzie, if the weather cooperates, would you like to take a walk along the shore tomorrow? It seems to me that you have something you want to talk about and we might best do so while we are walking rather than here in the house."

This curious comment ended what had been a great day with her mom — returning Sue to thoughts of questions that needed to be answered and fears of what those answers might be.

Sue woke to the smell of bacon and coffee. She pulled on her jeans, strapped on the running foot, pulled on a long sleeved t-shirt and headed to the kitchen. Her mom was sitting on a small window seat in the kitchen working on a large mug of coffee. "Breakfast is ready if you are hungry." Sue was certain that she was.

Breakfast was another visit to the past: pancakes, bacon, syrup, coffee, fresh squeezed orange juice and plenty of light conversation. After a quick cleanup with Sue washing and her mom drying and putting the china back into the pantry, Barbara looked out the window.

"It was a bit chilly outside during my run this morning, but the sun is shining and the bike path along the lake shore is clear of frost and ice from last night. Interested in a walk?" Sue agreed though she was not excited about the cold biting into her mid-Atlantic outdoor gear.

"Don't worry, you can borrow my Barbour hunting coat — it is loose enough on me that it should fit you and the sweater you will find in your closet."

Sue did as she was told, put on her trainers and headed for the hall closet for the coat. She walked up just as her mom was putting a two inch barreled Smith and Wesson .357 revolver into the right hand pocket of her very worn sheepskin lined leather coat. Barbara caught her look.

"Do you want something for your pocket?"

"Do I need something?"

"You never know for sure, do you?" Barbara reached into the closet and slid back a small false wall and pulled out a Glock 26 in a paddle holster. Sue took the small pistol, checked the magazine, loaded a round into the chamber and placed gun and holster on her hip. The sweater concealed the pistol completely.

"I bought it just for you. I figured you were more comfortable with an automatic than a revolver."

This was definitely not the mother-daughter conversation that Sue had had in the past with her mom or had expected this morning. It was out of place with the arts and crafts style, her mom's heavy wool beret and leather coat and boots.

"Let's go out the back door and walk down to the bike trail."

Sue watched as her mom locked the French doors and used a very discrete alarm box to set up a household security program. She was a little embarrassed that she hadn't noticed any IR sensors or cameras in the house, but they must be there if there was an alarm system.

Her mom was already 10 yards ahead of her heading down to the shore. It was a November day but the sun was starting to warm things quickly and before she got to the trail, Sue had opened her coat and briefly regretted wearing the sweater.

"I know you can run nearly as well now as you could before the operations, but you need to let me know if you want to slow down or speed up as we walk. It's up to you. Also, it will get chilly down by the lake, so you will be happy to have the sweater."

"Mom, let's start by talking about the sidearms. This doesn't seem like a high crime area."

"Dear, this area has one of the lowest crime rates in America. Don't you worry."

"Why the guns?"

"Same reason that we used to carry in the field and why you will carry sometimes in the field... just in case. Just because there are few villains out here, doesn't mean that there are none. And, honestly, there are other reasons why a former SOF operator and a former spy might carry. We have made some enemies over the years, no?"

The walk down to the lake front was easy enough and as Sue followed her mom along the footpath, she thought about how many times she had followed her mom in that leather jacket. Family history was Barbara O'Connell had bought the jacket new when the family was serving in Delhi — leatherwork from Kashmir. It had aged as Sue had aged. Packed away when they were in Nairobi, it was something that Sue had found in a box protected from pests with moth flakes. She remembered the smell of camphor mixed with leather as she sat in the air-conditioning in their embassy apartment in the late summer. As a young teenager, Sue walked with her mom in the same coat through the freezing fog covered streets of the Frankfurt Christmas market. When Barbara and Peter watched their children compete in soccer in late Fall in Northern Virginia, Barbara wore that coat. Now, over thirty years later, they were walking the shores of Lake Michigan and Barbara O'Connell was still wearing the same coat.

"Dear, are you alright?" Barbara had reached the bike path along the lakeshore and was looking over her shoulder at Sue. Sue realized she was looking into a mirror that showed her future face.

"Mom, I'm fine. I was just thinking about the Kashmiri coat."

"Not so stylish anymore, eh?"

"Not that. I was thinking about all the times I've seen you wear it."

"This old coat has been a good luck charm for me. It has seen some days and some places."

"Operational?"

"Some. Remember when we used to walk all over Frankfurt when you were a little girl and your brother was in the carriage?"

"Sure. We would go to Gruneberg park and walk toward the Palmengarten. You weren't working with us, we're you?"

"Sue, there is never a time that a case officer is not working in the field. In those walks in the park, we were collecting a signal from an agent's covcom. He was in the park as well."

"William was in the pram, I was running in the grass...we were... cover for your operation?! What about my dance classes in Moscow? Or the safaris in Kenya? Cover every time? Did we do our part to support your careers?"

Barbara realized this conversation was not going to end well. "Sue, you probably already understand that this work intrudes on everything you do in the field. We integrate our work with our normal life. I won't apologize at this point, because it is true that we were always preparing for an operation, working an operation, or building a cover for a future operation when we lived abroad. Our job was to keep ourselves and our agents safe and to do that we had to look normal. If we could match work with fun for your and Bill, we did. We often turned down work and even assignments so we could live something resembling a normal life. Still, the answer is yes, our family outings were often work related but you were never at risk and your activities were never essential to the job."

"Essential?"

"A poor choice of words. My point is you were never part of the plan. Rather, you and Bill were our family and to do our job we could choose to leave you behind with a tutor or send you to boarding schools as some of our colleagues did, or we could bring you along. We decided to bring you along. Unless you are going to be without a family in this trade, you have to make those decisions."

Up to this point, Sue had focused on work as separate from her life. It was easier with SOF — either you were on TDY working a target or you were back at Ft. Bragg leading a life in Fayetteville. Sue had never considered what this new life was going to mean. She would be living a full time life of espionage whenever she was abroad and living a cover story even when she was at Bragg. What in the world did that mean when you were trying to date someone? And, how could you be sure that any social contact was not constructed with you as the target? It made her head hurt almost as much as her leg was aching from the cold.

"Mom, I don't know what to say. I honestly don't know what to think at this point."

"Dear, we aren't out here freezing our nipples to talk about this complicated world we both live in today. I'm thrilled you are here, but you said you wanted to talk, so I thought we needed to do so."

Her mother had avoided the answer, shifted the conversation and now Sue had a choice. She could pursue one or the other of these uncomfortable topics, but she could see now that she couldn't pursue both of them. She realized that this was much like the training exercises at the Farm — not a real conversation, but structured elicitation where she was facing a master of the trade and she was still the novice. As a kid, she and Bill just thought all parents were just as omniscient as Peter and Barbara O'Connell. Now she knew otherwise. She had to at least put down a marker.

"Fair enough, Mom. But please, don't case officer me again."

Barbara looked pained at first, then smirked and eventually just stuck her tongue out like a little girl caught. Sue couldn't help but laugh.

"Mom, they talk about granddad at the Farm."

"Of course they do. He was a legend — though he hated being called a legend."

"He was investigated as a traitor! How did that make any sense?"

"It was another time, another place and not something that he ever talked about with us. We never learned about it either until we were inside the system."

"Did he hate the fact that Dad was not as good as he was?"

Barbara stopped and looked at Sue in a way that Sue didn't recognize at all. Her mom had turned hard — Sue had seen that face on SOF operators just before and just after a shoot. It was not a face she had ever seen on her mom and it was terrifying.

"Susan, never say that again. Your father was a terrific officer, brave, and received his own awards for his career and paid for his successes with his life."

Sue expected some degree of defense since she knew that her mother was the real success story in the partnership that was their marriage over the years. Barbara had traveled on tdys to nearly every warzone that existed in the 1980s and 1990s. She worked PLO, PLFP, and Abu Nidal terrorists, Iranian penetrations and Serbian war criminals. Meanwhile, her father stayed at home with the kids and worked in the embassy. It didn't seem fair that even years after her father's death, her mother wasn't able to acknowledge this.

"Mom, you were the one with the terrorist cases…"

Barbara touched Sue's arm. "Dear, I did have those cases and it was exciting. By now, you have to realize that sometimes the obvious is not the real in our trade. While I was traveling to Cyprus and Dubai, your father stayed with you two. That didn't mean he wasn't working, it just means you didn't see him working. Your father's problems with his father were not about his lack of success. It was about the risks he was taking. His father thought the risks did not justify the gain. I can't say which one of the two Peters was right because I was never in the compartment that allowed me to know. What I do know is my husband is dead and his father is alive and we both know that is because of your father's work."

"Dad died of cancer, you said so."

"Dear, your father died of cancer because he was poisoned. Your grandfather and I believe he was poisoned by someone on the other side who caught him in his work."

Sue felt her head would explode, her leg suddenly filled with pain and she was short of breath. Something as simple and as tragic as the loss of her father had secrets that were linked to his career. The arguments between her father and her grandfather hadn't been about his lack of success, it had been precisely about his successes and the risks associated.

"Mother, when were you going to tell me?"

"Dear, you know the answer. Never. All families have secrets that, once revealed, cause pain. In our family, secrets revealed can put your life at risk. That is the real world we live in. Now, what good would telling you have accomplished? Your father was dead and you were deployed in Afghanistan. The Agency and the FBI investigated, the CDC and Walter Reed did a chemical analysis. The poisoning could have occurred anytime in the previous five years. It is still an open FBI case, but it is a cold case. The only person still working on it is your grandfather and I worry that it is driving him mad. The ideas he comes up with are not rational and, sadly, he blames himself for your father's death. What part of that did you want to know before you returned to Afghanistan? I chose to wait until now."

"And Bill?"

"He knows it is an open murder case because it is a file in his squad. He asked me about it and I told him just what I told you."

Sue honestly didn't know what to say or think. Secrets in a family of spies had to be the hardest of all to understand. It made no sense but in the world of espionage, hardly anything ever did to Sue. Treason was an irrational act. Hunting potential recruits using deception, perfidy and the resources of the entire United States government was hardly normal. Pretending to be a quiet family assigned to an embassy while recruiting spies and hunting terrorists — not normal.

The clarity of SOF operations was profound. The targets were clear, they were enemies of the United States and often murderers of US citizens. S&R received a target package with a lead or a set of leads. They used their skills to observe and report from a distance. Once they had sufficient information, other parts of SOF were called in to complete the job. Either the targets were killed and their personal effects exploited for the next job or they were captured and ended up in interrogation and provided information for the next job. Sue missed the lack of ambiguity deeply but she knew there was no going back, only forward. Everything, including her past life and her future had to be framed within the context of "it depends." Nothing black and white. Everything gray. Sue and her mother walked for about a mile in silence before they turned around and headed home.

"What about the gun and the alarm system, Mom?"

"I have my own ghosts dear. Maybe they are all long dead or maybe they have forgotten me. But if they haven't forgotten and come looking, I don't intend to let them take me easily."

They both hurried back to the bungalow. Perhaps it really was getting colder or perhaps they were just tired of worrying if there was anyone out there watching or listening on the trail. The fire had burned down and Sue spent time rebuilding it. When she looked up, her mother was standing next to her, crying. She handed Sue a crystal glass with an ample volume of whiskey. It was only 3pm, but they both had no problems finishing their drinks by the fire.

Sue and Barbara worked together on a simple pasta recipe that night. Both avoided the topic until dinner was finished and they were working on the last of the red wine and chocolate.

"Why was granddad so hostile to Dad taking on a sensitive operation? Surely you guys had worked SAP projects before?"

"SAP?"

"Sorry, Mom, special access programs. I don't know what you call them."

"We call them lots of things depending on the level of sensitivity, but not SAPs. At least not when I was in the game. To answer your question, I don't know why Peter was so angry over this one. Your father and I had been involved in plenty of operations that I thought were far more dangerous. This was a CI case, I was not in the compartment, but it certainly didn't involve anything dangerous — at least that was what I thought. You have to understand that your grandfather had his own views on working against the Soviets and other Bloc targets.

Based on your comments about his time under investigation, you know his work in France in '44 included work with and against communists and, he said, against the NKVD — the old KGB, or SVR as you know them today. He also saw Soviet atrocities in Budapest in '56 and lost at least one agent during the uprising and lost two more agents when the Soviets rolled in to smash the rebellion. Finally, he was convinced the Soviets killed your grandmother, Judith O'Connell, in Berlin in '62."

"But you said that was a car accident."

"So it was, dear, but your grandfather never believed it was an accident. A large truck hit his car broadside on one of the side streets near their house; Judith was driving. Peter was on the street working that day. The driver of the truck was never found. It was winter and he was wearing gloves so no fingerprints for the German police to trace. Berlin station, the Berlin LKA, LFV and U.S. Army CI did a separate investigation. They decided it was an accident."

"Your grandfather couldn't accept the fact that sometime terrible things happen for no good reason. In our world, it is always easier to assume there is a cause. I don't honestly know if there was evidence that he was the target or that your grandmother was a target. Your father was too young to know what was true and what was false, but his father taught him from that day forward to never accept anything in life as just what it appeared to be. Your father lived through his father's investigation never knowing what was going on. By the time his father was assigned to Laos, Peter was in college and it really didn't matter anymore. Peter Senior was now on his way to becoming "COS world" and your father and I were in college and on our way to becoming case officers ourselves. Your father was not the most open person in the world, I can tell you it made dating your dad a pain."

"Harder still because you met at the Farm, right?"

"Indeed, another romance created by the most expensive matchmaker in the US: the CIA assessment folks. Put 30 young men and women together, most very much alike in their habits and their interests, run them through a series of shared hardships and, voila, you have tandem couples." Barb paused. "Speaking of romance, what about you?"

"Mom, it is so hard right now to even think about romance. I still have the nightmares and night sweats, the leg still hurts a lot, and I'm living in a program where they watch your every move. Not exactly the start point for a Broadway love story, eh?"

"Didn't you have a beau at Ft. Bragg?"

"Hardly a 'beau,' Mom. Earl was another warrant officer assigned to the CI section of my Brigade. It was an easy way to date — we were not in the same unit and we were the same rank, so no fraternization concerns. It was fun, and then I went to selection and he didn't. He didn't think I would make it and said so. I didn't take it well and he really didn't take it well when I completed selection. After that, it was one TDY after another and you simply don't date inside the Regiment if you want to stay inside the Regiment. Too complicated."

"Sue, you are still young and pretty and smart, you will find a guy."

"Or not, mom. Maybe the answer is or not."

The next morning over coffee, Barbara resisted telling Sue more details on either her father or her grandfather.

"Sue, you should visit Peter when you finish the course. He would be so proud. You know he stayed with me in Alexandria the first month you were in Walter Reed. Visited you everyday, though you wouldn't have known."

"Mom, that first month they had me so pumped with drugs, the President could have visited and I wouldn't remember."

"He sat by your bed every day and slept in the hospital every night. I couldn't get him out of your room except to shower and change clothes. He would only leave it I promised to stay by your side. Once he knew you were going to pull through, he just packed up and drove off."

"Where does he live now? I know he sold the house on the river."

"Actually, he rented the house on the river. That place is his legacy to you — you are now the co-owner with your grandfather. He loved sharing the place with you when you were at William and Mary. He made the change to the title in your senior year and promised to tell you sooner or later. It looks like it has been later. And, don't worry about Bill, it turns out your grandfather made a wonderful investment in a house in Georgetown in 1950. Your brother lives there now."

"So, does Gramps live in some tent somewhere?"

"Hardly. Peter has a small cottage on Chautauqua Lake south of Buffalo. He still has the boat and a small dock. He's from Western New York, you know. His father was in Donovan's unit in World War One and then Peter's dad did something or another for Donovan when he was the US attorney there — I never knew and Peter never said. That's how Donovan knew of Peter and how he ended up in the OSS instead of continuing with the 82nd. Donovan probably saved his life given the survival rate of paratroopers in World War II. At the very least, Donovan definitely changed his life."

"How is his health?"

"He is fit, he looks good and his mind is sharp. He is 85 and claims he will live to 100. Who knows? One thing, he really is obsessive when it comes to the Russians, Judith's death and your father's death, so be aware he doesn't need any encouragement."

Sue realized that he would be her first visit after graduation. Sue decided to change the subject.

"Mom, do you remember Mary Sanderson? She is my advisor at the Farm."

Barbara looked up from her coffee cup.

"Mary Sanderson. Now there is a name I haven't heard in years. How is she?"

"Mom, you have to understand my perspective is a little warped. She is part of my cast of characters in my nightmares — always asking hard questions that don't have answers. In the real world, she is supportive in an aggressive sort of way."

"She always was more than a bit aggressive, dear. That's what I remember about her."

"She is fit and healthy and looks like she could wrestle alligators if she had to. She terrifies the young male students."

"She terrified young male case officers in Kenya about a million years ago, so that is no change either."

"She said she owed you a personal debt, what's that about?"

"Mary was a young, attractive, aggressive female officer on her first tour in Nairobi. We helped her focus her efforts on good targets that she could recruit and I helped her sort out a personal problem that could have been trouble for her. She was meeting a Polish diplomat — remember this was Cold War days and Poles were good targets — but it seemed to me that the Pole was more interested in Mary for reasons other than work and, eventually, she seemed ready to accept that as well. Fraternization with any foreigner, much less a Warsaw Pact diplomat, was a career killer in those days. I simply made that point clear as a peer, before station management figured out this wasn't going to be a recruitment operation — at least not an espionage recruitment."

"Did she get the point?"

"You know, I think she never had considered the risk she was taking and, yes, after I gave her some sisterly advice, I think she did. Where did she go after that?"

"Mom, this is mostly a one-way street with her. I talk, she listens, she gives me corrective feedback, I listen. It isn't a real chatty time. I know her last job was chief of Base somewhere in the Gulf and she is an NE body. Other than that, I can't say."

"We tend to control access to ourselves over time. It stops being a work thing and becomes a habit. I suspect being a senior woman officer, she has to be "on" all the time. There are no "off" days for her."

"Is it that hard as a woman in the Agency?"

"It was for me. I did more than most men, had more recruitments and far more Intel reports every tour, but less encouragement. Worse still, as part of a tandem couple, the men in the office always talked to your father and rarely to me. I had to carve out my own niche and that niche was hunting terrorists. Today it is all the rage, in the 1980s it was considered a sideshow. Still, the work was good and the men in the office left me alone. It was about as much as I could expect."

Sue returned from Chicago refreshed and even more confused about her family history. Still, the farewell at the airport had been tough with both generations a little tearful. As soon as the students returned from break, literally as soon as they checked back into the Farm gate, they were tested with yet another set of meetings and the subsequent write up of the meetings. That finished and they conducted another street exercise where they faced a new, multi car surveillance team on the street. After that, they were out on the pistol range for day and night fire and the next morning they started a new block of instruction on cyber tradecraft.

Sue passed each of the training exercises, but as Fall turned into Winter, the aching in her wounded limb grew. The doctors at Walter Reed had warned her that this would happen as she got healthier and the blood flow returned to the extremity of her leg. They recommended she insulate her leg as much as possible in the Winter. Easier said than done when the training went from early morning PT, to a meeting, to a surveillance exercise, to an outdoor range, and then night work with computers. She would cope, but it wasn't getting any easier. She had refused the pain killers that the doctors prescribed and avoided hard liquor which she knew dulled the pain but had its own consequences. Ibuprofen, a bit of pain management meditation, and Mozart. Not as good as real drugs, but this technique meant she was clear headed all the time.

Sue's dreams got worse and far harder to understand. Her father entered dreams about Jalalabad, Jack entered dreams about her family and Mary remained the scariest character of all wherever the dream took her: Afghanistan, Ft. Bragg, college, or even her grandfather's home on the Potomac River. Mary's character in her dreams was so real and so…dangerous that Sue often caught herself being more careful and far less polite than she should be with her mentor. So far, Mary hadn't seemed to notice, but Sue wanted to pass this course and she didn't want to fail simply because her mentor hated her. Sue knew enough about surviving a "selection" course from S&R to know, your advisor could make or break you. Sue's caution was mixed with various questions rolling around in her head. Who killed her father? Who were the ghosts chasing her grandfather? Why on earth did her mother carry a revolver in Wonder Bread suburbia? What part of her childhood and teenage years were completely false? Did everything her parents said or did during that time period have a work linkage?

Also, what was that the life that Sue faced after graduation? She had never worked directly with the SOF intelligence teams when she was deployed. Chief Jameson was responsible for that linkup and at the time, she had been happy to leave it to her boss. Sue wasn't even certain that she had ever met someone from that team. She did know the "Klingons" had longer TDYs than the S&R teams and she now understood why that was. You couldn't recruit a good source on a timeline. She didn't know what life was like for the Klingons when they returned home. In fact, she didn't even know where "home" was for the Klingons.

Through all of this, the good news was that Sue didn't have to worry much about her new pals Melissa and Nancy. Melissa was in her element as the class began training on cyber tradecraft. She had a chance to serve as the guide after hours working with her peers, showing them the intricacies, opportunities and risks of working in a virtual world. Her engineering background was critical to the success of everyone in "wolf tribe" and she blossomed as she took charge. Sue was pleased to see this happen because so much of the other work had been out of Melissa's comfort zone that even when she did succeed in a task, she didn't see this as a building process and it didn't build her confidence. Now, she was confident of this set of requirements and able to explain to the others how the principles of espionage tradecraft applied just as much to the virtual world as the real world.

Sue also noticed that Melissa was spending more and more time "tutoring" Pigpen. There was romance in the air and Sue considered it good for both of them. Her mother had told her before that the Farm was the most expensive dating service in the US and Melissa and Pigpen were proving that to be true. Meanwhile, Sue was start-ing to feel closer to Jack and that had its problems. Jack was a SEAL

senior non-commissioned officer and Sue was an Army Warrant officer so there were questions of fraternization. Worse still, Jack was
going through a separation with his wife on his way, so he said, to
a divorce. This wasn't the first time Sue had watched that sort of
drama, but it was the first time she felt she was at risk as one of the
characters in the story. At least Jack, like all the SOF operators in the
class, knew about her prosthetic, so that wasn't a hurdle that she had
to handle.

Sunday's were generally slow days at the Farm. No events usually
before lunch. This morning, Sue decided to test her workout prosthetic and jog the two-mile forest loop near the dormitories. Just as
she started, Jack was finishing his run and he joined her for the two
miles — a "cool down" as he put it. Sue was happy for the company
and while they were running she outlined her family story. Like the
rest of the SOF crew, Jack knew that the Pete O'Connell in the lecture was likely to be a relation, so that made the discussion an easy
start. She ran through the news about her dad and waited for Jack to
comment.

"Sue, it sounds like some sort of Russian novel. Grandfather, father
and now you? Shit, can you get this more complicated?"

"So you have read a Russian novel, Jack?" Sue laughed.

"Does watching the movie 'Dr. Zhivago' count?"

"Nope."

"Can I change the analogy? How about a Dickens novel? Those I
have read."

"This isn't fiction, brother, it is my life."

"Sorry. So what do you want to do about it? Do you want to wait
until we get out of this prison?"

"I think some of the details are hidden in this prison and once I go
back to Bragg, I will never sort this out."

"Your ops, your plan, just tell me what you need. The gang will
deliver."

During the run, Jack told her that he was getting back together
with his wife after the class. They had decided to give it another try
and Jack was convinced that his new job would put less stress on the
marriage. Sue wasn't so sure about that, but she gave him all the

necessary encouragement. It was now clear why Jack had decided to continue his run with Sue. The "cool down" run gave him a chance to tell her and make it clear that their pseudo-relationship wasn't going to go anywhere. In the back of her mind, Sue was relieved. However, she was also hurt that he had decided to use a pretense to tell her.

Later that night, Sue had her Bose headphones on and listened to a Mozart violin concerto. The headphones had been essential on deployments. Inside the cargo aircraft, in the barracks, just about anywhere that she needed some internal privacy in the midst of the outside chaos, the headphones helped. Sue needed some time right now and Mozart was doing his part. She had contrived a plan that was starting to make some sense on how to collect information on her family history. Step one was convince the rest of her friends that they could and should help. Sue always had trouble asking for favors and this wasn't just asking to carry an additional load, it was asking to conduct operational acts at the Farm in ways that could get the participants sent back to their unit only a few weeks from the end of the course. She decided there was only one way to get through this. It wasn't going to be the way Jack had revealed his news. Sue decided she would explain once to everyone and then hope they would say yes. Jack seemed to understand, but there had been something between them. She already knew they wouldn't expose her, but that wasn't the same thing as getting them to say yes.

Sue found it interesting that she was basing her calculations on what they would say using the same skills she was being taught in class — evaluating risk versus gain, how she would design the "pitch" and how she had to explain why it was worth the risk. Sue didn't miss the fact that her mother had just told her that work took everything from you — your life, your friends, and, often your family. Now, she was facing the same risks with her friends.

Nancy stuck her head into Sue's room. "Hey, we are seriously short of chicks down at the bar downstairs. You interested in helping your peers keep the jokers away from us?"

"When have you had trouble telling men to back off?"

"Never. But, you could use some practice and I figured I could give you some pointers. Think of it as another practical exercise." Nancy barely dodged the pillow launched from Sue's bed.

"OK, wise guy. Guess what — you have just given me an idea on how to solve a problem that I have, so, yes, I'm ready for a beer and some instruction."

Sue went down to the bar with Nancy. The bar was originally a training venue. It had been designed in the early days of the Farm when Germany was the front lines of the Cold War. The cadre created a German pub of that era. It had the claustrophobic nature of the real venue — dark wood floors and walls, bench seating, shelves covered with old beer steins and hunting trophies. The bar was manned by two couples who were permanent party living at the Farm. The job was an easy enough job, but the hosts had to have one key skill. They had to speak near native German. During the class, the pub (or stuben in German) was a venue for some of the meetings between students and cadre role players. After hours, the pub was open until 7-10pm on weeknights and 7-11pm on weekends for students. The students were fairly certain that they were under observation both via the managers of the pub and video/audio surveillance, but no one knew for sure. As a result, the students always played the digital juke box as loud as possible and gathered as far as possible from the bar. Most of the conversations were equally loud, but barely understandable in the background din. They probably sold as much coffee as they did beer — but the beers were German and the wine French, so if you did have a drink, it was consistent with the bar.

Melissa, Pigpen, Jack, and Ginger were sitting at one of the round tables in the back of the bar worrying over a backgammon game. They looked up when Nancy and Sue arrived. Melissa turned to Pigpen, held out her hand, palm up and said "Pay!"

Sue raised an eyebrow.

"I bet her that nothing Nancy could say would get you down here."

"I hope it wasn't much of a bet."

"Dinner in DC when we get outta here."

"Yikes!"

"And I intend to select a very nice place. Any place where the food isn't served on trays."

Ginger looked up from his coffee cup. "She is such a sophisticate!"

"Yup, that's why we love her." Sue decided this was as good a time as any to break the ice.

"Kids, I need your help."

Pigpen looked at Melissa. "Maybe I don't have to pay up after all."

"No dice, big guy. She is here and that was the bet."

"Sue, if you need help, you know we are here for you." Nancy looked as serious as Sue.

"This isn't about the class, but it is about tradecraft."

"A challenge. Just what we need, more challenges." Ginger's sarcasm was tempered by his theatrical hand to the forehead and rolled eyes.

"Seriously, if you guys don't want to get involved, I understand."

"Just get with the pitch, we are already recruited." Nancy sounded interested.

"It's about my family and their operations."

"I told you she was from a family of spooks." Jack was never very subtle. Pigpen threw a peanut that hit Jack in the forehead.

"I need to get into the main online archive and possibly into the old, hard archives here on post."

"Well, I guess I know where I fit in." Melissa was grinning.

"Me too." Ginger was the best covert entry guy in S&R and had admitted working various locks on base: "just to stay in practice" so he said.

"So am I just a pretty face?" Pigpen seemed hurt.

"Diversion, mates. Diversion." Jack had his arms wrapped around Nancy and Pigpen.

"All in?" Sue was pleased, relieved and surprised at the same time.

"All in." They raised the mix of beer glasses, coffee cups and soda cans.

While everyone had glasses raised, Jack carefully bounced a peanut off Pigpen's forehead into his beer glass.

Sue and Melissa sat next to each other in one of the student computer work bays at the Farm. It was late, near midnight, but working late as the course progressed was nothing out of the ordinary. Sue had made a thermos of strong coffee and they were sharing a single cup. Next to the computer was a sign in red lettering: No liquids near the computers! "Do you think we will get into trouble with the coffee?" Melissa said with a smirk. She was dressed in jeans, an oversized Stanford University sweatshirt, sneakers and her ubiquitous black framed glasses.

"Compared to hacking into the Agency mainframe for personal reasons?"

"Think of it as extra practice in our cyber tradecraft."

"How are you going to crack the password requirement?"

"I'm not going to need to "crack" a password. By the way, you crack a code, you hack a system."

"Thanks for the lesson, Dr. Helpful."

"So, the answer is that I am using the password of our mentor, Ms. Tough-guy Mary. She logged on one time while I was in her office and I captured her password then."

"One time and upside down from the opposite side of the computer?"

"It's what I do. I don't comment on your shooting skills, do I? I know it's what you do."

"Speaking of shooting, where did you learn to shoot a handgun?"

"Hush. Genius at work. You see the logon isn't the hard part. The hard part is making the system think Ms. Mary is logging in from her computer. Then, when we are done, erasing all the foot prints of these two little members of the wolf tribe. That's the hard part and it is the part I am doing now. So, no stories right now."

Melissa's fingers flew across the key board, over to the mouse, back to the key board and back again to the mouse.

"It takes a few minutes to create the right back door and make the activities when we use the back door erase as soon as we do something else. This is important for you to know because you won't be able to return to a previous screen after you move to another image. Take notes and be quick about it, OK? I don't know if there are any time limits on this sort of thing on this system."

"So, you don't know everything."

"Not yet. OK, start your search. We are in the Agency's main archive database now."

Sue slid over and typed "O'Connell, Peter" and hit enter. "Your family?"

"My dad."

"Must have been an old guy. The first file is from 1948."

"Whoops, that's probably granddad."

"Family of spies, then."

"We prefer case officers, you know." Melissa stuck out her tongue.

"Set the date parameters, dummy, so you get the right Peter O'Connell." Sue typed the needful and a thousand files came up.

"Ugh. How am I going to sort this."

"Well, what do you really want to know because we probably only have a few more minutes given how slow you type."

"Feel free to drive." Sue slid over and Melissa took over.

"What is the key subject."

"Soviet Union". Melissa added that to the search.

"We are down to 150 files."

"KGB". Melissa looked at Sue, but typed in the additional search.

"Six files. One listed as restricted, closed, under the Operational title "AGAMEMNON.""

"OK. Let's call it quits. Back out and we will see if we can find the closed file in the hard copy archives here on post."

"Well, that makes it easier for me. Since we didn't open any files, our footprints are tiny mouse tracks." Melissa started typing again, more carefully. The screen reflected off her glasses as Sue watched.

"You are such a pal."

"Shhhh. I have work to do and I won't get anywhere if we starting hugging each other and crying. Save that for later."

"Promise?" Another smirk from Melissa, but she did not waver from the screen.

AGAMEMNON. Sue wondered what in the world is that file name mean — if anything. Sometimes they are chosen at random, sometimes not. Before they backed out of the electronic archives, Sue had noted the date of the file (1989-1992) and the date the file was archived (1999). It should be easy enough to find, if the files were stored by date. If not, it might be impossible to find.

The archives were located in a brick building in a glade of trees near the river. She had noticed it during one of the small boat training exercises where they simulated picking up an agents using a small Boston Whaler as an alternative. Sue assumed this was mostly for the instructors to have some fun and to demonstrate that the principles worked anywhere. At the end of the training session while she was tying up the boat at the docks near the boathouse, she noticed the red brick building in the trees.

"What's that?"

Sandy Jackson, a retired paramilitary case officer, instructor on driving and shooting and, in this case, small boat operations, looked up the hill.

"Archives. Beats me what else is stored in there. I have only seen annuitants and the Agency historians go in there. Old files I guess. Been there as long as the Farm. Certainly been there since I was a student here 40 years ago."

Now Sue would have to find out what was in there.

The office for Counterintelligence Center/cyber was in Old Headquarter Building in BB corridor — the first B stood for basement. After you entered the first door accessed with a cipher lock pin code, you waited in a small room while the office manager let you into the office. During that wait, the wags in the office said CIC/Tech was bathing you in low level microwaves to insure you were not carrying some electronic bug, or if you were, it would be fried. If that was so, most of the visitors were reluctant to visit more often than they absolutely had to. If it were not so, it was a great CI deception plan. Inside the office, the betting was deception. Jesse Markwell and Danny Jones were sitting in Danny's cubicle looking at one of the three monitors on his desk. Markwell was a 50 year-old with a shaved head, black turtle neck and jeans. He kept a full suit, shirt, and tie hanging in a suit bag on his office door in case C/CIC or a division chief, one of the "barons" in the building, asked the chief of CIC/cyber upstairs. When he was in his basement office and among the "methane breathers" as his staff liked to call themselves, he figured it made no sense not to be comfortable. Jesse had been in the gym when he got the call from Danny. His schedule was sufficiently predictable that any of his staff would know where he was at 0600hrs, Monday through Saturday.

Danny was one of Jesse's best. He was a farm trained case officer and now worked in CIC/cyber on technical recruitment operations against all of the adversaries identified by the U.S. as hard targets. Jesse had pulled him off a recruitment operation against Iranian radar designers over the weekend to support a joint CIC/FBI operation. Danny had been working all night and was in sweatpants, a t-shirt and flip flops. Unlike most of his peers, he did not drink energy drinks, much to Jesse's pleasure since the mix of long hours, energy drinks and small cubicles really did make much of shop smell like his staff really were methane breathers.

Danny was a pure espresso guy and spent one of his many CIC performance awards on a $2000 espresso machine which covered half of his desk. He was fastidious and Jesse was regularly surprised that Danny's cubicle smelled of nothing more than Simple Green cleaning supplies. Where he ditched his pounds of coffee grounds no one knew. Some of the staff were convinced he bagged them in bulk and threw them down the chute where the classified trash was deposited to an even lower level of the building. Others argued that Danny just ate them with his morning cereal that he prepared in the office kitchen. Jesse didn't want to know. The only other non-work related item on the desk which included three monitors, two separate hard drive columns and a laptop (glued to the desk so it could not be removed from the room), was an old yellow plastic tube. One of the remnants from the 1962 pneumatic tube system that used to link the entire Old Headquarter Building. Rare, hard to find, and just as eccentric as Danny.

"So, first she hacks into the mainframe. Brilliant job, used two different ghost hosts from here to do the deed and two more to erase her work. If we hadn't been warned and turned on the internal cameras and the key stroke logger on the room, we would never have known."

"Is she capable of this or did she have help?"

"Melissa Nez was recruited by our cyber team specifically for offensive operations. BS at Stanford, PhD at UC/Berkley. She is the heat."

"Great, Danny, but what was she looking at and did she do any damage?"

"Boss, harder to say. I know she went into the archives and she was searching the name O'Connell. She didn't touch any files, so I can't sort out which of the 10,000 plus documents that fit into the thousand plus files were the ones she was interested in when she did the search. The files track from 1948 to 2003. Who was this guy who worked so long?"

"Danny, it's not one guy. It's a family name and has two, soon to be three generations of players. Nez's pal who is sitting next to her is Sue O'Connell. Peter O'Connell, senior was in the OSS and his son, also Peter, was my first boss in CIC. His wife, Barbara, was one of the first case officers in CTC. This is very interesting and more than a bit confusing. I need to make a couple of calls. For sure, it is a positive development in our overall case."

"I suppose I don't get to know what that case is, right?"

"Danny, I will read you in later this morning, I promise. You are going to need to be fully in the loop."

"OK. So, now what? What should I do about Nez and should I let Ms. Sanderson know of the intrusion?"

"File the entire record in our offensive operations file for a future discussion with Ms. Nez. You will be the senior interviewer, so keep what you need, destroy the rest. Do not under any circumstances let Ms. Sanderson know about this. Got it?"

"Check, Chief. Are we going to be able to keep Nez on the books? She really is the heat."

"Relax, big guy. This is not going to prevent our using Ms. Nez."

Thanksgiving at the Farm was another work day. The students had a morning meeting with an asset, write up to the COS due by 1300hrs. and then casing to accomplish with corresponding casing reports due by 1000hrs on Friday. The sites to be cased were on post but required both day and night work. At 1500hrs, the students and cadre met in the mess hall for a formal Thanksgiving Dinner. Like many of the formal military holiday dinners Sue had attended, there was enforced sociability among the full cadre — all artificial but survivable. The post commander offered a series of toasts and each student table had one bottle of sparkling wine shared among eight students. Just enough for the toasts. The stuben would be open from 2000-2300hrs, but most of the students intended to get the night casing done and then gather for at least one football game on TV.

Sue met with her posse after the dinner. "Tonight is the night. We have all cased the archives day and night. There doesn't seem to be any cameras outside or camera leads into the building. The locks and alarms on the doors seem simple enough. After we complete the night casing, I want to get inside the archives and find my father's file. Now is the time to back out if you want to. We are within a week of the final problem and 15 days from graduation. Anyone who works with me tonight is risking it all."

Pigpen spoke before she had closed her mouth. "Really? We have to go through an Alamo speech at this point? Are you going to draw a line in the dirt with your pencil? Let's sort out the jobs."

Melissa spoke next. "I will monitor the mainframe here to see if there are any alarms or video surveillance files. If there are, they get deleted and turned into apparent power blips."

Jack added "I cover Melissa's back in the student computer room. We both will have casing reports going as well as Melissa's magic."

Nancy was next. "I will invite myself to the security office for a ballgame. I have been doing this a couple of times a week over the last month, so it should be reasonable that I would show up."

"It doesn't hurt that the security office has the full football ticket on their cable channel, does it? Jets game tonight, right?" Jack had to offer his advice.

"We all have our cross to bear, mate."

"Of course, I get to cover the entrance by hiding in the muck near the building. Night standing observation point — perfect."

"Hey, you didn't get the name Pigpen for nothing."

Ginger was next. "I do the locks, alarms and help search. If all else fails, I get the drop on anyone and we run like hell."

"Subtle, Ginger." Ginger held up his arms in surrender — arms that were twice the size of Sue's.

"OK. 2125hrs is our entry time; 2200hrs our NLT departure. Everyone backs off from there."

"Do we get to synchronize our watches? I always wanted to do that." Nancy looked around and then stuck out her tongue.

Sue expected Ginger to have little trouble with the locks and alarms and she was not disappointed. They entered the archives in blue booties and gloves — after years in S&R, Sue had a set or three in every bag she owned. The Farm had provided state of the art night vision goggles for their night casing exercises, so no flashlights were needed as they used their "green eyes." They both carried cameras with IR filters, so they could capture any file they found. Finally, both Sue and Ginger carried every possible type of tape and stapler they could think of so that they could seal any files they found and had to open. Their bags rattled like hardware store shopping carts.

The archives were in a brick building approximately sixty feet by forty feet. When they entered, they faced 15 rows of steel shelving the length of the building. Sue hoped that the files were in chronological order, but that had not been the case. After all, files had various start dates and finish dates, which would you choose? Then she checked to see if the files were in alphabetical order based on operation name. No luck. The files, it turned out were sorted by file number which, to some degree corresponded to the date the operation was opened. It took some racing up and down the aisles, but eventually they found it.

Sue let Ginger do the needful. He was the expert on opening things (doors, vaults, and envelopes) and she was too nervous. The file was in a folder that had probably been black, but was now faded gray, though colors were hard to judge in the green glow of the NVGs. Ginger headed her the file and held up 10 fingers. Like a jumpmaster telling the stick they had ten minutes to the green light, Ginger wanted her to know they had ten minutes to get the job done and start the process to get out. As he warned her before they started "we use our tools to get in, but we also have to use our tools to get out. If it takes me five minutes to get in, we need to budget ten to get out — just in case."

Sue placed the file on the floor and started to take photos — back to front. Page after page. About 100 pages. She then gave the file to

Ginger and he did the same with his camera. Sue remembered her chief instructor on clandestine entry in S&R.

"We are the department of redundancy department. If we have time we take four sets of pictures of everything going in and going out. If not four then three — but never less than two. I know you mugs think that is just because I'm a geezer and lived in the world of wet film where anything could go wrong and did. Sure enough, but anything that has batteries can and will fail when you need it the most, so humor me and be redundant."

Ginger finished and replaced the file in the envelope, replaced the seal using a glue stick that he had brought with him, and then replaced the file on the shelf. He checked his original photo of the file on the shelf to be sure it looked exactly like it did when they found it and gave Sue the thumps up. They backtracked slowly along the rows of files.

Sue sent a text to Pigpen, "7," meaning roger.

"77," he wrote back, meaning roger roger.

They cleared the building in 8 minutes. Ginger checked the alarms and locks twice and they disappeared into the woods and linked up with Pigpen.

"Mosquitoes suck."

"Brilliant, Watson." Ginger smiled.

Sue sat alone in her room looking at the photos on the memory stick. Ginger had given her his stick and replaced it with the stick he had used earlier in the evening for the casing report due tomorrow. Everyone agreed that the files were Sue's business and she could share them when/if she decided to do so. Once Pigpen sent the all clear, they went their separate ways to their rooms, confident that she would share…eventually.

Sue stared at the file — page one.

AGAMEMNON

PURPOSE: determine Soviet tradecraft used to handle American agents inside the intelligence community.

ACTIVATION DATE: 01 October 1989

PROPOSED LENGTH OF PROJECT: no more than two years APPROVALS: DCI, AG, D/FBI (initialed next to each)

SUMMARY: We assume that the KGB and/or the GRU have successfully penetrated the intelligence community. We further assume they are using the best possible electronic and physical tradecraft to handle their asset(s). Therefore, to catch the traitors we need to know this tradecraft. To date, none of the CIA or FBI penetrations of the Soviet services have had access to this information because they are not US agent handlers. To obtain this information, we have to risk a double agent operation where we offer up a U.S. Intelligence officer. We have identified an officer who has the right background and a plausible reason for treason. That officer is Peter O'Connell Jr.

BACKGROUND: O'Connell is a successful officer with multiple tours in both denied area and third world countries. He is part of a tandem couple. His wife, Barbara O'Connell is a counterterrorism officer involved in operations against known Arab terrorists. O'Connell is the son of a retired senior Agency officer who was accused during the Angleton era of working with the Soviets or, at least, having a pro-communist view. We intend to use this background to build a credible story for why O'Connell junior would approach the Soviets. The basic premise will be that he intends to get revenge for the false accusation of his father's loyalty and to gain additional information from the Soviets on Arab terrorist organizations — especially Soviet proxies in exchange for US classified intelligence.

BLOWBACK: The primary risk in any double agent operation is that the "feed material" given to the target is more valuable than the information provided. O'Connell will be assigned to Hqs and given job which will be interesting, sensitive, and filled with promise for future assignments in the field. We believe the Soviets will accept this as a seeding operation and focus on tradecraft issues while accepting our feed material as a bonus to building a future agent. There is no evidence that any of the O'Connells will be at personal risk during the length of the operation.

At this point, Sue put down the computer, pulled out the memory stick and hid it and its mate from Ginger in a small concealment she had made inside her prosthetic. She cleared the computer, initiated a recently added cleansing program courtesy of Melissa and shut down the computer. She then started to cry.

ue was busy enough with the last set of classes and exercises leading up to "the final problem" that she had little time to read the file. What she did read was the last pages in the file. When the USSR collapsed, it seemed a perfect time for the Agency to end AGAMEMNON. Peter told his KGB handler he was finished, based on the chaos that was happening in Moscow. Most of his interactions with the Russians was through electronic communications, but his last meeting in April 1992 was face to face along the Appalachian trail in western Virginia. The File offered little of the flavor of the meeting, but it was clear that Peter's handler explained that the KGB was becoming one of the most powerful crime syndicates in Europe and they were looking for Peter to help them in the U.S. Neither the FBI nor the CIA at the time wanted or cared about this option and Peter was extracted from the operation. He received the Intelligence Star for AGAMEMNON in a secret ceremony and a commendation from the FBI Director for his work. The file closed in June 1992.

The file raised more questions than it answered. Sue remembered her father and mother ending their careers in Headquarters as she and Bill headed to college. There was never any mention of the award ceremony or the operation. Sue didn't even know if her mother knew as much as she did about AGAMEMNON. Was there any link to her father's murder? The Russian mafia was famous for its ruthlessness in the late 1990s. Would they have decided to close out a "loose end" who knew too much? What about the SVR? Did they even keep the old files?

Sue had shared some of the questions and some of the answers with Ginger and Melissa, but the rest of her posse were focused on the class and pleased with their little Thanksgiving adventure that she didn't see any point in discussing the story with them all. Everyone wanted to finish the school and get on with life. It was like a long mountain hike with the summit just in sight. No one wanted to rest now, they just wanted to get to the summit and finish.

The final problem was 14 days long. During these two weeks, the students would operate in teams conducting operations outside of Zed station in an outlying city of Zed. The briefing took place inside the simulated station spaces in a very crowded conference room. At this point, the original class of thirty was now sixteen — an easy mix for four teams of four. Sue was surprised that there had been a 50 percent attrition, but not surprised at all that most of the departures had been individuals who quit rather than individuals who were told to go home. This was typical of all the selection programs she attended and had heard about in SOF — you make it hard enough that the folks who really don't have the desire just decide it is not worth the cost. Of course, the SOF students were still in place — you would have had to drop them in a lake with a cement block tied to their feet to get rid of them. There was no going back to your unit and tell them you quit.

"Wolf tribe survives as a team?" Melissa walked away from the formal briefing for the final problem. Like each of the students, she had received both a paper file and a memory stick filled with information on the overall mission and her specific role in that mission.

"Looks like some of us did." Sue was carrying her own file and noticed her file, like Melissa's, was labeled TEAM 3. They were walking down the stairs to the "embassy" basement where the team rooms were set up. As they walked down the hall, two others arrived from the opposite stairwell at the opposite end of the hall.

"It figures I would draw a weak hand." Ginger was looking directly at Sue.

"You shouldn't talk like about Stan." Stan looked puzzled and frustrated that he had walked into the middle of a joke where he didn't know if he was the subject, the object, or simply an accessory.

"Stan, you have to understand, these commandos are always rude to each other and to anyone in the blast radius." Melissa, as always, was committed to building consensus and community.

"Melissa, you don't need to apologize. I was a Marine before I was in the Agency. I had professionals try to make me cry."

Sue had heard Stan was a solid performer across every requirement. He would be a terrific addition to the team and would have no problem fitting in to the slightly tart version of team comraderie that they had already established.

"Now, Stan. The first thing you have to do is to join the Wolf Tribe." Melissa looked directly at Stan using her most serious face.

"Huh?"

"It's true, Stan. You need join our tribe. Have a knife? If not, you can use mine." Ginger jumped right into the joke and pulled a small clip knife out of his jeans and opened it. He was ready to cut open his hand like a little kid making a blood pact.

Sue decided it was time to clear the air before Stan decided he needed to take out one or more of them using some sort of standard unarmed combat technique.

"Stan, they are pulling your leg, brother. This is just a joke that started on day one and hasn't gotten any more amusing on day 100."

Melissa made a face at Sue. "I thought it was pretty good for at least the first 50 days."

"I think it went well past 50." Ginger was putting the knife back into his jeans.

They went into the team room and opened their files.

The final problem required the students to travel to another city, forcing them out of their comfort zone and forcing them to start all over again. Sue read that they were going to Buffalo and she thought immediately about her grandfather who lived just fifty miles south on Chatauqua lake. She doubted there would be time to see him, but you never knew what might take her outside the city. Sue had more reasons to talk to her grandfather than ever before and Sue decided to make time if at all possible. She had to remember that her personal agenda might affect her team, so she put that desire aside and focused on the program.

The files were linked together.

Inside the Republic of Zed, Buffalo is a port city famous for smuggling and some of the single most important extremists in the country. Each member had a specific mission to accomplish.

Sue — recruit a customs official who is a volunteer who wrote into the station and would be available for a meeting at a time/place yet to be determined. In the meantime, Sue would provide general support to the others. Melissa — handle a computer specialist who had direct access to servers that might be used by the extremists. The file on the computer specialist argued that he was a difficult person and that was why he had been put "on ice" for some time.

Ginger and Stan — identify the most likely warehouse in the city being used by the extremists as a safe house. The station files provided four different venues and two established agents who might be able to assist.

The files stated that the local arm of the Zed security service was suspected to be direct supporters of the extremists and profiting from smuggling activities. They could be expected to work hard to find the team and disrupt their activities.

"Well, that doesn't seem so hard, does it?" Sue figured this was the best way to start the team brainstorming.

"No, all we have to do is find the right people in a city of a half million, avoid a hostile intelligence service, surveil four separate buildings and you have to recruit a volunteer who might, in fact, be a dangle. Perfect."

"Stan, don't go with the negative vibes, brother. We know plenty from the files and just have to watch out for each other along the way." Ginger was looking forward to the challenge, though he was not pleased with the idea of working in Buffalo in December. "I heard one time that Buffalo has two seasons — winter and the 4th of July. Do we get extra money to buy snowshoes and parkas?"

Sue looked at him. "Wimp. How can you possibly think that the weather is going to be a factor in one of the great winter cities of North America?"

"Seriously, if you read to the bottom of the file, you would have seen a $1000 clothing budget to get you ready of the project. I suspect between here and Reagan National, we can find at least one outdoor store, no?"

The trip to Buffalo was uneventful which in December was surprising. The weather was predictable — cold, windy and plenty of snow on the streets. The teams were set up at a series of hotels around Buffalo International Airport — Team 3 was in an Embassy suites. December in Buffalo meant gray days with precious little sunlight to work with for days of casing.

The first few days were spent conducting area familiarization and making some surveillance detection probes to see if they were under surveillance from the beginning. The city was fairly easy to get around and the super highways mixed with old suburban roads and public transportation made the town a terrific venue for surveillance detection. On day three, Melissa got hopelessly lost and ended up nearly crossing the Peace Bridge into Canada when she confessed on the phone to Sue that she was lost. Sue knew how confusing that can be when you really get turned around in a city and, worse still, as you approach dusk and everything is gray. She told Melissa to pull over on a side street and wait. Stan found her parked in the parking lot of the Buffalo boat house and walking up and down near the river talking to herself.

Stan brought a coffee from his thermos over to Melissa, walked her along the river for a few minutes and then asked her to follow him back to the hotel. He pointed out that none of them wanted to add a real border control problem to their training exercise. Later, Stan spent some time with Melissa sorting out how she got so lost; Stan relayed to the team the next morning the only good thing about Melissa's travels around the city was that she had drawn surveillance.

The team met in Stan's room — their informal base of operations every morning at 0800hrs. Each day, someone got carry out. Today, Sue brought in a dozen donuts and a box of coffee from Tim Horton's.

"That gives me an idea! I think we need to case a hockey game. I understand the Sabres are playing Anaheim tomorrow night. Who knew Anaheim had a hockey team? Where do they get the ice?" Stan never knew if Ginger was being serious or joking.

"Really. Hockey? How does that work for us and how in the world did the donuts give you that idea?"

"First, Stan, you should know better — Tim Horton was a hockey player and all kids who have to go to hockey rinks at screwy hours in the morning live on donuts." Sue was completely puzzled. She thought she knew all of Ginger's background. Now what in the world is this link to junior hockey.

Ginger didn't wait to reveal his secret.

"Have you seen the Marine Midland arena pictures and environs? It is a perfect place to lose surveillance among nearly 20,000 spectators. So, when Sue finally gets the call for her linkup with the write in, we have options for her to get clean, assuming it is at night and the team is at home."

"And you have to walk around during a game because…"

"Stan, you are such a spoil sport. Because a map recon will not give up where the security cameras are located and… because I like hockey."

Melissa looked at Ginger. "Need a date?"

"Well, we might have to do some electronic checks as well, no?"

The team had no real team leader. It was a team of equals. Stan and Sue had no real reason to complain. It was their time and it actually sounded like a reasonable plan.

"See, it isn't so stupid after all. We have to sort out where we park, how we get in and how we get out. We might even see some hockey."

Sue jumped in to the discussion; she had been casing meeting sites for the team for the last three days and pulling counter surveillance at the meetings, There wasn't much on her agenda until the write-in established a meeting date and time. The cold and the rain/sleet mix over the last few days had been hard on her leg. The wind off the Niagara River was cutting and the sidewalks were slick. She had her best traction prosthetic on, but that didn't mean that she didn't twist and turn on the street.

"What do we know about our targets?"

Ginger said "I used a throw away cell phone to initiate contact with my guy. We met at D'arcy McGee's Irish pub tomorrow at 1400hrs yesterday. The location gave us multiple ways to use public transportation and the lunch crowd was finished by then. He gave me the list of the possible warehouses and their owners. The primary lead is a guy named George Paplow. I used Melissa's genius to find out as much as I can about the guy's background. Tomorrow, I need as much help as possible to get some eyes on the target — both the guy and the place. I will spend the morning doing the write up and then get out on the street doing some initial checks on the venues."

Stan was next. "I used another phone to call my guy. We are meeting as part of a formal tour at the Albright Knox Gallery tomorrow morning. I looked at the gallery and there are plenty of places to pull him off for a quiet discussion. He is a major player in the development of the Larkin district, so he should fit in OK. I am going to go down to Delaware Park today to see if I can sort out how surveillance might set up. After that, I will do some casing for the next meeting."

Melissa jumped in. "I figure the real standout might be you, Stan."

"Hey, it's a modern art museum. How hard can it be to look confused? And, I will wear a turtle neck with the black suit. Very hip in a California sort of way. Sorry, but I don't get to hang out with you in the old warehouse and grain elevator district tomorrow."

"My meeting with the tech geek was at a bar in Allentown. I did my best slacker disguise. He wasn't as hard as the file said. He just is an introverted tech guy who talks about his work with a passion and has little time for folks who don't get what he is trying to do. He gave me the basic material I needed to get into the suspect servers as well as giving me the email addresses. I will be working on this tonight. I will let you know what it tells me by tomorrow at breakfast. I will be available to help Ginger. I haven't gotten lost once in this town after the first day and I am ready to see the sights on the waterfront."

Sue closed the discussion. "OK, I'm on the surveillance gig as well. I still don't know crap about when, where or how I'm going to meet the write in, so a day in a car working a target will be a good use of my time. Just so you all know, the station will be texting me the meeting venue and time on my clean phone, so I may have to pull out of a run at a moment's notice."

"Or, you will be going down to the Anchor Bar for wings and just not telling us, right?"

"Ginger, if I do, I promise to bring you back some in a greasy carry out bag."

"Perfect."

Surveillance operations when the weather is crap are hard work. You have to either find a place where you can sit and have endless cups of coffee and watch the target location or you have to place a car in a location that allows you to stay put, but not look like you are a pervert or a criminal. After all, surveillance and espionage are criminal acts everywhere, so it is tough to figure out what to do and how to do it.

Sue was relatively lucky on the first location. There was an old diner in the area of the warehouse and it did have a plate glass window that looked out over the street. Sue had dressed appropriately — jeans, work shoes, a sweatshirt and a brown Carhart coat that she had dragged around the parking lot in the hotel and then dried out. Add to this a black watch cap and she looked like a truck driver just coming off a delivery looking for coffee and breakfast. She got the breakfast and got the right seat and worked over the plate of pancakes, eggs, sausage, bacon, and nearly a loaf of toast — stretching the meal to nearly two hours along with endless cups of coffee.

Just about the time she was ready to burst from the coffee, Paplow left the warehouse door and started to walk toward a lone SUV parked in the fenced parking lot. Sue had already paid for the meal and she ran for the restroom while dialing up Ginger. She got into the toilet and did the needful while talking on the Bluetooth.

"Stand by, Stand by. Bravo on the move from my Alpha. The Charlie is a gray SUV. I have the target, but will need to transfer soonest because I am going to be on the only car on Childs with him when he pulls out."

As Sue pulled up her jeans and started out the door, Ginger's voice arrived in the ear piece.

"Roger, I can at the corner of Ohio and Republic if he heads north."

Sue wished they had spent the time doing a spot map for the area so they didn't have to identify streets, but that was something that everyone forgot during the initial days of learning the Buffalo streets.

Melissa's voice arrived in her earpiece.

"I can if he heads south. I will pick him up on Ohio and Tift."

By this time, Sue was walking slowly out to her car — a Ford F150 rented specifically for the day's activities. No one expects a pickup truck to be the surveillance team… well, hardly anyone. She was pulling herself into the salt covered truck when the SUV went by heading north on Ohio.

"Ginger, he's yours. Black Tahoe. NY License Mike Victor Mike 323.

The vehicle looks gray because of the salt wash from the streets."

"Roger."

"I will cover up to Republic."

Sue waited until Paplow followed the curve of Ohio and headed across the canal and then pulled the truck out and did a U turn and headed North.

"Moving to S. Park and Louisiana."

After all this time, Sue still was surprised and pleased when Melissa figured out how to work surveillance. She would be ready for a hand over when Ginger asked for help.

Sue kept her distance and watched as her target moved up Ohio and passed Republic. She saw Ginger's minivan pull out from Republic.

"I have the Bravo."

"Roger." Sue pulled in behind Ginger and followed him for one street and then turned right and headed toward Louisiana and a probable linkup with Melissa.

The morning run went well. The weather helped as it switched from rain to sleet — making any effort on the part of the target to see surveillance just that much harder. Ginger and Melissa did one more handoff and then

Sue took Paplow to the second warehouse. At that point, they needed to set up a stakeout and Sue couldn't be that person simply because it would be too obvious to have her loitering around two different locations on the same morning. Ginger and Melissa found another diner near the warehouse and decided to have lunch together. A couple always looks less suspicious than a lone male or lone female anywhere and they could cover both ends of the street as well.

Sue drove to a layup position in a local strip mall, went to the 7Eleven for some water and a cup of coffee and then went back to the truck. She got in the truck, took off the blue tooth earpiece and pulled out the cellphone and put it on the center console with the speaker on and the voice muted. She expected she would hear from Ginger as soon as there was something happening, but it could be minutes or hours before that happened. She would have to move to a new layup position in about 20 minutes, so Sue set the countdown timer on her watch for 15 minutes and settled in with her coffee.

After 15 minutes, she started the truck back up and moved further away to a Starbucks location. Phone in pocket, Bluetooth earpiece in, she went to the Starbucks bathroom, bought another cup of coffee and walked back out to the truck. On the way to the truck, she slipped when her prosthetic caught some ice in the parking lot and spilled half the cup on her coat.

"Perfect. The elegant life of the spy."

When she got into the truck, she repeated the previous performance. Earpiece out. Speaker phone on. Then she changed the pattern slightly. She pulled out another throw away phone — this time purchased with her own money — and dialed up a number. The number rang for 10 times before there was an answer.

"Hello?"

"Gramps? It's Sue."

"Sue? My little Sue?"

"Yup. I was thinking about you and wanted to give you a call. I'm in Buffalo."

"Final problem?"

"Yes."

"Buffalo in December? Who did you piss off?"

"Lots of folks, Gramps, but that's not why I'm here."

"You think you would have time to see a geezer?"

"Probably not where you live, Gramps. I'm pretty tied up."

"Got that, dear. I will come up to town and we can try to linkup. It isn't that far and I'm still safe on the highway — sort of. The good news is I do still have a license. Or is that the bad news?"

"OK, but no promises. I just wanted to hear your voice and say how much I miss you."

"Dear, let's not get maudlin on the phone — I hate it when I have to cry into the receiver."

"That's what I love about you Gramps — you are such a charming guy."

"Yeah, that's what your grandmother used to say. Where are you staying?"

"Embassy suites near the airport."

"OK, here's a plan. We will meet at Schwabls in West Seneca tomorrow for lunch. Best beef on weck in the town. Small place, pretty easy to spot an outsider."

"I will try Gramps. I think I'm free tomorrow in the morning. I can't say about the afternoon."

"Fair enough, dear. I will come up to the city and you can call me on the following number — 716-652-6262. It's my throw away mobile so you can call from anywhere and anytime. You are the only one who has the number so I will know it's you."

"I don't suppose I can text you?"

The snort was clear over the phone. "No dear. Don't text me. Just call and say a time. We already know where. I suspect that will be faster than trying to text me."

"OK, Gramps. No promises, OK? I don't know how the problem is playing out."

"Do you have the recruitment target?"

"What?" Sue was still amazed at her family. They always seemed to know more about her life than she did.

"It only makes sense. The rest of the skills are too easy for you. The recruitment target is the only challenge, so I assumed you were the person from your team who drew that job. Remember, I ran the Farm kiddo. I can't tell you how many times I went through this exercise… but never in Buffalo in December. I still want to know who you pissed off."

"I guess I will have to bring the list tomorrow. No promises, right? I gotta go."

"Dear, keep safe. Remember, there are plenty of villains on the street who don't care about your exercise, but might care about you."

"Gramps, I can take care of myself.

"I know you can dear, but still keep your wits about you. It's not all play acting out there."

Just as Sue was about to try to say something glib, the speaker on the mobile next to her went off.

"Stand by, standby. Bravo leaving for his car." Ginger's voice was showing some strain. "I can if he heads north on Michigan."

"I can if he heads West on Seneca." Melissa's voice was garbled — she was probably in the middle of a sandwich.

Sue picked up the mobile, shut off the mute, and replied "I am on Seneca two blocks East of Michigan. I can if he goes that way." She switched to the other mobile.

"Gramps, I have to go. See ya tomorrow, maybe." She shut off the phone and put it inside the zipper pocket inside her Carhart next to her wallet.

The run ended uneventfully. Paplow made a straight route back to his residence which was in a neighborhood East of downtown in the city borough of Sloan. He went inside and Ginger called it good enough and they returned to the hotel.

Once they got back to the hotel, Stan was waiting. Nothing they had was critical so they decided to regroup at an early dinner before Ginger and Melissa headed to the hockey game.

Stan and Sue arrived at the same time at the hotel restaurant and staked out a table for four. Ginger arrived next and then Melissa. It was only 5pm, but they all were hungry and Ginger and Melissa had to leave by 6pm, so they ordered immediately and then got to work.

Sue started. "I got a message from station this afternoon. The write in wants to meet me at the Roycroft Inn in East Aurora tomorrow at 2000hrs. You guys will need to help me get clean tomorrow."

"Well, we will have some information for you tonight about the Marine Midland Center."

"Is there another game tomorrow night?"

"Nope, but there is an event — the Buffalo Bandits have an open practice in the Center."

"Bandits?"

"Box lacrosse."

Melissa looked excited.

"Finally, something consistent with Wolf Tribe."

It was Stan's turn to look confused. "What?"

"Lacrosse was a game played by the Iroquois here in Western New York. It was more than a game, really a method of conflict resolution. Box lacrosse has been a Native American game for years."

"Thank you, Dr. Science. Now how do we do this?"

"Too easy. We go to the practice together in a car. You ditch us, Stan picks you up somewhere near the auditorium and drops you off for a walking route to a prepositioned car. Then you drive to the site and do the needful." Ginger raised his hands to say — "voila!"

Stan added. "I get clean and get out to East Aurora before you. If there is anything that looks screwy, I call you on the mobile and you abort."

"OK, that's the plan. Now, let's here the rest of the story from you guys." Ginger was eating French fries so Melissa took on the next step.

"We forwarded some of our data right away to station today while we were waiting for Paplow to leave the second warehouse. It turns out that they can eliminate the first warehouse through another "means." Melissa stopped and pointed to herself. "Some brilliant electronic wizard work has identified the second warehouse as our target. Station wants us to stand by while they figure out what they want to do next. I have some additional work to do tomorrow on the network to collect what I can about what's going on inside the target." Ginger was finally finished with his fries.

"Just like she said." Stan was next.

"My guy was pretty open about his willingness to help and his unwillingness to meet again. He has access to the scheduled shipping dates of a shipment of guns coming to the warehouse. He didn't know it today and offered to pass the information and a list of two extremist facilitators who will be meeting with Paplow on the 10th. Luckily, we cased a bunch of dead drop locations in Delaware Park and in Forest Lawn early on and he accepted the drop at the base of Red Jacket's statue at Forest Lawn. He does the drop tomorrow at 1000hrs and I can pick up the drop shortly after that. I will need countersurveillance for the pickup."

"I can do that." Sue wanted to play.

"Nope. You need to focus on your case tomorrow. I will do the needful, Stan." Ginger had finished his plate and was finishing his coffee.

"He's right, you know. You need to take a drive out to East Aurora tomorrow morning to see what it looks like and then get back here in time for our effort to get you clean." Stan had his "I'm in charge" face on and Sue realized that this was not the time to argue. After hours on the street today, she was not about to be a tough guy.

"OK."

Stan looked at Ginger and Melissa. "Guess what? I just happened to score another set of tickets for the Sabres tonight. Different seats of course, but we could all sit together."

"Different seats?"

"Sometimes old contacts are useful. I have a pal from Cleveland who is a Sabres fan. He has seasons tickets in the Blue zone about five rows up from the glass." Stan displayed four tickets in his hand. "If we get clean, I don't see any reason not to use these tickets. He had no plans to attend the game against the Anaheim Ducks and it was too late to turn them in. Whatdya say?"

"I say let's get going." Ginger was always ready for anything.

Sue felt she had to be the voice of reason. "We can't go together. How about two cars."

"I'll ride with you in the truck and Melissa rides with Ginger in the mini-van. So far as we know, there is no surveillance on these two battlewagons, right?"

"Fair enough so long as we all do a surveillance run with an abort plan."

"We better get going then."

This was the last thing that Sue wanted to do tonight, but it seemed like the world was pushing her in directions she didn't understand anyhow and a hockey game might be the best way to deal with it. Still, she was limping slightly as she walked over to the elevator to go to her room and get her coat — this time the fleece/goretex. The Carhart still smelled of oil and coffee.

The game was exciting and ran into overtime. The Sabres won and the arena went crazy. Sue found the crowd's energy essential to stay awake. She had never been a hockey fan but Buffalo fans had enough energy to make it enjoyable and Stan was a Chicago Blackhawks fan so he could explain some of the nuances of the game that she would have missed as the skaters and puck raced up and down the ice.

They had breakfast together and then launched their separate ways. Stan and Ginger to work the dead drop. Melissa back to her room to work her electronic magic and Sue off to visit the suburb of East Aurora. The highway was clear and she got to the town in under an hour. She stopped at city hall on Main Street, got a village map and started to walk along Main Street toward the Roycroft. The recent rain/sleet had turned the snow piles into melted mush and the sidewalk was not friendly to Sue's prosthetic, but she did enjoy for a moment being free to just walk along a village street without thinking about surveillance or operations or a target worth following.

She found the Roycroft on a side street across from the brick three story middle school. The Roycroft included several stone buildings that looked like something you would see in rural England rather than western New York. The entire right side of the street was filled with half-timbered buildings with river rock facing and a large parking lot separate from the street by a three foot high river rock wall. To her left was the Roycroft Inn. According to the village map, it was originally part of a turn of the 20th century artists' colony and inn for visitors to the colony. Unlike the Tudor style buildings to the right, the Inn was a classic Arts and Crafts building painted forest green with a pergola that connected the two major parts of the Inn.

Sue went inside to see if she could determine how many exits and entrances there were to the building, but she was captured by the interior of dark wood and arts and crafts furniture and murals. She entered by the first door and walked into a sitting room and bar with a large stone fireplace heated by a strong fire of local wood.

"Mom would love this place."

All of the furniture had the simple lines of early Arts and Crafts with the Roycroft logo cut into the pieces. Sue walked through this main room, turned right and nearly fell down the three stairs that connected the main room to the restaurant. Unlike the dark main room, the dining room was awash in light from the floor to ceiling windows looking out into the small garden between the dining room and the pergola. The tables were under white table linen and the garden outside already had Christmas decorations. Sue was convinced she needed to bring her Mom here for a holiday. The staff wanted to seat her, but Sue moved quickly into the second lobby which was clearly the lobby for the actual Inn rather than for the restaurant. She got a clear view of the door in front of reception and one to her right which lead back out to the pergola and the street. This was not going to be easy to cover, but that was probably why the cadre chose it.

Challenges right up to the very end of the exercise. It figured.

Sue backtracked and headed back to Main Street and to her rental car she picked up this morning after trading in the pickup. As near as she could tell, she was clean of surveillance and could count on this car staying clean for the rest of the day. She looked at her watch. She called her grandfather's mobile.

"12"

"OK"

Sue arrived at the restaurant at 11:50. It wasn't super hard to find the restaurant, but it wasn't what she expected. It was an old house on a street corner in an old neighborhood of West Seneca. The sign said "Since 1837" and Sue believed it. The place looked that old.

Sue walked through the green door and up a flight of stairs into another dark, paneled room. There were only about a dozen tables surrounding an old wooden bar with a large steam table at one end with a chef cutting thin slices of beef. At the far end of the room was her grandfather sitting at a table for four tucked up against one of the corners of the bay window that looked out over the street. He was dressed in a tweed coat, a sweater and wool pants. His heavy wool coat and a wool cap were on a hook next to him. He looked healthy but thinner and much older than she remembered him. He still had a bristly little moustache and white hair that she remembered, but he looked like he was wearing clothes from another man. Her grandfather was shrinking.

Peter rose to greet his granddaughter and gave her a hug and a kiss on both cheeks. The moustache still tickled her skin and his hug was still strong. It was hard not to burst into tears from memories long past.

"Gramps, how do you know about this place?"

"Sue, I grew up in this town and Schwabls was here long before I was. My folks used to take the bus to West Seneca just to come out to the country and we stopped here to eat before heading back to the First Ward."

"Gramps, the First Ward of Buffalo is nothing but industrial park now."

"I know it and honestly, I don't miss anything about the old neighborhood. Buffalo was an industrial city when I was growing up and our family provided labor to the docks, the railroads, and the factories. My dad was a railroad engineer for the New York Central. The only reason I escaped to do something else was the war. After I got back, there was another option and I took it. General Donovan saved my life when he took me into the OSS as a courtesy to my dad who had been a sergeant in the trenches when he was Colonel Donovan in World War I. OSS changed everything about my life and here we are back in Schwabls eating lunch. Sorry, I forgot my manners and protocol. How much time do you have, dear?"

Time was everything for spies. How much time you have controls what you try to do in the meeting. Sue had to smile. The old geezer was still on his toes.

"Gramps, I'm good for about an hour and a half and then I have to go."

"Perfect. I already ordered for us, so all I have to do is give Ben the high sign and we can eat."

"But I haven't looked at the menu yet."

"Sue, you don't come to Schwabls and look at a menu. Trust me."

The meal arrived like a conjuror's trick. Suddenly, Sue had a full plate and a Molson's Canadian beer.

"OK, so it's a beef sandwich."

"Well, that's like saying a Rolls Royce is a car."

"So tell me."

"This is a Western New York meal. It is called beef on weck. The beef is two inches of thin sliced beef on a kummelweck roll that has pretzel salt on the top. You open the sandwich and put horseradish on the beef. You need the cold beer even on a cold winter day to cut the horseradish. The only thing you serve with beef on weck is German potato salad and that's what you have on your plate. I know everyone wants to say that chicken wings are the Buffalo deal and I certainly like the Anchor Bar wings, but this is the real Buffalo deal served at the best restaurant for beef on weck in the entire county. Enjoy."

Sue followed the instructions and put horseradish on the beef and bit into through the hard roll and the hot beef. The horseradish caught her by surprise, made her scalp itch, her nose run and her eyes water. She reached for the beer.

"Saw right away you put too much horseradish on the beef. Open the roll and use your knife. You can't taste the beef with that much horseradish."

Sue nodded and followed instructions. She eventually got her voice back after another sip of beer.

"Could have told me about the horseradish."

"Old men have to have their fun, no?" His eyes were still bright blue and his eyebrows still as thick as she remembered from the days staying at the house on the Potomac river.

"How is life on the lake?"

"Cold right now, but nice in the summer. You have to visit. It is a great little house on the water with a boat house. The speedboat is up out of the water right now, but it is still a great runabout. Next summer for sure, OK?"

"You got a promise. I will come to see you. I need to bring Mom to the Roycroft. I just saw the place for the first time today."

"The Roycroft. What were you doing at the Roycroft?" His voice was suddenly different, the eyes more focused and his expression was no longer the face of her grandfather.

"Its part of the exercise, Gramps. I have to meet someone there tonight."

"Well, it's a good place to meet, that's for sure. Just be careful."

"Gramps, it's an exercise and East Aurora is hardly a center for criminal activity. I suspect you could walk around that town with hundred dollar bills sticking out of your pockets and no one would bother you."

"Dear, there is no place 100% safe for any O'Connell. You have to realize this."

"Gramps, that's what we need to talk about. Mom didn't want to say and I found out on my own about Dad's operation. We need to sit down and talk about everything."

"We do, but" He looked down at the antique tank watch on his wrist. "We only have about 45 minutes left on your schedule. So, today is not the day for it. Just let me say that the O'Connell's have a problem with the Soviets, OK, the Russians now, and you have to realize that it is a family problem, not a problem that I had or your father had, but everyone in the family has. Your mother, young Bill and you. They don't ever forget and don't ever forgive."

"Then they caught Dad in the operation?"

"As far as I know, they never did. Your father's death had nothing to do with AGAMEMNON — which I suspect you already know was the name of the operation. It had to do with something that I did sixty-one years ago and they are punishing me for it to this day."

"Gramps, I don't understand."

"It is too long a story for us here. After your graduation, come visit me. Please." He grabbed her hand with a grip that was dangerously hard. He looked at her in a way that she thought a man might look at someone trying to save him from drowning.

"Here's what you need to know now. I killed a man in World War II who was in the NKVD — the name of the KGB at the time. He was the son of a senior NKVD officer and the brother of another NKVD officer at the time. I didn't have a choice. I killed him or he killed me. The other side didn't care. They just wanted revenge. They killed your grandmother in Berlin and they killed your father in Northern Virginia. Don't think they can't kill your mom in Chicago or Bill in Washington. And, you already know that your own job takes you places where it would be easy to create an accident."

"Gramps, I don't understand and, honestly, can't imagine they are coming after all of us."

"Perhaps it is an old man worrying about his family, but remember, your father was killed using a poison that is well known to the Russian services. How else do you explain that?"

Sue admitted it wasn't easy to explain unless you looked at what he did or what his father did to the Russians.

"Good. You are starting to understand the world that you are going to be part of as soon as you graduate. Now, one promise. You have to be careful. I know, you have been in a war and wounded and recovered and you think that is the last you will see of danger. I need you to understand that your life before the Farm was filled with danger, but danger that was clear. The enemy was to your front, your partners were to your left and right and you had the power of the entire US behind you in support. In your future job, you will be alone, on the street, with no clear enemies, no clear friends, only your wits and your intuition to keep you safe. Well, one more thing. I want to give you this."

Under the table, she felt his hand place something on her lap. Sue knew immediately what it was.

"Gramps, this is probably not the time for this."

"Sue, this is precisely the time for this. You need to put it in your pocket right now and take these as well." He handed her a box wrapped in tissue with a bow on it.

"I told Ben it was your birthday. He thought it was great that I was treating you to lunch. I told him not to make a cake for you, but he does have a terrific carrot cake in the cooler if you want some sweets."

"I've never been fan of carrot cake."

"That's because you suffered through my efforts to make you cakes when you were in college. This is real stuff. Please, share a piece with me." Sue knew her grandfather had a sweet tooth and it was hopeless to try to refuse. Again, the conjurer's trick and the cake and two cups of coffee arrived.

"Sue, you should know that what I just gave you is off the books."

"The books?"

"Not traceable. Not on anyone's records. It won't be linked to you, me or anyone else."

"OK, I guess."

"Just humor an old man. And eat your cake."

Sue had to admit it was terrific carrot cake and the coffee was strong, black and hot. If it hadn't been for this interlude with the gift, Sue would have had a perfect meal.

"Gramps, I got to go. I'm less than two weeks out from being free from the Farm and then I have about a month of leave saved up before I have to go back to Ft. Bragg. Can I visit you after Christmas? I want to spend Christmas with mom."

"Of course, Sue. Just call me on the phone and tell me what hour you are going to arrive. I will meet you at the airport. Remember, just call and tell me a time. I'll know it's you and I'll know it will be at the airport."

"I love you, Gramps."

"Love you to, Sue. Remember your promises."

"I got to go."

Sue stood up and swept the wrapped present into her left coat pocket while she put her other present into the right pocket. Standing up after sitting for a while was one of those times when Sue felt most vulnerable. The prosthetic always seemed to be in the wrong place and she had to shift her weight to be sure she was steady. Her grandfather looked at her and then gave her a hug.

"Don't forget dear, please."

"See you soon, Gramps."

Sue walked down the length of the restaurant, zippered up her coat and walked out into the Buffalo winter. When she got into the car, she reached into the right pocket and pulled out a 3" Colt Python. She checked to see if it was loaded, though she knew it was. She was slightly surprised to see it was loaded with Hydroshock .38 plus P rounds. Less recoil than the .357 magnum round, but just as deadly. What in the world was her grandfather thinking? What was it about this family and revolvers? Sue tucked the pistol back into her coat, buckled up and drove back to her team.

Stan serviced the dead drop without any problem and Ginger saw no surveillance at Forest Lawn. There were other student teams, so Stan and Ginger were convinced that the reason they were not seeing any surveillance was simply that they were not "in the gunsight" today. The dead drop was a modified flower arrangement that was near the Red Jacket statue in Forest Lawn — easy enough to identify in the snow and sleet that covered the cemetery.

When Sue returned from lunch, she met with the team in Stan's room and everyone had something to offer. Melissa started.

"My work on the extremists' servers provided me with a series of emails over the last two weeks between Paplow — who cleverly disguised his email as GPap — and two other targets with the screen name of Haroon215 and Majid1205. The two new targets have been working with Paplow to set up delivery of Christmas presents which he has promised them by mid December. His last email which was sent this morning says that he will have the presents ready for wrapping at his warehouse on 10 December. I have buried a very clever virus in Paplow's email account so when these two answer the email, they will be also downloading some geolocation software. It will tell us where they are accessing the internet. If they are dumb enough to access the internet through a smart phone, the geolocation software will tell us precisely where they are all the time." Melissa stood up and bowed to her audience. The others offered a healthy applause.

"Our source gave us more specifics on the delivery via the dead drop today. First, it looks like we have the names for Haroon215 and Majid1205. Paplow is scheduled to meet with two guys named Ali Daesh and Suleyman Majidi at 1100hrs on 10 December. The meeting venue is the warehouse we identified yesterday. I'm not saying our work here is done, but it looks like we are pretty close to turning the whole package over to station and letting them bring in the heavy guns to arrest the guys tomorrow."

"Stan, do you really think we arrest guys in cases like this?" Ginger had his "I'm pulling your leg" face on, but Sue knew for a fact that generally speaking the "finish" piece of this sort of operation downrange did not mean the guys were read their Miranda rights. Finish usually was quite final.

"My turn. I cased the Roycroft today. It is not an easy package. The Inn and Hotel are in one building but along a city block. You can access the hotel through the Inn by way of two different doors and by way of the hotel by two different doors. Unless you are in the actual hotel lobby, you can't see the stairs or the elevator to the rooms. If you go into the hotel lobby and sit down, the hotel reception is likely to ask if they can help. If you go to the restaurant which is the public area, there is no guarantee that you will be seated where you could see any of the entrance doors to the hotel. Parking across the street, you can see any cars that go into the Inn parking lot, but that won't do you much good."

Stan interrupted.

"So, I just get a room at the Inn tonight."

"You can try. There are only twenty rooms total — it is more like a very nice bed and breakfast than a traditional hotel."

"Early December, how busy could they be?"

"Beat's me. Here is the number. Give them a call."

Five minutes later, Stan came back into the room. "All set. I check in anytime. Its 1430hrs now. How long did it take you to get there and back?"

"About 40 minutes there and the same back." Sue said it with confidence knowing that she had no idea how long it would take to get back because she had taken a detour on the way back to the hotel today.

"Perfect. In an hour, I will leave for the Inn, check in and then return in time to pick you up at the arena at 1830hrs. Where are you going to pre-position your car?"

"At the Walden Galleria Mall."

"Good. I pick you up at the arena, drop you off at the Mall. I go directly to the Roycroft. You get clean and arrive in time for a meeting at 2000hrs."

"Sue, what do you expect to get from this Custom's official?"

"A hard time." Everyone laughed.

"I suspect it is designed in the scenario to make for a hard recruitment. Inside the scenario, I hope this target will give us more leads to more smuggling targets after we finish Mr. Paplow and his cronies. That's what I intend to push for, anyhow."

Stan stood up. "OK, I got to get an overnight bag packed and get going. See you at 1830hrs and see the rest of you later tonight. I reckon when we are finished, we will deserve a beverage."

"Ciao, Stan." Sue was ready for a bit of down time before it all kicked off again. She was used to long hours in S&R, but the yo yo effect of adrenaline then quiet then adrenaline over the space of 24 hours had taken its toll. She needed a bit of time listening to Mozart.

S ue had showered and put on what she thought of as her "street fighter" clothes — a blue turtleneck and black jeans with a pair of dress shoes that looked normal but had been modified by S&R to be as supportive as any pair of running shoes. She put a small clip knife in the left hand pocket of her jeans. Over that she pulled a navy sweater and added her Gor-Tex. She checked the pockets of the Gore-Tex, made sure she had her phone, a small digital camera and a flashlight. These all went into different pockets in the coat and balanced pretty well. She pulled on the black watch cap and was ready to go. She realized as she walked down stairs to the lobby that the reason everything balanced so well was because in the right coat pocket was her new gift from her grandfather. Too late to leave it behind.

Ginger, Melissa and Sue loaded into the minivan and headed to the arena. In the dark, it was easy enough for Sue to look for surveillance out the back window. There was no sign of surveillance as they headed into the city. The arena was filled with natural traps to reveal surveillance, so when they arrived, she was confident they were clean. The plan was to park the car in one of the ramps next to the arena and then Sue would take the stairs down to the street below while Ginger and Melissa went on to the lacrosse event. They didn't know how many people would be there and didn't want to take the chance that some diligent security professional noticed that they came in as three and left as two. Better safe than sorry.

As they left the car, Melissa reached out to Sue and grabbed her hand. Good luck, you. Make Wolf Tribe proud."

Sue was more than a little surprised. Melissa was not big on overt expressions of affection.

"Thanks."

"Yeah, what she said. Just remember, if you need us, just call. We are ready to be your QRF." Ginger's comment was far more typical of his normal response, though it had been a long time since she heard the term QRF — quick reaction force — used in an operation.

She couldn't figure how a QRF would be used in a cold pitch for a walk in. He must be as tired as she was.

Sue walked down the stairs — three flights of concrete steps along the outside of the building. The wind was blowing off the river and sleet was blowing through the breaks in the outside wall covering the inside wall of the stairs with a sheet of snow and ice.

"Perfect. I get to the end of the class, fall and break my neck. It just can't get much better than this." She used the handrail and slowly worked down to street level. It was 1827hrs.

She oriented herself and realized she was on the front side of the building so she just needed to turn left and walk along the sidewalk and look for Stan's sedan. They drove in silence. Sue had moved the right side mirror so she could help check for surveillance. Night operations were a nightmare when it came to catching surveillance unless you wanted to find some desolate road. They were on a time schedule and anyhow, there were no desolate roads in Buffalo available. So, they both checked to the rear, followed a route and arrived at the Mall on schedule.

"I will park the car in the main entrance parking lot of the Roycroft. If you see it, you know I'm there."

"Thanks, Stan. I don't think the cadre has any nasty surprises for me, but it is nice to know I will have a guardian angel handy."

"Be good, Sue."

"Thanks, Stan. See you on the other side." Sue caught herself. She hadn't said that phrase since she left Afghanistan. It was the standard there among the operators. Just a mantra that promised they would all get back alive. She shook her head. This was just an exercise after all. Realistic for sure. Hard work as well. But an exercise in the United States. She closed the door and walked into the Mall.

The drive was uneventful and her surveillance detection route made her confident that she was not followed. The town of East Aurora was decorated for Christmas and she came into the town from the West and entered the traffic circle heading up Main Street. In the center of the circle was a 30 foot Christmas tree aglow with lights. Each of the lamp posts were covered with lights and Christmas decorations and she drove up the street past all the churches with stained glass windows lighted from within the church. The town was so perfectly in the Christmas spirit, when she finally pulled into the parking lot across the street from the Roycroft, she had to pause for a second to get her head wrapped around the night's work. Sue went over in her head what she would ask and what she wanted from the write in. All she knew about him was he signed the letter as Captain C. He claimed to be a shift supervisor interested in a substantial salary in exchange for providing direct support to the USG counterterrorism mission, but it was also the perfect dangle operation and could be just enough to get an operator on the X so that the service could make an arrest. Sue expected she was over thinking this. It was an exercise and they wanted her to succeed, didn't they?

As Sue got out of the car, the Roycroft was in front of her, framed by the rock wall and surrounded by piles of snow. The sleet was changing to snow. Sue realized that living in this quaint little town might not be so nice around February after months of winter snow.

As she crossed the street, she saw Stan's Crown Victoria backed into the snow drifts in the parking lot — "combat parked" as her colleagues in S&R said. Sue pulled out her mobile and sent a text to a number provided by Captain C.

"I'm here."

"212"

OK, now she knew the room. She forwarded the text to Stan, Ginger, and Melissa's phone.

"chk"

Stan was not a great master at text messaging.

Sue entered the Roycroft via the side door, walked past the reception desk and into the hallway where the rooms were located. 212 was certainly on the second floor so she walked up the stairs using the oak rail as a guide and as support as she headed to the room. Just before she knocked, she took three deep breaths to wash some of the adrenaline out of her system. Not completely, but enough to take the edge off. This was the end of the Farm and she didn't want to look like a dope on her final problem.

She knocked on the door and it opened.

She looked into a room that could have easily fit in her mother's house. All period furniture, oriental carpets, lamps with copper shades. It was cool, but that was to be expected with all the windows that looked out over the town. It was a perfect setting.

Mary closed the door. Sue had some trouble at first getting the words to come given how unexpected it was to find her mentor in the room.

"Captain C?"

"No need for that, Sue. You have passed and the exercise is over. I have been watching your performance all along and figure you don't need to prove anything to me, to the cadre or to yourself. Have a seat."

Sue realized that the suite was set up so the sitting room had two Morris chairs separated by a round table. On the table sat a crystal bottle filled with amber liquid, an ice bucket and two matching crystal glasses — one half full, the other empty.

"Sue, this is a celebration. Relax. Have a seat and please pour yourself a drink. I have a lot to tell you and not a lot of time to do it, so we need to get started."

Sue had trouble accepting this new version of Mary Sanderson. She had always been remote and critical. Suddenly she was friendly, even collegial. So, which was the real Mary? Remote, calculating or warm and engaging? Working with these folks — including her own parents and her grandfather — was becoming more challenging as she realized that good actors could make any character "real" to their audience. Right now, Sue was the audience and Mary the actor. To what end?

To be polite, Sue poured herself a drink. She could smell the Scotch in the glass and, now that she noticed, on Mary's breath. This was not Mary's first drink of the night. Sue put two ice cubes in her glass. Scotch had always been too "grown up" a drink for Sue. She was more of a beer drinker, but if pressed had joined her friends at Ft. Bragg in a glass of bourbon, but only with ice and water. Mary topped her glass off and took a drink. No ice.

"First, I want to congratulate you on your success in this course. We aren't allowed to put our SOF in class ranking. Still, if you were in the mix, I'm sure you would be ranked one or two. You have it all.

You are smart, you are willing to manipulate, you can appear to care even when you don't, and you are very, very security aware — almost too cautious in that regard, but some divisions really like that.

Your parents' division for one. They like cautious people to face off against the main enemy, the Russian service. They want people who are reliable, who are diligent, who are… well, safe. I come from another division which is filled with men who think of themselves as buccaneers.

They see the world filled with opportunities and they are convinced they can guide the fate of people, of countries to do their bidding with little or no risk to themselves. Personally, I find most of them windbags and their historic successes as so much drivel, but that's me."

Mary stopped to take a drink. Sue joined her. The ice in Sue's glass had melted enough that she could drink the scotch without revealing her lack of enthusiasm for malt whiskey.

"You know, this is my last class here. I am going to go out as COS, Tunis this summer. My own station and on the Mediterranean as well. Not bad after nearly 30 years."

Just to get a word in, Sue said, "Congratulations! It is a great assignment and filled with all the targets you could ask for from terrorists to hard targets."

Sue would have been hard pressed to name a single thing of importance in North Africa, but she figured it didn't hurt to be enthusiastic.

"Yes, it is a good assignment and it will free me from this job of watching class after class of young officers go out to do the work that I love to do. I have been very careful in this last few years. I haven't been friends to many of my students or, for that matter, many of my peers, and Sue that is something I can say to you. Keep yourself to yourself. Don't reveal too much of who you are to your peers. Especially to your male peers. They are not much interested in your career and see you as a threat. A strong woman is always a threat."

Sue was already starting to see where this was going. Radical feminism had never been something that she saw as useful. Her mother had taught her by example that if you were good at what you did, you would succeed. Her female commander in the MI detachment at Ft. Bragg had been hard to live with, but no harder than her male counterparts. In SOF, if you did your job, you were rewarded — male, female, white, black — everyone was purple as far as SOF was concerned — a blend of Army and Marine Corps Green, Navy and Air Force Blue.

"Sue, you are joining your family in a tradition that is so deep that you probably don't understand how much a part of your DNA the work is. Your father and mother, your grandfather all part of the espionage world."

"Yes, it is a bit creepy, isn't it?"

"Not creepy. Glorious. Espionage is the ultimate human endeavor. We are manipulating people for the good of the service, working every day to keep them alive and productive and at the same time playing a game of chess against security services. But, here is a secret that you don't know." Mary paused for a moment and Sue wondered if she was aware of AGAMEMNON, if she was going to "reveal" the secret to Sue and how in the world Sue would sell the fact that she was surprised.

"You are also part of a family of spies who have worked for the good of Russia since 1943."

At first, Sue had no idea what this meant or where Mary was going with the discussion. Was this still part of the exercise?

"I know you are confused about this, Sue, because you have been raised to believe that your family are loyal Americans. Well, they are loyal — up to a point. But they are also servants of the Russian special services as I am and now it is up to me to pass the baton to you. Take up your rightful position, Sue."

"Mary, I may be dim, but I don't think I understand."

"Of course you don't understand! How could you?" The stern Mary was back. At least that was something Sue could understand.

"Up till now, your family has been lying to you. You think your family are all loyal members of the CIA. They were, in fact, loyal members of an espionage service, but that service was the KGB until the USSR went away. They backed the wrong horse in the world of double agentry. They were linked to the service that seemed to be the most powerful in the world. They were spies for the KGB for years.

I know this because I have seen their files. Of course, the KGB is defunct. There is now two services where there was one: the SVR and the FSB."

So Mary didn't know about AGAMEMNON? What in the world is going on?

"In the 1990s when you were still a child, I decided to follow a different track. I agreed to work with a more professional, tougher, but smaller service and I have never regretted it. Your mother tried to talk me out of it when we served together. She thought she was doing me a favor — I didn't understand until I saw the family file and realized she was pushing me toward your father's company. I ignored her. My lover opened my eyes to the service which was more professional and more dedicated than my own. I joined the GRU and have never regretted it."

"What?"

"Why not? After all, your grandfather was accused of working for the Russians during the war and I know for certain that your father worked for the KGB for nearly ten years — at the direction of his father. Espionage is a game, dear Susan, and you want to be on the best team. The CIA has had its moments, but at its heart, it is a bureaucracy which has little in the way of professionalism.

"America doesn't understand how confusing and complex the world is and it doesn't ever see the value of espionage, subversion and sabotage. It believes in open source intelligence and think tanks. Russians understand the outside world is a created reality — a reality created by politicians and business leaders so that the average citizen is content with his lot. Russians understand that the real world is a world of secrets, backroom deals, deceit and theft. They value their secret services. For nearly one hundred years, the GRU has been the most secret and the most professional of the special services.

"How many GRU cases has the FBI ever uncovered? How many GRU cases has any security service ever uncovered? None. KGB? Well, of course. They are very bureaucratic. Very much like their counterparts in the US. We don't get caught and that is because we are professionals first and foremost. We care about the trade of espionage not about careers as intelligence bureaucrats."

Sue stood up. She was not certain what was happening, but it certainly wasn't part of any normal scenario. Mary stood up and stood between Sue and the door.

"I am offering you a chance to work with the best service in the world, dear Sue. It is in your family tradition. Except, you have the chance to better your father and your grandfather because instead of the KGB, you are going to be working for the best. Think of it as moving up from the minor leagues to the big leagues. The opportunities are greater, the organization is run better, and the challenges are the best in the world. When you leave here, SOF is going to put you in some small intelligence unit which will be interested in nothing more than small time criminals that they will conflate with terrorism and reward themselves when they eliminate these criminals who they have made into "real" terrorists. You will be handling nobodies who will only give up other nobodies to insure you don't kill them.

"The GRU wants so much more from you. They want you to become a senior intelligence professional in the US defense community. They will create opportunities so that you can excel in ways that your peers will not be able to imagine. The GRU network in America will be working for you because you are the next generation. Your family links are deep and trusted in Russia. You have a career ahead of you that has literally no boundaries. You could be the next head of DIA or the next DNI for that matter with the help of the GRU. You have given up much for your country — you have sacrificed your body for your country and what have they done? They have simply offered you an opportunity to sacrifice again at a tactical level with no hope for advancement past that. For goodness sake, they have kept you at the rank of a warrant officer — after all this, can't you see they don't care? The GRU can change that for you.

"I am here as a messenger. It is the first time I have ever offered this opportunity to a student at the Farm. Believe me, it wasn't easy for me to convince them that I should break cover and offer you this opportunity. Sue, I know in your heart, you have always wondered why you were different and your family was different. Now you know. You were different because your family was playing in a league far beyond their peers and far beyond anything you could imagine. I watched you throughout the course. You are good and you are tough. I had to be sure. I needed to see you under real pressure and real pain. You handled it beautifully. In your family history, the only thing for certain is their work for the KGB. Everything else was simply a charade — make believe to insure their success. Now it is your turn to step up."

Sue tried to remember what her CI classes in the Army had said. If you were pitched, you listened to the entire pitch, then you turned them down flat. Leave no doubts that they have picked the wrong person. Personally, Sue wanted to stick her thumb in Mary's eye and dial a number, but a rejection would have to do. Sue wanted to be sure this was the entire pitch; Sue just couldn't stand it any more.

"Mary, you have made a grave error. You picked the wrong girl and you need to know that right now. Whatever you think about my family, you are wrong. Now, you need to let me out of this room."

Sue took a step toward Mary and suddenly was looking down the barrel of a Makarov automatic with a five inch suppressor. A small copy of the Walther PPK, it fired the same sort of round and at this range was as deadly as any pistol on earth. It was designed to be the pistol that Russian officers used to execute Russian soldiers when they disobeyed orders.

"Sue, you have made an error in judgment. You need to say yes or you won't be leaving here at all. One of the reasons why we are here and not in some hotel in Buffalo is that if you are foolish enough to reject my offer, then I have instructions to eliminate you and then cross into Canada. My exfiltration team is waiting on the Canadian side of Niagara Falls and I will be out of North America before dawn Sue, I don't want to end my career here, but I will if I have to do so. You need to make a decision…"

Sue started calculating how she was going to handle this situation. She was certain that the suppressor on the Makarov would mean that no one in this hotel would ever hear the shot. At this range, Mary would be able to kill her with the first shot. She had no time and decided to act.

"Don't shoot me!" She cried as loud as she could and raised her hands. Mary's eyes followed her hands just as the instructors said she would and Sue followed the move with a short hard kick with her prosthetic into Mary's right knee. The titanium prosthetic was over 100 times harder than any human bone and Mary's knee shattered with an audible crunch. Sue's left hand came down on top of the Makarov and she used a wrist lock to free the pistol while breaking at least two fingers of Mary's hand. The pistol fell to the floor as Mary collapsed under her destroyed right leg.

Sue lost her balance about the same time Mary did. Her prosthetic had shifted under the stress of the kick and Sue found herself on one knee face to face with Mary. She reached into her right pocket and pulled out the Python and pressed it, hard, against Mary's temple. She used her left hand to pick up the Makarov and placed the barrel just under Mary's left eye while she put the Python into her pocket. She heard the oak door splinter.

"Let's think about what happens next, OK?"

Sue realized the voice was familiar. Stan was in the door with a Glock out as the lead in the stack of FBI officers in raid vests and multiple Agency Security officers in trail. He looked at Sue and slowly walked over to Mary and pulled her out of Sue's reach. He holstered his pistol and gently pushed the Makarov down so it was pointing to the floor. Sue had never put a finger on the trigger, so he wasn't afraid of her firing the gun, but he was not entirely certain that she wouldn't pistol whip the woman that was now in federal custody. That would be bad form in the initial indictment. Behind him, Sue could hear federal agents reading Mary her Miranda rights as they hand cuffed her. One of the agents was calling for an ambulance as they realized that Mary's right leg was sitting at what was clearly an unnatural angle and her right hand was already swelling because of the broken fingers.

Mary eyes locked on Sue's. "I never would have shot you. You have to know that. You are too valuable to us."

Sue couldn't think of anything clever in reply. She said nothing and slid off her one knee and sat on the floor. "So, that was fun, eh?"

"How did you know to come in here?" Sue suddenly realized that in the doorway was Lester Bayard.

"Sir, what are you doing here?"

"Ms. O'Connell, I'm sorry to say that we have been watching you for some time — not as long as we have been watching Ms. Sanderson here, but we were concerned that you might have been recruited by her months ago. After what you did with Ms. Nez and your SOF colleagues last month, we just couldn't be sure."

"We added Stan, who is an Agency CI Center officer, to your team to insure we had a handle on what was really going on here. When Mary asked to be your target and picked this lovely though rather remote location for the final exercise, we decided to rent the room next door and wire this one for sound. After all, we did tell you in advance that everything that you did would be monitored."

Sue looked at Stan. "Creep."

"But a lovable creep, no? By the way, Ginger and Melissa are downstairs waiting for their beer. We have to do some serious debriefing tonight, but I think Mr. Bayard will let us have a beer first."

Sue looked at Stan. "Was everyone on the team aware of this except me?"

"Not until this afternoon. We decided they needed to know." Sue looked at Stan and decided this was not the time or the place to argue.

"Help me up will you? I have to adjust my leg." Stan looked down and realized that Sue's leg was just as twisted as Mary's.

"We need to get you down to the ambulance."

"Nope, just hold on a second." Sue reached down and pulled up her pants leg and grabbed the prosthetic and readjusted it with a jerk. It was painful, but felt much better once the prosthetic was back in place. She looked up and saw Stan's face turn white. Sue looked at him.

"You look like you could use a drink."

The graduation took place at the same auditorium where they first started the class and had suffered through so many classes. The students sat in the front and the cadre and select members from CIA and SOF sat in the audience. No outsiders were invited. Like most graduations, there were introductions followed by the guest speaker. In this case, it had been the Director of the Central Intelligence Agency. He gave a good, short speech. No surprise given the fact that he was formerly a senior Congressman and a former case officer. He knew his audience and knew that they all wanted out as soon as possible.

Sue and her SOF cadre members were obvious in the crowd because of their uniforms. Sue hadn't seen Jack in uniform and didn't realize he had the Navy Cross nor did she expect to see Ginger wearing a silver star, but then again, as former SOF operators, it wouldn't be a surprise to find real heroes in the bunch. Sue was not comfortable in her dress uniform. As a member of SOF, she could count on one hand the number of times she had worn it. She had to ask Melissa's help in arranging her ribbons. She had never put the purple heart or bronze star in her ribbons and had to look up precedence to be sure she didn't embarrass herself or anyone else from SOF. Melissa was very moved helping Sue put on her ribbons, her wings and her foreign decorations — including foreign jump wings she earned while on trips for both her old MI unit and joint training with British counterparts.

Sue concentrated hard as she climbed the stairs to the stage. It wouldn't do to trip on her way up or down. There was no diploma. Just a handshake from the Director, Mr. Bayard and Ms. Anderson. The ceremony took less than an hour and they were done. Free. Graduates. Sue wasn't entirely certain what was next other than a short meeting in one of the classrooms with Commander, SOF, his senior officer responsible for all SOF intelligence operations, and one other full colonel that was part of the SOF contingent.

"I am going to make this as brief as possible so we can all get out of these monkey suits and get home." Commander SOF looked as uncomfortable as any of them in his dress uniform.

"I am proud of you and know that you have worked hard to complete this course. You are all a credit to your units and to SOF. You are scheduled for six weeks block leave and you deserve it. Unfortunately, we need you sooner than that — actually we needed you a month ago. So, I want you to take some days off and report back to SOF headquarters on 05 January. We have plenty to do in the world and you are going to be part of the cutting edge of this work. We have orders for you reassigning you from your respective units in SOF to a new unit we are creating that will focus on recruiting targets that will give us better access to the networks that are making and deploying IEDs that are killing our troops in Iraq and Afghanistan. Clear?"

All of the SOF graduates said "Check, sir."

"Now, get out of here."

As they all walked to the door, one of the SOF colonels Sue assumed he was the J2 — grabbed her gently by the arm.

"Chief O'Connell. I need to talk to you before you go."

"Sir." Sue looked at the Colonel. He was about her height, in his late 40s, and was wearing master jump wings, Military Free Fall wings, a silver star, bronze star, purple heart and two rows of campaign ribbons. This was no intelligence geek. His right sleeve had a 1st Battalion 75th Ranger scroll. He was definitely not what she would expect from a SOF staffer. His nametag said "Smith."

"Chief, I am the new commander of a unit that we are building which will use the skills you have spent the last few months learning. I wanted to talk to you before you arrived at Bragg next week. I have been instructed to ask you to volunteer for an additional duty. This is not something that I want to do nor do I agree with the request. Your answer will in no way affect your assignment. I am looking forward to working with you and I don't think this additional duty is worth your time or effort. However, I know how to follow orders and this is what I am doing."

Sue wasn't really sure where this preamble was going, but she was sure that she needed to be polite to Colonel "Smith."

"Sir."

"I have been briefed on the events at the end of your final problem. CIA, DIA and the FBI would like you to consider taking on the role of a double agent while you are working in my unit. Specifically, they want the GRU to believe that you accepted the pitch and are ready to serve as their penetration of SOF. They have explained to Ms. Sanderson that if she didn't want to live in isolation in a supermax prison for the rest of her life, she had to communicate with her handlers that all went well and you were on board with working for them. She has a vested interest in saying yes.

"You, on the other hand, have no good reason to say yes and I am reluctant for you to do so. However, I have been told that this operation has been briefed up the chain to the SecDef and the Attorney General. They agreed with the plan. That said, we have no idea what methods the GRU will use to validate you as an agent and we don't know what they might ask you to do. If you agree, our CI folks in partnership with the CIA and DIA will give you material that you can share with the GRU to validate your access. No matter what, you will not be allowed to travel to any location where you might be placed in additional danger. I will already be asking for you to do that in your day job and I can't afford to put you at additional risk.

"Now, if you volunteer, I have been promised that the operation will last no more than two years and it will not pull you away from your work for our new mission. Rather, what it is going to mean is that you will be giving up your leave time, whenever you get it, to work for a joint Defense, Agency and FBI team as they hunt GRU agent handlers. It is important, but it is a dangerous game. I told them I would ask, but I didn't promise you would say yes."

Sue looked him in the eyes.

"Yes, sir. I am willing to do this."

"Then you will meet with your CI team after hours in one of our SCIFs in SOF headquarters on 10 January. We will start work that day as well and you will start with them that night. I appreciate what you are doing here and I want you to know that if at any time you want out of this, you can reach out to me and me alone and say you are done. No harm, no foul. SOF wants you and we honestly don't care what the Pentagon or the FBI think. Clear?"

"Check, Sir."

"One final note. From here on out, this is a special access program and you need to sign these forms to agree to the restrictions in this SAP."

Sue looked down at the paper. It was similar to every one of the other Special Access Program documents she had signed in the past. She noticed the SAP program name. ELEKTRA. "Well, that is appropriate."

"Excuse me, Chief O'Donnell?"

"Sorry, sir. That was just my inside voice talking out loud."

"Chief, do me a favor and try to keep that inside voice inside, OK?"

"Yes, Sir."

"Enjoy your block leave for Christmas. You won't be seeing much leave time once you are back with SOF. Congratulations and see you in a month."

Smith turned and walked out the door. Sue was left behind and lost in her thoughts. ELEKTRA. The daughter of Agammenon and his avenger. Somebody on the inside knew what they were doing. She wondered if it was inside DoD, FBI or the CIA. Did it really matter?

Ginger poked his head into the classroom.

"If you are done pondering your future, the rest of us are going to go to the bar and have some beers. No carrier landings on the pub tables, but we do intend to celebrate. Are you in?"

"Always." Sue walked out the door and down the hall with her new team mate.

ELEKTRA

Sue started block leave immediately after graduation. All of her classmates promised to stay in touch and most exchanged personal emails so that they could do so. Sue knew that this would be a promise made but never kept so she restricted the email exchange to just three people — Stan, Melissa, and Nancy. She didn't need to exchange contact information with her SOF partners. She would be seeing them soon enough at Ft. Bragg.

Along with the revolver, the box her grandfather had given had a set of keys to the house on the Potomac river, a letter from her grandfather, a note on the passcode for the security alarm and a memory stick. The letter was simple:

Sue, please accept the house as a graduation gift. It was a good place for me to hide and I suspect you will use it for the same purposes. Check out the wine cellar when you get there — especially the woodwork on the wine racks. I hope to see you soon in Chautauqua.

All my love, Gramps

Sue loaded her clothes into her vintage T-bird and drove up I-95 to the house overlooking the Potomac River. It was an old farmhouse built in the 1880s. Originally, it had been the center of a larger dairy farm, but now was simply a few acres of woods, a house, an old carriage house that served as a garage and a boat house on the river. Sue opened up the house, cleared the alarm system, and then proceeded to walk around the house. Like all houses that hadn't been occupied in some time, the house smelled of a mix of stale air and old memories. The memories got stronger as she walked up to her bedroom that she used when she was at William and Mary and Peter was in residence.

The house was small enough that it could easily handle one owner and one guest and little else. When Peter was the occupant, the house was filled with memorabilia from his tours as well as his extensive library of first editions of travelers' tales from the Far East, old maps,

and a collection of leather bound works of Roman and Medieval classics as well as translations of Tolstoy (Peter's favorite Russian author).
The living room was now less cluttered — Peter's favorite chair, table
and reading lamp were probably in his place in Chautauqua along
with most of the books, but still had a small collection of the classics
and enough furniture to make the room comfortable.

Sue noticed that Peter had left her a well-stocked liquor cabinet
and following his recommendation, she went to the basement to find
a wine cellar with about 100 bottles of various French and California red wines. Sue assumed the reference to the woodwork implied a
concealment of some sort and after tracing the wood along the back
of the rack, she found the concealed lock. What she hadn't expected
was a complete false wall and a full sized room behind the wall.

Sue turned on the light and a series of standard 60 watt light bulbs
illuminated the room with a slight yellow glow. She realized the room
was a Spartan mix of armory and computer research center. There
was an old oak desk and rolling desk chair that belonged in a movie
set from the 1930s. There was a Tiffany glass desk lamp on the desk
and a large, antique Caucasian rug on the floor and then the walls
were covered with book shelves and a large gun cabinet. In the gun
cabinet, Sue found two short barreled shotguns (one pump, one auto-
loader), two rifles, and at the base of the glass covered case was an
oak pistol rack that included a .22 High Standard, a 1911 .45, and a
slot which Sue determined was designed for the Colt Python that her
grandfather had given her in Buffalo. She pulled the pistol out of her
shoulder bag, unloaded it, and put it back in its place. Below the pistols was a fine oak cabinet with three drawers. The first drawer held
shotgun, rifle and pistol ammunition. Sue put the .38 ammunition in
the box in the drawer. The second drawer held cleaning gear for all
of the weapons. The third drawer closest to the floor was empty.

On the wall across from the gun racks was a large LCD television
screen that was mated to a desk top computer that looked to be an
ear ly Macintosh. Sue booted up the computer and the room went
suddenly from the 1930s yellow light to the strong blue light from the
screen. She used the passcode from the security alarm to access the

computer which to her surprise already had her listed as one of the users. It was empty of files. Nothing.

For the first time since she left the Farm, Sue wished she had Melissa with her to see if there was some sort of virtual concealment on the computer. She could find nothing with her basic computer skills, so she inserted the memory stick that came with the keys and the instructions. The stick held a number of files including files on the various "special" modifications of the house (including several other concealments) and a file which outlined her grandfather's notes on both his previous encounters with the NKVD, then KGB, and his suspicions regarding the death of her grandmother and her father. Sue opened the word file.

Sue, I prepared this brief so that you know what you are facing as you enter this new world. It is a world where you have to be prepared for friends to be enemies and enemies friends.

You need to understand the O'Connell legacy as well. I want to tell you the whole story when I see you next, but for now, you need to know the following:

I killed a man in France in 1944. He was a member of the Russian intelligence service and worked for a department called SMERSH. Yes, I realize you thought that was a creation of Ian Fleming's imagination, but it was not. SMERSH was a counterintelligence arm of the NKVD and it was filled with killers. I killed the man because he was trying to kill me and my partner. The man's name was Boris Vladimirych Beroslav and he was the son of Vladimir Beroslav, a Soviet KGB colonel who rose in the ranks after the war to General officer status in the Second Chief Directorate — the Counterintelligence directorate. Boris Beroslav had a younger brother, Vladimir Vladimirych Beroslav who was a First Chief Directorate Colonel when the USSR collapsed.

I believe the Beroslav father and son killed your grandmother. We were in Berlin at a time when the Cold War was nearly World War III and the Soviets were conducting black ops in the American sector — trying to eliminate our sources as fast as we were trying to recruit new sources. I was known as a good recruiter and we knew that they knew I was their biggest American problem in Berlin. There were two attempts on my life which were reported as criminal acts because we didn't want to be the ones who started a shooting war at the Berlin Wall. I found out later that Beroslav the elder was trying to kill me when your grandmother was killed in the car accident. As you know in our trade, there are no such things as coincidence.

By now, you know about AGAMMENON. I tried to talk your father out of the operation, but he was convinced that he needed to do the job. It was a dangerous time in US-USSR relations and there is no doubt his work allowed the FBI and CIC to track down key Soviet sources in the US and in NATO countries. The problem was that after the USSR collapsed, most of the KGB field operators ended up in the Russian mafia. I think one of the seniors in the Russian mob was Vladimir Beroslav. I think he killed your father both as part of the vendetta against me and because your father did not agree to work with the Russian mafia. It was never in the AGAMMENON mission to work against the mafia and your father paid for this with his life.

Sue, you are now the only O'Connell in the field and you need to know that the SVR and the Russian Mafia are dangerous adversaries who will eventually find out that you are the new case officer in the family. You need to be careful and trust no one except your closest friends.

Please come visit me in the new place as soon as you can. With love,

Gramps.

The note ended and there were no files attachéd. Sue was convinced there was more material, somewhere. Perhaps the material was in the house or with her grandfather in Western New York or secreted someplace else. There were no clues and Sue was not ready to start a room by room search. She had a plane to catch tomorrow for Christmas with her mother and brother and, if there was time after that, a brief trip to see her grandfather. If his premise was correct and this was a vendetta that had started in 1944, Sue was convinced a few more days wouldn't make much difference one way or the other.

S ue spent the night in the house on the river. She had trouble thinking of it as "her house" at this point, but that was certainly how her grandfather viewed it. There was little in the pantry for breakfast, so she made some black tea, ate a granola bar that she carried in her overnight bag and then called the Dulles airport shuttle. Sue had decided to keep her car and the majority of her clothes locked up at the house and just take the carry-on bag to Chicago. Sue had no interest in leaving her vintage Thunderbird in airport parking over the holidays — there were too many ways that that could turn into tragedy. She would return to the house after the holidays and drive from the house to Fayetteville a few days in advance of her reporting date.

The shuttle arrived on time and took her to Dulles. The Southwest flight to Midway airport had one stop, but no plane change and Sue slept from the time they closed the door at Dulles until the aircraft landed in Midway. She hadn't realized how tired she was and how weird the last few weeks had been. She needed to talk to her mom, but wasn't sure how much she wanted to tell her. ELEKTRA was out of the question — it wouldn't help to talk about it and it would only make her mom worry. Sue hadn't thought about what she was going to tell her mom about Mary. It certainly fell into the category of need to know, but Sue also needed to talk to someone about the betrayal and treachery. Sue realized that she would have to share her time with her brother and while he had clearances, he definitely didn't have a need to know. These were the thoughts that ran through her head as she road in the taxi to her mom's house.

About a mile out from the house, Sue realized that her world was now entirely different. Instead of wondering about the normal "Christmas holiday" issues of presents, meals, and family conversations, she was suddenly worrying about compartmentation, tradecraft and how or if she could have a heart to heart with her mom about her new life or her grandfather's view on his family's "curse." Was this the way that life would be from now on? How does a case officer share all of her concerns? Does she ever share her concerns? And what about her mother? Does she still carry these around with her?

Barbara answered the first knock on the door. She gave Sue a hug before she even got inside. Through the narrow entryway, Sue could see a Christmas tree waiting to be decorated, a fire in the fireplace and Christmas cards on the mantle. The holidays were certain to be relaxing and free from all of the concerns she had during the flight.

They spent the first few hours talking about the Christmas plans, last minute shopping trips and how good it was going to be to have the family together. Her brother Bill was scheduled to testify in the US District Court in Washington court on 15 December, so they had tomorrow to be together and then Bill would arrive late on 16 December and they would have a few days to be a family again. Sue started to cry. Normal was something she hadn't expected and the emotion of it all was hard to take.

After a bath, a bowl of her mother's beef stew, and a glass of wine, Sue felt more relaxed and decided it was time to have a conversation with her mother that needed to happen before Bill arrived.

"Mom, I need to tell you some things before we go shopping tomorrow and before Bill arrives." Her mother nodded and waved them away from the table and to the living room near the fireplace.

"Mom, the final exercise was not what I expected." With this ice breaker, the story flooded out. Sue told her mom about the trip to the archives, her meeting with her grandfather, Mary's treachery, and the final confrontation in the hotel. She stopped short of ELEKTRA simply because she didn't know how her mom would respond. The story was weird enough without the addition of double agents and future operations.

Barbara sat on the couch and listened. She never interrupted and didn't touch her wine throughout the whole story. When Sue was finished, she shook her head.

"My God, what a twisted life Mary must have had. I never suspected she would become a traitor. What do you think they are going to do with her?"

"No one said and I didn't ask. I was just happy to be out of there."

"No doubt, dear. I find it interesting though that the FBI hasn't made it public yet. I wonder if they are going to try to double her back against the GRU? It would probably save Mary from isolation in some supermax prison, though she is certainly going to pay for her crimes, eventually. The Russians will be after her eventually as well. Ugly. Just ugly."

"Dear, I have to admit, I knew more than I told you about your father's last operation. We shared everything, but it didn't seem to make sense to try to explain it to you over Thanksgiving. You had plenty on your mind and I had planned to tell you after graduation. In the long run, you probably learned more than I would have told you even now. It was not something I wanted to share with you or Bill."

"Mom, we are a family. Don't you think you owed it to me?"

"Yes, I owed it to you, but it is hard to stop keeping secrets once you get started. I suspect you already know that by now."

The comment hit Sue hard. She had just accused her mother of not being forthcoming just after she was very selective of the truth about her own operational commitments. Of course, she could argue in her head that her mother no longer had the "need to know" but that just an excuse.

Her mother was right, once you started keeping secrets, it was hard to stop that internal voice from asking the question "does she have the need to know?"

Sue thought about all the years that her mom and dad were in "the trade" and how many times they kept secrets from each other, from their family and, especially from Sue and Bill. What sort of people do case officers become as they work year after year in this environment? Surely the most successful had to be slightly sociopathic. This was not a relaxing conversation inside her head and she could see her mom was waiting for her to continue the conversation. Sue decided to use a classic technique — misdirection — to keep the conversation alive, but away from what was stomping around inside her head.

"Mom, I need to see Gramps before I return to Ft. Bragg."

"I think you should. In fact, I thought that maybe we all should visit him for New Years Eve. I haven't raised it yet with him or with Bill, but we could easily drive from here on the 30th then spend New Year's Eve and New Year's Day with him and the return to Chicago on the 2nd or you could go directly from Buffalo to Dulles and then on to Ft. Bragg."

"Sounds like a plan, Mom."

The next morning, Sue awoke to a completely silent house. It was early morning, false dawn as some call it and she laid in bed enjoying the quiet for some time. Eventually, she heard her mother in the kitchen and she decided to join her. She pulled on her sweat shirt and sweat pants, attachéd the running prosthetic and wandered into the living room. It was at that point she realized why the house was so quiet. Overnight, it had snowed another eight inches and was snowing hard still. Not a blizzard, at least not a blizzard by Chicago standards. There was no wind and the snowflakes just drifted slowly by the windows as they fell to the ground. The house was insulated by the snow and Sue thought it was lovely.

"Good morning, dear. Did I wake you?" Her mother was filling the French press with hot water from a copper kettle on the stove. The smell of coffee filled the room. Two cups and hot milk were already on the counter. "Would you like me to add some cocoa to the mix?" This was how Sue learned to drink coffee and while she had stopped making it that way when she joined the Army, she was filled with nostalgia as soon as her mom said it.

"Yes, please. And, no, you didn't wake me up. I was sitting in bed enjoying the early morning silence."

"Snow storm last night off the lake. I would guess we will have a bit of trouble if we want to go downtown today. Still, the trains should be running and the station is only 10 minutes by car."

Sue realized that she had no presents for either her mom or for Bill and she knew that this might be the only chance she had to get them if she wanted to go into the city.

"Mom, I need to do some Christmas shopping, but I don't need to go into the city if you think we can find things in your town."

"Sue, you can find just about anything in the local stores. That will make it easier for both of us and, once Bill gets into town, if we decide we want to go see the city decorations, we can do so anytime in the next two weeks."

Barbara used a tablespoon to put cocoa in Sue's cup. Then she added some hot milk and stirred. After that, she added the coffee and additional milk. It was perfect.

"We may be a bit snowbound today, but the Rover will easily get us into town for some shopping. We will enjoy breakfast, let the snow-plows clear the roads and then we will head into town. Did you bring anything resembling winter gear? And, not to be too blunt, but what do you wear on your prosthetic?"

Sue took another sip from the coffee.

"Mom, I honestly don't have any Chicago winter kit. Can I borrow your sweater and coat again? As to my foot, it is waterproof, but I have a pair of hiking boots that I just wore in Buffalo. I doubt the Chicago weather is worse."

"I still wonder why your grandfather decided to stay in Western New York in the winter. He could live anywhere and instead he is living in a place where there are two seasons: winter and the 4th of July."

"Mom, you were the one who told me he was from there. And he certainly knows the city. He talked about growing up there when it was a tough, industrial city. I suppose he doesn't mind the snow. And, after all, what sort of schedule does an eighty-five year old man have to keep? If the weather is crap, then he just stays at home, right?"

"Don't count on it. Last winter, he complained they didn't get enough snow for him to use his cross-country skis. He also skates at the local rink which is about a mile away and he walks to the rink. He is not about to spend his time housebound."

Barbara's cellphone rang. It was a distinctive ringtone — the open-ing two measures from the 60s TV show "Dragnet."

"It's Bill."

"Mom, don't even tell me what my ringtone is, OK?"

"Chicken." Barbara picked up the phone. "Hello, dear."

The conversation didn't last long and it didn't sound very promising.

Sue started her second mug of mocha coffee and waited for her mom to come back into the kitchen.

"Our snow last night turned into a blizzard in DC this morning. Well, it is about three inches of snow but that is on top of an inch of ice. The city is closed. Bill's testimony will be delayed by a day or two. He wanted us to know as soon as he heard. He will be here by the 20th for certain because if he hasn't testified by that time, the court will be taking a Christmas recess. So, its just us girls."

"More time for shopping, baking, and, assuming you are up to being beaten, games!"

"Well, let's think about breakfast and then go downtown. Cheese and bacon omelettes sound OK?"

The trip to her little bit of suburban Chicago was almost too wonderful. The village had multiple coffee shops, boutiques and bookstores. Sue was able to purchase gifts for both Bill and her mom and still had time for a coffee and a Danish pastry that tasted homemade because it was made at one of the coffee shops while she was waiting over her first cup of coffee. The second cup was perfect with the warm from the oven pastry.

"Mom, how do you stay slim with these temptations?" Sue said after the last crumbs were gone and she was working on her third cup of excellent coffee.

"It isn't easy. In the summer, it is easier because I walk to town and walk back. Its 10km round trip, so a pastry doesn't seem too much of an indulgence. During our long dark winter, I try to get to the gym at least three times a week and workout at home another three on the rowing machine that is in my bedroom. Bungalow life does not allow for a home gym."

Barbara's cellphone rang. This time the ringtone was a simple buzz. Barbara looked at the phone before answering. Sue could see the screen — it just said NO CALLER ID.

Her mom answered the phone. Sue watched as her mom's face went from puzzled to surprised to crying. She hung up and turned to Sue.

"We have to get to the Rover and get home. I'll explain in the car."

They walked quickly to her mother's Range Rover, put the packages in the truck, closed the hatch and entered the front seats. Barbara reached across Sue and opened up a glove box and pulled out a silver fabric bag.

"Sue, put your cellphone in the bag and take mine and do the same. Seal the bag with the zipper. Put the bag in the glove box."

"Mom?"

"Please do it now." Sue followed instructions.

"Now, in the back of the glove box, you will feel a small latch against the right hand side. Pull the latch to the left."

Sue did as she was told and a false wall in the glove box opened to reveal a Beretta .25. She pulled it out and handed it to her mom.

"Sue, the Beretta is for you. I have my Smith in my pocket." Barbara started the Rover. As the display screen appeared, Barbara reached along the console next to her right knee. Sue couldn't see what she did, but suddenly the screen went black.

"Disabled the GPS."

"Mom, what is going on?"

"Just a second. Let me get on the road."

Barbara pulled the Rover out of the parking lot and headed out of town and away from her house. She got onto a limited access parkway headed North along the lake front. Barbara was quiet for the first few miles and turned right off the parkway into a neighborhood called "Lakefront Estates." Barbara worked her way through the "estate" and came out in a county park which had a one-way loop road that ran counterclockwise along the lake. Barbara continued to drive the loop and pulled into the last parking area at the end of the loop which looked over the entrance to the park and the road to Lakefront Estates.

"OK. We'll stop here for a minute."

Sue looked at her mom. A very serious face offering little in the way of clues as to what was going on. Sue knew enough to wait. Her mom would talk when she was ready.

"Sue, the call was from the watch office in Langley. They wanted me to know that Peter was found murdered in the house in Western

New York two hours ago. He had one round in his head — looks like a sniper shot. He had a pistol in his hand and appeared to have been trying to get out of his house when he was shot. The FBI has been called in. It looks like a professional hit."

Sue was stunned. She could only think of her last moments with her grandfather in Schwables. The dark room, plates and coffee cups on the table, and the old man looking her in the eyes and giving her a hug. Now he was gone. Sue started to cry.

"Sue, the reason Langley called was they wanted both of us to know. Me because of what happened to your Dad. You because of what they called ELEKTRA. Sue, what is ELEKTRA and why does it have anything to do with your grandfather?"

"Mom, it is complicated and I think we are going to have time to talk about this as we drive to Chautauqua Lake to Gramps' house. For now, it is an operation that I agreed to do with the Agency and the Army after I go back on duty in January. It is a CI operation."

"Oh, Lord. Not again."

"Mom, it was the right thing to do and it is certainly the right thing to do now. What I want to know is, what do we do next? This is your turf, mom. I get the route and I get why we are here. But, can we go home or do we leave for New York from here?"

"I have a neighbor who is the head of Cook County Sheriff SWAT. I will give him a call as soon as we can find a Kroger's where I can buy a throw away phone. He will help."

They drove to a local Kroger's and picked up two phones which they paid for with cash. The phones were pay as you go and came with 100 minutes preloaded. One phone was on the Verizon network, the other on ATT. While her mom did the purchase and bought some basic food and travel essentials, Sue opened the bag with the cellphones and added both her and her mother's credit cards. Barbara returned, started the car and headed to another park in the area. This one was directly on the lake. She pulled up at the first parking space that allowed her to face the Rover toward the entrance way. She called her neighbor in Cook County Sheriff's Depatment. The call was short, to the point, and Sue was surprised how easy her mother convinced her friend to help. When Barbara hung up, she saw Sue looking at her with the "Well?" face.

"Jim is dispatching two undercover detectives in a panel van to our neighborhood right now. They will provide overwatch until he can get over to the house with a pair of his SWAT guys. No lights, no sirens, no uniforms. Jim has a key to our house and I have a key to his so he will just enter the house and do a room by room check. He will call when that's done. Probably have an hour and a half to wait. I know a place where we can hang out for that time."

"Mom, you had a plan all along, didn't you?"

"Something like that, dear. I certainly didn't expect it would be needed because of your grandfather. That was a shock."

"So, let's get to the safe site and start planning our next move."

"That's my girl," Barbara started the Rover and pulled back on the road. It took 20 minutes to get to the new site. It was a diner along the state road heading North named Dorothy's. It was a throwback to the 1950s. The front of the diner was clearly an old Pullman dining car that had been on blocks since sometime after World War II. Squared off behind the "dining car" was a small building that served as the kitchen. There were six stools at the counter and two tables at the windows with only two seats at each table. There were no cars in the parking lot. "Open?" Sue didn't see any signs of life.

"Open for us, dear." Barbara walked to the back door on the building behind the dining car. As she approached the back, Barbara pulled her wool, Turkish scarf over her head, just covering her hair, but not covering her face. Sue followed and did the same with her paisley wool scarf. Barbara knocked on the door and a short, stout man in his sixties with an enormous mustache and not a single hair on his head answered the door. He was in a t-shirt and very old work pants — Sue's father would have called them dungarees — and lime green Crocs.

"Anna, what can I do for you? You need a cut of good halal meat?"

"Mike, can my daughter and I sit down in the diner for a while? We need some peace and quiet and we need to be someplace where no one can find us."

"My good friend, if you need peace and quiet, Mike can give you this. Pull your truck to the back, we enter here. Your friend was cleaning after a long day of feeding stew to customers. Still enough stew for three and always there is tea."

"Mike, you are my most trusted friend. I knew you were the right man for me."

Barbara handed the keys to the Rover to Sue and walked into the building. Sue pulled the vehicle into the back parking lot, combat parked the vehicle so it could drive away quickly and returned to the door and knocked.

"Ms. Janice. You do not need to knock at Mike's place. You are family. You are Anna's daughter. You come in anytime."

Sue entered a very small, but very clean kitchen area. She immediately kicked off her boots and placed them next to her mother's boots. She hoped "Mike" would not notice the difference in shape between the left sock and the right sock.

Mike took her through kitchen area and then into a small room at the very back of the building. It served as the office, the living room and, if Sue had this correct, Mike's bedroom as well. The floors, walls and couches were covered with Central Asian carpets. Barbara had already sat down and Sue joined her. Mike arrived almost immediately with a tray of pistachios, cashews, dried fruit and two glasses of very hot, very sweet tea. He said nothing as he entered and said nothing as he departed.

"Mike, please let us know if you see anyone come by who does not belong."

"Anna, do not worry. Mike will protect you. Mike will be your guard. I have the shotgun you gave me. Beautiful gun. Do not worry." He left and closed a parquet door that was also covered in a very thin, very old Persian silk carpet.

"Mike?"

"He was an Iranian Kurd who worked with me years ago. He was an asset in Northern Iran and I used to meet him in Istanbul about once every six to eight weeks. Among other things, he was a carpet dealer. I made sure he got out of Iran when we stopped working together. We put him in the relocation program and he ended up here. He was the one who decided to run a diner — he had more than enough money from his final payment to do anything a middle class American might want to do. He liked to cook. I never knew where he was until one summer day I was cruising along this highway and pulled over to see what sort of meal you could get at Dorothy's. It was a surprise to find Mike."

"What is his real name?"

"He is a Nestorian Christian so he really is 'Mike,' well, Micah."

"Are we safe here?"

"We are safe here for now. My only concern is that we don't leave a trail of breadcrumbs that brings someone here who might harm Mike. He has risked too much already."

That was obviously a story that would have to wait. Sue picked up the glass cup and carefully tasted the hot tea. It was sweet tea with apple juice. It was delicious. Sue grabbed a handful of pistachios and dried apricots and started to eat.

"Danish and coffee and now tea and dried fruit?"

"Mom, you know the rule one of any operation — always eat when you can."

"I thought rule one was always pee when you can."

"Well, OK. So always eat when you can is rule two."

"Agreed." Barbara started drinking her tea and eating pistachios. "Now what?"

"We wait for Jim's call. If we don't get a call by 1800hrs, we have Mike give us dinner, we drink tea with him until we get a call or we decide that there is some trouble at the house. I promised to call Jim again at 2100hrs if he didn't call before that. If the house is under surveillance by these villains, then we leave from here and head to Buffalo."

"And Bill?"

"The watch office said that FBI headquarters had already informed Bill and he would head West as soon as his testimony was complete. He will drive there in his Bureau car since this may end up being a case that has a link he needs to know about. If nothing else, we may need his access to LEO databases and his trunk full of guns."

"Don't you have a trunk full of guns, mom?"

"OK, your interrogation techniques are too much for me. Yes, the

Rover has a shotgun and two more pistols in a cavity next to the spare tire. It has a cipher lock. Don't forget the number — it is 7229."

"Got it."

"We need to sort out what happened at Peter's house and that may be hard if the Buffalo FBI Field office has already taken over the case. Bill may be able to help, but we are going to need to play the role of grieving relatives so we can get into the house as soon as possible. We need to sort out why Peter was killed."

"Did he ever tell you the story of his series of run ins with the Beroslav family?"

"No, Sue. How did you find out?"

"He gave me the keys to the Potomac River house and down in the basement is a secure storage room. I pulled up a letter he wrote to me on a computer in the room." Sue proceeded to describe the details from the note. Sue started to quietly cry.

"Dear, Peter had a good long life and it appears he died fighting. I'm not sure he would want us to grieve."

"But he would want us to find his killers."

Less than an hour later, Jim called Barbara and told her that the Cook County team had identified surveillance on the house. If the individuals involved broke into the house, the SWAT contingent working with the Cook County sheriff's office would arrest the individuals and sort out the rest downtown. Barbara said thanks and rang off.

"Time to go" was all she said. After farewells to Micah, Barbara asked him to give her the duffel bag he was holding for her.

"Sure, Anna. You need my help? You need some muscle?"

"Mike, the kind of trouble we have right now is like the old days. We need to just disappear for a while. Our friends in the police will help, but it will be easier for them if we all disappear. Can you afford to go away for a few days — someplace where no one knows where you would be?"

"Anna, I am a Kurd. I know how to disappear. I will leave right after you. No phones, no mail, no credit card, no problems. After Iranians chasing me in Shiraz, don't you think Mike can disappear?"

"Of course, my friend. Just for a few days. You can be back by Christmas. By then, the police will have done their job."

"Just like the old days, Anna. I will follow instructions."

Sue walked out to the Rover with her mother. Once they got to the vehicle, they opened the back and accessed the compartment near the spare tire. Sue took the shotgun out and put it in the low visibility set of clips under the dashboard. She left the two pistols in their concealment — if they needed that many guns all at once, they were in far more trouble than Sue figured. Barbara opened the duffle bag and pulled out $5,000 in $20 dollar bills and passed half to Sue. She pulled out a new purse and a set of New York license plates.

"Can you put these on front and back while I make the change over in docs?"

"Sure, Mom."

"By the way, there are three changes of clothes in the duffle, they should fit both of us, at least well enough, and an overnight kit of toothbrushes, hair brushes and soap. The rest is going to have to be acquired on the road."

Sue was busy using her swiss army knife screw driver blade changing the plates. Once they were changed, she handed the old Illinois plates to her mom.

"We will store these with my docs in the concealment in the spare tire compartment. Don't worry, the NY plates are current and registered to the VIN number on the Rover and in my new name. Well, another old name: Anna Percheron. It's one of the aliases I used years ago. Home, Fredonia New York. Occupation: Adjunct professor, Fredonia State."

"Does that hold up?"

"Well, for now it will. Fredonia State is on Christmas holiday. Once we are back in New York and matched up with your brother, we will return to Illinois plates and my identity. It is just to be sure that we don't leave too easy a trail of breadcrumbs." Barbara pulled out a curly red headed wig from the bag and put it on. She handed Sue a New York Yankees baseball cap.

"With your short hair, no one is going to notice two women in the car until we get out. If there is any question, you are just going to have to be my butch partner. You OK with that?"

"No problems, mom. I've been worse."

"Sue, from now on, its Anna. Remember, Anna."

"No dramas, Anna."

"OK, then. You drive. Remember — no speeding or anything that gets us into a traffic stop. We need to be the most boring pair of dykes on the road."

"I can do boring. I would like to do boring, but it seems it doesn't come with the O'Connell name."

"Not for now."

Sue felt surveillance before she saw it.

"Mom, we have some guys following us. Three Caucasian males, dark jackets.

"I thought so. Turn my mirror out a bit so I can watch from my side." Sue used the cruise control on the Rover to slow down one mile per hour per half mile. In about two miles, the vehicle appeared in the mirror. Black Explorer. Illinois plates and a rental bar code on windshield. As soon as they saw Sue had slowed, they did the same.

"Friend?"

"Sue, my pals would be driving classic police undercover vehicles — gray Crown Victorias or black suburbans. I have been trying for years to explain they weren't real discrete and, honestly, they replied, they didn't care all that much. They definitely don't use to rental cars."

"So, what's the plan, Anne?" Sue smiled at her mom.

"This is a fairly lonely highway, so I want you to accelerate to 65 for about a mile and then stop in the middle of the road. OK?"

"Didn't you just say something about being discrete?"

"We can't get to New York with this tail." Barbara's voice was muffled as she reached under the dash for the shotgun and Sue pushed the Rover to its red line. Barbara pulled the shotgun out and then dropped her seat back to almost flat, unbuckled her seat belt and crawled into the back seat as Sue continued to accelerate.

"When you stop, I want you to use the hatch release. The hatch will go up on its own. When you hear my shot, accelerate immediately. Clear?"

"Check. By the way, what if it is just a couple of tourists?"

Barbara put the shotgun into battery. Sue heard the reassuring sound of the pump locking into place.

"Oh, well…"

Sue stopped at the first curve and popped the hatch. "You might want to cover your ears, dear."

They could both hear the Explorer accelerating to catch up. As the Explorer came around the curve the driver saw the Rover stopped in the middle of the road and skidded to a halt about 10 meters from the Rover. Sue covered her ears.

Bang. Bang.

Before the Explorer had stopped, Barbara had put two rounds into the radiator of the SUV. Sue accelerated and Barbara reached over and closed the hatch from the back seat. Two passengers got out of the Explorer and opened fire. The 9mm handgun rounds were never accurate enough to hit the Rover.

"All good?" Sue's ears were still ringing from the noise of the shotgun. Barbara crawled back into passenger seat, cleared the shotgun and returned it to its home under the dash. She then reached up and pulled the earplugs out of her ears.

"What did you say, dear?"

"You could have given me a pair of those." Sue was shouting — over compensating for the ringing in her ears.

"Sorry. Only one set in the Rover. You know the ringing will stop… eventually. I think we are good for a while. Two in the radiator means at least one ended up in the engine block. No one hurt, and I doubt the followers are going to report to the police given their response by shooting at us. Eventually, they may have some real explaining to do to the rental car company, but that's not our problem."

"Just another quiet weekend with the O'Connells, eh?"

"Exactly, but we recommend tourists don't get too close for comfort." Sue could see her mom's smile reflected in the glow of the dashboard as they saw the I-90 East on ramp ahead.

The rest of the drive on I-90 was uneventful and just about as boring as a drive can be when you are on the run. Barbara got a call from Jim about 0200hrs saying that they had two characters in custody who were known felons suspected of working for an organized crime boss with the attractive street name of Bluto. They had lawyered up fairly quickly and had nothing to say. But, given the fact that they were caught inside her house with two suppressed Beretta submachine guns, Jim was convinced the Cook County district attorney would win a fight to keep them in the jail without bail. Jim said that as near as he could tell, nothing had been tampered with and he promised to keep the house identified as a crime scene with police surveillance for the next week.

Barbara was relieved and told Sue the story as she crossed into Pennsylvania. She had taken over the driving in Ohio and had encouraged Sue to get some rest. It didn't happen, but at least Sue had a chance to stretch a bit when they refueled outside of Cleveland. They were just a few hours from the Fredonia exit on I-90 and then they would stop for the morning at a truck stop along the highway that had showers and a full restaurant. Not exactly the ideal situation, but Barbara did not want to arrive at an FBI crime scene looking more like a felon than a victim. Sue agreed.

A shower can be a wonderful thing after a night on the road. They had a high protein breakfast of bacon, sausage, and eggs with about two pots of coffee between them and two travel mugs to go. Sue returned to driving and headed on to Chautauqua. About ten miles out, Barbara told her to turn onto a county road. They pulled over and changed the plates back to their originals and "Anna" became Barbara again.

"At this point, we either are in real trouble or we are safe for a while.

Either way, alias docs and plates aren't going to matter."

"Too true, mom. What about the guns? I understand New York State is mucho strict."

"Once we are inside the law enforcement bubble around Peter's place, I am not real worried about a gunfight. Still, I have a concealed carry license for New York courtesy of Peter's friends in the sheriff's office, so I will keep my Smith. I recommend you return the shotgun to its home in the back and the Beretta to its home in the glove box. I doubt anyone is going to argue with a SOF operator, but you never know how long it would take for them to find out that you are who you say you are."

"Mom, this is not what you call a normal reunion."

"Nor is it going to be a normal funeral, dear, but that's just the way it has to be."

They arrived on site at 1100hrs. It took a bit of work to get past the initial perimeter of State Police, but Barbara eventually pulled out a credential from her jacket and that broke the ice. Sue showed her military ID and Barbara vouched for her daughter. The State Police sergeant in charge of access stepped back and they headed into the neighborhood. "Credentials, mom?"

"Sorry, I forgot to tell you I still do some work in Chicago for the Agency. They are Agency credentials that they issued to me when I agreed to work with the relocation folks. That's why I am still in contact with Micah and have the alias package. After your dad died, I just needed to return to the game — even if it was just a little easy bit."

"And... you were going to tell me when?"

"Sue, it was supposed to be over the holiday. Sorry."

The next few days were some of the most painful in Sue's life. There was the regular intrusion from the local police, state police and FBI as they questioned Barbara and Sue. They both know that the lawmen had a job to do and they both also knew that there was no way they could explain the real story. So, they followed a simple Agency rule — "everything we say is completely true, just not truly complete." It would do for the time being — they were in Chicago when they heard about the murder. There had been a similar attempt at Barbara's house which was prevented by the Cook County sheriffs. They didn't know what to think about the murder. "Compartmentation" was the word of the day.

Meanwhile and once they were allowed to access the house, Sue and Barbara spent their time boxing up Peter's papers and any other items which might be better secured for the family. The police said Peter was looking out over the frozen lake when he was shot. He had an old Browning Hi-Power in his hand, hammer back, safety on. He appeared to be looking for trouble. The shooter was likely out on the lake and the round hit Peter in the forehead. The State Police captain shook his head when he told them.

"Scary boys did this. One shot, uphill, probably 300 yards, no evidence on the lake at all. I was in the Marines in Desert Storm — our snipers were good, but honestly, I'm not sure they were that good. How the hell does that work?"

He was talking to Sue when he said this. "You know he was mighty proud of you, Ms. O'Connell. Talked about you all the time when you were in Afghanistan. Told me about your gunfight. Do you think this has to do with Al Qaida? Are they here?"

"Captain, this isn't about terrorists, this must be something else." Sue was looking down at her boots.

"Something else in the old guy's past?"

"Don't know, Captain, but if it is, the guy is long gone."

"You are not gonna let this go are you?"

Sue looked him in the eyes. "Not a chance." Barbara came up after the Captain left. "Was that wise?"

"He needed closure, mom. I can't just play the ninny. I can't lie as easily as you can." Sue was surprised how quickly Barbara responded.

"Young lady, if you don't learn quickly, you are not going to help solve this. You know why? Because if they realize how much you know, they are going to start hunting you just like they hunted Peter and they have been hunting me. They killed your father and now they have killed your grandfather. We have got to get this to stop and telling civilians that we know what's going on doesn't help."

"I just can't be so calculating." Sue's comment came out as a mix of a whine and a snap punch to Barbara's chest: unexpected and painful. Barbara took the "punch" and grabbed Sue by the arm and pulled her close.

"Decide right now if you are going to be part of the solution or a victim. I have lost two men in my life, I'm not going to lose my daughter." Now it was Sue's turn to recover.

"Mom, I'm in."

"OK. From now on, this is an O'Connell family affair. Bill needs to know, but no one else. I mean No One. Not your command, not your Army handlers, no one. We solve this ourselves. If we need help, we get help, but the full story stays with us. A small circle of trust."

Barbara smiled and hugged her daughter. As she did, she said "Sue, we are going to have to work on this ourselves. You are on the inside now so that is going to be where you belong. Don't lose sight of your real job. But, there are plenty of opportunities to use the system to help us. I'm on the outside and I have a bit more...flexibility, but no access. This is going to work if you are willing to partner with me."

The first weeks back at Bragg with the new unit had been fairly typical of Sue's experience in the Special Operations Community. After basic inprocessing at SOF headquarters, Sue and her Farm colleagues from SOF were told to go home, change into civilian clothes and meet back on post at a warehouse off Honeycutt Road. They were told that once on post, they were to tell anyone who asked who they were that that they were new logistics contractors hired to manage the deployments of 18th Airborne Corps units for Afghanistan and Iraq. Bragg had become one of the major locations for "Brigade Combat Teams" that were heading to Afghanistan and Iraq and money supporting these deployments had transformed the post from a place filled with soldiers and run down 1950s barracks prior to 2001 to a ghost town of new high rise buildings for administrative staff and troop barracks, but where troops were either downrange, conducting block training to go downrange, or on block leave having just returned from downrange. New buildings, especially warehouses to handle the transitions were everywhere and Sue realized that she needed to pay close attention to the street signs because all of the landmarks that she had used before 9/11 were now gone.

The warehouse was down a graveled road and behind a grove of pines. It was far more than the normal sized military warehouse with tin sides and a tin roof. This was more like the size of the aircraft hangers used at Pope AFB for servicing the C130s. It was large. The gate on the fence had a phone. Sue picked it up and gave her name. The gate opened electronically. She parked her T-bird in the gravel lot next to a red Corvette. Sue arrived about ten minutes before the time scheduled for the in-briefing and she was told to sit and wait near the entrance on a set of seven folding chairs near the door. Half her colleagues were there already and the other three arrived within a minute of Sue.

Once everyone was there, they received their in-brief from Colonel Smith. He was in jeans and a long sleeved turtleneck and had about a week's beard that would not pass any Army grooming standard. He looked more like he belonged on a dockyard or railyard than a SOF

223

compound. Next to him was his newly arrived Command Sergeant Major. Sue recognized a friendly face, albeit with a shaved head and under a beard that would be best described as belonging on one of the crew of Shackleton's arctic adventures. Jim Massoni.

"OK, welcome to Logs Unit 171. As you recall from our last meeting at the Farm, my name is Jedediah Smith." He paused to see if anyone was going to roll their eyes over the name "Jed Smith." No one was that dumb even if they did know about Jed Smith the mountain man. "You can call me Jed or Boss. Starting now, we don't use any ranks or any "sirs" because we are supposed to be civilians and need to act like it here and anywhere else."

"This is the next step in the global war on terror and you are part of the pathfinders for this effort. We already have ten 171 case officers in the field and you will complete our compliment — at least for now. My goal is to use some of you to expand our network into Central Asia and Southeast Asia. Given your backgrounds, I suspect you have all had your fill of Iraq and Afghanistan and you will be glad to hear that, for now, there is no plan to send anyone from 171 to either combat theater."

Sue watched as Pigpen did a little happy dance. Sometimes, he just couldn't help himself. She wondered how the Smith/Massoni team would handle that.

Smith looked directly at Pigpen but said nothing. "I will be working up travel plans and target packages for all of you you can expect to get your first files by the end of the week and be on the road by the end of the month. We work as singleton's here, so don't expect to spend a lot of time together except when you are in the warehouse. All of your peers are currently on TDY, so pick a cubicle in the warehouse that is empty and get to work with the admin staff to get your docs, your kit and any other paperwork in order. Jim, they are all yours."

"Thanks, Boss." Massoni turned to his seven new players.

"Welcome to 171. You can expect to live about 20+ days a month on TDY. Most of our trips are 10 days long and you will return again and again to various locations where your sources live, work, and play. We are considering a move sometime this year to an airbase somewhere in NATO, so don't get too comfortable. We need to be nearer our targets and stop wasting government money on airfare. I saw from your 201 files that all of you, but one, are single and that is a good thing. This means you aren't going to be too much trouble when we PCS you to someplace else. Now, here is your first instruction."

Massoni handed out a brown clasp envelope to each of them. "Open it, morons."

They did and out fell a ID card on a lanyard. No names, no identification, just a picture of Bozo the Clown. Sue couldn't help but laugh.

"Yes, you are the clowns today and until I am sure you know the ropes here. This tells everyone on the admin staff that you are new, you don't know anything and they have to help you no matter how stupid your request. OK, put them on."

It got better as the day went on.

Massoni introduced them to the analytic staff of 171. Three men, two women — all about twenty and each surrounded by three computer screens and two keyboards, wearing headphones and looking at what appeared to be live feeds from multiple locations around the world.

"This is the brain trust. Deke, Pluto, Blaster, Hawkeye, and Flash. Brain Trust, meet Peter, Joe, Jerry, Sandy, Ginger, Sue and Pigpen. These are your new collectors. Deke and Flash looked up from their screens and acknowledged Massoni and the new team. Pluto, Banger, and Hawkeye raised their left hands from their keyboards just long enough to make it clear that they heard Massoni.

"Friendly bunch, perfect at cocktail parties" was all Massoni would say as he walked away from their cubicles.

The next stop was a caged off area with a cipher lock on the door. Massoni hit the cage hard with the flat of his hand. "Hey, Marconi, you got visitors."

Another twenty something walked out from the rows of metal shelving. He was wearing what looked like a baker's toque, mask, gloves and hospital scrubs.

"Marconi, here are the new crew. They will be reaching out to you later this week for their computer kit and the standard issue."

He pulled down the mask. He looked like he belonged in a metal band as the drummer. He had a sleeve tattoo on his left arm that appeared to be some sort of design from the Northwest Coast Native Americans. Sue thought it looked like some sort of fish, but it could be a very stylized hawk or raven. For sure, it was mostly blue.

"Welcome to the madhouse. Don't let Massoni's friendly demeanor fool you. He is a slave driver."

"Thanks, Marconi. Get back to work."

As they walked away, Ginger asked Massoni. "Is Marconi his real name or do you call him that because of his job."

"Yes" was all Massoni said.

By 1600hrs, the introductions were over and Massoni was satisfied that they were not going to mess up his world, so he let them take off the ID, hand it back to him and return to "normal." They had pictures taken for their new passports, received their DoD contractor ID cards and had appointments with Marconi to get one on one tutorials on their new computer communications systems, their concealed camera and voice capture units and several other items that Marconi promised were well worth the wait. Massoni met with them at 1700hrs.

"So, that's it for the day. Do whatever you want at this point — go workout in our stylish gym facility" he pointed to a corner of the warehouse where there were pullup bars, two benches with free weights and a rack of dumbbells and kettlebells sitting on what looked like 1950s wrestling mats. There were two heavy bags in the corner of the "gym" — one of which was currently in use by Smith.

"Or, if you want to have stimulating conversation, you can always join us at our café for an espresso." He pointed to a folding table and chairs and a classic military coffee pot which probably had yesterday's coffee still under heat.

"Seriously, get outta here. You won't have a lot of free time in the near future, so you need to enjoy what little time you have left. Next meeting is 0900hrs tomorrow. Shoo!"

Massoni waved to them and they broke up. Ginger and Pigpen walked over to the gym. The rest left the building.

"Not precisely the Republic of Zed, but I like it so far." Sandy said as he was walking to his Harley which was parked next to Sue's T-bird. January in North Carolina could be ice storms or perfectly clear days with temperatures in the 40s. Today was the latter and Sue wasn't surprised to see Sandy had a bike.

"Did you move your family down from Virginia Beach?"

"Yup." Sandy started zipping up his jacket and pulled on his helmet with a shipping container logo on the back stating "this end up." Before he closed the face shield, he said "Janet said she would give it another try and I said it was what I wanted as well. The kids are happy so far — starting yet another semester in yet another military school, but they are used to that. I hope that Smith is right and we keep our schedules pretty regular. Janet was fed up with the 120 downrange, 60 home, 120 downrange game. I just hope she can get used to having me around more."

"Good luck with that." Jerry added a slap on Sandy's helmet for emphasis. Jerry and Sandy had always been at each other throughout the Farm — nothing nasty Sue could tell, just classic macho dude banter. Jerry got into his new red Corvette and drove off. Joe smirked at the exchange as he got into his Jeep Wrangler. He was the quietest of the SOF bunch at the Farm, a steady performer, but not the most social guy.

Sue waved to Joe as he pulled out and then got into her T-bird and drove toward the main gate on the compound. Admin staff had given them proximity badges for the gate and the main door which meant that they could go in and out of the compound at any time of the day or night. They also had individual four digit codes they had to punch in to shut down the alarm system — easy enough and consistent with what Sue had used at S&R during the few times she was back at Bragg.

The rest of the week was one administrative briefing or training after another. Marconi provided each of them with some modified computer equipment, a satellite phone which looked like a regular NOKIA phone, an encrypted external hard drive that looked more like a Swiss Army knife than a real Swiss Army knife and a pair of concealments plus one messenger bag and one day pack to carry it all in. The brain trust conducted briefings on the AQ international network with names, dates, places, and maps that were hard to follow because they flashed so quickly up and off the screen. Massoni was there to make sure no one zoned out during the briefings and he promised that this background briefing was simply a start point for the more detailed briefings they would get once they were given a target deck to work. All seven of the new members of 171 were given a language test on whatever language was listed as their second language and, more for fun than for any training value, they were taken to a small pistol range inside the compound and worked on close quarter battle drills inside a house made of old car tires with a Glock 26, a Sig Sauer P228, a Makarov and a .22 Sig Sauer Mosquito. Both Smith and Massoni attended this training.

Smith was the range master throughout the drills and walked on the catwalks above the "tire house" with Massoni. He offered some tactical advice, but basically let the newcomers shoot the house. "Depending on where you are and who you are working with, you are going to have a station Glock or a NATO pistol or no pistol at all. We are trying to get the protocols set up so you can carry anywhere when you are on TDY, but so far, that's not possible outside of Africa or the Gulf. Still, I want you to stay current and we will have a formal qualification at the end of next week before you are deployed so that it is in your records. You will qualify on the Glock since that is the weapon that the Agency uses as their service weapon. The rest of these are just in case you have to pick up something else."

Sue's second week as a member of 171 focused much more on a set of cases which appeared on her desk on Monday morning. Before she got a chance to even open the files, Massoni used his "sergeant major voice" to call a meeting in the middle of the warehouse.

"OK, here's the deal. You have already found the case files on your desk. They are up to date as of Sunday night. The cases are already being handled by your counterparts in the field right now. You will read the files, sort out your plan, brief the Boss on Thursday and be out the door and on the road NLT Sunday. Admin is already processing travel for you — tickets, country clearance, and accommodations. Don't be surprised that you are not going to open new locations for us. You are too new to work that challenge. After you have demonstrated to everyone here and in the field that you are not dangerous to yourself and to others, we will work up new cases and new areas for you. It will probably take about six months for that to happen, but since it doesn't look like AQ or any of the other terrorists groups are going away anytime soon, I suspect you have job security. Think of yourselves as novices who just joined a Medieval guild. You have to work to be journeymen and once you are journeymen, you will be given more challenges. I have posted the briefing plan for Thursday. Check with admin tomorrow to pick up your itinerary and your docs — passports, any identification cards, military TDY orders and anything else you might need to get you from here to your destination. Clear?"

Everyone said check and went to work. Four days was not a long time to read and understand files and to make sure you didn't get lost the first day on TDY. Sue had three files on her desk. Two established agents to run and one access agent who was providing leads to new cases. All of the cases were based in Cyprus and both active cases focused against Lebanese Hizballah. This was the first time that Sue had even seen mention of the Shia terrorist group and she was surprised. Everything that Smith and Massoni had said so far had focused her attention on al Qaida.

At least the cases were consistent with what Smith had said on day one. Sue was picking up the cases from a long time HUMINT operator named Dave Daniels. Like many of the more traditional Army HUMINT operators, Dave was an exceptional linguist who spoke both Arabic and Turkish. He had been working Cyprus as his TDY home since 2003. The two agents he had recruited were both providing material support to a Hizballah/Iranian network working throughout the Eastern Mediterranean. Sue was pleased to see that the cases could be handled in English which was not a huge surprise since English was the lingua franca in Cyprus. Her Arabic was limited to a few working phrases in street Arabic she had picked up while working targets in East Africa and her Persian was an Afghan dialect that likely would draw more attention than cooperation.

File 206 was a Lebanese expatriate who ran a small shipping company out of Larnaca running guns and explosives from Europe by small freighters to the Lebanese coast and, eventually, to the Beka'a. 206 was recruited based on a simple financial incentive and a full understanding that he was going to spend a very long time in a Cypriot jail if he didn't cooperate.

File 207 was a Palestinian who worked as Hizballah's penetration of the port facilities in Limassol. The Palestinian was an administrative clerk for the Port police. 207's motivation was based on revenge. His family had been in a refugee camp in Southern Lebanon at the time Hizballah rose to power. His entire family had been killed by Amal — the predecessor to Hizballah — while he was in Cyprus looking for work. He was determined to do what he could to damage Hizballah and, ideally, find and kill the murderers of his family. A control issue for sure, but about as solid a motivation as you could find.

File 208 was Daniel's most recent contact. He was not yet recruited but had potential as a good reporting source on any threats in the Eastern Mediterranean from radical Sunni groups associated with al Qaida. He was a young Egyptian linked directly to the Muslim Brotherhood. He had escaped several Egyptian government dragnets for Muslim Brotherhood followers by stowing away on an eastern Mediterranean cargo hauler and eventually ended up running a coffee shop in Cyprus. The only complication was 208 lived north of the Green line in Turkish Cyprus. Crossing over the green line was nearly impossible for 208 and equally difficult for Daniels. He had four meetings with 208 in the past year, but they were short and Daniels had not been able to develop the case beyond identifying background and eliciting possible motivations. Daniels had yet to reveal his intelligence background to 208.

So, Hizballah. Sue knew next to nothing about this organization other than it was a Lebanese Shia organization, run by families and clans who were secretive in ways that were more like an intelligence service than a terrorist organization that grew up in the 1980s and that they had killed plenty of Americans in the past. Sue walked over to the Brain Trust and found out that Flash was the analyst handling Daniels' cases and she was more than willing to talk about Hizballah over several cups of black coffee. In the first few minutes, Sue realized she had made several incorrect assumptions about the analysts. First, Flash was no 20 something punk rocker. She was 28 though her brushcut died jet black, black t-shirt, black fatigue pants and black jungle boots argued for a different age if not a different planet. Flash didn't offer her real name, but did say she had a PhD in Islamic Studies from Columbia and had joined the Army in September 2001 after several friends were killed in the Towers on 9/11. Due more to luck than wisdom, the Army recognized that she was best suited to the Intelligence Corps. Once in the system, SOF found her file and she had been in one intel cell after another in Bagram, Balad and now back at Bragg.

This biography took the first cup of coffee, so Sue refilled the cups and started asking questions.

"Why is Daniels going after Hizballah? I thought 171 was hunting AQ?

"Don't believe the broad brush description you got from Jed. We are here to go after any terrorist organization that the CG wants to go after. The Shia militias in Iraq — especially in Baghdad and Basra — are deadly and killing far more Americans and Brits right now than the shitbirds in Anbar. Our collectors in Iraq are telling us that the militias are being trained by Iranian al Qods — the Special operations side of the Islamic Revolutionary Guards Corps or IRGC and by experts from the armed fighter side of Hizballah. So, they become a target for us."

"Got it. So if Iran is the bankroller and the arms dealer for Hizballah, why is Daniels looking at smugglers in Cyprus?"

"Because, some of the most dangerous weapons in use right now in Iraq and we fear eventually in Afghanistan are very sophisticated anti-armor weapons called EFPs — explosively formed penetrators. The first time we ever saw these things, they were used against Israeli armor in Southern Lebanon — devastating. Iraqi Shia militia are using them now against US troops. These weapons take lots of electronics for their remote detonation system and those parts are limited by lots of embargos. Most of the material is dual use and Lebanon has no such embargo. In fact, most of the Iranian industrial complex uses either Dubai or Lebanon as their big box supply company.

Remember, we are strategic collectors — we don't want the shooters, we don't even want the shooter's bosses, we want to take down the network that supports the shooters and their bosses. Dave thinks we have a nexus here from Cyprus to Lebanon that includes money and electronics. 206 is supposed to help with that and 207 is supposed to give us a time and a place where a ship filled with the shit is headed to Lebanon. Early days so far, but I think he is on the mark."

Flash paused for a moment, finished her coffee and added "You realize Daniels is an asshole, right?"

"How am I supposed to know that?"

"OK, here's just a couple of things to put in your "just for me" file from the Flash. Daniels is a retired Army CI officer who was working on 9/11 as a DoD civilian at 18th Airborne Corps CI shop. He is a good, Farm trained case officer and SOF grabbed him early on to run some of their cases in Iraq. He is an Arabist and he was good at the interrogations of the early AQ captured guys. His CI background came in handy — sometimes he was an interrogator, sometimes he was a debriefer. All good and when 171 was formed, he was picked as number one case officer during playground selection for the team."

Flash pointed to her coffee cup. Sue walked over and filled it.

"Here's where it gets painful. Daniels is convinced that he is the boss around here and he had a couple of discussions with Smith about how things should be run. Smith needed Daniels so he put up with this civilian telling him how this unit should be run. He makes a couple of tdys and each time he returns, he acts like some Roman general returning from capturing a large chunk of Europe. He gets more and more belligerent each time he returns. He makes it clear that he is the 171 star and no one can afford to tell him what to do."

Flash took a drink from her mug. She smiled.

"Then that cat Massoni arrives." Flash pointed over at the "front office" of 171

"And?"

"Daniels tries one of his tirades on Massoni. Massoni quietly invites him into the cage where Marconi lives and invites Marconi to take an early lunch. When Massoni and Daniels come out of the cage, it would appear that Daniels has decided that Massoni is not someone he wants to talk to… ever again. Word in the warehouse is that when Daniels returns from this tdy, he is going to be given a chance to transfer back to his old CI unit or, as a civilian, he can just be transferred to some other CI unit someplace else. The brain trust is voting for someplace nice like HOA. You dig?"

Sue wondered what Daniels had done to the analysts that they would want to send him to the US military facilities supporting the Horn of Africa — HOA. There were few places there that were pleasant and many that were downright unpleasant. Still, an Arabist could legitimately be sent to HOA if that was what command wanted to have happen. "So, I should watch my six, eh?"

"Count on it."

On Thursday, Sue was more than a bit nervous when she arrived at the only office in the warehouse. Smith and Massoni shared an office with white painted sheetrock and plywood walls and a real door framed out like it belonged in a construction site. Marconi had previously told Ginger that originally they didn't have an office but after a couple of serious arguments with some of the first case officers that filled the warehouse with expletives, they decided to frame out the commander's space. After that, it was all good until one of the case officers slammed the door on the framed space and two walls fell down. Finally, Massoni got some of the admin staff together and they drilled down into the concrete floor, bolted a frame to the floor and then framed out the office with real 2x4s and the office was more or less sound proof and anger proof.

Sue knocked on the closed door precisely at 1600hrs. She was the last briefer of the day.

"Enter."

Sue had not been in the office before. All of her views of the room had been framed around the door. She knew there were two military style metal desks and two computers on the desks, but that was it. What she hadn't realized was that on either side of the door were covered two large flat screens topped with cameras to support secure video teleconferencing. The other three walls were covered with

1:100,000 scale Maps of the current 171 AOR: Europe, HOA, Iraq and Afghanistan. Red pins marked what Sue assumed were the 171 field officer locations.

"Boss, I'm here to give you my deployment and turnover plan. You ready for me?"

"Yes. Here's how I want you to do your briefing. I want to know how you are going to get there and back, what you think is going on with your cases, and how long you expect the turnovers to take. Finally, I want to know how long you think this TDY is going to last. Jim?"

"Works for me, Boss."

"Start talkin,' O'Connell."

Sue walked over to the map of Europe and pointed to the red pin in Cyprus.

"Boss, Dave Daniels is currently based inside RAF Akrotiri in Southern Cyprus. While he coordinates his work with station in Nicosia, he doesn't seem to spend much time in that part of the country. 206 and 207 live and work in the Southern Part of the Island. I know Dave traveled to Cyprus by military air, first catching a C17 from Pope to Mildenhall and then shifting to an RAF C130 supply flight to Akrotiri. That made sense at the time, but I think it might do us some good for me to go commercial air. The reason I think this makes sense is because I want to at least introduce myself to the COS as soon as possible and work out any kinks we might have with the Klingons before I start working 206 and 207 and especially if we get some traction and are able to pitch 208." Sue paused to see how Smith and Massoni took that discussion.

Smith looked up from the notebook that he was using to take notes. "One of the things that we have been dodging over the past year has been the issue of Title 10 authorities versus Title 50 authorities. Do you think you can avoid any confrontation with the COS?"

Authorities were one of the legal issues that SOF operations addressed all the time. The Secretary of Defense was the manager of Title 10 authorities in the US Code — preparing and executing war. The legal authorities associated with Title 50 — intelligence operations — were less clear and there was always a multi-player game of tug of war which included the Directorate of National Intelligence, the Director of the Central Intelligence Agency, the Director of the Defense Intelligence Agency, the Director of the FBI and virtually every senior general officer in a theater and, most especially, the Commander of SOF.

"I do. I understand that we are operating under Title 10 in most cases because we are looking at supporting the larger SOF combat mission, but I have been reading some of the CG's notes about partnership and his praise for the work between our outfit and both Baghdad and Kabul stations. I honestly think that at least giving the COS a briefing as soon as possible is better than holding agent meetings and then telling the COS what we are doing."

"Diplomatic answer, O'Connell." Sue had never thought Massoni was anything more than a combat leader, but over the last week, she had enough contact with him to know that he paid particular attention to two areas: operational security and coordination with the other agencies in the field. "Daniels has had some run ins with the station and we came close a couple of times of pulling him out of Cyprus simply to cool everyone down. I think it makes sense to engage the station first and then go down to Akrotiri, but I don't want the Chief there to use the meeting to veto the program. Clear?"

"Check, Boss. Do you want Dave in Nicosia to introduce me?"

"Nope. He can stay in Akrotiri and prepare your introductions to the Brits. The MILATT can do the job. I went to Carlisle with Jack Williams. I will talk to him before you leave."

Sue realized that it was a small world in the senior officer corps of the Army. Regardless of branch of the Army, all seniors would go through Ft. Leavenworth for Command and General Staff College and, assuming they made full Colonel, to the War College at Carlisle Barracks in Pennsylvania. If Smith had that sort of connection to the Military Attaché in Nicosia, it would be a serious help to her.

"OK, lets go with your plan on getting there. Now, what are you going to do when you get there…"

The next hour, Sue outlined her understanding of the cases, the operational security issues related to Cyprus and her tentative plans on what to do once the cases were hers to run. Smith and Massoni didn't have any problems with any of this and Sue was ready to finish up and get out of the commander's "gunsite" when he interjected.

"OK, now lets talk about ELEKTRA."

Sue had been so focused on the cases, planning on how to get to Cyprus and then focusing on her first briefing to Smith that she hadn't thought at all about this part of her new life. She wasn't surprised that Massoni was read into the case. After all, Smith didn't make full bird colonel and not understand that his sergeant major was the most important guy on his team — compartmentation be damned.

"Boss, I don't know squat about what's next with ELEKTRA. I haven't given it much thought."

"Well, here's something to consider. What if they contact you while you are on TDY? Are you going to tell station? Or, given the fact that you are living and working on Akrotiri, are you going to tell the Brits? If so, who will you talk to?"

"Shit." Sue hadn't thought about any of this and was seriously pissed at herself for not considering how complex this double agent mission was going to be.

"Exactly, O'Connell. That's one of the reasons why I didn't want this to be part of your job here and I said so. Needless to say, my view didn't count for crap. OK, sit down and let's work through this process."

Sue probably should have realized that Smith was an experienced case officer in his own right, but she hadn't thought about it at all. She had just assumed SOF simply had a good Colonel on the J2 — Intelligence staff and put him in charge of 171. In the next few minutes, she realized that she was mistaken.

"OK, here's what we are going to do. I will reach out to my colleagues who are working on ELEKTRA. They will tell me who is read in to your program. I know they asked me to assign you to Europe, so that means someone in the Klingon empire of Europe knows what's going on. Meanwhile, one of the ops managers in the Army CI staff in Germany worked for me, so I will engage them as well to sort out if anyone has been read in to this program. If you are contacted, they are going to expect you to have some material to pass almost immediately. I don't want them to know about 171, so the ELEKTRA team needs to give you feed material — like, yesterday."

Massoni chimed in, "Boss, how about I get in touch with my contact in FCI at the Hoover Building and sort out if any of the Legal Attachés in Europe know anything — at least anything about ELEKTRA. Sue needs to know who will be her backup if anything goes sideways. I really don't want to have to put together a rescue team from here or from SOCEUR." Special Operations Command Europe (SOCEUR) was the only place that Sue knew of in Europe that would have a SOF contingent.

"OK, O'Connell, what are you going to do about this? We can't carry your water forever."

"Kinda busy recently, Boss."

"Well, get busier. Now." He used both hands to wave her goodbye and Massoni chimed in with his best effort at a posh British accent — "Toodle Loo."

Sue walked out the room and heard Smith shout — "Shut the door!" She did and leaned against the frame while she did a couple of deep breaths to sort out what to do next. Pluto walked past and offered his own views over his shoulder.

"It's always like that when you enter the linear accelerator. Don't worry, you aren't the only particle being pushed around. It doesn't get any easier, but it does get more normal."

It was 1800hrs and 171 was still full of people working in their cubicles. You could also hear Marconi working something on the lathe in the back of the cage. It was a busy place and Sue was about to follow Smith's instructions and "Get busier."

During her last visit with Smith before leaving the warehouse and heading to the airport, Smith delivered a curve ball that she wasn't expecting. "O'Connell, pack your Class A uniform and two sets of ACUs. I think you know that Daniels is a civilian and he has not been all that well received by either the US embassy folks or the Brits. We need to up the ante a bit — you are going to do that, clear?"

"Check, Boss. A bit of spit and polish then for the locals?"

Sue was dozing in the Lufthansa frequent flyer lounge in Frankfurt waiting for her connection to Nicosia. It had been a bit of a rush to get out on the schedule that Smith required, but they had eventually accomplished it as a team. The admin folks in 171 had been unable to arrange a space available flight on any USAF aircraft leaving Pope AFB or any other East Coast AFB to the UK or to Germany, so they had arranged a simple flight from Washington Dulles to Frankfurt and then Frankfurt into Nicosia. Smith sorted out the connection to the Military Attaché in Nicosia who set up both country clearance from the Ambassador for Sue's trip as well as scheduling a meeting with the COS early morning the day after she arrived.

The big shortfall had been with the ELEKTRA team. They didn't have anything to offer Sue to answer any of Smith's questions or her own concerns. Sue had lived inside government bureaucracies long enough to know that they were not prepared for the speed that SOF moved and they were stalling so that they didn't seem completely stupid. Sue knew that the COS was not going to be a happy camper with a SOF case officer operating in his turf and, worse still, that same case officer playing the role of double agent on a sensitive USG operation against the GRU. She could imagine how much fun the meeting would be tomorrow. In the meantime, she was trying to catch a few minutes sleep in the lounge before boarding the Lufthansa Airbus flying non-stop to Cyprus.

"Is this seat occupied?" A dishelved, overweight man in his mid-50s looking even more jet lagged than Sue was asking to sit in the chair that was currently hosting her carry-on bag. He wore a dark suit and wool overcoat, black shoes and white socks. Everything he wore looked to be nearly as old as he was. Sue looked around and in the last few minutes the lounge had filled with passengers and there were precious few seats left. She could be rude and say that it was occupied, but Sue didn't have the energy to be rude.

"Please sit down. I will move my bag." She placed her bag in front of her, resting her legs on the case and closed her eyes. All she needed was a lonely old man bothering her for the next hour. She hoped he got the message. He walked around Sue's outstretched legs and placed his briefcase in front of the chair and walked over to the counter to get some of the ersatz coffee offered in the lounge. Sue heard rather then saw him return as he slumped into the adjoining chair.

"Too much travel for these old bones," he said. Sue kept quiet. Perhaps he was talking to himself or, perhaps, if she did not respond he would get the message. She felt him shift towards her. He smelled of tobacco and garlic. Perfect.

"I have a message from Mary for you. You remember Mary, of course. Your friend who served in Kenya?" Sue went from near sleep to full alert. She opened her eyes slowly and turned to face the man. He was about six inches away from her face.

"Are you sure you have the right person?"

"Of course, I have the right person, Ms. O'Connell." Sue could feel her temples pounding. She took a deep breath and tried to make it sound like a normal sigh that a person might make just waking up. She needed to get into the game, and quickly.

"So, how is Mary? I haven't seen her since before Christmas."

"As it should be, Ms. O'Connell. As it should be. Now, we don't have a lot of time here. I have a plane to catch as do you."

"OK, so what's the message?"

"Very good. Very direct. That is what we expect. The message is that when you get to Nicosia today, after you check into your hotel, we need you to stop at your hotel shop at 1900hrs tonight and buy a convenience item, toothbrush or something similar. The shop closes at 2000hrs so be precise. If there is any flight delay, you will go to the shop tomorrow at 1900hrs. We will contact you there. The contact will simply ask you if you are Austrian or Swiss — remember he will ask Austrian or Swiss. You will answer "I am neither. I am not a European. Why do you ask?" After that, simply follow his instructions. Do not worry, he is very good at what he does and will not ask you to do something foolish. You understand?"

"I understand, but Mary never told me what I was going to do for your firm. Can you tell me, please?"

"Ah, Ms. O'Connell. I think you know the general idea, but your contact will tell you the specifics. Please don't worry, you will know the details soon enough. Now," he looked up at the monitors on the wall across the lounge "I have a plane to catch. Enjoy the rest of your time here in Frankfurt and have a good flight to Nicosia." He got up, grabbed his bag, sighed as if the effort was too great, and shuffled off to the exit of the lounge.

Sue watched him leave. How many of the other patrons of the lounge were with him? If she was running the operation, she would have had at least two in place before she arrived watching her both before and after. She certainly couldn't be seen using the phone right after her contact departed. In any event, she had to process what he said, remember everything about him and then, eventually write it down somewhere in private — perhaps on the flight.

Sue drank three demi tasse cups of strong, black coffee in the lounge as she thought through all the details and tried to figure out how in the world she could contact the ELEKTRA team before she arrived in Nicosia. It seemed unlikely — her flight left in 45 minutes and she would arrive in Cyprus at 1700hrs local. She had to collect her bags, clear customs, get a cab to the Hilton Cyprus, check in and all before 1900hrs. It seemed pretty tight. Luckily, she had the time on the aircraft to think it through.

The admin team obtained a first class seat for the government rate, so as Sue boarded the aircraft, she almost immediately found her seat — 4D — window seat in the last row of first class against the bulkhead. Not a reclining seat, but then again, Sue wasn't going to get much sleep anyhow. She put her bag in the overhead bin, got into the window seat and put her laptop case under the seat in front of her. The Lufthansa flight attendant in her blue and white uniform reached over and asked

"Was drinken sie, bitte?"

"Mineral wasser mit gasse, bitte." The flight attendant turned and walked toward the galley.

"Nice accent, Ms?" Sue was reaching into her bag when she heard the voice. Oh, great. Another annoyance… she looked up to face Stan in an English cut suit and tortoise shell glasses.

"O'Connell. And your name, sir?"

"Baker. Stan Baker."

The Lufthansa attendant interrupted this charade long enough to deliver Sue's water, a napkin and a small cup of mixed nuts. Stan ordered an orange juice and a glass of still water in nearly perfect Swabian German. The flight attendant smiled and left.

"Mr. Baker, you speak very good German. Where did you learn it?"

"I grew up in Germany. My father was in the US Army in Germany for nearly 10 years. My mother is German and I have a German passport."

"How interesting. Why are you going to Cyprus?"

"Business. I work for a German company that services ship engines. Mostly diesel fuel injectors. The good news for our company is diesel engines need the injectors and they wear out often."

"Hmmm." Sue wasn't sure how long this was going to last, but she decided that a discussion of fuel injectors was designed to end the conversation not sustain it. "Please excuse me, but I am writing a letter to my brother about my trip to Germany and I want to post it as soon as I get to Nicosia."

"Of course."

Sue reached into her bag and pulled out a simple composition notebook and pen and started to write.

Dear Bill,

It has been a short visit to Germany in my job as a courier, but I am now going to Cyprus for some sun…

As soon as the flight took off and the seat belt signs were off, Sue walked to the lavatory, leaving the pages of the "letter" that described the events in the lounge, the contact plan and a description of the German contact. When she returned to her seat, the first page of the letter to Bill was still there, but the other pages were gone.

"I hope your brother appreciates a letter. Most times, I don't even get a chance to write a postcard."

"Well, it helps if you have something to write about."

"I'm sure that's true. Now, if you will excuse me, I have some paperwork I have to prepare before we arrive in Cyprus, so I have to leave you to your letter writing."

Sue watched Stan pull out and open his brief case and place the Economist he was reading in the top compartment. She noticed that he had left a small bit of her letter visible so that she could see that he had recovered the note. He then took out what looked to be fairly detailed schematics for large scale diesel engines manufactured in the US and sold around the world. He took notes in a small notebook as he flipped through the schematic. Twice during the flight when the attendant came by, Stan engaged her in his perfect German while Sue stumbled enough that the attendant shifted easily to English. The attendant was polite to Sue, but gave Stan the look that implied "tourist." He simply answered "Genau" — exactly.

Once the seatbelts sign was back on and the plane began to descend into Cyprus, Stan began to put his things back in the brief case leaving a 3X5 card visible that said "We'll be watching." Once he was sure Sue had read the note, he closed the briefcase and put it under the seat in front of him.

The flight arrived on time. Sue watched on the final approach as they crossed over the turquoise waters of the Eastern Mediterranean, did a wing over the rugged terrain of the former salt lake that Larnaca was built on and landed back toward the Sea. Sue's official passport, military orders and her one roller bag translated into an easy trip through immigration and customs. Waiting outside the arrivals lounge was a fifty something embassy driver in a white shirt and black trousers holding her name on a 8x11" whiteboard.

"I'm O'Connell."

"Good afternoon, Miss O'Connell. I am Mr. Tsapiras, I drive for Colonel Williams. I have been driving for the embassy for thirty years and now I drive for the military attaché. Let me take your bag. I understand from the Colonel that you have a set of meetings tomorrow in the morning, so today we will let you rest in your hotel and I will pick you up at 0730hrs tomorrow. Is that acceptable?"

"Thank you, Mr. Tsapiras. That sounds great." They walked out to the parking lot and loaded Sue's rolling duffle in the back of an armored Suburban with US embassy plates. Sue got in the passenger seat on the right side of the vehicle. It had been a while since she loaded into an armored vehicle and she barely pulled the door closed due to the weight of the armor. Tsapiras got into the driver's seat and started up the vehicle. Sue had never quite understood why the US seemed determined to buy left hand drive cars for their embassies where the driving laws stipulated driving on the left — Britain, Pakistan, India and Japan were the most obvious, but Cyprus was another. Tsapiras seemed to have no problem negotiating the drive, though it meant that as the passenger, Sue was always facing the oncoming traffic. An armored Suburban is one of the safest and heaviest vehicles on the planet, so after a few minutes, Sue relaxed for the short drive to Nicosia.

Tsapiras was an excellent driver and he pulled up to the hotel in just under 40 minutes — amazing given the Cypriot traffic. Sue thanked Tsapiras, got her luggage and entered the hotel. She checked in with about an hour to spare before her scheduled contact with her GRU handler. She went up to the room, showered and switched into a navy running suit and black tennis shoes, made a cup of coffee from the coffee bar in her room and worked through her plan. She had a small shoulder bag which she loaded with her passport and wallet, her 171 issued electronics, a Moleskine notebook, pen, and both her Leatherman tool and a 2 1/2" flat blade and sheath which normally hung on a lanyard around her neck. She hung the bag crossways over her shoulder keeping the bag over her left hip. She was as ready as she was going to be. She entered the elevator at 1858hrs and headed for the lobby.

The Hilton lobby like most modern hotels was designed more for the visual pleasure of architects than for the use of the patrons. In front of the main desk were a series of chairs clustered with no apparent plan other than to look good around the flower displays and the fish tank that anchored the center of the room. The elevators were off to the left of the main desk and across the great room was the convenience store/newsstand that was the site for Sue's meeting. She walked across the hall just as her mobile phone alarm silently vibrated 1900hrs.

The room was narrow and divided by a single aisle which on the side toward the entrance handled newspapers and international journals in every European language and on the side toward the back wall of the shop handled all the necessary conveniences that a traveler might have forgotten from bathroom products like toothbrushes, razors, deodorant to electronics accessories like multipronged wall outlet adapters, small headphones and phone cases.

Sue greeted the shopkeeper with a nod and walked over to the bathroom products. She paused for a moment to sell the cover story of looking for the right bathroom necessities when a voice said

"Entschuldigen sie, du bist Osterreicher oder Ungarisch?"

Sue looked up from her search to see a man in his mid thirties, very fit, olive complexion, dark hair and hazel eyes. He was dressed in a very finely black tailored wool trousers and a maroon silk pullover sweater and a black silk jacket. He looked the part of a wealthy, young European businessman.

"I'm sorry, you are completely mistaken. I am an American." He switched to perfect English with a very slight British accent.

"I'm apologize. I thought you were a lady that I saw in the City today at my offices. She spoke German with an accent, so I thought she might be from Southwestern Austria or possibly from Hungary."

"No problem at all. Excuse me, but I am going to make a purchase here."

"Of course. Still, would you care to have a coffee with me in the lobby café? I would like to at least apologize for what seems a very rude way to meet a young lady."

Sue realized that so far the dialogue sounded like something out of a soap opera on television. There was no way to get it to stop than to just say yes. "Of course, just let me make my purchase."

Sue met him outside the shop and they actually did head to the lobby café which was much to her liking. She had been afraid that this contact would want to move to another location immediately and she was not real happy about letting the GRU completely control the situation until she was certain that they were unaware that she was a double agent. They ordered two coffees — he ordered Greek coffee, she ordered café mélange — a Viennese version of café au lait in honor of the completely silly parole the GRU had used for this meeting. They were sitting at a table in the corner of the café a discrete distance from any other customers and to the outside observer, they looked very much like two young people engaged in the beginnings of a love affair.

"Ms. O'Connell, I have to complement you on your precision. I was watching you walk into the shop as my watch clicked to 1900hrs exactly. A good start for what may be a very interesting relationship for us both."

"Do you really think this is such a good idea meeting in a hotel lobby? I am the one taking the risks you know." Sue just mimicked the lines she had heard at the Farm from one of her instructor role players. The lines seemed much more credible now as she looked around in what appeared to be a clandestine meeting being held in the open.

"Please don't worry about this, Ms. O'Connell. Everyone in the café at this point are my people. We have surveillance on the door and on the elevators. We are being watched but only by members of my team."

"Who are you exactly and where are we going in this? Mary was vague, All she offered was the opportunity and then she just disappeared from my life. The next contact was completely useless other than giving me instructions for this meeting. Please don't think I am any less interested, but I would like to have a better understanding of what is going on. You know I am a special operations soldier. I survive by knowing what risks I am taking."

His answer was carefully modulated and he didn't seem to be in the least bit willing to let any emotions filter into this meeting. Sue realized this was not the first time he had run a case and, it seemed to her, it was also not the first time he had run into a SOF operator.

"My name is Jan Bachmann. I have been selected to work with you on this case because of my own special services background. We can talk about this in the future, but for now, I just wanted to meet you and let you know that I will be your contact with the service in the future. We know that you are currently scheduled to stay in Cyprus for the next 10 days and we know that you will be moving to Akrotiri the day after tomorrow. Your mission for the US is to conduct operations against terrorists in Cyprus and to uncover their links to other countries in the Eastern Mediterranean. We can help you with that work and, in exchange, we simply want to know what you find out. You see, in Russia we have our own terrorists and our own efforts to destroy them. They have killed women and children in schools, hospitals, and theaters. They have no mercy and we are hunting them like the animals they are. You can help your own country while helping us as well. Does that make sense?"

Sue was careful to listen to the entire approach. She knew she would have to provide the details tomorrow. She had to admit it was an approach that she hadn't expected. Bachmann was basically outlining a "liaison" relationship not an espionage relationship. Very well crafted and designed to get her used to working clandestinely with a "colleague" before she was actually tasked to deliver US secrets.

"I understand and it is, more or less, consistent with what Mary said was the objective. She did say that I would be challenged and pleased to work with professionals from your service."

"Our service now, Ms. O'Connell. Our service."

"We shall see, Mr. Bachmann. Again, I am the one taking the risks here, so I need to be certain that I can survive first contact with your service before I agree that it is our service."

Bachmann lowered his eyes and let out a small chuckle.

"I can understand that you are trying to decide how much you will give up — at least until we have demonstrated that we can keep you safe. It is a reasonable point of view and one that I am happy to hear from you. The short answer is that we are ready to accept any relationship that you offer and we promise you that we will use the resources of the entire service to keep you safe."

Sue realized her head was starting to fill up with more questions than answers and her inside voice was taking over her actions outside her body. She took a deep breath to clear her head and slow her brain down. One thing at a time, sister. One thing at a time.

"Bachmann, it is not that I don't trust you, but I will need to see something sooner rather than later that shows me that you are serious about this relationship. In the meantime, I need to know how I can get in touch with you for any future meetings. I don't know where I am going to be or how much time I am going to have while I am in country."

"Of course, we need to set up our arrangements." He moved his hand over the round table and placed it on Sue's. She had not expected any contact and was surprised to find his left hand was cold as ice.

"I'm sorry. Sometimes I forget that my prosthetic is so lifelike that people don't realize…"

She looked down at his left hand. Now that she was studying it, she realized it was a very lifelike prosthetic with hinged joints on the knuckles. No telling how much he could move the hand, but it was clear that he was as used to his prosthetic as she was of hers.

"Yes, we also have our wounded warriors in Russia. I lost my hand in Chechnya."

He raised his hand and under it was a small electronic device the size of a matchbox. Too small to be a pager, but clearly a bit of electronics in "spy black."

"It is a simple, two-way communication device — more or less a pager with some modifications made to the device to make it useful for us. The device has a GPS chip in it which means that as long as you have it with you, I will know within 50 meters where you are located. You can send 20 characters in an encrypted message. You set the time and the date and the amount of time in minutes you will have for the meeting. So, if we are going to meet tomorrow at 1600hrs for 30 minutes you will send 26/01/1600/30. I will track you to within 50 meters and then I will trust you to select a place which is discrete for our meetings here in Cyprus. We need to meet at least once more before you leave — after you get to Akrotiri and before you leave so you can tell me where you are going next. You will return this to me at that last meeting and we will have a more permanent device to use in the future. Ten days is not a long time to work in Cyprus. I suspect you will be coming back on another trip — possibly even to replace the other officer assigned to Akrotiri, but that is for the future. Do you understand?"

Sue nodded.

"Please repeat it to me."

Sue repeated the instructions to include the example. The device itself was easy enough to use — there was a small LCD screen and two toggle switches — one for numbers and one for placement along the screen. She added, "But what if you want to set up a meeting?"

"First we have a meeting in Cyprus and then we sort out the next steps where we have two way communications."

Sue realized that part of this was a test to see if she can follow instructions and given the fact that the device might be something that was more or less off the shelf, the GRU was taking no risks in giving her this device.

Of course, there could be far more inside the device as well and they were likely testing her to see if she was going to pull it open to see what was inside.

"Bachmann, I have a long day ahead of me and I would like to get some sleep. If it is acceptable to you, I would like to call it a night. I promise to arrange another meeting, whether it will be here, Akrotiri, Larnaca or someplace else, I simply can't say at this point. Is that satisfactory?"

"Ms. O'Connell, we are very pleased to be working with you and we understand that you have had a chaotic few weeks since your graduation. I think you should leave now. My watchers have said that they are tired of looking like normal people in this abnormal setting. Please send my condolences to your mother on the death of your grandfather. I hope someday to get a chance to meet her. She is described as the role model of the perfect officer in several of our case studies at the Aquarium. Now, good night and I will see you again soon."

He stood up, did a slight bow and shook her hand and left the lobby and the hotel. As Sue finished her coffee she watched two businessmen and one couple leave the café and depart the hotel. Their departure was timed sufficiently that it was never clear to Sue if they were part of Bachmann's team or just "casuals."

Sue got up from her table and walked right to the elevators. She realized she was very tired, but didn't expect she would get any sleep at all tonight.

Sue opened the door to her room and was immediately grabbed from behind and her mouth was covered by a gloved hand. The room was dark, but she was certain there were at least two men in the room involved in the attack. She sagged a bit to shift her weight and twisted enough to grab the testicles of the man holding her. She was about to squeeze hard when Stan appeared in front of her waving his finger to tell her not to injure his partner. Sue let go of the man and straightened up. He backed away quickly.

Stan placed his finger over his lips and pantomimed placing something on the nightstand next to the bed. Sue realized he wanted her to place the GRU device on the table. She did so and then watched as Stan acted out what he wanted her to do. First, go to the bathroom, then take a shower, brush her teeth, etcetera. Stan pointed to his watch. 2145. He then placed his hands in front of Sue and fingered 823. Sue's room was 822. She nodded. Stan and his partner left silently and Sue turned on the lights and started to act out the plan.

Forty minutes later, Sue walked quietly across the hall and into the already opened door of room 823.

"Sweet Jesus, Sue. You almost gave Matthew kittens."

"Sorry, I just assumed you were bad guys and if I didn't act straight away, I was going to end up in a trunk of a car with a bag on my head."

Matthew spoke from across the room "I thought for sure I was going to end up in the hospital tonight."

"Matthew, I am sorry. Not exactly the best introduction. I'm Sue."

"Got that."

"Sue, we don't need to take much of your beauty sleep tonight. We got most of the conversation from the boom mike we used based in the mezannine in the second floor. Just in case you wondered, they have your room bugged but don't have any video in the room. So, be careful when you return to the room to be sure it sounds like you just went out for some ice from the ice machine. You get to use our ice bucket." Stan smiled his quirky, uneven smile.

"I just wanted a chance to let you know that we know what is going on and will meet you in the Embassy tomorrow afternoon. I will brief the LEGATT and the COS in the morning, so you won't be headed into an ambush before your first coffee. Your only job is to sort out whether you want to brief the MILATT."

"Is it necessary?"

"I don't think your boss wanted him in the ELEKTRA compartment, so no, I don't think it is necessary. He has enough on his plate here handling his own operations and your operations down in Akrotiri."

"OK." Sue realized she was really tired and losing her concentration. "Get back to your room — after you get some ice — and get some sleep. You look like you need to crash."

"No kidding."

Sue left, walked down the hall to the ice machine, got a half bucket of ice and returned to her room. She dumped the ice into the sink and bent over and stuck her face in the sink full of ice. She toweled off and walked back into the bedroom. Before she crawled into bed, she opened her suitcase and pulled out three metal triangles — door chocks from her S&R days — and put two in the door and one in the sliding glass door that opened to the small patio that overlooked the city. "Better safe than sorry" said her inside voice as she slipped off her prosthetic and she slipped into the sweats that she always used on work trips as her pajamas. She pulled the knife and lanyard over her head and put it down next to the GRU device and shut off the light.

Sue opened her eyes at 0500hrs. A little less than six hours sleep and a jet lagged brain. Perfect. Still, she got up and started a daily routine that she had developed over the years as a TDYer in S&R. First, ten minutes of yoga while the hotel room coffee maker made a cup of coffee. Next, black coffee, two sugars down the throat. After that, she started a more formal exercise routine which could be accomplished in a hotel room, a small room inside a TDY house, or even a ship or submarine. It was fifteen minutes of calisthenics which would raise her blood pressure just enough to wake her up and enough if conducted every day to maintain some degree of fitness for however long the TDY took place. After she was finished, she called room service and ordered a high protein breakfast to be delivered in 30 minutes. Enough time to shower and get dressed.

The trip to and into the Embassy was without any drama. As she walked past Marine Post One and through the bullet proof glass door, she noticed the Marine corporal delivered a salute which she returned. It has been some time since anyone had delivered a salute to Sue, but it was not a surprise to her since she arrived at the Embassy in her class B uniform — trousers and jump boots, white short sleeved shirt with ribbons, short zip jacket with rank, and her maroon beret.

As she passed into the Embassy proper, the Marine Detachment commander, a Gunnery Sergeant named Westfall walked up to her.

"Ma'am. Colonel Williams asked me to get you set up properly at the Embassy. We need to take a trip downstairs to the RSO's office and we'll get you an Embassy ID card. After that, I will take you up to the Colonel's office. That sound OK to you?"

"Gunney, I am in your charge. Let's do it."

After she received her Embassy ID, Sue and Gunnery Sergeant Westfall walked up two flights of stairs to a steel door with a cipher lock, combination dial and a telephone. Westfall gave Sue the cipher combination on a post it note.

"This is where all the intel side of the embassy lives. The MILATT and the Station. I suspect you will be here plenty. If we had turned to the left, the Embassy seniors are down that hall ending with the Ambassador's office. Now, its all yours. I will get back to my job. I do want to give you an open invitation to the Marine House. We have a good gym and a decent bar. The gym is open 24/7, the bar is open on Friday nights. You can use the MILATT cipher to get through our doors. I hope we see you there."

"Count on it, Gunney. I suspect you know I'll be down in Akrotir most of the time, but if I'm up here, you can save me a place in the weight room. See ya."

Westfall left and Sue proceeded down the hall to the office of the Military Attaché. She knocked on the door, entered and faced a middle-aged Air Force Master Sergeant at his desk. His nametag said Andrews.

"Chief O'Connell. Good to meet you."

"Master Sergeant Andrews. Pleased to meet you as well. Is the boss in?"

"Waiting for you." Andrews nodded to the office to his left. "I will have Brody get you some coffee or a soda. Which?"

"Coffee, black will be fine."

Andrews turned to the office on his left and shouted in his best parade ground voice. "Brody, you lazy squid, forget those electronic gizmos for a moment. Get a cup of coffee for the Chief and one for the Boss."

A younger voice echoed from the back of the room. "Yes, Sergeant."

"Brody is our Navy petty officer. He actually works for the Naval Attaché who is based at the port, but we decided he could work here a couple of days a week as well. I needed someone to boss around and he drew the short straw."

Sue smiled and turned to the Attaché's office. She knocked on the door frame and entered.

Colonel Jack Williams was older than Sue had expected. He was tall and bone thin. He was dressed in Class B uniform as well which gave Sue a chance to do a quick scan of the medals on his shirt. Sue saw the one medal that she rarely saw on an officer — especially a full colonel — the Good Conduct medal. This meant Colonel Williams had started his career as an enlisted man. She also noticed his Master Parachutist wings, Pathfinder badge and Ranger tab. It didn't take long in the Army to sort out a person's pedigree.

Sue decided to make a formal start and performed a hand salute. "Sir, Chief Warrant Officer O'Connell reporting."

Williams stood up, returned the salute, smiled and offered Sue a seat. "I don't know that you will ever need to call me sir again or render a salute to me, Sue, but thanks for the courtesy."

"You are my new boss, sir. It seemed only right."

"Well, there is a debate on whether I am your new boss or Patty is your new boss, but for now, let's just say I am definitely your top cover to prevent any shit from running down hill and hitting you."

She had heard from Smith that he was a good old boy from Appalachia, but the accent was definitely flat, hard to place Midwest. On the other hand, she had also heard that he was in an established turf war with the station chief, Patty Dentmann. Dentmann was convinced that she had the DNI's authorities for all intelligence operations and, according to Smith, Williams accepted that but still answered the mail when it came to DIA requirements.

"Sir, I wanted to see you and the COS on arrival. You know my mission and the fact that I am going to be working down at Akrotiri — I'm taking Dave Daniels' slot there."

"Sue, we are very pleased to see you and I do appreciate the fact that you came to visit the Embassy first. Dave is a good case officer…" This was the second time Sue had heard this followed by "but, he can rub folks the wrong way. We are hoping that you can smooth some of those bureaucratic rough edges left by Dave while keeping his cases just as productive."

"I will do my best, sir."

Brody walked in with two mugs of coffee. Both mugs had jump wings on them. One of the mugs had the scroll from the 75th Ranger Regiment on it. Brody put that mug on the Colonel's desk. Sue realized that Brody was hardly a young guy and hardly someone who looked like he needed supervision. He was a very fit man with an anchor tattoo on his right arm and a submariner badge on his duty uniform.

"Thanks, Brody. Has the Master Sergeant been beating you up today?"

"No sir. He just doesn't like it when I fiddle with the equipment. I don't think he understands that there is more to electronics than the ON/OFF button."

"Now, Brody, you are confusing him with me." Brody smiled and left.

"Sue, I know the 171 mission in detail and I want you to know that we are here to support you any way that you need. I know of Dave's cases and I realize that 208 is across the Green Line. The area is safe, but can be a little treacherous from an operational security standpoint. We can help you on that front if you need it sometime in the future."

"Sir, thanks for that. I don't know enough about 208 to know what we are doing. The file is not entirely complete and I will need to talk to Dave to sort out what needs to be done."

"That's Dave. Everything we tell headquarters is completely true…" Sue completed the saying "It's just not always truly complete." Williams took a drink of his coffee.

"Here's the plan for the day. You need to get down to the COS's office. I am to deliver you there and move out smartly. It's just something that Patty does and I don't need to fight her on that. After that session, come down here and we will go to lunch. After lunch, we can take a drive around the city and I will introduce you to my British counterpart. He will be your nominal host down in Akrotiri. It's just a courtesy call, but that will get you off on the right foot. Unless you have anything else you have to do here in Nicosia, I will arrange for you to go down to Akrotiri tomorrow and you can get to work. Sound good?"

"Excellent, sir. Any advice on the COS?"

"Patty Dentmann is a super Chief and an even better case officer. As near as I can tell, she has been working her way up the Agency through one successful field tour after another. She is an Arabist and has been working for CTC since it started in the 1980s. She focused her early career on Palestinian terrorists and then transitioned in the 1990s to Hizballah. After 9/11, she did a tour in Yemen and then two tours in Iraq. She doesn't have an ounce of fear in her body. When seniors from the Agency come to visit, they tell me stories of Patty that sound like they belong in novels — running sources in the West Bank, Gaza, Lebanon, and then running paramilitary teams grabbing AQ guys in Yemen. Sheesh!"

"She is very turf conscious. She has a strong opinion of Dave and it isn't a good one. I don't know if she just doesn't like him or if she thinks his cases are problematic, or both. You have to understand, I'm not a Klingon by training, I'm just a simple Ranger who knows how to conduct a recon patrol and leave no any sign that I was there. So, maybe you will get more out of her than me. If you do, let me know what you can about the Akrotiri operations since DIA periodically asks my opinions and I haven't contributed shit yet."

"Sir, I may be able to help on that simply because I am a Klingon more or less by birth. It might give me a start point."

"Yeah, Jed told me you were a third generation Klingon. I wonder if that's why he sent you here — to figure out what's up in Akrotiri. He also said you were a S&R operator before that. Where?"

"Lots of places, sir. Bosnia, Kenya, and Afghanistan."

"See, there is more than enough to talk about today as we roll around Nicosia. For now, you have to get down the hall to Patty's office. I set up the appointment for 0930hrs. Done with your coffee?"

"For now, sir. There is always the microwave later."

"Too true."

They got up and left the office and walked down the hall.

The station offices started immediately after the MILATT spaces. Most of the doors were closed and locked with cipher locks, but the station front office was open and Williams walked in to be confronted by the office manager.

"Jack, what are you doing now?" The station office manager was a lady in her early 60s, nearly as thin as Williams, sitting at a desk surrounded by computer screens and two separate bowls filled with M&Ms — one bowl had nothing but red M&Ms and the second blue M&Ms. Behind her was a picture of a large family gathering with the office manager in the center of the picture.

"Debbie, we have an appointment with the Chief. This is Sue O'Connell."

Debbie stood up and shook Sue's hand.

"O'Connell? You wouldn't be Peter O'Connell's daughter would you?"

"Yes, indeed."

"You don't seem old enough. Peter was my boss in Laos."

"Oh, you mean my grandfather." Sue realized that was probably not the most polite way to say it.

"Sadly, dear, I do mean your grandfather. How is he?"

"He died last month. He was murdered in his home in Chautauqua." It was still hard to say that out loud.

"Oh, my god. I'm so sorry. We haven't been in touch for the last couple of years. I've been on the tdy circuit and bounced around a bit."

Williams interjected "Debbie is an Agency rover — she runs stations into the ground and then goes to another one."

"Jack, if you were older, I would do you harm." This was obviously an ongoing exchange.

"Sue, I move from station to station to cover for folks who need to be home for some reason. I've been here since just before Christmas and will stay through February. Are you PCS?" The Agency used the old military orders acronym for "permanent change of station" as a noun and sometimes as a verb meaning permanently assigned to a post.

"TDY, just like you Debbie."

"Then we need to go down and cause trouble in the Marine House while you are here, kiddo." Sue had to laugh. She had no doubt that Debbie could and would cause trouble in a Marine house anytime she wanted to do so.

"It's a date. I'm down in Akrotiri, but we will definitely cause some trouble together before I leave."

A raspy voice entered the conversation.

"If you are done distracting Debbie from her real job, I would like to talk to you."

Patty Dentmann was a square built, 50 year old woman with short gray hair wearing a well tailored blue suit, a men's Rolex watch, and sky blue pumps. She had three inch heels and was still only about 5'4." Sue could see why she was considered according to Williams "a force of nature." She had startling blue eyes which peered at Sue over her half glasses and standing in the door to her office with her hands on her hips, she seemed to be challenging anyone within shouting distance to a fight.

"Jack, you have done your part. I want to talk to Sue on my own. Like Debbie, I have some catching up to do with her about her family."

"Sue, you are on your own. Just remember, she might kill you, but I don't think she will eat you afterwards."

"Great, thanks."

Williams walked out of the office and Dentmann immediately shut the door and invited Sue into her office and to the pair of carved wooden chairs matched with a small table near the windows of her office.

"Debbie, can you get us some coffee and some water?"

"Right, Chief."

"It isn't her job to fetch coffee, but if I don't ask when we have visitors, she just hovers around until I ask for something. My previous experiences have been as chief of myself in various places where no one ever visited. I actually think headquarters sent her here to teach me how to be a chief in a place that actually matters."

Debbie returned with a small tray with two china cups and saucers, a polished brass coffee urn and a small sugar bowl and milk pitcher.

"See what I mean. I didn't even realize we had this stuff in the station."

"Chief, for now, just let me take care of this stuff for you and you can fake the rest."

"No respect either…"

"I respect you Chief, but I also need to make sure you don't do dumb stuff." Before Dentmann could say anything more, Debbie had left the room and closed the door behind her.

"Sue, I know you are probably tired of hearing this, but I trained at the FARM with your grandfather and worked on a CTC fly away team in Frankfurt when your parents were stationed there. Your mom taught me plenty as a peer in Frankfurt and then as my supervisor in CTC when she was in Headquarters as deputy chief of ops and I was a senior CTC case officer assigned to Cairo. She was definitely the heat."

Sue was tired of hearing about her family legacy, but this was the first time she had heard much about her mother, so she encouraged Patty to go on.

"Among other things, your mother was a chameleon when it came to personalities. Working against any macho culture — and believe me Arabs have a very strong macho culture — you have a choice. You can either be their mother or their sister — either way you have to be something other than the young female officer that you are. You must never play the role of peer because it will take you down the road of sexual innuendo that is not productive for the relationship and definitely dangerous to both you and your asset. I watched your mother play both roles. In fact, during one interview in a Lebanese police station, I watched her switch from mother to sister and back to mother. The Hizballahi wasn't sure what to do except he knew he needed to follow her instructions or he was going to be punished. It was brilliant."

"Didn't make it any easier being her daughter, I can tell you that."

"Most probably. I never saw anyone better at detecting deception."

Patty poured the coffee, added sugar to hers and then let Sue take a moment to pour her own.

"Enough pleasantries for now. I need you to come back here sooner or later because Jack and I need to introduce you to our counterparts in the Cypriot government."

"Oh, dandy."

"Actually, given your mission here, if your unit hadn't made that decision, I would have made it for them. The counterterrorism mission is one that is entirely compatible with our liaison partners and they have proven that they have plenty of diligence when it comes to either Sunni or Shia extremists. Well, you have to expect that given their history on this island and their anger over the Turkish invasion and capture of the northern part of the island in 1974. It is complicated, I figure this is an extension of a fight that started under the Ottoman Empire, but for now, it means we have a cooperative service." Dentmann paused for some coffee. "You are going to Akrotiri tomorrow?"

"Yes, Chief."

"OK, I'm not about to get in the way of your operational plans, but when you come to town next time, I want you to spend two nights here so we can get you integrated into the station. Also, I understand from Jack that you are taking over Dave Daniels' accounts, so you are going to be a regular visitor. Right?"

"Yes. My unit has decided that Cyprus is my work home for the next year or so. Even if they do move to Europe, Cyprus and the Eastern Med will be my turf."

"At the last COS conference back at the Asylum on the Potomac, I heard that 171 was trying to move to Europe to cut travel time. I think it is a great idea and I would support it. Sadly, we don't have any US bases here, but if they wanted to set up shop at the Army base at Vincenza or Sigonella Naval Air Station, I am sure I could talk the current COS into supporting the deal. We are old classmates and he owes me a favor or two."

"Sue, I am not going to ask you about 206 and 207 right now simply because you don't know anything more than I do from reading the files. Dave plays very close to the chest and I suspect you will find some surprises when you get to Akrotiri. As to 208, I want you to think hard about how to proceed on that case. Dave didn't want station or liaison to have anything to do with his developmental. I have tried to explain to him that none of us "own" our cases and we need to work together. He is too set in his ways to see any reason to collaborate and I just gave up trying. However, you do need to understand that if we worked together, I can facilitate 208's travel across the green line and that will mean you can move more quickly to turn this developmental into a recruitment. Just think about it."

"Check, Chief." Sue was pleased that Patty was thinking about her cases and seemed to be a more inclusive COS than she expected. It might be a function of her gender, her links to Sue's family, or simply being pleased to have Daniels leave country. In any event, Sue was willing to take whatever she could get.

Patty stood up and opened the door.

"Debbie, please get the rest of the folks in here now, OK?"

"Sure, Boss."

Patty closed the door and turned back to Sue. Sue was about to meet a different Patty.

"Now that we are all friends, I want you to know that I am seriously pissed that you have brought a GRU operation to my country and didn't even ask permission." Patty was leaning over other the table about three inches from Sue's face. Sue hadn't been intimidated for a long while — basically since her first years in the Army — but she was definitely intimidated now.

"I am going to wait until your Agency CI contact, the LEGATT and Jack come into the room before we talk about ELEKTRA, but I want you to know I am irritated." Sue could see that. "This doesn't mean I won't support the operation. It has enormous potential, but I just don't like surprises and this was a surprise party that I found was being hosted in my country without my permission. Bad form, Sue."

Sue was saved from trying to defend her position. There was a knock at the door and three men walked in. Debbie brought in another tray of coffee and water. It was clear this was going to be a fairly long meeting. Patty walked over to the windows and drew the heavy drapes. She then walked over to her desk, pulled out what looked to be a television remote control and pointed to the ceiling. The walls of the room started to vibrate with a low frequency hum like an old tube radio from the 1950s.

"OK, gentlemen. The coffee and water is on the table — help yourselves.

Stan began the meeting." Chief, I am Stan Cyzneski from the CIC. I am one of the team leaders for ELEKTRA. I know you have been briefed in on the case, so I will jump to the last night's operation.

"Last night?" Patty and Jack said the same thing at the same time and both looked at Sue in a less than collegial manner. If Sue could have pulled up the wall to wall carpeting and started digging a foxhole in the floor, she would have.

"Chief O'Connell was approached in the Lufthansa departure lounge in Frankfurt yesterday morning. The contact was eventually identified as a GRU agent based in Rome who was in transit on his way to Oslo. We had Sue under surveillance from the time she left 171 on Monday."

This time it was Sue who looked at Stan in a less than collegial manner. She had no idea that she was under surveillance — which was embarrassing for a former surveillance expert. Still, she hadn't expected surveillance from 171 to her home and then from her home to the airport.

"I boarded the same Lufthansa flight and I arranged to sit next to Chief O'Connell. She gave me some of the instructions she received in the lounge and we took it from there."

Stan sat back and turned to the Legal Attaché who was dressed in formal FBI uniform — dark suit, red tie, white shirt, black shoes. The only thing that prevented him from looking like a character out of a 1950s G-man story was his Brietling Navigator watch which hung loosely from his left wrist. The LEGATT turned to Sue.

"Chief O'Connell, my name is Supervisory Special Agent

Benjamin Nelson. I am the Legal Attaché here in Cyprus and part of the ELEKTRA team. We set up surveillance in the Hilton last night and captured the meeting between O'Connell and the GRU agent. He called himself Jan Bachmann. We haven't been able to identify his true name. He gave O'Connell a simple communicator — basically a pager with a simple tracking device that uses the cellphone network — which she is to use to set up a meeting sometime in the next ten days at her convenience. While the meeting was taking place, the GRU also bugged Ms. O'Connell's room. That's all we know at this point."

"My turn?" Patty was obviously working hard to control her temper.

She was civil but clearly angry. "OK, so ELEKTRA is a double agent operation using O'Connell as the bait. I understand from the call I got today that the goal is to establish the GRU procedures for handling an American intelligence officer and, secondarily, to feed them disinformation. I would have been better prepared if I had received this information sooner than two hours ago."

She paused to drink some coffee and, Sue was convinced, to count to 100 so that she didn't say something she regretted. Sue only got to 50 by the time the COS continued.

"I have a number of operational questions that are not clear in my mind. Who is going to be able to answer?"

"Not me, Chief." Sue realized that she should have kept quiet, but it just came out. Now that ELEKTRA was in play, she realized how useless her briefings had been so far. She was being treated like an asset. She got only enough to do the job and nothing more.

"I wasn't asking you, Sue. I suspect you don't know more than I do about any of this."

"Chief, I can offer a headquarters perspective if you like?"

"And, Lord knows, we all need a headquarters perspective, don't we gentlemen…" Patty had jumped on Stan before he had a chance to continue. After a few seconds where no one knew what was coming next, Patty said "If you would like to answer some questions, that would be lovely, Cyzneski."

"Yes, Chief."

"OK. Here are some basic questions I need answered:

Do you intend to actually do anything in Cyprus other than have one meeting?

Do you have any feed material you intend to give Sue or are you just going to let her make shit up. Personally, I hope the answer is you have feed material.

How big is your surveillance team and will you be able to avoid both Cypriot and Russian teams in country?"

Finally, how long do you think this is going to last? I ask that question because I have agreed to have Sue serve as the 171 case officer in Cyprus for at least the next year. I need to know if ELEKTRA is going to be part of my world."

Patty picked up her coffee cup, realized it was empty and reached for the coffee pot. Sue could see she would make a mess, so she reached the pot first and poured a cup for both Patty and herself. She then raised the pot and offered to fill other cups. Only Jack accepted.

"Chief, I don't have any good answers for most of your questions. I don't expect anything more than one meeting in Cyprus at this time. Since Sue is going to be able to set the meeting time and place, we will be able to expand our coverage to identify the larger GRU team supporting Bachmann. The ELEKTRA team in Washington is working on feed material which will be consistent with Sue's real world job. Bachmann made it clear that he wants Sue to detail her CT operations, so we are going to create some CT operations for her that will be consistent with the environment here in Cyprus. As to the rest of your questions, I don't have the answers at this time."

Patty focused her attention on Cyzneski and the LEGATT. "OK, gentlemen. Here is how I see this operation going down and I intend to make it clear to the ELEKTRA team that this is how it will go down in my country. I will get my techs to build some type of tag that we can sew into Sue's clothes so we know where she is at all times. I don't buy the GRU plan is to just wait for Sue to engage. I suspect they are going to pick her off the street at a time and place of their choosing. The tag or some other gizmo my geniuses are going to manufacture will have an alarm switch which will be available to Sue even if they have her handcuffed."

"Sue is not going to be surveilled. Not by you and certainly not by me. I have no doubt your team is good, but the Russians have more official and mafia assets in this country than we have people assigned to this embassy. We are not going to be able to be in the right place at the right time and anything less than that puts Sue at risk of being identified as a fink. Remember, we are dealing with the GRU here. They don't treat finks nicely. In fact, they rank right up with the old IRA in how they handle spies in their midst. We are going to have to trust Sue to gather the sort of information you need to make this a success." Patty was clearly done with the men in the room. She looked at Sue.

"You are going to go down to Akrotiri tomorrow and you are going to stay on base until we have the gear ready. No agent meetings until then, no matter what Daniels says. If he pouts or complains or whines or anything else, he can take it up with Jack or with 171 directly. I don't give a crap. Once the gear is ready, Jack and I will bring it down to you and we will have a meeting on base to clear up everything we can."

Patty turned back to Stan and the LEGATT. "Your ELEKTRA team needs to deliver feed material by next Monday. We should have some of the gear ready by then, so I can deliver it to her when I see her with the tag. Cyzneski, you and however many of your guys who came with you need to leave country in dribs and drabs as soon as you can. I don't need the local service or some Russian penetration of the embassy wondering why we have a large Agency contingent in country. I think if they notice the team they are going to do the math and figure out that Sue is a dangle and they are going to do some harm to her and then leave before we can stop them."

"Now, go do what you need to do and let me beat O'Connell up some more. If you need to talk to her later, just let Jack know. He is her boss."

Patty stood up and shook Stan and the LEGATT's hands, punched

Jack in the arm (hard) and opened the door. They left on cue. Patty closed the door and looked at Sue.

"I think that went well, don't you?"

If Patty thought that her meeting with the ELEKTRA team went well, then Sue figured her meeting with Daniels went equally well. The 171 office in Akrotiri was a 10 x 10 office built inside a shipping container placed in one of the more remote aircraft hangers used by UK Special Operations troops when they were called to deploy to the Eastern Mediterranean. No one looked twice when Sue arrived in her fatigues and red beret, got a ride from one of the RAF military police Land Rover Defenders to the hanger and knocked on the door of the shipping container. From the inside it looked like a small shipping container made even smaller by computer gear, a three drawer safe, a small weapons locker, two chairs and a desk.

As promised, Daniels was a very serious, very detail oriented case officer who was not real interested in the views of other people and especially a newly minted, female case officer. He decided on her arrival to make it clear that he was in charge of "his office." Based on everything she had heard, she was prepared for a bit of turf struggle as the experienced case officer intended to be sure that the new case officer didn't mess up his cases. Sue had been through enough rotations with S&R to understand how personal any special operation became over time and let him play the role of the boss for a time. After all, once he left, he would have nothing to do with the operations in Cyprus, so Sue figured it was not worth arguing about something that would change as soon as he hopped a military flight out of Akrotiri.

However, once Daniels heard that Sue was in a "wait" status until the COS and the MILATT cleared her for operations, Daniels transitioned from simply being an annoyance to being a real jerk.

"Do you think I give a shit about what Smith thinks about our relationship with the Station? He is so many time zones away, he has no visibility into our relationship with anyone. All he cares about is that we build this network, produce the kind of strategic intelligence that SOF needs and we don't get caught. Punto. The rest of this is not my problem."

At this point, Daniels made an error and put his right hand on Sue's chest. Sue never did figure out if this was to emphasize his point or to push her out of the way so that he could leave their box and get some fresh air. It really didn't matter. Sue had tried to be nice, she had tried to be professional and at this point, she decided to solve the problem the way that she would expect Massoni, Creeter and her other mentors in SOF would appreciate. Sue used her right hand to put Daniels' hand in a very quick and, she expected, painful wrist lock, spun on her prosthetic and placed her left hand on his right elbow. It would take very little pressure to break his arm at this point. Sue used this pressure to gently "guide" Daniels against the wall of the box that had a large map of Cyprus pinned to an even larger caulk board.

Sue leaned over and whispered into his ear. "Mr. Daniels. I don't know if you realize that it is a federal offense to assault a uniformed officer, especially a female officer. Now, I am assuming that you just got carried away in the heat of the moment and that you weren't thinking. So, if you have cooled down a bit, I will let go of your arm and I hope you will let us both move on. If not, we can continue to mix it up, or I can press charges. Whatdya think?"

Daniels was not in the best shape. Too many years, too many beers, and too little time in the gym. Still, he had at least 70 pounds on Sue and she had learned a long time ago that you didn't take any chances with a wounded male ego. She only let him go when he agreed. Even then, she stepped well clear of him when he turned away from his introduction to "Mr. Wall."

As he rubbed his right arm, Daniels said "I still don't like Nicosia having any input in my cases."

"Mr. Daniels, I understand that completely, but there are probably reasons why they want me to wait a bit and those reasons may have to do with operational security or some criminal threat that we just haven't heard about yet. Either way, it isn't going to be forever, just a couple of days as I understand it from Colonel Williams." Sue tried to put on her best conciliatory face and voice.

"Well, I'm scheduled to leave on the RAF flight the day after tomorrow. If they don't sort it out by then, you will just have to do a set of cold turnovers." Sue figured that that might be the best solution of all. She had heard of case officers who could be brilliant with assets and jerks with their peers, but somehow, she figured Daniels was just 100 percent jerk.

"I guess we will have to wait and see."

There was a ten day wait for the delivery of the specialized tag for Sue, so Daniels left. Sue was left with cold turnovers between her and 206 and, eventually, 207. While Daniels was a jerk, he was a professional and the communications plans he had for his agents was thorough and included plans for missed meetings and for introducing a new case officer "cold." Sue watched Daniels get on the RAF Hercules headed to the UK with nothing but relief.

Williams and Brody came down to Akrotiri on 08 February and delivered the package from Station. Sue was very impressed. The Station had purchased a very stylish leather jacket with a tight European cut, but just loose enough for Sue to carry her Glock on her right hip. It was dark brown leather and cut with two outside pockets and an interior zip pocket over her heart. Sue tried it on and it fit perfectly. There wasn't a ton of room inside the shipping container to move around, nor was there a mirror, but Sue was amazed at the fit.

Brody offered the answer. "Debbie bought it for you at one of the higher end leather shops in town. She has a calibrated eyeball for measurements. She said the she had been buying gifts for the wives of tdyers for years and you were too easy since she actually saw you instead of working from some picture."

Williams then challenged Sue to find the concealed tag and the concealed alarm trigger. Sue turned the coat inside out and started working the seams. There was nothing to reveal where it was.

"Patty told me ELEKTRA must have some juice back in Washington. They actually flew two techs to station to make this happen. One electronics guy and the senior seamstress inside the Agency concealments unit. Just for security reasons, none of us get to know where the tag is or how it works. All you need to know is that it is working right now and it is a signal emitter and a GPS tag that works off the mobile phone network here on the island. What is important is the buttons sewn at the cuffs of the jacket set off the alarm. All you have to do is force one off the jacket, it breaks the circuit and you are sending a GPS based alarm to Station, CIA headquarters, and the ELEKTRA team at the Hoover building. Do me a favor and don't accidentally break one of those buttons, OK?"

"Check, Boss."

"Now you get to go out and play and, without Dave Daniels. How cool is that?"

"Knowing Patty, she probably planned it that way."

Williams looked at Sue. "Ya think?"

Williams and Brody departed the next day and Sue did go to work. She used a non-attributable phone to make a pretext call to 206 to generate the meeting for sundown that night. It was a car pickup along the docks of Larnaca. Sue picked up a car from the inventory that 171 had on base, a very old, very well-maintained Mercedes C class diesel. She was wearing jeans, a sweater and her new jacket. Under the jacket was her Glock26 and under her sweater was a flat throwing knife similar to the one she carried in Afghanistan.

The run to the car pickup site was uneventful and Sue was pleased to see she made the turn onto the street just as the car clock turned 1817hrs — sunset according to the local maritime logs. 206 was walking toward her dressed in "smuggler chic." He was wearing a black leather jacket, black jeans, black boots. She knew 206 was a character, but the clothes and the swagger were almost enough to make Sue laugh. Too many film noir movies was all she could think as she pulled up.

As she approached 206, Sue had thrown a switch under the steering column which turned off the right headlight. It was their signal that this was the right car. Sue pulled up and rolled down the passenger side window.

"Where is the Maersk container section?"

"No Maersk on this dock. Only Haager."

Sue unlocked the door from the control panel on her side and 206 got in.

"Where is Mr. Jason?"

"He had a family problem, his father is dying and he wanted to get home to say goodbye."

For all of his tough guy pose, 206 immediately responded with a sigh and his eyes teared. "We all face that day. Inshallah, he will make it home in time."

"Our office arranged a jet for him. He will make it." The little white lies came quickly and easily for Sue. She wasn't sure if it was training or family history or what, but 206 seemed to be responsive and that was all she cared about.

"Hussein, my name is Maryam and I'm here to take Jason's place until he can return. I have worked here for about a year and over two years in Turkey. I want to keep our good relationship going while Jason is gone. He is like my brother and I must help him."

206 looked at Sue as she drove along the docks. She was wearing a knit watch cap and no one would think she was a woman. He noticed she had some sort of weapon on her hip and she drove better and faster than his previous contact. He would work with her — at least to test her skills.

"We can work together for Mr. Jason. I have promised."

"Thank you. Please tell me any information you were going to pass to Jason last week."

The rest of the meeting worked well and, honestly, Sue was surprised at how close it was to the simulations at the Farm. 206 offered a series of detailed reports that he had written down and loaded into his concealment. Sue had a duplicate concealment, a men's shoulder bag, which was empty save for his monthly salary. The meeting ended without a glitch and Sue headed home feeling quite pleased with herself.

Sue pulled into RAF Akrotiri back gate, showed her base ID and drove into the parking lot maintained for the UK SOF units. It was dark on most of the base, but in the SOF areas, it was well lighted and patrolled by yet another crew of RAF military police. This crew recognized Sue and after they did a check of the trunk and the underside of her car, she was allowed into the lot filled with four different 171 vehicles and twenty UK SOF vehicles which were covered in tarps. No UK SOF on base at this point, so the maintenance crew simply serviced the vehicles once a week and then covered the mix of Land

Rovers and sedans. Sue left the parking lot, gave a wave to the MPs as she headed off to the hanger.

Sue dropped her bag with the electronics (mobile phones and her ELEKTRA equipment along with her specialized leather jacket) into a locked wall locker outside the container. She then cleared and unloaded her Glock with the gun pointed into the clearing drum filled with sand — located next to the container. Sue had never had a negligent discharge with any firearm and she was not about to have one on this tour. She reholstered the empty firearm and then entered the container using her personalized code. She unhooked the paddle holster with the Glock, did the same with the two magazine holster on her left side and put them in her desk drawer. She turned on the coffee pot and sat down as the pot began to gurgle and fill with coffee.

"Let's get to work." Sue said to no one.

Sue never enjoyed the write up of reports as much as some of her classmates, but it wasn't a chore either. She had a good memory, had the notes written by 206 and the format for the reports were easy enough. 206 had identified a series of high tech switches and memory boards purchased by a legitimate Cypriot buyer that were being diverted by a separate Cypriot smuggler and delivered to a Lebanese cargo ship that was a known front for Hizballah and, by extension, the Iranians. 206 made it clear that the Hizballahis involved were not pawns in the sale. Instead they were working for a high payoff once the electronics arrived in an Iranian warehouse in Beirut. As 206 pointed out "No one works for free in this world. The risks are too great and the loyalties too weak."

After Sue finished the report and sent it out on the secure server, she set up the web camera in her computer and booked a secure video teleconference with 171. She wanted to let Smith and Massoni know that the cold turnover with 206 went well. While she was waiting for the time window for the conference, she made herself another pot of coffee and a bowl of oatmeal. Massoni's face popped up on the screen just as she was shoving a spoonful of oatmeal into her mouth.

"Nice to see you are taking care of yourself, Sue."

"Jim, it's the first meal in about twelve hours. I needed something to protect my gut from the second pot of coffee."

"Just drink a third pot and it will all be fine."

"I don't have a sergeant major gut, Jim."

"If you train, you can approach excellence." Sue nodded as she pushed another spoon of the oatmeal into her mouth. SOF rule number two — always eat when you can.

"By the way, are we using up satellite time to address diet and health and let me watch you eat?"

"Jim, I just wanted to report the meeting with 206 went fine and there is a report on its way for the brain trust."

"Excellent. I knew there was no good reason to listen to Dave Daniels. He wanted everyone here to think you couldn't make it happen. He is such a turd."

"No argument here, though if 206 is his creation, he certainly knows the trade."

"I know. It is a shame that he can't be consistently a shit. By the way, no one listened to his whining before he left country."

"More business: The next meeting is with 208 tomorrow evening on this side of the green line and then 207 next week near Larnaca."

"Check. By the way, we got a very nice note from the Klingons about this operator named O'Connell. You have some relative in country?"

"Nope. I'm the only Irish chick here. I just bonded with the Klingons when they heard I had to deal with Daniels. I suspect they were so happy to see him leave that they would have been thrilled with anyone short of Attila the Hun."

"OK, I will pass your message to the boss and warn the brain trust that your scribbles are on the way. Anything else we can do from this end?"

"Nothing I can think of Jim. I'll give you a shout after the meeting with

208. I know he is not recruited yet, so don't expect much but a report on building the relationship."

"Check. Watch your six. Out." The screen went blank.

Sue finished her oatmeal, pulled off her clothes and slumped into her sleeping bag on the cot. She was just too tired to drive over to her quarters on base.

Inside the container, it was always dark, so Sue slept well into the morning when she heard someone pound on the door.

"Daniels, get your body out of that container and face me like a man!" The container door was solid enough that that voice was muffled, but the pounding wasn't. Sue pulled on a set of sweats, her running foot, grabbed a wet one from the desk and ran it over her face and pushed her hair into something that probably resembled a red fright wig. She opened the door and faced a pair of British SOF operators in desert camouflage trousers and dark brown t-shirts. As soon as they saw her face, they stopped their noise.

Sue took charge of the situation. "Mates, I always wanted to know what the Brit term 'gob smacked' looked like. Thanks for the display."

"Sorry, we just want to see Daniels." The older of the two had finally recovered.

"Well, you are about a week late. Daniels is gone, replaced by me. I'm Sue O'Connell. Officially, Chief Warrant Officer O'Connell if this is an official visit. And, I was up all night, so I'm not terribly respectable. You SAS?"

The younger of the two said "You said that just to hurt our feelings, right? "

"SBS?"

The older added "Precisely. So, we stopped by to see if Daniels wanted a brew with his mates. My guess is you could use one."

Sue looked at her watch. 1030hrs. She had been asleep about five hours. She definitely could use a brew of strong English tea.

"Give me a half hour and then a brew would be brilliant."

"Right. The team shed is next door. Looks just like yours, but we have to fit five inside. You host the next brew up. See you in 30."

"Deal."

Sue went back into the container. She must have been tired last night — inside her hanger was a Gazelle helicopter and five Land Rovers in the space that had been empty last night. She grabbed her shower kit, a uniform on a hanger on the back of the door and walked to the small shower at the far end of the hanger. Sue had worked with the Brits in Bosnia and Afghanistan, so she was happy for the diversion, though she needed to keep track of the time. She needed to start prepping for her coffee with

208. Still a British brew would be worth the time.

The Brits were located in a similar looking shipping container that they referred to as their "porta-cabin" which was located in the next hanger on the base. When Sue entered, she realized how luxurious her accomodations were. This container had rucksacks, firearms, computers and cots for five operators. In the center of this crowded space, Sue saw a small folding table and six folding chairs. Five SBS operators were already working on tea and biscuits, dressed in black gym shorts, tan t-shirts and nylon sandals. It didn't exactly fit her image from English literature of a tea party, but she wasn't exactly dressed for a lawn party anyhow in her fatigues. In all honestly, she felt overdressed with this crew.

"Gents, thanks for the invitation. I really need a brew and to get out in the sun. It has been a long few days trying to learn to do Dave's work in a new country."

The operator who had pounded on her door a half hour ago opened the conversation as soon as he finished a long drink of tea. "OK, Chief, time for formal introductions. I'm in charge of these ruffians. I'm George. Around the table are Mac as in MacSween," a square shouldered, square headed man raised his hand that held a tea biscuit, "Paddy," a black haired, blue eyed, very sun burned man who had been pounding on Sue's door a half an hour before raised his mug, "Dozer" the largest man in the room with very short cropped blonde hair nodded just long enough to separate his mouth from his mug, "and Brian." Brian was a much smaller and younger version of Dozer. "Gents, this is Sue."

George passed a biscuit tin over to Sue. It was a green Harrods tin that had probably last seen London in the 1980s. Still, the biscuits seemed fresh and the brew they handed Sue was strong tea with more milk and sugar than she used, but certainly welcome after last night.

"When did you killers get in last night? I was up working until about 03 and I didn't hear you arrive."

Brian offered "We got in at 06 local, just off the plane from Basra.

First a good de-lousing, burned our uniforms, reported to the local Rupert and started to brew up some tea."

"Rupert?"

George responded."The Army officer in charge of this section of the base. You know Sandhurst graduates — always Rupert or some such posh name. They aren't from the Regiment, so we don't spend a lot of time learning their names. Just, "yes sir, no sir" and then get to the porta-cabin as quick as we can before he decides how he can use us on the base. How about you?"

"I had about a week with Dave…"

"Lucky you." Dozer obviously had something more to say about Daniels, but Sue realized she would have to wait to find out what. George gave him what could only be described in the US Army as the "stink eye" and he returned to his mug of tea.

"…last week and now I'm on my own doing the same sort of work. Mostly night work, so I suspect we won't be seeing much of each other."

"Depends, mate. Dave used to keep us on standby when we are here just in case there something a bit dicey. He didn't seem too handy with a firearm and, well, that's one skill we bring to the table wherever we are."

"Well, he and I come from slightly different backgrounds, so I'm pretty handy as well, but I won't turn down help if you have free time in the future. This is not exactly friendly turf outside, is it?"

"Too true. I understood from Dave that he was hunting the buggers that are helping the Iraqi Shia build IEDs. That isn't exactly a friendly crew, eh?"

Sue was now in dangerous turf. She didn't know how much Daniels had told his Brit neighbors. They were definitely allies and US and UK SOF were partners in Iraq and Afghanistan, but that didn't necessarily mean they had the need to know specifics of her work. Still, since Dave had already revealed the basics, Sue decided to follow guidance that she got from Massoni back in S&R: Sua Sponte which was one of the Ranger regiment mottos and was most easily translated by Massoni as "use your initiative!"

"Exactly right. So far, there hasn't been much of a threat that I couldn't handle but you never know. I come from an outfit that is, more or less, like your SRR so I'm more than a little used to shitholes."

"Daniels was a bit more of a café society guy as near as we could tell. Glad you are here Sue. Just remember, all you have to do is ask and we're ready to help."

"Thanks, George."

They made another round of tea and then everyone started going in different directions. Sue needed to get back in touch with 171 to sort out what Daniels had said to the Brits because she had read nothing at all about him using them as his quick reaction force. It sounded like a great resource, but she wasn't so sure Smith or Massoni would think so. Either way, she needed them to give her some left and right limits. After that, she needed to get ready for the meeting with 208.

It turned out that Massoni knew of the SBS team in Akrotiri and he was supportive of using them as Sue's QRF — "just in case" something went wrong. Daniels hadn't been clear about his relationship with the Brits on the base. Massoni still didn't have a good understanding of how the SVTCs worked, so his head filled the screen and he talked way too loud. Sue tried not to appear too amused.

"For once, I have to admit that Daniels was right, Sue. I was always concerned about the work next to the Green line with 208 and now that I know that Daniels was working with something resembling a QRF, I suppose I didn't need to worry as much. So, if you think you need the Brits and they are willing, I'm good with you making those decisions locally. The obvious problem is related to comms — how do you talk to these guys if you have a problem and, more importantly, where do they wait while you do the 208 meeting? As to their knowing what you are doing, well, that appears to be something that really doesn't matter anymore since they are clear about the project in Cyprus. If you can sort out the specifics on what they know, great. If you can't and they are still willing to help, I'm sure the Boss is going to support your decisions. However, I would not use them with 206 or 207 — you are in control in those cases since you are doing car meetings and I have no doubt you can handle a goober in a car."

"Thanks, Jim. I will go over to the Brits now and sort out what they are willing to do to help. Meanwhile, the next meeting with 208 is set for tonight at a café on our side of the Green line. I will let you know my assessment of the case tomorrow. All good?"

"Check, Sue. Out." Massoni's "big head" disappeared and the screen went to screen saver. Now Sue had to get to work. She had six hours to prep for the meeting and get across the island to the Green line. First thing was to talk to the Brits.

George was outside of the container sitting on a workout bench lifting weights when Sue walked up. "More tea already, Sue?"

"George, I wanted to ask you about how much you helped Dave when he was here."

"Sue, honestly, Dave acted more like a Rupert than any of us could stand. He didn't ask for anything, he insisted on plenty. Still, we were told that if he needed assistance, we were to help on this project. Too many of our mates are being maimed and killed because of the IEDs in Iraq. If we can stop that by disrupting the network, we need to do so."

"I would like your help, but I realize you have just come back from downrange, so if it is a bad time, I get it."

"Sue, you just need to ask and I'll tell you what we can do for you and what we can't do for you. I have a fair bit of latitude here, but I'm not going to start killing or snatching guys for you if that's what you need."

"George, I have a meeting set up on the green line tonight. The guy is not on our side...yet. I need to sort out if he is willing to help on the program, but I don't know if he is legit or was simply stringing Dave along for some other reason. I'm not really worried about him; I'm pretty confident I can take care of one guy. What I don't know is whether he is one guy or simply a guy leading me into an ambush on the Green line."

"You want a QRF, just in case?"

"Exactly."

"You have a car we can use? All we have is our Defenders and they are not exactly low profile."

"Sure. I have a Fiat which is a bit too small for you guys, a Mercedes sedan and a VW van. Mercedes or van, your call if you want to play — but I need your help tonight and we have to leave in about an hour."

"Too easy, Sue. The mates are already restless and this will keep them from busting up some pub on the base. Sidearms OK or do you need long guns?"

"If you have at least one long gun with a night scope, that would be useful." Sue pulled out a British army map of the island and laid it on the ground. "The café I'm meeting the guy is about 5km from the Green Line. I looked at the map and there appears to be a couple of overlooks along this road that parallels the Line, but honestly, I defer to you on how you would want to set up. I am meeting the contact at 1930hrs local."

"Sue, don't worry about our position. We'll figure that out. What about comms?"

"That's a problem. I don't have any comms except the mobile phone because I'm a singleton here. Nothing like the comms I had in Afghanistan."

"OK, we have some local kit that works up to about 5km. Nothing fancy, simple HF radios with remote mike and earbud. Will that work?"

"Perfect. I will be back in an hour for a final check with you and to pick up the comm gear. Deal?"

"Too right. It will keep us from causing too much trouble here and we always say a change is as good as a rest."

Sue left the airbase at 1530hrs using the old Mercedes as her vehicle. She had picked up the communications gear from the SBS team, did a quick commo check and then launched. George and the team would follow an hour later in the van. They identified an observation point that would be close enough to the café to observe the meeting but far enough away that anyone watching the café would have to be looking hard to find them. George and Dozer would be on a hillside overlooking the café with two long guns, one M4 and one sniper rifle. Mac, Paddy and Brian stayed in the VW on a roadside layby about a kilometer away. For the first time since she left S&R, Sue felt certain that she was safe.

Sue ran an indirect route to the café to assure she was not followed and she arrived at 1915hrs. It was a dusty little roadside stop that overlooked a valley and then another ridge line which served as the quasi-official border between the Republic of Cyprus and Turkish Cyprus. Sue could see the various UN peacekeeper patrol vehicles driving along the ridge. It was transitioning between dusk to full dark when she sat down at the outside table, placed a newspaper and a Michelin guide on the table and ordered a coffee. Sue realized that 208 would be expecting Daniels and that he was not recruited, but she hoped that 208 would recognize that she was in the right place at the right time, so with luck, he would sit down and ask her if she was waiting for Daniels.

1930hrs came and went. Sue realized that a contact who was not recruited might not realize that 1930hrs meant 1930hrs not "around dark." She waited. 1945hrs. Still no contact. The café was closing at 20hrs. She was the only patron and the owner was working as hard as he could to get her to realize he was ready to close down for the day and go home. He slowly, patiently folded the other tables and chairs and started to close the shutters with a degree of energy that probably did the ancient wood no good, but certainly made his point. 1950hrs. No contact.

Sue got up, walked over to the café and handed the owner her coffee cup and some change. So far, she hadn't had to use any English — she had ordered in French and thanked him in the same language. There was no reason to leave any trail of an American hanging out on the Green Line.

Sue keyed the mike. "Mates, looks like it is a wash. I'm going to RTB."

George's voice was in her ear. "Roger, Sue. Return to base. We will watch you leave and then follow."

Sue got to the Mercedes, opened the door and suddenly from the right front she saw 208. The lights from the café barely illuminated the parking spaces, but she certainly recognized 208 from the photo in her file. More importantly, she recognized that 208 was raising a small pistol in his right hand.

"Die, Jew." 208 fired the pistol. Sue instinctively dropped to one knee behind the car and the round zipped past. Later she realized the pistol must have had a suppressor because there was no noise except that sound of the bullet breaking the sound barrier near her head.

Sue stayed on one knee, drew her Glock and tried to decide what to do next. A gun fight across a Mercedes seemed a bit on the ridiculous side as well as dangerous since she didn't know if 208 was simply waiting for her to jump up or if he was moving around the car for a clearer shot. Sue opted for the former as the most likely and started to move toward the rear of the car. At the same time, she keyed the mike.

"Ambush!"

George's voice was calm in her ear. "Roger. We see the little shit. He is still at the front of the car. If he moves, Dozer will cap him. Meanwhile, you need to get farther away. Move away from the car and toward the highway. He moves, he's dead. He tries to engage, he's dead. Check?"

"Check."

Sue worked her way along the back of the Mercedes and then sprinted across the road to the brush along the far shoulder. She heard another round pass over her head. 208 was obviously an amateur. No one had taught him to aim low at night. Sue heard what sounded like a backfire from some distance. One shot from Dozer.

Dozer's voice in her ear was just as calm as George's. "Shooter down, Sue."

Sue stood up and looked at the scene behind her. 208 was sprawled over the hood of the Mercedes. He wasn't moving and wasn't likely to move anytime again.

Sue keyed the mike. "Thanks, mate."

An agitated voice in her ear bud."Sue, behind you!"

Later, Sue couldn't remember the blow that came from behind. It must have been a hand strike of some sort because it was sharp enough to take her in one blow, but didn't open the skin around her neck. She wasn't bleeding, that was for sure.

She woke up in a dark, confined space. She had duct tape around her ankles and wrists and then her elbows and knees were roped together with some sort of nylon cord so she was in a fetal position on her left side. When she moved her head, she hit a very hard, unforgiving metal surface. It felt like she was in some sort of metal box. Hitting her head simply made her dizzy and nauseous. She recognized the signs of a concussion. The good news was she was still in her clothes and that meant that so long as she kept calm, she likely wouldn't start down the dangerous spiral of shock.

Sue decided to spend a little time exploring her surroundings. She could still move her hands, sort of, and her foot, sort of. Her prosthetic hurt — a lot — so that meant that at the very least, she didn't have any serious injury. She could feel her toes on her right foot, so no spinal damage. She could also feel the fact that her holster was empty as was the magazine carrier on her left side and the radio clipped to her belt was gone. As near as she could tell, the one thing that wasn't gone was her small knife hanging around her neck under the sweater and her long sleeved t-shirt. Better still, she still had her jacket on.

Sue used a rough edge of the floor of the metal box to pop one of the buttons off the sleeve of the jacket when her world was flooded with light. The transition from complete darkness to a spotlight on her face was nearly as nauseating as when she hit her head. She looked away from the light and realized that her metal box was the trunk of a car. The transition from darkness to light was caused first by raising the trunk lid and then turning on the spotlight.

"Good evening, Ms. O'Connell. I hope I didn't hit you too hard. The idea was to incapacitate but not to damage. I want you quite conscious."

Sue would have argued about full consciousness. The voice was familiar, but her brain wasn't working all that well. Scrambled. She could understand the words, but she wasn't entirely certain that she could say anything.

"One of the results of this type of concussion is that it will take you some time to speak. Don't worry. All your mental skills will return, eventually."

Sue still couldn't see the face behind the spotlight. Her frustration mounted as she tried to sit up. A mix of nausea and restraint. She was somehow tied to the trunk as well as roped and taped into place.

"The paracord that has you forced into that position is also tied to the bolt that used to hold a spare tire in this wreck. We had to take the tire out to make sure you could fit."

Sue was fighting fear. Adrenaline can be a friend or an enemy. If you let the adrenal glands empty, you get tunnel vision, lose any sense of hearing and become a victim. Fight or flight. If you can't do either, then you go into mental collapse. Literally, you can't think straight and you can go into shock and cardiac arrest for no reason at all. Her training at Ft. Bragg at the survival, evasion, resistance and escape school came back to her. Take a few deep breaths. Focus on your pulse and your breathing. Take a few seconds to control your limbic system. Survive!

"Very good, Ms. O'Connell. I want you to live. No need to let shock take you too soon. Oh, and by the way, your team of shooters couldn't follow us. I kept them busy while you were moved here. Now, they have the entire island to search for you, but not much time."

Finally, it came to her. "Bachmann."

"Very good, Ms. O'Connell. That's right. You know me as Bachmann. I was supposed to be your GRU contact. You were supposed to be my penetration of SOF. We all know that your side of the story was fiction. Would it surprise you to know that my side of the story was fiction as well?"

Sue continued her internal fight. Shock comes in many forms and she needed to focus on her breathing and her surroundings. The best news so far was that if Bachmann wanted to kill her, she would be dead already. In the real world, villains didn't gloat over their victims until help arrived. They simply killed their victims and left. So, she was alive which meant he wanted her to be alive. That meant they intended to take her to some place for interrogation. One step at a time, she said to herself. Remember SERE school. One step at a time. Keep your wits, don't irritate your captor. If you want to stay alive, remember… your wits. "Bachmann, why?"

"First, the name isn't Bachmann. But you already knew that. And I am not in the GRU. I suspect you didn't know that. Bachmann was GRU and supposed to be your contact, but he is dead and buried nearby and as you can see, I am very much alive. I am not even part of the Russian special services. I am a very successful businessman who works in the gaps and seams of this world you think you understand. It is a dangerous world as you suspected when you realized I am missing a hand."

Bachmann paused. Sue couldn't see his face, he was still a shadow behind the spotlight.

"One last thing, Ms. O'Connell before I say goodbye. My name is Nikolai Beroslav." Sue had trouble understanding what that meant. Beroslav? As in the family that her grandfather thought had a vendetta against him?

Beroslav turned the spotlight away from Sue just enough so she could see his face. He leaned over the trunk lid.

"Now, I have to say farewell. I have real work to do. This was simply a distraction, but a useful one to be sure. I hope you find your last few hours uncomfortable. I don't honestly think anyone is ever going to find you to grieve over your body. Very much like my grandfather."

The trunk lid slammed shut. Sue was so surprised, she couldn't even shout. She did hear Beroslav walking away.

Sue had expected the car to either explode or to be filled with bullets in the few minutes after Beroslav left. Instead, there was only silence and darkness. Sue returned to her breathing exercises for several minutes after she realized that she was not about to die, at least not yet. After she calmed down enough to think relatively clearly, she started down a checklist.

What is his plan?

If the car is located in some remote place, he expects me to starve to death. If remote enough, he doesn't expect anyone to find me even after I am dead.

What is the best-case situation?

George and his team observed what was going on and may be searching for me. Assuming the Patty's signal system is working, I have triggered a signal which can be tracked.

What is the most likely situation?

If I am to survive, I have to get out of this myself.

Sue focused her attention on some basics. First, she needed to free herself from the bonds. She slowly closed herself into an even tighter fetal position. When she did that, she could just reach the thin chain around her neck. She worked the chain slowly out of her sweater. The knife sheath pulled out of the front of her bra and slowly worked up her chest and then out of her sweater. She had the knife.

Even with a knife your hands, you have to be careful as you try to cut duct tape on your wrists. Too little pressure, the duct tape doesn't cut. Too much pressure and you have just slit your wrists in a perfect way to commit suicide. Sue was just happy Beroslav didn't use flex cuffs. Getting out of them with the knife would have meant blood even if she did it right and she couldn't spare any right now.

Once her wrists were free, she could cut the bonds linking her elbows and her knees. Finally, the duct tape on the ankles. Sue was covered in sweat at this point and decided it was time to take a breather, return the knife to its sheath and the sheath back under her sweater and then return to deep breaths. She was still locked in a trunk. And, Sue realized she didn't know for sure if Beroslav was just waiting outside to shoot her as soon as the trunk lid opened. Just to be sure, she pulled another button off the opposite sleeve of the leather jacket. No telling if the beacon would work, but she believed in the old military adage of "two is one and one is none." She had been tossed into car. There was no guarantee that the wires linking the buttons and the beacon weren't damaged.

Next step. Turn to face the front of the car. Sue had no idea what sort of car trunk she was in, but most cars were not all that well insulated between the trunk and the rear seats. Many European cars had release locks to allow skiers to pass a ski bag through the trunk into the rear seat area. It was dark and she needed to be careful. Trunks were never made for comfort and just as with the knife, a wound at this point could be the beginning of the end. One hand at a time and from one side of the trunk to the other, Sue ran her hand along the trunk lid and along the side facing the passenger compartment. She was relieved to find a knob that appeared to be linked by a cable to the back seat of the car. She pulled the knob gently. The seat in front of her popped down and the trunk was no longer pitch dark. The night sky was visible from the right rear passenger window.

"Well, that's progress."

Sue moved her hand down near her knees. Another nob. Another pull and now the left rear passenger seat popped down. There was enough room now for Sue to slide out of the trunk into the passenger compartment without showing her head or torso out the back window. She worked hard not to move too quickly and to keep her balance so that anyone looking at the back of the car would not see any shifting of the car. While laying on the floor, she replaced the seats in the locked position one at a time. At that point, she realized she was in her Mercedes and sitting in the front seat was 208. Dead as he could be, in the driver's seat, keys in the ignition.

Now the good news was that the Mercedes had a number of concealments built into it courtesy of Marconi at 171. Mostly, they were designed to hold documents and, possibly a small laptop computer in a pinch. However, Sue had found the one concealment at the back of the arm rest between the front seats that was just big enough to hide a Sig Sauer Mosquito .22 automatic that was one of the three pistols normally residing in the weapons locker at the base. She checked and the Sig was still there, resting quietly in its holster. Sue quietly cycled the slide on the Sig and clipped the holster inside her pants. Not a lot of rounds and what rounds it had were in .22 caliber, but at least a few rounds of hollow point ammunition that she could share with any visitor who might be watching.

"OK, kiddo. Now what?" Sue realized that sooner or later, she would have to take the risk and look out one of the windows of the car to determine if there was anyone out there watching and waiting to see if she got free. She looked at her watch. 0300hrs. She did some math in her head. The gunfight had been at 2000hrs yesterday. She was hit around that time. Depending on how long she had been unconscious and where she was, Beroslav would have been waiting for her to regain consciousness for at least three hours. She hadn't looked at her watch until she cut her hands free at 0230hrs. At least three hours until daylight.

Sue decided that it was worth the risk to take a peak out — first out the front windshield and then out the back. Out the front was relatively low risk because she could lean up against 208's body and peer just past his head. She realized that they were parked in a junk yard filled with cars. The Mercedes was just one of dozens sitting on the lot. Next out the back window. Again, more cars silhouetted against the night sky. No sign of life. Of course, that's what it is supposed to look like when a sniper is waiting for his prey.

Sue decided to move at 0400hrs. She spent about 10 minutes before the move working some basic muscle stretches. She needed to be as limber as possible in case she had to run as soon as she opened the door. She had checked and the slot between the right side of the Mercedes and the next car was just enough room to open the door and roll out. After that, she would work her way toward the front of the car and see what happened after that. No way to tell, so she just decided to go for it.

Sue felt a bit foolish afterwards because it was clear in the first few minutes of her effort that the junk yard was as abandoned as you would expect any junkyard and any cemetery in the last hours of darkness. Once clear that she was alone, Sue went back to the Mercedes and pulled out a red filtered LED flashlight from the glove box. She walked around the car and looked underneath the car. Sure enough, she found what she had expected to find. Beroslav had wired the car so that if anyone started the car or even moved it, a balance switch would ignite a small charge and the gas tank would explode.

Sue turned to 208 next. "Well, it doesn't look like we are driving out of here tonight." Sue decided to check 208 — both for information and, possibly for a small IED. After several minutes, she didn't find an IED, but she did find another pressure switch between 208 and the driver's seat. Beroslav hadn't had time to conceal any of this work, but then again, he probably didn't expect anyone but the junkyard attendant or possibly a policeman to check the car in the morning.

Sue did find 208's identification papers, his wallet with a mix of different currencies, and a notebook in his breast pocket. Luckily, George's shot had been a head shot, so death was instantaneous and 208 didn't spend much time bleeding. All of the documents were intact, including a letter. Sue had to give Beroslav credit, he was thorough. The letter was in English on stationary from a Gaza hotel.

Habibi,

You have an appointment with an American tonight. You are warned — your "American" is an Israeli. They will capture you tonight and take you to their prison. The Israelis are sending a woman so you will be unafraid. Do not go. If you do go, you must protect yourself. They will do anything to stop you.

We can help you to safety. Meet us tomorrow in Kyrenia at Pier 117A. We will take you to safety.

Your brothers

Beroslav set up a perfect knight's cross gambit. If 208 had followed these instructions, Sue would have waited and Beroslav would have arranged his own ambush. If 208 decided to take the fight to the Americans and the Israelis, then 208 would handle Sue and Beroslav would handle 208. Luckily, Sue had invited the SBS to the party and that meant Beroslav had other problems to deal with before he got Sue into the trunk of the car. One thing was certain, the Mercedes and 208 were going to stay right where they were for now. Sue knew the basics about military and terrorist explosive devices, but this sort of threat was more than she was going to handle in the dark with a red filter flashlight and her knife. Since she was going to walk out, Sue checked the car to see what, if anything had been left behind by Beroslav. He had checked the obvious places — glove box, map slots on the door and the back seats, but had missed all of the concealments. Sue made a mental note to thank the 171 team when she got back home. The concealments delivered a pocket knife, another magazine for the Sig, and her military ID and credentials authorizing her residence at RAF Akrotiri. She still had some Euros in her pocket, so life was as good as it was going to be. Sue walked out of the junk yard hoping that she would be able to sort out her location sooner rather than later and start to head back to her new home at RAF Akrotiri.

It was just after dawn when a three-car convoy arrived to pick up Sue about 5km from the junkyard. She recognized the first vehicle. It was her van from Akrotiri filled with her SBS partners. The second vehicle was the armored Suburban driven by Brody with Williams and Dentmann in the vehicle along with an individual with a laptop open in front of him. The third vehicle was a Land Rover Defender with RAF Akrotiri plates. It had three men and a woman in plain clothes.

The van hadn't rolled to a complete halt when George was out of the van. He was dressed in hiking boots, jeans, a Barbour rain coat and a wool watch cap. He looked relieved, worried, and peeved all at the same time.

"I know, I owe you a round at the base club."

"Sue, I suspect you owe more than that, but still we are happy to see you vertical."

"Hey, tell Dozer the shot was brilliant and then ask him why he didn't shoot the bastard that hit me." George smiled and Sue smiled back.

"He was afraid he would hit you. The bastard was dressed in black and approached in a crouch. We didn't see him until he hit you. After that, we got into a bit of trouble all by ourselves with some locals. Villains with small arms. Not hard work, but distracting. By the time we had sorted it out…"

Williams and Dentmann had arrived and they were already giving Sue a piece of their mind before they were even in earshot of their newest operator on the island.

"Before we get too far into the ass chewing, Boss, I need to let you know that my Mercedes is in a junk yard about 5km away and it is very much wired to explode the first time anyone tries to move it. Do you think we might want to let the authorities know?"

George looked at Sue and then at the two Americans.

"If you don't have any trouble with me helping on this, I can call the Akrotiri anti-terrorism unit which has a bomb squad. They can come up here in a Gazelle in about an hour and we can call it a terrorist bomb threat. It helps explain the noise to the locals. Meanwhile, we can secure the site."

Dentmann spoke to George. "SBS?"

"Yes, governor. Station commander?"

"Got it in one. Please proceed. I will call your chief at Akrotiri and we will smooth out the rest of the story on the fly. Of course, it might be in everyone's best interest if the bomb squad determined that it was safer to blow the car in place than to try to defuse it. What do you think?"

George got the message.

"Ma'am, I think that makes good sense. No reason to risk anyone's life just to save an old Mercedes placed inside a junkyard. The squaddies will know what to do."

Dentmann nodded.

"Meanwhile, we are going to have to get out of here pronto. Jack, you and Brody take care of Sue for me if you would. I will engage the folks in the Defender, explain a bit and then we will regroup with them back in Nicosia tomorrow at 0900hrs. I reckon it makes sense that we will meet in the British High Commission since our newest secret agent in Cyprus has now laid bare our operations to our best allies. I do want to see Sue tonight before we start the show. Just let me know when. Sound like a plan?" Sue didn't think Patty was actually asking for approval. Jack and Brody were already making an approach to Sue. George had taken off the watchcap on his head and was rubbing what little hair he had on his head. Still, he was smiling so that was a good sign.

Sue was ready to get in the Suburban as soon as possible, but thought she might have one thing to add. "Chief, the car that is wired also has a dead body in it.It might be convenient if everyone was convinced that he was the terrorist and the SBS team eliminated the threat before he did something terrible on the island. Oh, and by the way, there might be another car there with a body. I don't know if it will be rigged with explosives or not."

"O'Connell, you are starting to demonstrate some skills after all. The team from Five in the last car will think that works well. They always want to show the British are doing bad things to bad people anywhere they can." Dentmann was already walking toward the Defender. She turned to look at Sue.

"Well done and, by the way, I'm glad you aren't enjoying a dirt facial."

"Thanks, Chief." Williams came up to her and gave her a hug. Brody was out of the Suburban and did the same. Brody also had a stainless steel thermos travel cup which smelled of strong, over-brewed coffee. He handed it to Sue and she was very pleased to take it. Sue was tired, but it was clear there was plenty of work left to do before she could get some sleep. Coffee would have to do.

Colonel Williams worked hard that afternoon to keep Sue away from all the madness that she would face the next day. He knew that if Sue was just "hanging around" the Embassy, Patty would insist on a one on one with Sue. He knew the Patty-Debbie team well enough to know that if they got Sue alone for an hour, they would know everything before anyone else. He and Brody drove Sue down to Akrotiri so that she could pick up her dress uniform and some additional clothes in case she had to stay more than one day in Nicosia and he intended to put Sue in the small apartment on the embassy compound that served as visitor's quarters. It was nothing more than a room with a desk and a bed and a bathroom, but it would mean that Sue wouldn't have to start early the next day to get to the big conference at the British High Commission compound.

On the drive down, he decided to do his own debriefing of Sue. As Brody drove them in the armored Suburban, Williams and Sue rode in the back.

"Sue, I need to ask some questions that are for my own bureaucratic survival in Nicosia as well as to protect you from the Klingons. I realize you would prefer to talk to Jed first, but I'm not sure we can set up a secure VTC when we get back."

Sue took a moment to gather her thoughts. She had been silent for most of the trip so far with plots, plans and ideas rolling around her head like bees swarming out of a bee hive.

"Sir, here's what I recommend. To be fair to my commander, I would like to have a chance to give him the story the same time I give it to you. I can set up a VTC in my quarters on Akrotiri and you and Brody can sit in on the VTC. That way, if the COS goes high and right when we brief her tonight, at least my boss has a little time to protect 171 from the blast radius. OK?"

"Sue, that's good for me."

They rode the rest of the way in silence. Brody had a full thermos of coffee and sandwiches that he had made ahead of time, so Sue used that time to eat and, for a brief time, to doze as the Suburban blasted along the main highway to Akrotiri.

On arrival, Sue set up the VTC, plugged in two headsets — one for her and one for Williams and shortly there were two heads jammed into the computer screen with Smith in the front and Massoni in the back. She was certain that their screen looked the same: her in the front, Williams in the back. Brody was outside in hanger. The VTC started well.

"Shit, O'Connell, did you really intend to start killing people right away in Cyprus? I thought you would wait a few weeks at least."

Clearly, 171 headquarters knew some of the story. Sue had to fill in the details and get some guidance. It was 1400hrs in Cyprus which meant it was ten hours since she left the car. Enough time to figure out what would make sense and what wouldn't make sense. The rest would have to be a discussion that she would have with her mom at some future date. It worked against the grain to mislead all of these men supporting her operation, but, honestly, she didn't see any way not to give them some misdirection. Otherwise, she would have to say that her operation was disrupted as a result of a multi-generational conspiracy to wipe out the O'Connell family because of actions conducted in World War II. Now, wouldn't that make sense? Not really.

"Sir, in all honesty, I didn't kill anyone. I was ready to do so, but my SBS colleagues did the shot."

"SBS?"

"OK, let me start at the beginning."

Massoni chimed in. "Boss, I approved the use of the SBS team just in case. I just didn't get around to tell you… yet."

The little face in the front of the screen reached up and smacked his head. "It is a conspiracy of silence around here among you madmen."

"Sir, you ready?"

"O'Connell, go ahead before Massoni tells me he recently dispatched a team to the Kremlin to steal Russian nuclear secrets."

Massoni, ever the wise guy, decided he would add one last thing.

"Boss, I promise, I was going to tell you about that later today." This time, Smith grabbed a rolled map on his desk and smacked Massoni in the head. On the computer screen, Sue could not tell if it was a light tap or not.

"Sir, the deal was as follows. 208 had a note in his pocket that suggested to him that Dave and I were Israelis setting him up for rendition to an unspecified location. 208 came to the meeting intending to kill me and then cross the line into Turkish Cyprus. The SBS team had overwatch on the meeting and their sniper took out 208 after he sent two rounds in my direction."

"OK, that sounds reasonable. Well, at least reasonable for an O'Connell operation. Now what is this I heard about you in the trunk of our Mercedes and the fact that they had to blow the Mercedes up to cover up the entire deal?"

"Boss, that's a little complicated and here is where I get into trying to figure out stuff rather than telling you anything I can prove."

"Go ahead, O'Connell. Anything you tell me is better than anything I am going to hear from the Klingons."

At that point, Williams interjected.

"Jed, the Klingons don't know anything yet. We made sure you heard the real story first. We will have to brief them later today, but it should give you time to do some damage control there."

"Brilliant. Damage control is not my forte, but OK. O'Connell, what are you waiting for?"

"Boss, just about the time that I heard the SBS shot, a guy hit me from behind. The SBS guys said he was dressed in black and approached in a crouch in the classic sentry take down. They couldn't see much. They were then engaged by a small number of shooters and lost track of me. I don't know what happened to the shooters, I haven't had much time to talk to them."

"O'Connell, I don't give a shit if they killed them and buried them on some beach in Cyprus, I want to know what happened to you."

"Just trying to give you the picture Boss."

"Painfully slowly, I might add."

"OK, so I wake up in the trunk of the Mercedes. I'm tied up and roped to the trunk. Around 0200hrs, the trunk opens up and I'm hit with a spotlight. The individual there doesn't say anything other than imply ELEKTRA is compromised, the supposed GRU handler is dead and then the individual slams the trunk lid down on me. I assumed he intended to shoot me while I was in the trunk, but he didn't. I figured at that point, he just intended to let me starve to death. I worked my way out of the trunk through the back seats and I find 208's body in the driver's seat. I'm in a junkyard about 10km from the Green Line. I recovered my kit and my backup gun from the car concealments and then did a quick exam of the car. I identified that it was wired to explode if I moved 208, if I started the car or if anyone from the junkyard had moved the car more than a few inches. I had previously triggered the emergency beacon that was attachéd to my coat. I started walking and the team picked me up about 5km from the site."

"So, bottom line. We lost 208 to someone who wanted to compromise the operation and it looks like whoever did that also decided to compromise ELEKTRA, but actually we don't know crap other than we have lost a firearm and nearly lost you. Does that sum up the situation?"

"Yes, sir."

"One last question, O'Connell. What did you do to Daniels?"

"Sir?"

"Daniels was supposed to report to 171 yesterday. No dice. We checked all flights including Air Force and commercial from the UK. No dice. We know he arrived at RAF Lakenheath and headed to London. We don't have any evidence he left any UK airport headed to anywhere. I am not ready to engage CI or the Brits to track his travels using the CCTV system, yet. I just figured along with disrupting our relationship with the Brits and the Klingons and probably the Republic of Cyprus, you decided to help us with Daniels as well."

"Not me, Boss. I saw Daniels get on the RAF Hercules and never looked back."

Williams spoke. "Jed, I can confirm that Daniels left the island. The Brits confirmed that manifest and sent me a courtesy copy. What he did when he landed in the UK is anyone's guess."

Smith responded. "Perfect. Well, O'Connell, the only good news you have offered is that we no longer have to work this ELEKTRA stuff. Oh, and of course, the fact that you don't have any additional holes in your body is a good thing as well."

"Thanks, Boss."

"Jack, you take care of O'Connell out there. Make sure the Klingons don't get too stupid and we'll have to see if we need to pull her out. At this point, I don't know enough to know. Do you?"

"Jed, I think as long as the Brits hold up their end of the bargain and take credit for stopping a terrorist attack, then there shouldn't be any trouble on the island. I can't say what the COS is going to say."

"Really, and I thought that was your job to sort?"

"Jed, you got it so easy there in your warehouse. You want to trade places?"

"No dice, kid. I like my little world even if I have to put up with Massoni." Massoni made a face into the camera.

"OK, Jed. Enough small talk, I have to get O'Connell back to Nicosia, she definitely needs a shower and a change of clothes and then she gets the chance to explain her story to the COS. All before we call it a day. Unless you have something else for her, I say we shut down."

"Jack, let me talk to O'Connell alone for five and then you can let her get clean and ready for the Klingon inquisition. Thanks for helping on this one, brother."

"No worries, Jed. I'm going to unplug now. You definitely owe me a beer when I get back to CONUS."

"At least one, Jack, at least one."

Williams unplugged his headset, laid it on the desk, and walked out of the container.

"O'Connell, I know there is more to this story than you just told me, but honestly, I think it is as good an official story as we can get out of this mess. Save the rest of the story for your next face to face with us. Do not vary from this story when you talk to the COS because if you do, you will sink Jack and then I will choke you when you get back here. Got it?"

"Yes, sir."

"One last thing. I'm very glad you are OK, Sue. I personally attribute this entire shit storm to this double agent crap which was none of your doing. Plus, I would hate to make Massoni do the paperwork if you were hurt again. He can't spell for shit."

"So unfair, Boss. I definitely can spell shit."

"Sue, get cleaned up and just ride this one wherever it takes you. Don't argue with the COS or any of the other yoyos involved in ELEKTRA. If we can keep you in Cyprus, great. If not, then I have more than enough work for you in other places. By the way, don't mention the news about Daniels disappearance. It will only get the spy catchers involved before we know what the heck happened. For all I know, he is asleep with some sweetie in London."

"I would doubt Daniels had any sweetie anywhere, Boss."

"Well, I still don't want this getting out until we know what we are dealing with on the Daniels front. Let the MILATT know as well. Got it?"

"Check, Boss." The screen went blank.

Shit. That was all Sue could think. Shit, shit, shit. No good answers, lots of leads running nowhere and plenty of dangerous possibilities. Was Beroslav really Beroslav or was he Bachmann? Was this a GRU plot or a vendetta? If the latter, what would happen when Bachmann didn't turn up? Would the GRU assume he defected? What would happen if they ever found Bachmann's body? What if Beroslav really was Bachmann and… well, it just got stranger and stranger.

Years ago, her grandfather had said that James Jesus Angleton used a line from T.S. Eliot to describe counterintelligence operations as "a wilderness of mirrors." "Whether true or just a story about a man he hated, for the first time, Sue realized how well the line matched the world she lived in now. Worse still, there didn't seem to be any way out or any way to return to the clarity she had as a SOF operator in S&R. In S&R, they were simply finding bad guys, fixing them in place and letting others in SOF handle the finish. But, the great thing was there was always some sort of finish — good or bad. Sue couldn't see any good conclusion or, for that matter, any conclusion. The ideas racing in her head offered many routes but no clear solutions. The one thing she did know now was she didn't have time to work out the best possible route because Williams and Brody were waiting to take her to Nicosia.

The meeting at the British High Commission was formal and Sue spent most of her time listening to Dentmann and Williams outlining the current situation and what they saw as the way forward. She had worked with British SOF in the past, but not a "liaison" session. She was initially introduced to them in Bosnia before selection and then in Afghanistan. The relationship among the uniformed SOF units was cooperative, competitive but focused on getting the mission accomplished. In the High Commission, it was clear that getting the mission accomplished was only one part of a larger chess board where strategic intelligence issues were as much a part of the discussion as the local issues related to identifying the links between the Hizballah, Iran, the Iraqi Shia militias and the IEDs that were killing US and UK troops in Iraq.

In Dentmann's briefing to her British colleagues from the Secret Intelligence Service (SIS but still referred to by its World War II name MI6 or 6), the British Security Service (BSS but still referred to by its World War II name MI5 or 5) and SBS started by framing the entire set of events from the previous two days as an intelligence operation gone bad with someone inside the Shia or Sunni extremist networks in Turkish Cyprus determined to kill an American intelligence officer. Dentmann then opened the discussion for comments and recommendations on the "way forward." Sue became aware at that point that the Station and the British intelligence team were also running parallel operations against the same networks. "Need to know" was all Sue could think of as she heard for the first-time source names and networks discussed and an overlay on a map of Cyprus showing the dozen different cases involved. She further noted that neither 206 nor 207 were listed on the map. The only 171 case discussed was the failed targeting effort against 208. It might mean that Dentmann and Williams intended to keep her on the island and Sue wanted that to happen for one reason. She intended to find out if Bachmann/Beroslav was still on the island and, if so, to offer to repay his hospitality with some of her own.

The meeting ended with Dentmann thanking her British colleagues for their considerable assistance in keeping Sue alive and framing the "flap" and the subsequent Cypriot investigation along a route that would make it easier for the two services to continue their operations. Sue had little to say during the meeting other than describing the actual shootout with 208 and her escape. She wasn't sure the Brits believed the story, but they seemed to accept the fact that this was the only story they were going to get, so Sue's report was accepted with a few nods, some comments about her bravery and resilience and then, as far as the meeting went, she was simply part of the furniture.

Later in Dentmann's office, over a cup of strong Turkish coffee, Dentmann looked over the table at Sue and Williams and let out a long sigh.

"So, Jack, do you think they bought the story?"

"Nope."

"Will they do anything about it?"

"Nope. Based on the cover story you concocted out on the highway, they end up looking like heroes to the Cypriot government and they know you aren't going to tell them anything else, so for now they will accept it. The real question is will they continue to work with us on SLINGSHOT and with Sue after this."

"I agree. We will know soon enough because I am going to recommend that we keep Sue here. She has a relationship with 206, she has to get the turnover with 207 and she has a very secure location at Akrotiri that allows her to conduct operations there without any linkage to the station or your office — which gives us some degree of deniability if the Cypriots start to wonder what the station is up to here. As to SLINGSHOT, we probably need to decide if we are going to reveal 206 and 207 to the Brits and when that is going to happen. I leave it to you to talk to the 171 team to sort that out. OK?"

"Will do. Anything else?"

"For now, I think we have managed to save our skins to fight another day, so if you will engage 171 as soon as possible, that will be great."

Williams got up. Sue was slightly miffed that even in the COS's office she was being treated like furniture, but she started to get up to follow Williams. He put a hand on her shoulder and gently pushed her back in her chair.

"Not so fast, Sue." Patty clearly wasn't through with her. Debbie came in as Williams left, picked up the empty coffee cups and replaced them with two filled cups. The aroma of hot, strong and sweet Turkish coffee filled the space across the table. Debbie closed the door as she left.

Here it comes, thought Sue. She hadn't received an ass chewing yet from anyone, so she figured this was the time it was going to happen.

"OK, Sue. Here's where we get serious about what we do next. I have to decide if it makes sense to keep you here, how we are going to do it and how I am going to keep you from getting killed." Dentmann paused. Sue wasn't sure she was expected to say anything so she waited. Dentmann didn't say a word. There was a bit of uncomfortable silence which Sue decided to fill.

"I want to stay, but I have to follow orders from 171. If they will let me stay, I intend to get a meeting with 207 as soon as possible and continue to run both 206 and 207 until we determine whether they can help on the IED issue. Any chance you are going to tell me what SLINGSHOT is?"

"Sue, it is simply the worldwide program on IED defeat efforts. It is a joint CIA-DIA-NSA program with links to 5 and 6 and UK SOF. I assumed 171 called it the same thing since SOF is central to the program, but I guess not. Now, the real question is what are you going to do about Beroslav?"

Sue was stunned silent. She hadn't mentioned anything about Beroslav to anyone and she knew 171 or the CIA-FBI ELEKTRA team didn't know anything about the "family business." Where did Dentmann get that name? There was another, long uncomfortable silence, but this time Sue did not fill it.

"Sue, certainly you have heard CIA officers refer to "the Barons" meaning the seniors in the organization. They are the ones that make the big decisions regarding resources and people and the strategic decisions on what we collect. The Farm teaches you that the President and the NSC ask questions and we are here to answer those questions if someone needs to steal the answers. True up to a point. However, the NSC spends a lot of time asking questions and someone has to prioritize the requirements and sort out the strategic questions from the politically motivated questions. That's something the Barons do as well." Dentmann paused, drank some coffee and continued.

"Historically, the Barons were all men. That has changed over the years and slowly women are becoming part of that select group. In part, that process of forcing change has been accomplished because women in the Agency have banded together: collaborating, mentoring, teaching a generation of female officers to play an appropriate role in the decisions of the Agency. We call that "the sisterhood." Dentmann paused. "It's not a secret society, it has no special handshake or special ring, but it is an organization that works both inside and outside the Agency to promote capable women. Your mother was one of the early members of the sisterhood and she has been my mentor for years."

Sue remained silent. It seemed like her family secrets changed every time she moved, like the kaleidoscope she had as a child changing pattern with the twist of the wrist. Now her mother was part of a larger network of women spie — perhaps one of the founders. What did that mean? For that matter, how did that affect Dentmann?

"It's a small outfit, Sue. There are only a few hundred of us in the field and probably five senior women in the entire Directorate of Operations — fewer than that when I joined. I chased targets in the Middle East, your mother was the pathfinder for us. When your mother started, men were convinced that a female case officer couldn't work an Arab man, a Persian man and especially an Islamic extremist. She showed us that not only was it possible, but she could excel. At that point, the Barons had to accept that women could, actually should, be in the mix against these targets."

"What does that have to do with Beroslav?"

"Ah, well, actually, not much. When you were reported kidnapped, I figured I owed to your mother to tell her what was going on. I called her on her secure phone in Chicago. I talked to her in some detail and she told me about the Beroslav angle to the death of your grandfather, your father and how she was convinced there might be a Beroslav angle to your disappearance."

"Her secure phone?"

"Sue, Barbara is still working as an annuitant for the Agency on several old cases. She has a pair of cases that she has been handling for a dozen years and the Agency is smart enough to understand that she has to be the one that handles them. She has a secure phone locked in some safe somewhere in her bungalow. I'm sorry, I thought you knew."

Sue wasn't sure if she was blushing or on her way to a stroke, but she felt her face turn red and her body started to sweat.

"Too much Turkish coffee, Sue?"

"Too much family history, Chief."

"OK, let's get some of the facts out for now, draw a line under the column for today and regroup tomorrow."

Sue nodded.

"Was Beroslav the one who put you in the car?" Sue nodded again.

"What did he tell you?"

"That he had killed Bachmann, replaced him before I arrived, and intended to leave me to die in the car. He said the fact that my body wouldn't be found was the same as his grandfather."

"So, ELEKTRA was compromised somehow by Beroslav. Did he say he was SVR or GRU?"

Sue thought hard. His voice came back to her. It was hard to avoid the emotions also coming back — emotions of fear, claustrophobia, frustration, anger. She took a few deep breaths to drive some of those demons back into the past.

"He said he was an international businessman whatever that meant."

"Mafia probably, but who knows."

"So, what does this all mean and how does it fit with my real job?"

"Real job? Sue, you don't realize this is your real job?"

"171 wants me to work against the Iraqi IED target. I want to work on that target. I don't want to work on anything else. I never wanted to work on anything else — except to find my father's and now my grandfather's killer."

"One thing at a time. I used some resources earlier today to sort out if Bachmann/Beroslav has left the island. The answer is, not by any means that I can track. He may still be here, he may be in Turkish Cyprus or he may have left by some boat from a dozen docks across the island. One thing we do know from SLINGSHOT is that the Russian Mafia is making a fair bit of money selling electronics to the network that is building the EFP IEDs. They acquire the electronics in Germany and Austria using their front companies, move them to here, and then turn them over to the Lebanese network that turns them over to Hizballah for delivery to Iranian and Iraqi technicians building the weapons. So, you see, this might very well, be your target. Just in an odd sort of way."

"Nothing about being an O'Connell appears to be straightforward anymore."

"Sue, you can count on the fact that nothing about being an intelligence officer appears to be straightforward, ever. Now that you are inside the labyrinth, you don't get out…ever. The best you can hope for is to finish your career, find a safehaven in retirement and hope that old enemies don't catch up to you. As an O'Connell, it appears you have more enemies than most of us. Honestly, I don't know if there was ever any going back for you or your family. It seems to me the labyrinth was built in World War II long before you or your parents were born. Sorry."

Dentmann walked over to her desk. She pulled out a bottle of Raki, a bottle of water, and two small crystal glasses. She poured about a half a glass of raki into each crystal glass, then added the water. The liquid turned from clear to milky white. She handed Sue a glass. Sue smelled the strong anisette aroma of the raki.

"To the sisterhood." Dentmann drained the glass. Sue did the same.

THE SISTERHOOD

Sue was sitting at her desk inside her shipping container back inside the hanger in RAF Akrotiri. It had been a tense few days as the COS, Williams and Smith back in 171 engaged every level of the chain of command to keep Sue in country. In the CIA, nearly every position in the chain of command was filled by someone who had served in the field and who Dentmann knew or knew someone who knew someone. Dentmann was relentless. It was never clear to Sue whether the chain of command at the CIA agreed with Dentmann or simply wanted Dentmann to stop annoying them. Either way, the COS got what she wanted which was to have Sue remain in country and expand the effort on SLINGSHOT.

On the other hand, Williams had to deal with multiple layers of DoD bureaucracy which was filled with uniformed officers, civilians, lawyers and political appointees. Just when a position was agreed upon, some additional complaint, caveat, or concern was announced and delayed a decision. Luckily, Smith's role as commander of 171 carried the day. He and Massoni drove over to SOF headquarters, got in front of the SOF chief of staff who briefed the SOF commanders in Tampa and Washington. Finally, Smith called someone (no one knew who) in the Pentagon and, suddenly, DIA agreed with CIA that Sue was going to be invaluable to SLINGSHOT operations in Cyprus.

Smith and Massoni's faces appeared in the small screen on Sue's desk. "O'Connell, even though you have probably destroyed both of our careers, we have been able to keep you in the field. I hope you are happy."

"Boss, you never seemed to me to be a careerist anyhow."

"Perhaps, not O'Connell, but both Jim and I want eventually to become mere, wretched federal pensioners and that means, at least, completing our military career. No pressure, O'Connell, but you have to do well out there or Massoni is going to be living out of his mini-van."

"Jim, I never knew you had a mini-van."

"Just for storage, Sue."

"OK, here's how this works. You are now part of the larger SLING-SHOT operation run, unfortunately, out of station. Our operations — meaning 206 and 207 since you killed 208…"

"Remember, Boss, I didn't kill 208, he was killed by my SBS backup."

"Whatever, O'Connell. 206 and 207 are your responsibility and we are your managers here. However, you will take requirements from station as well as from the brain trust here and you will coordinate your meetings with station to make sure we are maximizing the take from our cases. It isn't optimal, but it was what the SOF commander wanted, so that means its perfect. Check?"

"Check, Boss. Does that mean I can set up the cold turnover with 207 now and proceed with the next meeting with 206?"

"Exactly. Get to work. Out." The screen went blank. While Smith never was much for pleasantries, Sue was happy to hear that he was on board with her staying in country. She and the COS had a plan designed to both disrupt the entire Cyprus node of the IED program and, with a little luck, capture a member of the Beroslav mafia network — perhaps Bachmann/Beroslav himself.

Over the next ten days, Sue ran a series of tests to determine if she was being followed if/when she left the airbase. She always wore her now repaired leather jacket and always carried a pistol wherever she went. Slowly she became more comfortable with her surveillance status: it appeared that she was not being followed. The tech support personnel at station had determined that her remaining two vehicles, the van and the Fiat Abarth were clean of any electronic surveillance devices. She had asked for a third car from 171 and they just laughed. "Rent a car, O'Connell," was all Massoni said.

Once Sue established it was safe to return to work, she established contact with 207. Another car pickup in Limosal. 207 wasn't quite as pleasant a person as 206. He was all business and all about the money. They spent the first few minutes arguing about whether Sue should give him money up front or get his reports first. Eventually, Sue realized this wasn't getting her anywhere, so she gave him the envelope full of cash, passing it over with her left hand.

207 looked in the envelope. It included two months salary in Euros and an additional $500 in US currency.

"Too much," was all he said.

"A little bonus for being willing to meet me and continue the relationship."

"Good. It is acceptable that I should be rewarded. Now, what do you want to know."

"I need you to shift your focus. We are no longer interested in the ships being used by Hizballah. We are interested in the people delivering the goods to the ships. We have decided that it will be safer for you if we focus on those people who are not your regular contacts. We want to keep our relationship strong. Too much information about Hizballah means you could be at risk."

207 smiled. He had five days' beard growth, nearly a shaved head and yellow and broken teeth. Too many cigarettes and too many fights.

"I told Mr. James this before, but he never listened. Now, you come here, give me more money and agree with me. I like you."

"I like you too."

"I am too happy. But, it will take work to answer your questions. The delivery crew is very secretive, very dangerous. Not dangerous like Hizballah. Hizballahis, they are loyal. They will believe you because they see you as a brother. The Europeans who deliver the packages, I think they just kill you because they wonder if you are a risk. Maybe like the mafia you see in your movies. They are big men, dressed in suits, interested only in profit. They threaten you with their words and then some night they kill you in your bed. I don't like

305

them. I think it will be good to help you. These men will hurt me sooner or later just because I am a Palestinian."

"Why do you think they will hurt you because you are a Palestinian?"

"One night, the leader comes in. He is young, good looking, but has a weak left hand. He doesn't use it for anything. He doesn't talk until I take the delivery and move it to the other side of the warehouse for pickup at the docks. I wait in the shadows as I come back. I hear him say "We can't trust any of these Muslims. Their money is good, but they are not worth taking the risk. We will make two or three more months of profit then we kill them all. Especially the Palestinian. He probably is working for the Port Police as well as anyone else who will pay him."

207 took a long drag from the cigarette and exhaled. The blue smoke was filling the little Fiat interior. Sue's eyes were watering and her lungs were crying for fresh air. She finally gave up and opened her window. It only made things worse for a time as all the smoke in the car exited through that window. Next car would have a sunroof, she promised herself.

"Have you seen this boss before or since?"

"He comes all the time now. I don't like that. He looks at me in a way that a cat looks at a mouse."

"The next delivery?"

"Mid May. I will tell you when they have delivered the next."

"No, I need to know when they are going to deliver them. I want to be there to protect you."

"You would protect me?" The question passed through the exhaled smoke from 207's fifth cigarette in the last 10 minutes.

"Yes, I will protect you. I need to be there to be certain that this man is not going to finish his game with you."

"OK, I tell you as soon as I know. You have a phone number I can call?" Normally, Sue would never have sent or received messages from any source via the telephone. It was completely insecure in a modern world where nearly anyone can intercept a mobile phone conversation. Still, if she was right about this, she could expect the Russians to only report about the delivery at the last minute and there would be no time for a face to face meeting. She passed 207 a number with the name written in Greek letters.

"Alexis?"

"That will be me. Anyone asks you, you tell them you have a new girlfriend — a Greek girl who loves you. Alexis Andropolos. You met her in a bar. It is her number. You call me at that number, you make sure you always ask for Alexis first. It is my phone, but you must ask for Alexis. That way, I know you are OK. If you don't ask for Alexis, I know you need my help immediately. OK?"

"I love you too much for this. I promise to call as soon as I know." 207 laid his right hand on her left knee and leered at Sue. Sue used her left hand to reach into a small slot on her trousers she had cut and reinforced on the calf side of her left leg just above her prosthetic. She pulled out a gravity knife, opened it with a flick and jammed the point down on the arm rest about a half inch from 207's right arm.

"You are my very best friend and if you touch my leg again, I will cut your throat and throw you in the sea."

207 smiled and moved his arm carefully away from the blade and back to rest in his lap. "OK, I still love you too much."

S ue caught a ride with Brody in the MILATT Suburban headed to the embassy in Nicosia. After Sue was integrated into the SLINGSHOT program, one of the methods to get Sue back and forth from the Embassy was to establish a regular visit by the military attaché to RAF Akrotiri. Sue wasn't entirely certain who they were trying to deceive in this effort, but she wasn't about to complain that she didn't have to drive the Fiat or the van. Plus, she could talk to Brody on both legs of the route which made the trip go faster. The Marine at post one was suitably impressed with Sue in her class As and rendered a very formal salute as she walked through the secure door.

"Ma'am. Good to see you again and, honestly, great to see you in uniform."

"Thanks, Marine. Hope to see you at the Marine house this go round, OK?"

"I'll provide the first beverage."

Sue met up with Colonel Williams and provided him with the same back briefing on the 207 meeting that she had offered via SVTC to Smith. Once they were finished with the briefing and a coffee, Williams called the station on the internal line and asked to see Dentmann. Debbie told Williams to come down and he and Sue walked down the hall to Dentmann's office.

"Looking sharp, Sue." Debbie gave Sue a long look from highly shined jump boots to her dress jacket with the various awards and decorations.

Dentmann shouted from inside her office. "Get them in here. We have work to do."

"Yes, Chief." Debbie winked at Sue as she let them in, brought in the tray of coffee and sandwiches and closed the door behind them.

"Patty, this must be serious if you are offering food as well as coffee. Are we your hostages now or, perhaps, victims?"

"Jack, you are always my guest. I realize that Sue doesn't get to eat anything resembling real food down in Akrotiri so I figured she might like a working lunch courtesy of the Embassy Club."

"Patty, you need to get down to RAF Akrotiri. The officer's mess on post is like something out of a movie. Real china, linen napkins and table cloths. We need to introduce you to officer's life in service of the Queen." Sue decided to end the pleasantries. "I don't get to the mess all that often — they also require formal dress. It's mostly ramen noodles, with periodic mix of local cheeses, wine and bread courtesy of the SBS blokes next door. Luckily, they don't see me as a Rupert and that means we share and share alike."

"Enough about etiquette in Southern Cyprus. What do you have to tell me." Dentmann walked from behind her desk toward the round table where Williams and Sue were seated. She was dressed in a navy pants suit. The jacket was hanging over her chair and the sleeves of her white blouse were pushed up to her elbows. "By the way, Sue, you can take off the jacket. I'm sure Jack won't mind since he is wearing his sweater combination."

"It is part of the uniform, Patty, as you well know. And, you are correct, I won't mind if Sue gets comfortable." Sue unbuttoned her jacket and laid it carefully on the couch nearby. She rolled up her long sleeved green shirt — not exactly regulation to do so, but certainly more comfortable. She had her pocket notebook out and her Mont Blanc roller ball pen.

"207 has given me information on how the Russians are providing the electronics to Hizballah. Since 207 has access to warehouses due to his position in the harbor police, they use him to move material after hours from the warehouses near the docks through the customs house to dockside delivery locations. He has promised to provide a date and time for the next delivery. He is motivated by the fact that he heard the Russians talking about one or two more shipments and then they pull the plug on the operation and, by extension, pull the plug on 207. He is ready to help and can manufacture a story to Hizballah if they don't get the next shipment of material for the EFP IEDs. It is a win, win as near as I can see."

"Will 207 still have utility if we disrupt this network?"

"I certainly think so. He won't be as useful as 206 since he will return to being just a penetration of the harbor police, but certainly that is still useful to SLINGSHOT once the Hizballahis find a new

source for the equipment. We will have to design a disruption operation that doesn't put him in the middle of the take down, but that
shouldn't be that hard, no?"

"OK, so what sort of disruption do you think works?"

"Obviously, I would like to set up some type of capture operation on the mafia types so that we can trace back their sources in
Europe. Meanwhile, we control the new electronics just long enough
to beacon the boxes and, perhaps, fiddle the equipment. The electronics continue on their way and we end up tracking the route back
to wherever they are manufacturing the EFPs. Then, well someone
does the finish piece."

"You think you can arrange this opportunity?"

"Well, 207 says he loves me…"

"Yeah, well, all my male assets love me too. So what?"

"Just joking Chief. He sees this as a way to get out from under a
death threat. I suspect he will deliver. I just don't know what sort of
finish piece we can set up in Limossal."

"Patty, I think I can work with the UK SOF commander to free
up Sue's SBS pals for this operation. What about the gang from 5,
will they insist on some sort of Cypriot participation to build their
equities?"

"Not if I point out that mafia types are Russians. The Russian
mafia money is all over this island and I'm not sure who we could trust
in the equation. It's not that 5's contacts are corrupt, but who knows
who they would have to report to both up and down the Cypriot
chain of command. We need to keep this a US-UK operation, full
stop."

"What about a US SOF role?" Sue needed to get back into this
discussion or once again, she would be about as useful as Dentmann's
office furniture.

Dentmann raised an eyebrow and turned to Williams. "Do you
think we can get a SOF team in here quietly and have them wait until
we get a go signal? I'm OK with that if we are certain that the package will be small and patient."

"I don't have a clue, Patty. We can use the SVTC in my office
to talk to Smith back at 171 and see what he says. SOF is pretty

stretched right now in Iraq and Afghanistan. We might be able to get some Rangers…"

Dentmann looked skyward. "Don't get me wrong, I know they are capable. I'm just worried that they come in packages no less than 120. I don't think we can keep 120 Rangers hidden from anyone for long. How about an SF team from Germany? I can live with 12 guys if that's all they bring to the party."

"I thought you would never ask, Patty." Sue knew that Williams had been in 10th Special Forces Group before the collapse of the USSR and when the 10th was responsible for Western Europe.

Once again, Dentmann took charge.

"OK, here's the deal. I don't honestly care who is involved in the finish piece at this end. Sue is a 171 asset which means a SOF asset which means you, Jack, have to figure out the monkey puzzle of who gets to play where and when. I just want one thing — I want to have it end up quiet enough that the Hizballahis don't think there is any trouble and they take their new set of electronics — specially prepared by my folks — back to their secret club house in Lebanon or Syria or Iran or Iraq or wherever. We have a chance to disrupt as well as collect on this mission and my vote — and I suspect the vote of all the seniors involved in SLINGSHOT is to collect so that we can disrupt at the far end of the pipeline."

"Sue, your job is to make sure we have both the right time and place and 207 gives us backdoor access or you get us backdoor access with your former S&R skills so that the warehouse is ready for the party before the Russians arrive. Jack, you figure out who gets to come to the party from the military side. We have to keep this small — not military small, which usually means less than 100, but Agency small which in this case means less than 20 total including the force inside the warehouse and the blocking/security force outside the warehouse. I will have three techs inside the warehouse ready to start their magic as soon as we are done with the Russians. Finally, I don't want an international incident here. I don't want a room full of dead Russians that we have to sort out. No telling how many of these guys who 207 thinks are mafia types are actually Russian SVR, FSB, GRU or Spetsnaz. It could get ugly if I have to explain to our Ambassador why his Russian counterpart is pissed at us for capping a few of his citizens. Clear?"

Jack had a been taking notes with his right hand and eating a club sandwich with his left hand. He paused just long enough to nod his agreement. Sue had been unwilling to eat anything until and unless she was certain that Sue didn't intend to ask any further questions. It seemed clear that this was the end of the meeting and Sue looked longingly at her sandwich and chips as she said "Clear, Chief."

"OK, Jack get started. I have a couple more questions for Sue and I want her to get a chance to eat something as well before you put her in front of a computer for the rest of the day and, likely, the night. OK?"

"Patty, I got plenty to do before I need to see Sue again, so just send her down the hall whenever."

"Thanks." Williams left and closed the door behind him.

"Eat your sandwich, Sue. You are going to need some food for the work you have to do for the next few hours. No beers at the Marine house for you tonight. One of the disadvantages of living in Z+1 is that we are a full seven hours ahead of Washington and Ft. Bragg. I reckon we are going to be up all night."

"Now, I want you to know that we are not going to do this operation so that your best friend Bachmann/Beroslav or whatever his name is meets with a sudden accident in the warehouse. I need to be sure you understand that before we go any farther. If he comes to the warehouse, he gets treated just like the rest of the mopes that are part of the mafia side of this equation. Just like the rest, right Sue?"

This time, Sue really did have a mouth full of club sandwich, so all she could do was nod. Sue was convinced that Beroslav was going to be treated precisely like the rest of the mopes. At least if she had anything to do with it.

For the last two weeks, Sue had been the operational focal point for the US-UK team that would disrupt the operation. As 207's handler, she was the one who had the information on the where, the when and how the smuggling operation worked. She watched as Dentmann, Williams and Bruce Sykes, SIS Station commander in Cyprus, juggled the political and logistical effort. It was an interesting lesson for Sue in bureaucratic competition. In the long run and to the surprise of Sue, Dentmann ended up controlling the operation including the deployment of resources into Cyprus. Dentmann simply staked out a reasonable position and never gave any ground.

Dentmann's plan was simple, low profile, and covered all the necessary bases for success. All they needed was a little luck and it would work. SIS used their local assets at the dock to obtain the observation point that Sue was sitting. Sue's five SBS pals from RAF Akrotiri along with two members of UK Special Branch assigned to the High Commission were serving as the "muscle" for the takedown of the mafia after delivery of the material. Williams arranged for an Special Forces team to fly into Akrotiri and they were serving as the quick reaction force/blocking force in case of trouble either inside or outside the facility during the takedown. They were located in two travel vans just outside the port facility. 207 provided additional keys to all the gates so that they could control access in and out after the Russians arrived. Finally, SOF provided Sue's former S&R team to serve as surveillance coverage of 207 for the past week. Dentmann's team would be inside the warehouse ready to do the modifications on site so that the Hizballah delivery could be tracked wherever it ended up and so the electronics would never work properly once added to the EFP.

When 207 called Sue yesterday to report the transfer of the material was going to take place at 2300hrs tonight, Sue had already established an operational tempo with Brody, who had insisted he wanted to play and Williams had agreed to let him join in. Twelve hours on, twelve off, sleeping on site, eating British rations provided when they moved into the location, and generally making the room smell awful. Sue would be happy to be out of the room, but she was equally pleased that she was back in the comfortable position of being a hunter in the game.

Sue was sitting in a folding chair next to the folding desk that held the computer linked to the long-range video camera watching the sliding service doors of the warehouse. They had drilled a hole in the wall of their position and inserted a pinhole camera that provided the intelligence feed. Six hours ago, Sue had replaced the standard camera lens with a lens mated to a night vision optic provided by station. This optic was smaller and provided a brighter image than anything that she had used at SOF, but it was hardly military hardened and only good for one night at a time before all the batteries needed to be recharged. Normally, Brody would be in the cot on the other side of the room, snoring, until he took over at 0200, but this night no one was sleeping.

Dentmann's voice in Sue's ear bud.

"2230 — radio check." She and her two tech officers were located in one of the small offices inside the warehouse. Waiting like everyone else. No one had appointed Dentmann as the leader, she just assumed responsibility and no one argued. She was SLINGSHOT6.

"Mike6. Our Bravo is almost to the main gate of the facility. No complications." It was great to hear Jameson's voice again. On arrival at Akrotiri, Sue had a few hours to catch up with him. Nate had been promoted and was assistant team leader and a new female surveillant named Beth had been in Sue's position for the last year. Otherwise, the rest of the team was intact. They had been in Baghdad for the last six months and were happy to spend a little time in a country where they weren't facing the IED threat.

"Uniform6. In place." Williams was manning the commo in the lead van with the SF team. The team leader, a Captain, didn't like having the Colonel on board, but he didn't get a vote. Williams was going to be in the game somehow and Dentmann told him that she needed him with the QRF — just in case.

"Able6. Set." George and his team plus the two Special Branch officer were secured inside a large wooden crate inside the warehouse. The crate would collapse on a signal, preceded by two flash bangs, and assuming there were three Russians as planned, they should be secured in seconds.

"Tango 6. We have a clean look at the door." Sue spoke into her headset. "We also have a good feed from the remote camera on the back side of the building. No sign of life on dockside. Standby, standby 207 is rolling up in front of the building now."

Dentmann reiterated Sue's message. "Stand by, stand by. Tango6 reporting arrival of 207." She paused.

"Mike6, please move your team to your blocking positions. Tango6, watch for our other guests."

"Mike6"

"Tango6"

As Sue watched the screen, 207 walked to the warehouse door, unlocked it and stepped inside. He seemed comfortable and showed no signs of nervousness.

"Standby, standby." Williams' voice was excited.

"We have one vehicle coming to the open gate. Black Mercedes GLW, driver, two passengers visible. They are entering the compound."

"Standby, standby. That was Uniform6 reporting arrival of what looks to be our guests. Three Bravos sited. Charlie is a black Mercedes GLW. Confirm."

Two clicks — most probably from George in the box.

"Mike6"

"Tango"

Dentmann again, this time in a whisper.

"Uniform6, on my mark, block the entrance with one van. Doors open, but none of the team comes out unless needed. Check?"

"Uniform6"

Sue watched at the Mercedes pulled up next to 207's Skoda. Three individuals got out of the Mercedes. One moved to the back of the Mercedes and pulled out a large crate. He didn't seem to have any trouble carrying the crate, but then he was a large individual himself. When he picked up the crate, his jacket opened to reveal a Russian folding stock AKS74U submachine gun.

Sue keyed her mike. "Standby, standby. Three bravos leaving the

Charlie coming to the front door. One carrying a large crate. He has a Krinkov in a modified chest carry. Right handed. No other weapons visible."

Dentmann's voice — a whisper. "Roger" Two clicks from George. "Uniform6"

"Mike6"

The Russians entered the warehouse.

Brody was working a third computer. He accessed the remote camera they had inside the warehouse. He could see 207's back and the faces of the three Russians. Sue looked over his shoulder. The lead Russian was Beroslav. Brody turned on the remote microphone inside the warehouse. Based on where they were standing, it was only picking up about half of the conversation from the Russians and none from 207. Brody sent the feed through the entire team's network.

"We have… on time." Beroslav's voice. English with a British accent. 207 nodded and said something they couldn't hear.

"Our money…"

207 picked up the briefcase with his left hand. He handed it to Beroslav. Beroslav handed it to the man on his left. The man on his right still held the crate. The Russian opened the briefcase.

Bang. The dye bag linked to the money exploded covering the Russian's face and chest with bright red dye. Stunned he dropped the case.

While everyone was looking at the case, Beroslav had pulled a Makarov with a suppressor out and fired two rounds into 207. 207 fell like he had been hit with a bat.

Dentman's voice in their earpiece. "Go go go."

Sue and Brody watched as the screen flashed bright and their earpieces overloaded. Boom, Boom. The flash bangs went off and the crate collapsed revealing the five man SBS team and the two Special Branch officers in a modified stack formation. George in the lead followed by Mac, Dozer and Brian, the two Special Branch officers and Paddy covering their back. They had been watching the feed while inside the box so they were prepared to engage immediately. The Russian carrying the crate was the quickest. He dropped the crate and reached his SMG. He was shot before his hand reached the pistol grip. Two rounds in the chest from George's MP5. He was stunned, but clearly wearing armor under his coat. He dropped to one knee and released the Krinkov from its harness. Two more rounds from Mac's pistol fired over George's right shoulder finished the job. There were two matched rounds in the Russian's forehead.

Sue realized that Beroslav was no longer in the frame. Where did he go? She could see the Special Branch officers handcuffing the Russian with red dye all over him and George and Mac securing the weapon from the dead Russian. Where was Beroslav?

Sue looked at the first screen. Williams and crew had secured the Mercedes. No one there.

George and his team were working through the warehouse. "Third Bravo is free. No joy in the warehouse."

"Uniform6. He didn't come out the front."

Sue pointed to the third screen and shouted at Brody. "Tell them!"

"Tango2. The third Bravo is outside the warehouse on the dock side. Tango6 in pursuit."

Dentmann's voice in Brody's headset.

"Standby, Standby. We need to clean up the warehouse and we need to get the equipment repackaged. Uniform6 and Mike6 — seal the area. We are in a fenced compound, our Bravo is going to have to either climb a fence, go out a gate, or swim. If our third Bravo gets away, that's the least of our worries right now."

"Able6"

"Uniform6"

"Mike6"

Dentmann's voice in Brody's headset. "Tango6, confirm."

All Brody heard in his headset was "Shit."

Brody heard another voice, Mike 6 this time, say the same thing. "Shit." Sue had her earpiece in and had heard the entire discussion, but she was too busy running down the stairs to answer. Of all the skills that she had mastered since losing her leg, Sue had never mastered going down stairs quickly. After the first landing, she decided the only good way to accomplish the job was to slide down the metal bannister and hope she didn't get entangled when she hit the floor.

Sue came down hard on the ground floor. She had taken the shock on her right leg and could feel that she had twisted something — ankle probably but possibly her foot. Either way, it hurt, but her leg didn't give way, so she pushed through the back door of the warehouse and headed along a parallel alley toward the water.

Just as she approached the dockside from her alley, she saw Beroslav cross the alley, running down the dock toward the fence line. Sue knew that this was the fenceline covered by the S&R team.

"Mike6, Tango6."

"Mike6"

"Third Russian running toward your position." She took a breath. Gathered herself and drew her Glock.

"Male, 6 feet. Dark overcoat. Short hair. He has at least one pistol though it is holstered right now. He is right handed. Headed toward the junction of the fence and the dock on your side."

"Check. We'll stop him."

"Tango6, SLINGSHOT6" Dentmann's voice in her earpiece. Sue drew a breath. "Tango6"

"Let Mike6 handle this."

"Roger."

Sue took off after Beroslav.

He was approaching the fence when he looked back. He saw Sue in pursuit.

"O'Connell" was all he said. He turned and drew his Makarov. Sue was closing, fast, but was still 20 yards away. She realized that this was not going to go well. She stopped, drew her weapon and dropped to one knee. The first round of the Makarov passed over her head by less than an inch. He had aimed for her chest and would have hit it with the Makarov at 20 yards. Sue's brain was racing. All she could think was "he is a very good shot."

The second and third rounds hit her in the chest. The lightweight body armor stopped the Makarov round with no trouble at this distance, but it hurt and it did push Sue over on her left side. She had the Glock up and Beroslav in her sights.

He dropped like a rag doll, tried to get up, and then fell into the water. Sue realized that there was a green laser dot on her chest. She rolled quickly, got up and ran to a series of containers nearby. Two rounds blasted into the containers. And then, silence.

Sue had expected a serious ass chewing from Dentmann immediately after the operation finished. So far, she hadn't received one, but then again, Dentmann was busy working the electronics end of the operation. Sue and Brody had picked up their kit and driven to Nicosia in silence. Brody drove, Sue sulked.

They held the larger team meeting this time in a conference room in the US mission. All of the players sat at a very long table in the basement of the embassy. Sue arrived with Williams and Brody. Sue had expected Dentmann at the end of the table and she wasn't surprised to see the position to her right open for Williams. What she was surprised to see on her left was Melissa Nez in a formal suit, wearing very professional black framed glasses with her hair cut in a very short pageboy haircut.

"Hey you." Melissa looked at Sue across the table and pushed the glasses off her nose.

"Hey, you!" Was all Sue could say.

They sat down, the SOF and the Brit team came in with their Escort Required Badges and under the observation of a very diligent member of the Marine Security Detachment. The Marine walked out, closed the large ciphered door and flipped the red light on and the paper sign that said "Conference in progress."

Over the next hour, Dentmann worked the table demonstrating her skills again and again. Sue watched as Dentmann encouraged her counterparts to brag a bit while they told their part of the story. The important points nearly everyone already knew, but that didn't mean it wasn't good to hear the story from the perspective of the team.

The Russians turned out to be members of a Europe based organized crime family that traded in everything from drugs to people to high tech equipment. The British were very pleased because in the long run, both of the "Russians" on site were, in fact, holding British passports. Ethnically, it was not yet clear if they were Russians, Central Asians, or Europeans. The detained Russian was on his way back to the UK on an RAF aircraft with two Special Branch officers for interrogation and prosecution because his documentation showed a

London residence and the electronics in the crate were from a British firm. All legally purchased and all illegally smuggled out of the UK.

Even 207 had a relatively happy ending. On 207s arrival in the warehouse, Dentmann had come out of her secure location and insisted that he put on a lightweight armor vest under his shirt. Williams reported to the crowd that during the cleanup, 207 looked at Dentmann as they loaded him into one of the SF vans.

"I love you." Was all he said according to Williams. Dentmann looked none too pleased.

Dentmann ended the meeting by offering the rest of the story regarding the electronics. The tech team lead by Melissa Nez imbedded a beacon into the box and another into the wrapping material that protected the electronics. They also modified the electronics so that they would survive a simple bench test, but would fail once emplaced in any device of any sort, but especially if linked to a firing sequence for any EFP. At 207's instruction, they put the box with the appropriate shipping documents in the established dockside location and, as of 0800hrs, according to the beacons, the box and the equipment were on a ship headed toward Lebanon. Given the fact that the equipment had been rendered inert, a joint US-UK team decision had been made to let the equipment reach its final location. Once bench tested at the arrival location, a third beacon would engage and that information would be passed to a joint US SOF and UK SOF headquarters in theater and they would decide how to proceed.

Dentmann closed by stating that a thorough search of the dockside had not uncovered the third Russian or his body. She said

"We can all hope that the third Russian is fish food at this point, but honestly, we don't know and I, for one, don't care. His operation was disrupted by this team and even if he survived, we have already have a deception campaign in place which will blame him for any failures in the electronics. It is definitely a good day. I recommend we adjourn and regroup for dinner tonight. I have set up a catered dinner at my house for everyone involved. More of a buffet than a sit down dinner given the size of our team, but I hope you will all come."

The room emptied after multiple handshakes, back slapping and hugs. Sue was looking forward to conversations with George,

Jameson, and Melissa, but she didn't get far before her shoulder was grabbed by Dentmann. Dentmann was a small woman and she had to reach to grab Sue's shoulder, but her grip was painful and Sue knew that it wouldn't let go until she sat back down. She waved to Williams and sat back down.

"You didn't follow my orders, O'Connell."

"Commo was poor."

"Bullshit. Discipline was poor, Sue." Sue got ready. Ass chewing time.

"If you are going to succeed in this business, you have to realize that there are going to be times when you simply have to trust someone. And you have to realize that sometimes you don't know everything because you don't need to know."

"He was going to get away."

"No, dear. He wasn't going to get away." Dentmann paused. "Remember the green laser dot?"

"Yes."

"The Brits did a quick bit of forensics at the site. They found two rounds of 7.62 x 39 embedded in the container where you took cover. Russian ammunition. Most likely shot from a Russian sniper rifle."

"Eh?"

"Hard to imagine why a Russian team might have been shooting at a Russian mafia figure, but it would appear that that was what happened."

"And when they shot at me?"

"Who is to say? However, I suspect that anyone who could hit Beroslav from a boat in the harbor, in the dark, probably could have hit you as well. Don't you think?"

"Maybe so..."

"Maybe so, Sue."

J.R. SEEGER is a western New York native who served as a U.S. Army paratrooper and as a CIA case officer for a total of 27 years of federal service. In October 2001, Mr. Seeger led a CIA paramilitary team into Afghanistan. He splits his time between western New York and Central New Mexico.

THE MIKE4 SERIES
BY J.R. SEEGER

MIKE4

Friend or Foe

The Executioner's Blade

Available in bookstores and at Amazon